Point Blank

Point Blank

By Philip Rosenberg
and Sonny Grosso

Grosset & Dunlap
Publishers • New York
A FILMWAYS COMPANY

For "Jeannie" and the kids,
because we hope the truth helps.
And for Detective "Luke Antonelli,"
who wanted the story told.

"Cara Mia" words and music by Tulio Trapani and Lee Lange
Copyright © 1954   Leo Feist, Inc.
Rights controlled by Leo Feist, Inc. for North and South America
Used by permission

Contents

Preface   vii

Part One   The Trap   7

    Chapter   1   Fish Fry   9

    Chapter   2   Carlo Danzie   24

    Chapter   3   The Washington Connection   36

Part Two   The Investigative Plan   57

    Chapter   4   A Man of His Word   59

    Chapter   5   The Caruso Taps   67

    Chapter   6   Missing Link   88

    Chapter   7   "Some Other Consideration"   105

    Chapter   8   The Passport Gambit   121

    Chapter   9   The Split   149

    Chapter 10   The Stakeout   168

    Chapter 11   The Plant   183

Chapter 12 Point Blank   200
Chapter 13 Advice of Counsel   217
Chapter 14 Palm Sunday   236
Part Three Of Accidental Judgments Casual
            Slaughters by Sonny Grosso   253
Chapter 15 Good Friday   255
Chapter 16 Point of No Return   264
Chapter 17 A Dead Man's Name   273
Chapter 18 Property Clerk   291
Chapter 19 Tip From a Dead Stool   303
Afterword by John J. Meglio   310

Preface

This story is true. The incidents depicted here really happened. Some scenes have been dramatized, and dialogue has been supplied in instances where our sources and research did not disclose the actual words spoken. But every effort has been made to give an accurate and fair presentation of the facts. We have chosen to present the story in the form of a novel because this seemed the most intelligible way to tell so complex a tale of intrigue and double-dealing. But it is not a work of fiction.

For obvious reasons, many of the names have been changed. The following real names appear in the book: Jack Anderson, Michael Armstrong, Shirley Bassey, Governor Hugh Carey, Vic Damone, Philip D'Antoni, Charles De Gaulle, Detective Eddie Egan, Patrolman Gregory Foster, Patsy Fuca, Sidney Greenstreet, Detective Sonny Grosso, Lorenz Hart, Howard Hughes, Clifford Irving, Senator Henry M. Jackson, Detective Randy Jurgensen, Ted Kluzsewski, Whitman Knapp, Patrolman Rocco Laurie, Mayor John V. Lindsay, Tony LoBianco, Lucky Luciano, John Meglio, Attorney General John N.

Mitchell, Police Commissioner Patrick V. Murphy, President Richard M. Nixon, Pelé, Patrolman William Phillips, Governor Nelson A. Rockefeller, Judge Sylvester J. Ryan, Roy Scheider, Patrolman Frank Serpico, Whitney North Seymour, Assistant Attorney General Laurence H. Silberman, Frank Sinatra, Patrolman Mike Treanor, Albert Wilkins, Ted Williams.

The authors are deeply grateful to a number of people who helped in the preparation of this book. Many individuals who came forward with information cannot be publicly thanked; they have our gratitude nonetheless. Of those who can be publicly acknowledged, we would like to thank Detective Randy Jurgensen, who made a number of valuable suggestions; Phil D'Antoni, who graciously provided us with encouragement, advice, and support; Stuart Rosenberg, who read every page of every draft and made irreplaceable contributions at the marathon editorial sessions when the manuscript was hammered into shape; Charlotte Rosenberg, whose sensitive and sympathetic judgments helped us in a number of places; John Meglio, for whom the tragedy of "Joe Longo" is an ongoing crusade, and without whose cooperation this book would not have been possible; and Susie Friedman, the perfect secretary, who not only typed and retyped draft after draft but also kept our spirits up by asking for the next chapter, and kept the tea hot, the soda cold, and the interruptions to a minimum.

The dull-green Plymouth crossed the Williamsburg Bridge into Manhattan, cut south toward Canal Street, and then circled twice through the chaos and construction of Confucius Plaza. It pulled to the curb opposite the foot of Mott Street and the two men inside talked briefly, picking up a discussion that had begun on the Brooklyn side of the river. Then the car slid out into the midmorning traffic and made its way slowly up Bowery to Delancey and back onto the Williamsburg Bridge.

The driver, a slender, nervous man in his mid thirties, didn't know Brooklyn. He drove slowly, smoking cigarette after cigarette and letting his passenger direct him through a maze of broken streets. It was a cold bright day toward the end of March 1972, less than one week into spring.

Except for giving directions, the passenger had said nothing since the stop at Confucius Plaza. A large handsome man with thick black hair and heavy hands, he sat stiffly upright and looked straight ahead. As they drove through the Williamsburg section of Brooklyn, down

3

streets where he had played as a child, he refused to look to either side. The course he charted zigzagged erratically, lefts and rights in a seemingly random sequence, so that on more than one occasion the driver noticed that they were on a street familiar from but a moment before.

That morning the driver had put two guns in a brown paper bag and deposited them in the trunk when his partner picked him up. As an afterthought he opened the trunk again, unfolded the bag, and added his gold detective's shield. He saw his partner's black leather briefcase next to the spare tire but didn't have to ask what was in it.

"Take the next left," the big man said firmly. Something in his voice hinted that he had made a decision and was now directing the car toward a specific destination. After a few more turns he asked the driver to stop just past an intersection. Without a word of explanation, he climbed heavily from the car, walked back to the intersection, and disappeared around the corner.

The driver turned to watch him go but then turned back to face the windshield, moved by an instinctive tact that warned against intruding. In that brief glance backward he had seen a street sign that told him his partner had gone down Hope Street, but he was in no mood for ironies.

In less than five minutes the other man returned, his massive athlete's body swaying in the stiff wind as he walked. "We'd better get going, don't you think?" the driver asked as soon as his partner was seated in the car.

"Fuck him, let him wait," the other man said.

Soon they were movng quickly down a broad avenue, once again heading for the bridge.

"Do me a favor."

"Sure," the driver said.

"Call my brother, tell him I want to see him."

Again the driver followed directions, past Spanish stores and two-story frame houses surfaced in asbestos tile, past vacant lots and bright brick brownstones, west on Fourth Street, past Driggs, then right on Bedford, right on Seventh, past the bulky gray back of Saint Vincent de Paul Church, where the parishioners were still the Italian families the big man, who was calling all the turns, had grown up with. Years ago the priest once told his mother that someday her son would be another Joe DiMaggio but it hadn't worked out that way.

At Driggs the big man told his partner to make a right and pull to the curb at a bus stop, down about twenty yards from the mouth of the subway station.

"What's his number?" the driver asked.

The candy store at the corner across from the subway consisted of one small square room with a counter to one side and pinball machines and public telephones along the opposite wall. Repeating the number to himself, he asked for change and went to the phone.

A woman's voice answered. When he delivered his message she said, "Sal's at work, he knows that." There was a pause. Then she said, "How come he had you call? Is he all right?"

The man hung up and hurried from the store, a vague presentiment growing at the back of his mind. When he got to the street and saw that his partner was still in the car, he slowed his pace, momentarily reassured. Then, suddenly, he broke into a run, his eyes locked on the window through which he could see his partner slumped in the seat, his head resting on the back cushion.

When he got to the passenger door he didn't even open it. He saw at once that his partner was dead, knew it as certainly as if he had felt his lifeless pulse. He looked away so quickly he didn't even see the small bright splotch of blood that gleamed on the dashboard, pumped there in one violent thrust when the bullet sliced into a corner of the big man's heart.

He raced back to the candy store, confused. "What precinct am I in?" he shouted, a question so irrelevant that later he couldn't understand why he had asked it. He got his answer and dialed 911. "My partner's been shot," he screamed into the phone, "corner of Driggs and Seventh."

Alone in the suddenly empty store, he closed his eyes and held his hand over them to blot out everything. Then he walked out to the sidewalk and staggered unconsciously around the edges of the crowd that had collected there. He hesitated a moment, listening to the urgent, curious whispers of the men on the sidewalk as though he were no more a part of what had happened in the car across the street than they were. Then, his head down so he wouldn't have to see the car, he crossed to it and stood by the trunk, legs apart at parade rest, waiting for the sirens he already could hear crying toward him.

Part One
The Trap

And Satan answered the Lord, and said, Skin for skin, yea, all that a man hath will he give for his life. But put forth thine hand now, and touch his bone and his flesh, and he will curse thee to thy face.
—The Book of Job 2:4–5

Chapter 1
Fish Fry

FIRST THERE WERE the bad guys, the gangsters, the kilo connections, the street dealers, each running his own game, cutting it a little thinner down the middle, skimming a little off the top. Then there were the good guys, the law. But some of them ran their own games, too, getting paid up front or just taking a slice from the junk that passed through their hands. So there had to be a new set of good guys, police to police the police. And they ran the most vicious games of all.

If Gil Lacey had any pride at all, it was the pride that came from knowing he had doped it out so he could play it all three ways. In his first ten years in the job his record as a cop had been solid but unspectacular, starting with patrol in Brooklyn's Seventy-ninth Precinct, followed by three years in Tactical, the Department's elite goon squad, and from there to Narco. But his record on the street was something else. The word was out that Lacey was doing business, and Lacey himself did everything but advertise the fact. If anyone had cared, that kind of talk could have cost him his shield, but no one did care—at least through most of the sixties no one did—and he was cool enough

9

to know that a reputation for dealing greased the wheels.

He was right, too, except that he should have known that when the Knapp Commission hit town things were going to start heating up. Suddenly it was a bull market for corrupt cops, and a smarter guy than Lacey would have known enough to slow down. It was the one thing he blamed himself for, because all at once they were coming down hard on him from every direction.

Before he even knew what hit him, he was jammed up, but even so he managed to land on his feet. Better than that, in fact. When they gave him the choice of turning or doing time, it had taken less than a millisecond to make the decision, although he didn't want them to get the impression he fell easy so he did his best to make them think he was thinking it over. For one tough week they grilled him, with an assistant D.A. doing most of the questioning while two inspectors from Internal Affairs listened and took notes. When it was over he was theirs. He hadn't told them everything by a long shot, but he had given them enough to put him away if they ever wanted to. And what they gave him in return was a set of wires that would have impressed General Sarnoff. His car was miked front and back, with a transmitter in the trunk. The buckle of his seat belt completed the circuit, giving him the option of terminating transmission whenever he wanted to talk off the record. As easy as that and he was back in business. Only now his ass was covered in case anyone tried to sneak up behind him.

Not that any of this passed through his mind as he sat behind the wheel of his tomato-red Pontiac in the parking lot adjoining the Mays department store in the Jamaica section of Queens, the motor idling and the fan blowing hot air for all it was worth in a losing struggle to take some of the sting out of a vicious January afternoon. He held his hands over the air vent and rubbed them together, his mind blank as he waited. Five minutes passed, and then, about ten cars away, coming from the direction of the station house across the street, he saw Sergeant Patrigno striding toward him, walking rapidly, his coat unbuttoned but pulled closed with his hands deep in the pockets, his head down and white steam pouring from his mouth. Lacey waited as long as he could and then switched off the motor. The hiss of the blower cut out immediately and by the time Patrigno circled the front of the car to the passenger side, Lacey could hear the crunch of his shoes against the thin crust of snow.

Inside, Patrigno spoke first. An affable man, large and demon-

stratively friendly, he bore a certain vague and disconcerting re-
semblance to the much younger Lacey. Both were broad and stocky
with powerful bodies, though far heavier than they should have been.
Both had, too, the same wide, flat face and both wore their thick hair
straight back from the forehead, although Patrigno's black hair
was well along toward gray. In dress, however, they contrasted sharply. Lacey wore no overcoat. His sport jacket was so rich and deep a
brown that it seemed almost red in the sunlight. That, a Cardin tie,
cream shirt, light trousers, and brown shoes that gleamed like patent
leather established the difference between him and the rumpled Patrigno, whose overcoat billowed in front of his chest when he sat. Still,
they could have been taken for a working-class father and his successful son. If Patrigno had ever been brought to trial they would have
made a striking pair as they confronted each other in the courthouse.

"My sister asked me to pick up some pants for the baby," Patrigno said. "You know, them corduroy things. With the suspenders," he
went on, his hands describing suspenders in front of his shoulders.
"She's all the way out in Yonkers so I figured I'd take off a little early,
get the pants here at Mays."

He would have kept talking, but something in Lacey's lack of
response stopped him, seemed to make friendship or even sociability
impossible. Pete Patrigno saw the benefits of doing business with
Lacey as almost his due after twenty-four years of service, but he was
a man of the old school and the idea of meeting in parking lots never
sat right with him. That was for younger men, greedy, ambitious
punks, but not for him. He would have liked it better if Lacey had
come to his office, but times had changed and he accepted the fact that
under the circumstances it couldn't be done that way.

Lacey understood this but had no patience with it. He didn't
know whether to believe the story about the corduroy pants, which
just happened to be true. But Patrigno always managed to find something to say to make it seem that meeting in out-of-the-way places was
merely a convenience. If he had been capable of being amused, Lacey
might have found Patrigno's gambits amusing, but the best he could
manage was to mask his contempt with an impassive face. He knew
what he was, and people who didn't know themselves irritated him, so
he waited until Patrigno fell silent and then said, "I got info on a good
gun collar if you want it."

Patrigno nodded.

"You want it?" Lacey asked, unwilling to accept a mere gesture.

"Sure. What's the details?"

"Guy named Barrera, some kind of high-class messenger. What I hear is he always carries a piece and he could have ten grand on him, maybe more, I don't know. Anyway, he should be good for something."

"When?"

"What's today . . . the twenty-sixth?" Lacey asked rhetorically. "He's flying in tomorrow, staying at the hotel out by Kennedy. He's connected pretty high up, so it's for sure he's not gonna want to do time on a gun thing. Maybe he'll give you some names, he could be a goldmine. If he turns you onto anything, give me a call. But even if he doesn't, it'll still be worth your while just for him."

As Patrigno listened he found himself, just within the last few seconds, suddenly becoming glum and withdrawn, like someone who had just been waked up. He felt an almost overwhelming need to get out of the car and away from Lacey. "Yeah, I'll take it," he said, his voice thick, like it came from far away. The change was so striking that when the tape was played back later in the United States Attorney's office, the federal prosecutor wondered if something had happened that Lacey didn't tell him about.

"Fine," Lacey answered, "then I'll see you next week. Who you gonna take?"

"Why?" Patrigno snapped, refusing to answer Lacey's question. The next sound on the tape was the car door slamming.

Ramon Barrera was not surprised when the police entered his room, for he had come to New York for the specific purpose of being arrested. Not a drug dealer at all, he was in fact a federal agent for the Bureau of Narcotics and Dangerous Drugs on undercover assignment to the United States Attorney's office for the Southern District of New York. After Lacey's meeting with Patrigno, Barrera was notified that arrangements had been completed and the operation was set to go. The next morning he flew from Washington to Kennedy Airport, checked into the International Hotel, and settled in to wait.

In addition to his clothing and personal effects, his suitcase contained a nickel-plated Browning automatic and a manila envelope with twelve thousand dollars in hundred dollar bills. He had packed the gun in his suitcase so he wouldn't have trouble with it at the airport.

When he got to his room he removed it, putting it under the pillow on the bed but leaving the bedspread wrinkled where he had moved it. He left the manila envelope in the suitcase under his shirts. Both the money and the gun were government issue, the bait with which Sergeant Peter Patrigno would be hooked and landed.

In another sense, however, Patrigno himself was the bait. Although he was the immediate target of this operation, Special United States Attorney Paul Scala, who controlled Lacey, was looking higher. It was a luxury he could afford because Patrigno was already jammed up without knowing it. His had been one of the first names Lacey had given when he originally turned, and in the year since then Lacey had led the sergeant into half a dozen bribery and shakedown incidents. Patrigno could be reeled in whenever Scala wanted, but for the time being he could be more useful on the outside. In effect, Patrigno served as a double agent working under the deepest cover of all—so deep that he himself was unaware of it.

Early Thursday evening Patrigno picked two detectives from his squad to make the arrest on Barrera. He didn't tell them about the deal with Lacey. To do so, he would have had to have trusted them far more than he did, for there was no one Pete Patrigno trusted that much. He simply counted on the fact that when the time came they would see how it was going down.

The three officers arrived at the hotel shortly after eight o'clock and secured a passkey from the manager. They learned that a dinner had been sent to Barrera's room less than an hour before. He hadn't turned in his key at the front desk and the desk man hadn't seen him leave.

After conferring briefly, Patrigno and the two detectives took the main elevator to the fourth floor. As they walked quietly down the carpeted corridor, Patrigno handed the passkey to Tim Conrad, the younger of the two detectives. When they reached Barrera's room, Ralph Hutchinson, Conrad's partner, positioned himself against the wall just beyond the door while Patrigno took the near side. All three had their guns drawn. Conrad slid the key silently into the lock with his left hand. When he felt it seat, he nodded to his partner, who reached over his shoulder and knocked loudly twice. "Room service," Conrad called out, turning the key in the lock. "You finished with your tray?"

He swung the door open and stepped in, his gun scanning the

room for less than a second before it locked on the slender dark-haired man in the upholstered chair on the far side of the bed. "Police," Conrad announced. "Move and you're dead."

Barrera had no intention of moving. In what seemed almost an involuntary gesture, his right hand flicked out a few inches toward the pillows on the bed but stopped even before Conrad had finished speaking. In his left hand he held a cigar, the moist tip of it just a few inches from his forehead as his elbow rested on the arm of the chair. In a moment there were three cops in the room. Barrera knew that the big one in the middle was Patrigno. With a shrug he indicated that he was willing to do as he was told.

"All right, get up and get against that wall," Patrigno ordered.

Without using his hands, Barrera rose awkwardly from the soft chair. Hutchinson plucked the short stub of cigar from between Barrera's fingers and tossed it through the open bathroom door. There was a splash and then a hiss as it died. Barrera stood without moving while the detective patted him down for weapons.

Patrigno's voice said, "Okay, you can turn around." When he did, he saw that the third detective already had begun searching the room. He started with the suit coat that hung over the back of the chair at the small desk by the window. From the inside pocket he removed a tan leather billfold, which he flipped across the room to the sergeant.

By this time Patrigno had holstered his gun. He caught the billfold with his left hand and began to inspect the contents. There was a New York State driver's license, some credit cards, and a few hundred dollars in cash. "Why don't you make yourself useful?" he said with understated sarcasm to Hutchinson, who hadn't moved since he finished frisking the suspect. As the detective hurried across the room to the suitcase, which stood unopened on the luggage rack, Barrera winced almost imperceptibly.

"Just relax, Ramon," Patrigno said.

"Sergeant," Conrad called. He had thrown back the bedspread and flung the pillows to the side, leaving the nickel-plated gun exposed on the coarse starched sheets.

"I don't know nothing about that," Barrera protested.

"That's what I figured. Must've been left there by the tooth fairy," Patrigno answered softly, his deep voice expressionless.

"You're lucky we got here in time. If you went to bed you could've blown your brains out."

Barrera turned away in disgust. On the other side of the room Detective Hutchinson was rifling through his suitcase, scattering the contents on the floor after shaking out each shirt to make sure nothing was folded into it. When he got to the manila envelope he held it up for the sergeant to see.

"Open it," Patrigno ordered.

The detective ripped off the sealed end of the envelope and looked inside. "Jesus Christ!" he said, then turned and dumped the contents onto the bed. Six small bundles of money fell out. Patrigno walked to the bed and spread them out. Each packet was bound with a paper seal around the middle. Picking up one packet, Patrigno counted it. There were twenty hundred-dollar bills in each packet, two thousand dollars, a total of twelve thousand in the six bundles. "I suppose you don't know anything about this either?" he said to Barrera.

"Since when's it a crime to have money?" Barrera answered.

"It's not," Patrigno said. "It's just where you're going you won't need it."

This was the moment the undercover federal agent had been waiting for. His whole manner changed abruptly. His surliness disappeared and he was suddenly frightened and deferential. "Look, sergeant, could we talk?" he asked.

"Sure, talk's free," Patrigno said. "Read him his rights, Conrad. I don't want him talking about anything he doesn't want to talk about."

"Fuck that," Barrera shot back. "I know my rights. I just thought maybe we could talk."

"All right, talk."

"Alone?"

Patrigno took three steps forward until his jaw was just inches in front of the smaller man's eyes. His left hand shot forward and grabbed Barrera's shoulder, squeezing painfully into the muscle and against the bone. He could have picked Barrera up with just that one hand if he had wanted to. His right hand came up to Barrera's throat and his thick fingers fumbled awkwardly under the knot of his necktie. A forefinger probed under the collar button until Barrera could scarcely breathe, and then Patrigno ripped downward, tearing the shirt open to the waist. "All right," Patrigno said, releasing him and stepping back, "say your piece but say it in front of everyone."

Barrera took a moment to compose himself. In Washington that morning they had talked about sending him in wired, and he was suddenly aware with excruciating clarity that he would be in serious trouble right now if he hadn't convinced them that it wouldn't be safe. The buttons of his shirt hung uselessly in their button holes while the other side of the shirt dangled like an old flag with frayed edges. He tried to pull it closed but it wouldn't stay. The picture he had of himself at that moment, with his necktie dangling against the pale white skin of his naked chest, reinforced his sense of his own vulnerability.

"Look, sergeant," he said, "maybe if I could do something for you, you could do something for me."

Conrad and Hutchinson glanced quickly at each other and then at Patrigno, who waited for a long time before answering. "What can you do for me?" he asked.

"It's right there, sergeant," Barrera said, gesturing toward the bed. "There's twelve grand there. I can't see doing time on a gun charge. Be worth it to me."

"Barrera, you're going to be carrying your nuts around in your hand if you keep talking like that," the sergeant snapped. He turned and walked to the bed, where he started putting the packets of money back in the envelope.

"Hey, look, sergeant," Barrera pleaded. "I got a lot of things going, man. I can't face time."

Patrigno replaced all the money in the envelope, which he left on the bed. "I'll tell you what you can do, Barrera," he said in a low voice. "You can think about what you just said. Think about all the things you got going and whether you really need all of them. Maybe you can see your way clear to some of it you don't need. Then we can talk. Conrad, cuff him and read him his rights."

"Wait a minute, wait a minute," Barrera cut in, his left hand raised to stop Detective Conrad. "I can see that," he said. "Just let me think a minute."

Patrigno nodded and Conrad stood his ground, about five feet from Barrera.

"Yeah, okay, look," he began tentatively. "If I give you something nice, maybe we can just forget about this, huh?"

Patrigno shrugged noncommittally. "Let's see what you got, I'll see what I can do," he growled.

"Awright, look. There's a guy gonna be in town next week. He's big stuff. Works out of Milan, hundred kilo class, I'm not shitting you. He's not any fucking courier either. He won't have that kind of weight on him—don't get me wrong, I'm not telling you that. But that's what he deals in. This is straight. You get your hands on a guy like that, it's up to you what you do with him. But you're playing big league ball, yknow what I mean. You interested?"

"Yeah, I'm interested," Patrigno said, but he didn't like it. It was just instinct, but an instinct developed over twenty years in the job, and it told him something in this whole setup was wrong. All at once the room felt close and he could smell his own sweat. He wanted to get out of there, with or without Barrera. A wormy little messenger like this didn't deal in hundred kilo shipments and didn't mess with those who did. If he had to give up something to beat the gun rap, he would give up some of his own people, but he wouldn't be stupid enough to hand up someone near the top.

Patrigno's head felt like it was being crushed from the sides in, and it was only with an immense effort of will that he restrained himself from running out of the room the way he had fled from Gil Lacey's car the day before.

Just from looking at Patrigno's face, Barrera could see that something was wrong, but he didn't know what. Suddenly he was afraid that the whole operation would fall apart if he didn't start talking quickly to get control of the situation. "Listen," he said, speaking rapidly, "the guy's name is Danzie, Carlo Danzie. He's from Milan. He's gonna be in New York next week. Tuesday, I think. Yeah, Tuesday. He stays at the Americana. He'll have some stuff with him, I don't know how much but I'm telling you the guy deals in hundred kilo lots. Now can we forget about this thing?"

Patrigno walked to the chair where Barrera had been sitting when they came into the room. His huge body collapsed into it and he spoke softly without looking up, his hand in front of his mouth. "I'll tell you what I can do," he said. "I'm taking you in, there's nothing I can do about that. But if this thing comes through and it's anything like you say it is, I'll see what I can do for you."

"Hey, look," Barrera objected, "I don't want anything like that.

What're you gonna do, get me a suspended sentence for cooperating?
Fuck that, mister. I'd be better off in the can the rest of my life. I'd be
dead, yknow that."

"Don't sweat it," Patrigno said. "We'll fix it up some way so it'll
look all right."

Barrera knew he could accept that, but he still thought the money
was worth another try. "Listen, sergeant," he said, gambling that Patrigno wouldn't smell a trap. "I'll give you this guy, right? Now there's
the bread, the offer still stands." He walked to the bed and took two
packets, four thousand dollars, from the envelope and stuffed them
into his hip pocket. "There's eight grand there," he said, indicating the
envelope that still lay on the bed. "Between that and the other thing it
ought to be enough for you."

"Okay," Patrigno answered sharply, looking up at Barrera for the
first time in a long while, "this is the way it's gonna be." His composure seemed to have returned and he stretched his legs in front of
him and crossed them as though he were comfortable with things now.
"If this thing comes down next Tuesday," he said, speaking carefully
with great emphasis, "I'll do what I can for you on the gun rap. But
I'll level with you," he went on, his right hand reaching out toward the
bed, where it came to rest on the envelope. "You got other problems,
too. There's bribery of a police officer, for example. But on the other
hand, look, if you're into as much as you say you are, maybe there's
some of it you could tell me about that would help square that."

Son of a bitch, Ramon Barrera thought. In half a dozen years
working under cover this was the best performance he had ever seen
and he was impressed.

*Barrera's operation had worked to perfection. It cost the United
States government one airline ticket to New York, a forty-five automatic, the price of a shirt, and eight thousand dollars. When Barrera was
taken from his room in handcuffs, Uncle Sam in effect stiffed the International Hotel for his room and dinner.*

*In return for its investment, the government got everything it had
wanted. After being booked, Barrera was sent to the Queens County
House of Detention. With a good word from Patrigno and a portion of
the four thousand dollars left to him, he was able to enlist the cooperation
of an assistant D.A. in the Queens County district attorney's office. Ultimately, this assistant D.A. would be indicted, tried, and convicted for*

accepting a bribe to fix the Barrera case by falsifying records so as to make them show that the gun seized in the raid was inoperable. In 1974, however, the conviction was reversed on appeal.

Additionally, in November of 1972, ten months after the incident at the International Hotel, Sergeant Peter Patrigno and Detectives Timothy Conrad and Ralph Hutchinson were indicted for violation of state anticorruption laws. Patrigno, however, had a long history of mental instability. In 1945 he had been discharged from the army on grounds of "psychoneurosis." Although his friends and associates knew him as an affable, outgoing man, he was subject to periodic fits of intense suspiciousness and deep withdrawal. Through 1971 and the early part of 1972, these bouts of quasi-paranoiac derangement had been growing more frequent and more persistent. By June of 1972, when Gil Lacey's role as an undercover agent for the federal government was publicly announced, Patrigno was no longer able to maintain his precarious balance. After the indictments came out in November, a court-appointed psychiatrist pronounced him unfit to stand trial and his case was separated from that of the two detectives who worked under him.

Conrad and Hutchinson were brought to trial in the spring of 1974. Testifying in their own defense, they contended that although Sergeant Patrigno had indeed taken money from Barrera and had divided it with them, to the best of their knowledge he had done so in order to cement a relationship with a potentially valuable informant. In addition, accepting the money gave Patrigno a bribery charge he could hold over Barrera to ensure his further cooperation. Insisting that they knew of no prearranged shakedown deal between Patrigno and Gil Lacey, Conrad and Hutchinson explained that they hadn't reported the incident because they assumed it was their sergeant's responsibility to do so. Although the prosecution put both Ramon Barrera and Gil Lacey on the stand, the jury believed the detectives rather than the undercover men. Conrad and Hutchinson were acquitted.

Sergeant Patrigno was never brought to trial. As of this writing he is still confined in an institution for the mentally ill.

By Tuesday morning Sergeant Patrigno still hadn't decided what to do about the Danzie tip. He had lied to Lacey when he met him on Monday morning, saying that so far Barrera had been unwilling to talk.

This put Lacey in a bind. He knew Patrigno was lying because

Barrera made bail late Friday and reported on the bust to his control agent over the weekend. But the most Lacey could do if he didn't want to give away the whole show was to remind Patrigno firmly that if Barrera ever cracked, he, Lacey, deserved to be in on whatever his tips produced.

When he left Patrigno on Monday morning, Lacey raced from Queens to the West Side of Manhattan, hurrying across town at 125th Street. Even on a cold February morning Harlem was still Harlem, the sidewalks almost alive with grim-faced black people moving purposefully against the wind or bobbing listlessly in place to keep warm. When he was in Narco he had worked these streets a hundred times, but right now they held no interest for him and he sped on toward Broadway. Turning left, he drove south toward Columbia University, then west again to Riverside Drive. Pulling to the curb in the no-parking zone in front of Riverside Church, he hopped from the car and jogged across the Drive to a small, hilly park with a crust of unshoveled snow on the sidewalks. Ahead of him, in the deep shadows of a doorway to Grant's Tomb, he could see Special United States Attorney Paul Scala, who had ordered this meeting and picked the location. When he saw that Scala had no intention of coming out of the shadows to meet him, he slowed his pace to an almost leisurely walk, consciously enjoying the feeble warmth of the sunlight as he kept his boss waiting.

As Lacey climbed the three stone steps to the Tomb, Scala nodded a greeting but didn't offer his suede-gloved hand. Posed stiffly a few inches from the stonework wall in a gray overcoat with clean, almost military lines, he could have been taken for one of the male models who often use this site for fashion spreads in the Sunday magazines. Except that his face was all wrong. His small, soft eyes were ludicrously close together and his nose looked almost too large and round to be real. If it weren't for the thin-lipped, cynical mouth that gave some measure of the man's intense determination, he would have looked like the sort of homely person who is easy to get along with. As it was, the net effect of his features was disconcerting, like someone had crossed a grizzly bear with a koala.

"Look," Lacey began with a tone of urgency, "we may have a problem here. I don't know if Patrigno's running some kind of game on me. I just came from talking to him and he said Barrera didn't give him a thing. Not a word about Danzie."

"Maybe he's getting greedy, wants the collar for himself?" Scala said, offering the hypothesis as a question.

"No way. He's out in Queens. How's he gonna make a bust in Manhattan?"

There was a long pause. "Well, maybe Barrera didn't give him the information," Scala suggested.

"Says he did," Lacey answered. "He's your man. You got any reason not to trust him?"

"No. Do you think he burned you?"

"Patrigno? I don't know. I don't wanna think about that," Lacey said. But the idea had been running through the back of his mind ever since he left the sergeant about an hour before.

"You just better hope he didn't," Scala said icily. "Because if he did, I don't see what use you're gonna be to us."

Lacey let the threat pass. He knew that Scala was not a man who liked to be disappointed. Just one mistake and that son of a bitch would pull him out of the operation and leave him facing a suitcaseful of charges.

"I'm gonna send Danzie in anyway," Scala went on. "Maybe Patrigno's got someone of his own he wants to give it to. You leave your bait out long enough, you gotta catch something. One way or the other we got ourselves a fish fry."

Paul Scala had been in the middle of the guerrilla warfare being waged against police corruption ever since the first shots were fired two years earlier. When the Knapp Commission was formed in May 1970 he was named as an associate counsel on the staff, working directly under Michael Armstrong, the commission's chief counsel. The very formation of the Knapp Commission led indirectly to the resignation of one police commissioner and directly to a number of major departmental shakeups. Its televised public hearings provided a forum for Patrolman Frank Serpico, who until then had been struggling against corruption for years with no discernible results other than a bullet in his head. Besides giving Serpico a chance to tell his nightmarish story, the hearings produced three days of sensational testimony from Patrolman William Phillips, a garishly corrupt cop whose shocking revelations generated headlines that lasted for weeks.

In the end, however, the Knapp Commission went out of business having accomplished little besides making the public aware of police cor-

ruption and hostile to cops. Its chairman, Whitman Knapp, accepted his commission's demise with equanimity, as did Chief Counsel Armstrong. Knapp was rewarded with a judgeship, while Armstrong was appointed to fill the unexpired term when the Queens County district attorney was indicted on corruption charges. Paul Scala, though, elected to play the game out to the very end. From the start he had realized that a commission appointed by Mayor Lindsay could not reasonably be expected to dig very deeply into Lindsay's Police Department. Thus, in the summer of 1971, while the Knapp Commission was still in existence, Scala presented his credentials to the Justice Department in Washington and argued convincingly that the issue of corruption in New York should not be under the exclusive jurisdiction and control of New York's mayor.

Political considerations may have played a part in the Justice Department's decision to give Scala what he wanted. At the time Mayor Lindsay, on the verge of shifting from the Republican to the Democratic party, was making presidential noises that undoubtedly grated on the sensitive ears of the Nixon administration. A generous application of scandal obviously would go a long way toward quieting him down. So Paul Scala was appointed as a Special Assistant United States Attorney for the Southern District. Nominally he was, like all assistant prosecutors, under the jurisdiction of the U.S. attorney in his district—in this case Whitney North Seymour. But in fact Scala's status as a "special assistant" gave him a unique degree of latitude, so that to a large extent he was answerable directly to John N. Mitchell's Justice Department.

In addition to his title, he was given a corps of agents from the Bureau of Narcotics and Dangerous Drugs to use for his investigations. His most important investigative tool, however, was not supplied by the Justice Department but was Scala's own contribution to the operation. This tool was Detective Gil Lacey, whom Scala had in effect stolen from the Knapp Commission. Without him, Scala wouldn't even have had a job, or would have had to go back to being just another assistant D.A. when the commission folded. With him, he was suddenly one of the most feared and powerful men in New York, though few people in the city had ever heard of him.

It was only by the merest chance that Patrigno called Joe Longo instead of Gil Lacey. His involvement with Lacey was making him increasingly uncomfortable and he still couldn't get over the feeling that Barrera had given him a tip he had no business giving. The possibility that Lacey was working for the Justice Department or that Barrera was an undercover agent never explicitly occurred to him. His mind didn't work that way. Instead, he made simple distinctions between what felt right and what didn't, and then stayed away from the latter.

Acting on this principle, he let the Monday meeting go by without passing the tip on to Lacey, figuring he would just let the whole matter drop. But Tuesday found him still brooding on it. The problem was that Barrera would be bargaining with the D.A., who would want to know what had come of the tip Barrera had given. Patrigno would have to have an answer.

He reached for the telephone and dialed Lacey's number in Manhattan, then hung up before it rang twice. Where's my head, he thought. The solution to his problem was so clear that he was annoyed at himself for not having seen it before. He didn't want to call Lacey, but he couldn't sit on the tip. So he made a typical sergeant's decision. He would give it to someone else, someone who would handle it the right way. He called Joe Longo.

Chapter 2
Carlo Danzie

THE JOINT TASK Force on Narcotics, founded in 1968 as part of President Nixon's highly touted war on drugs, was a group of federal, state, and city law enforcement officers headquartered on three floors of a federal office building at 201 Varick Street in southern Manhattan. In the early evening hours, groups of men often collected there for a few minutes of talking and joking together before breaking up for the night. Although they worked in civilian clothes, their humor was the locker-room humor of uniformed men. Cops, like soldiers and athletes, relate to one another with a loose camaraderie that manages to be intimate without presupposing friendship. Indeed, like athletes, the men at 201 Varick Street lived their jobs, so that there was about these end-of-the-day sessions an element of mere hanging around, a restless reluctance to go home.

When the phone rang the officer nearest the desk answered it, then passed the receiver to Joe Longo.

"Pick up a loaf of bread and a quart of milk," someone teased from across the room.

Joe identified himself, listened briefly, then held up his hand to silence the joking in the room. After a few minutes he passed the telephone back to the man who had given it to him, stood up, and walked to the wall rack where his coat hung. "Anyone wanna make a bust at the Americana?" he asked. All six men in the room volunteered.

They drove uptown in two cars. Joe's partner, Luke Antonelli, drove his own Plymouth, with Joe in the passenger seat and a federal agent named Bill Kane in the back. Joe didn't say who had called, and no one asked, but he did point out that the information he had received was contradictory. Pete Patrigno had told him that the man he was looking for had ten kilos of heroin with him and was supposedly a high-level emissary who had been sent to New York to pass out samples.

The sample procedure was a normal part of the narcotics traffic. A traveler from a European or South American syndicate would arrive in New York and set up shop in a hotel. Representatives from the major local syndicates would call on him and would be given small packets of heroin, which they would take away with them for testing. In a day or two they would get back to him, a price would be set, and orders taken for delivery of anything from ten to a hundred kilos. Thus there was no reason for a sample man to carry heavy weight, and Joe was puzzled by this discrepancy in the story Patrigno had given him.

"We'll see," he said. "Either way. Ten kees would be a nice collar, but busting a sample man's gonna do us more good in the long run." Kane and Antonelli agreed.

The two cars arrived at the Americana simultaneously and pulled around to the Fifty-second Street entrance. Before he got out of the car, Joe spotted two wise guys he knew loitering under the awning of the Pier 52 restaurant, which stood directly across Fifty-second from the hotel. He poked Luke and nodded in their direction. "Tomasa and Santini," he said. "Looks like we're in the right neighborhood." (A few hours later, when he brought Danzie out of the hotel in cuffs, Joe noticed a carful of federal agents parked beyond the hotel's loading platform. Assuming they were waiting for Tomasa and Santini to come out of the restaurant, and not wanting to blow their cover, he made no sign of recognition to them. Weeks later, as he remembered the incident, it became clear to him that they were there because of

Carlo Danzie. Only then did he realize that in effect he himself had been the object of their surveillance.)

When the seven officers rendezvoused on the sidewalk, Joe detailed two city cops to stay outside in the car. Antonelli, Kane, an agent named Leo Wiley, and a detective named Jeff Stallard followed him into the hotel, where they waited in the lobby under the hostile watchfulness of the desk clerk while Joe went in search of the security officer. It was well past show time but there was nevertheless a steady traffic of desultory-looking men and overdressed women circulating around them.

In ten minutes Joe returned with the security man and made introductions all around. The man they were looking for had checked in that afternoon with no luggage, giving an address in Milan and using an Italian passport for identification. The security man, a retired cop in his late fifties who knew Joe from Joe's years in midtown Mounted, was well aware that they had no warrants for Danzie. If they had had them they would have shown them to him, so he didn't ask. Instead, he explained that he couldn't give them a passkey but would let them into the room. The terms seemed fair, and the men fell in behind him and Joe as they led the way to the service elevators.

On the twenty-fourth floor they followed the long brightly lit corridor until it branched to the left. "It's the third door on the right, twenty-four sixty-six," the house detective whispered.

Joe asked him where the stairs were. There were two sets nearby, one in the branch corridor three doors past Danzie's room, the other in the main corridor just beyond the branch. "Maybe we wait an hour, see if there's anything to see," Joe suggested, figuring it would make a better bust if they observed traffic in and out.

Antonelli, Kane, and Wiley were detailed to the staircase off the main corridor, and Joe took Stallard to the one beyond Danzie's room, pausing as they passed to listen briefly at the door. They heard nothing. The security man, who said he didn't want to wait, promised to return in forty-five minutes and shuffled back in the direction of the service elevator.

The time passed quickly, a total waste. If Danzie was doing any business, this wasn't the night for it. Two or three times the detail in the stairway off the main corridor heard the elevators open but they were all false alarms. Nothing went in or out at twenty-four sixty-six. It was almost ten o'clock when the house detective returned.

The six men gathered silently outside Danzie's room, Joe positioning them with hand movements. Normally the lowest-ranking man on the raid is the first one in, but no one was surprised when Joe took the job himself. Standing tensely in front of the door, his right hand on the knob, he raised his left to a ready position for the go signal. Reaching past him, the security man slid the passkey into the lock without making a sound and turned it slowly until he felt it click. Joe felt it, too, jerked on the knob, and slammed his shoulder into the door with enough force to get through if the chain lock had been on. It wasn't, and he stumbled into the room, the others pouring in after him with guns drawn.

In front of him he saw a sturdy, well-built man in shirt sleeves, probably in his fifties. "All right, hold it right there," he barked, but the man ignored his order. In that first moment of confusion, as the police rushed in, the man strode across the room toward the wall to Joe's right. "I said hold it," Joe shouted, his voice hard and commanding. Yet the man took two more steps and for an instant the thought flashed through Joe's mind that he had come to the wrong room. He was only a few feet from the man now, and as he looked into his face he saw two gray eyes staring back at him with a look of perplexity that mirrored his own.

This exchange of glances lasted less than a second, and then at the edge of his vision Joe caught a fleeting blur of motion as Carlo Danzie's left hand darted outward over the television console that stood against the wall. It was a rapid movement, like flicking at a fly, but at the end of it something shot from Danzie's hand, something small and white that disappeared behind the television.

Behind him, Joe heard the other men shouting—"Back of the tv, Joe," "No you don't," "Get your fucking hands up." But he didn't need them to tell him what to do. He lunged forward, his forearm raised like a charging lineman. It caught Danzie square in the chest and sent him reeling to the side, where he fell off balance on the bed. Turning his back on Danzie, Joe grabbed the set in his powerful hands and pulled it away from the wall, snapping the cable with a sharp report that cut through the voices of the other men like a gunshot on a busy sidewalk. The tiny parcel, which had landed on the horizontal portion of the picture tube that projected from the back of the set, fell silently to the carpet.

Joe scooped it up and examined it. A small plastic envelope, it

contained what felt like less than an ounce of heroin. Wheeling to face
Danzie, who still lay where he had fallen on the bed, he thrust the
envelope under the man's eyes and demanded, "Is this it? Is this all
there is?"

Danzie said nothing.

"All right, search the place," Joe ordered, without taking his eyes
off Danzie. "Him, too."

He grabbed Danzie's shirt in both hands, pulled him up physically from the bed, and shoved him backward in the general direction
of Jeff Stallard, who quickly frisked him and reported, "He's clean,
Joe." Within a few minutes the other detectives and agents had completed their search of the room. Except for the one packet Danzie had
tried to hide behind the television, they found nothing.

"All right, sit down," Joe ordered, grabbing the wooden chair
that went with the writing table and slamming it in behind Danzie's
knees, knocking him into a sitting position. Then he sat on the bed
facing him and began his interrogation, his face barely six inches from
his prisoner's, his green eyes flashing with the impersonal hatred a
soldier learns to feel toward an enemy soldier. Danzie remained utterly
silent, his face a mask of fear and bewilderment.

Before long Joe was rattling off his questions in a rapid-fire stac-
cato, punctuating each one by jabbing sharply at Danzie's chest with
the heel of his hand. "What's your name? Who gave you the junk?
Where's the rest of it? Who are your buyers? When are they coming
back?"

Then, frustrated and angry, he stood up and walked across the
room to his partner. "Maybe the bastard doesn't speak English," he
said. "Why don't you give him a try?"

Antonelli took Joe's place on the bed. His family came from
Bologna and he spoke fluently in a northern Italian dialect. As soon as
he said a few words Danzie cut him off. "My name is Carlo Danzie,"
he said in Italian. "I am from Milan and I will not answer your questions." With that, he lapsed back into silence.

Even though it was now clear he would get nothing out of Danzie,
Joe was reluctant to leave the hotel room. Since Danzie still had a
sample on him when they came in, it seemed reasonable to expect that
someone would be showing up to collect it. So the five narcotics investigators and their prisoner waited until nearly midnight, the agents
and detectives talking quietly among themselves, Kane with his head

out the door listening for the elevator, and Antonelli making small talk with Danzie in Italian. It was after two o'clock on the morning of February 2, 1972, when the group finally arrived with their suspect at the Varick Street office, where he was booked and fingerprinted. Joe did the paper work himself and then personally delivered Carlo Danzie to the Federal House of Detention on West Street.

The moment Joe Longo and his men burst through his hotel room door, Carlo Danzie knew something had gone wrong. The plan called for him to be busted by New York City policemen and put in the Tombs, the notoriously overcrowded prison attached to the courthouse at the north end of Foley Square. There he would attempt to bribe his way out of the case by working on corrections officers, judges, and members of the Manhattan district attorney's office. Because the arrest was supposed to have been made by Gil Lacey, there was no point in attempting to bribe the arresting officers. Thus the government hadn't supplied Danzie with money, as it had done for Ramon Barrera the week before.

Perhaps, too, they simply didn't trust Danzie. Unlike Barrera, he was not an agent. He was a civilian, not even an American citizen, who worked from time to time for the Bureau of Narcotics and Dangerous Drugs as an S.E., "special employee"—a polite euphemism for a paid informant. For over twenty years he had been making his way through life on favors owed and owing. In his native Milan the police knew of him as a major contrabandista, *or smuggler. Years ago he had been arrested by American drug agents in Lebanon and had worked the case off by betraying colleagues. Since then he had made it a practice to cooperate whenever he got himself jammed up, and the authorities in turn had granted him a certain latitude for conducting business.*

Even to a knowledgeable insider, the idea of using an S.E. for an operation such as this seems outlandish. Sending agents into prison to work under cover was nothing new, but getting a bona fide member of the international narcotics network—even a cooperative one—to go into an American jail for the sake of an investigation must have taken some very fast talking and some very heavy promises.

In any case, at the moment of his arrest Danzie immediately saw that things were not going according to plan. As soon as he saw five men charging through the door with drawn guns he realized that someone didn't know the score. It didn't take five cops acting like the Gestapo to make an arrest that was a setup in the first place. In his confusion,

Danzie figured it would be best to say nothing. This accounts for his otherwise inexplicable behavior in pretending he didn't speak English, when in fact he was fluent in English, Italian, Spanish, German, and Arabic. The dumb act gave him time to think, to figure out where he stood before he said anything.

When he was taken to West Street instead of the Tombs, there could no longer be any doubt that something had gone wrong. He didn't know enough about the intricacies of jurisdiction in America to understand how it could have happened, but he did know that he was in a federal prison instead of a New York City jail. Was it some kind of a trick? He had been supplied with heroin and then arrested according to plan. But perhaps Paul Scala, who devised the whole operation, had betrayed him? He was supposed to be working for the federal government, making cases against the city, but instead he was a federal prisoner, locked up by agents who seemed to represent the very people he had agreed to help.

In fact, the explanation was simple. The mix-up had come about because Pete Patrigno had done the one thing no one had counted on. If Patrigno had made the collar himself or given it to practically any other New York City cop, it all would have come out right. But he called Joe Longo, a cop he had met when he was working in the Brooklyn D.A.'s office half a dozen years before. Although Joe was still a city cop, he had been assigned for the past five months to the federally funded Joint Task Force. Because of this assignment, Joe's participation automatically made the arrest a federal case. To Patrigno, who wasn't in on the scheme, this didn't matter. He was simply getting himself out of a situation he didn't like and at the same time doing an old friend a favor. He had no way of knowing that in the end it would turn out to be a favor that would cost his friend his life.

After depositing Carlo Danzie at West Street, Joe drove back to the Joint Task Force headquarters. All six of the men who had been in on the arrest with him were still in the office. As soon as he walked in, his partner Luke told him that all the information they had on Danzie, including his fingerprints, had been sent to the Police Department's Bureau of Criminal Identification and that already the BCI had called back to say that as far as they were concerned Carlo Danzie did not exist. He had no record of arrests in New York and there were no wants on him.

"Maybe the International Group knows something about him," Joe suggested.

The International Group was a collection of federal agents working out of the Bureau of Narcotics and Dangerous Drugs offices at 90 Church Street only a few blocks away. Kane put in a call to them, but the man on the night desk there told him not to expect an answer until the office opened in the morning. Since it was almost five o'clock by this time, the men decided to call it a night. Before the squad split up, though, Joe remembered that he was scheduled to be in court that morning on another case. Figuring that he might be tied up there all day, he asked Antonelli and Kane to handle Danzie's arraignment for him.

Because of the time and because it was almost an hour's drive from the office to his home just beyond the Queens border in western Long Island, Joe elected to stay at headquarters, where he could get a few hours sleep on one of the cots kept for that purpose on the fourth floor.

He woke up a little before seven thirty, stiff and sore from the cot, which hadn't been designed for a man of his size. Jeannie and the kids would be up by now, so he called home to let them know he was all right. Then he made himself a cup of instant coffee, sipping at it gingerly as he carried it back to his desk. He removed his shirt and threw it over his chair, took a razor and a can of aerosol shave cream from his bottom drawer, and went to the men's room to wash up and shave. A few minutes later he strode back into the office feeling as refreshed as if he had slept all night.

Two federal agents from the International Group were seated at his desk. One of them, Bert Poole, was leaning back in Joe's chair, his ankles balanced on the corner of the desk. Joe didn't know the other. They had helped themselves to coffee.

"You guys get up early," Joe called with a light laugh from across the room. There was an edge of sarcasm in his words, but his voice and smile hid it so completely that neither Poole nor the other man took offense. Like most New York City cops, Joe did not have a high opinion of federal agents, who were generally regarded as arrogant, selfish, and pampered. Over the years he often had been called on to cooperate with the FBI and the Bureau of Narcotics but the cooperation always seemed to go only one way. Invariably something would happen that left a bad taste.

"Congratulations," Poole said softly as Joe moved around behind the desk and stood bare-chested, towering over him.

"What for?" Joe asked, bending over Poole to take a clean shirt from one of the desk drawers. The white expanse of his broad, almost hairless chest loomed over Poole like an insult, and even in repose the heavy muscles of his upper arms bulged with ominous potency.

Poole waited until Joe stepped back and pulled his shirt on before answering. "Carlo Danzie," he said. "You got him. Congratulations."

"Yeah, we got him," Joe laughed. "What've we got?"

It took Poole more than ten minutes to spell it out. Before he was halfway through, Joe was seated on the corner of his own desk listening raptly, his shirt still unbuttoned, his spirits soaring, and his mind racing miles ahead of what Bert Poole was telling him. According to Poole, Carlo Danzie was one of the major drug traffickers in Europe. He was not a money man or a dealer. He operated as a high-level factor or intermediary, negotiating major deals between Middle Eastern laboratories and European syndicates that did a large-volume drug business.

What was even more exciting was that Danzie went back a long way with the Bureau of Narcotics as an informant. "The guy'll work," Poole said. "At least that's what the form sheet on him says. Whenever he gets himself jammed up, he always works it off. So far as I know he's never done time anywhere." To the best of Poole's knowledge, this was the first time he had ever shown up in the United States.

"If he's so good over there, then what's he doing here?" Joe asked.

"Expanding, I guess," Poole said tentatively. He himself had been taken by surprise when he got to the office that morning and learned that Carlo Danzie was under arrest in New York. He hadn't had time to check with any of the bureaus in Europe and at this point could do no more than guess.

"Could be anything," he went on. "But look, the guy's hot as a pistol, has been for years. He can't take a piss or a crap without checking to see where it lands. We're all over him. But he's a terrific guy, yknow what I mean. Dynamite. He brings deals down, we find out about them six months later. We got him covered every way there is, but the guy moves like a roach when the lights come on. Smooth son of a bitch. But look, he's not perfect yknow, so every once in a while we nail him—every year, I don't know, two years, three, whatever it is. And each time it costs him something. He's gotta work it off, he loses some friends. It's a tough way to do business. So it could be he's sick of the whole thing and he's looking to get himself some territory where maybe he's not so well known. Except for the bunch of us down at International, I don't think anybody in the country's ever heard of him. Poor schmuck, now he's back in it again. Gets himself busted first time he comes to town."

As Poole talked, Joe realized he had made what might well turn out to be the most important collar of his career. Involuntarily, his memory brought him back to the day, now ten years ago, when he first ran into Sonny Grosso on the sidewalk on Forty-seventh Street outside the Taft Hotel. Joe was in midtown Mounted at the time, twenty-eight years old and happy with the job. As a young man he had had more ambitious dreams, but that afternoon he thought they were behind him.

He had been signed out of high school by a scout for the Cleveland Indians and had gone to play for one of their minor league teams in Wisconsin. At six-one and two-ten, with immense strength in his arms, shoulders, and back, he was the type of left-handed power hitter the scouts were always willing to take a chance on. He had trouble hitting the curve, but then kids often do, and he knew that if he learned to handle the pitch he would hit with the power of a Kluzsewski. He was making progress, too. Then, in late July, he was playing first base when a batter hit a pop foul that started out just over the line and then began hooking toward the bleacher stands. Joe gave chase with all the abandon of a rookie in a low minor league and never even heard his catcher's warning. As he cracked into the bat rack just beyond his own team's bench he heard what sounded like two distinct explosions in the distance and then crumpled to the ground in pain. Both legs were shattered just above the ankles. The season was gone, and when the next spring came he knew his legs would never carry him to the major leagues and didn't even report to camp.

He stayed home that year and worked intermittently in his father's contracting business. There are some sons who can work easily for their fathers and others who cannot. Three of his brothers were there, but Joe didn't feel like he fit in. He was inducted into the army and sent to Korea. When he came back he joined the police force.

For the first few years on the force he was as restless and dissatisfied as he had been when he worked for his father. Then, on a whim, he volunteered for mounted duty. Although he had never been on a horse in his life, he was a superb athlete and mastered it quickly, soon becoming one of the best riders in the division. The job involved mostly patrol duty in Central Park and crowd and traffic control assignments in the midtown theater district. For the first time since his baseball career had been destroyed, he seemed to be approaching some kind of peace with himself. Later he would describe his two years in Mounted as the happiest of his life.

Always a bit of a show-off with more than a touch of vanity, he frankly enjoyed the picture of himself on his beautiful chestnut stallion riding the streets off Broadway. Tall and handsome, with a square, open face, candid green eyes, and an easy deep-throated laugh, he quickly became a well-known figure in the theater district. He went backstage whenever he got the chance and he soon knew and was known by most of the theater people as well as the men who ran the expensive restaurants, nightclubs, and bars that still flourished in the neighborhood. He was married by this time and his son Joey was almost two years old. On his nights off he would have Jeannie get a sitter and they would go to the Copa or to catch Shirley Bassey at the Royal Box at the Americana. The coatcheck girl would greet him by name and flatter Jeannie, and the maître d' would rush up and say, "Hey, it's good to see you, Joe. I'm holding a nice table for you. Terrific show tonight."

Joe didn't fool himself about what he meant to these people, didn't imagine he was really part of their glamorous world. He was just a popular cop on their beat, and they had the business sense to know it was smart to be on good terms with the police. But to a young man in his twenties who had once thought he would someday be a celebrity himself, it was fun and it was exciting. One night at Jilly's the manager brought Vic Damone over to his table and Damone had a drink with him and Jeannie.

It went on like this until that cold Wednesday afternoon in April of 1962 when he met Sonny Grosso. Afternoons Joe usually worked in the park, except on Wednesdays and Saturdays, when there were matinees. He was ticketing a car on Forty-seventh in a no-parking zone across the street from the Taft when a nervous young man approximately his own age charged up to him like he was going to pull him from his horse. "Hey, what're you doing!" the young man shouted.

"This your car?" Joe answered.

After a few minutes of discussion back and forth, the man explained who he was. He didn't show any identification but he said his name was Grosso and that he was a detective. He was working on a case and needed to leave the car where he could have access to it. Joe agreed not to ticket it, and Grosso asked him to keep an eye on it and make sure no one else did either.

Over the next week he saw the car there on a number of occasions but didn't run into Detective Grosso again. Then the car was gone, and a few days later there were headlines in all the papers about a mammoth narcotics case. At the time it was the biggest single seizure ever made, and later it would become famous as the "French Connection" case. Grosso's name was featured in all the stories, and that night Joe excitedly told Jeannie about his encounter with the man who had been in the middle of it all.

Toward morning, Joe woke up with a knot of tension in his stomach and an unpleasant realization growing at the back of his mind. Suddenly the life he had been leading seemed flat and dull, the Broadway friendships no longer glamorous. What the hell am I doing with myself? he thought. He's out making cases like that and I'm writing him a parking ticket!

For a day or two he brooded about it and then, without telling Jeannie, he applied for transfer to narcotics. And now, ten years later, Bert Poole from the International Group was telling him he had a stool with the potential to give him cases bigger than the French Connection.

Chapter 3
The Washington Connection

As soon as the two agents from the International Group had gone, Joe drove to West Street and had Danzie brought down from his cell. The moment the prisoner appeared he seemed like a different man. He greeted Joe warmly if not effusively in both Italian and English. To Joe, this meant only one thing. Danzie had had time to think and had decided to abandon the stonewalling strategy he had used the night before. When a man you arrested wanted to be your friend, it meant he wanted to work.

"Hey, don't you have a coat?" Joe asked as they walked from the prison to Joe's car. It was a bright, clear morning, bitingly cold.

"In my native Milan we have many cold days in winter," Danzie announced grandly, articulating each word precisely. "A person must accustom himself."

"Or get a coat," Joe said, and both men smiled.

In the car Danzie said, "This is what we hear about America, the pace, the rush. Do you always do things so early in the morning?" Even when he spoke softly, his voice was deep and sonorous, a true basso without a trace of the growl deep voices often have. His English was lightly accented but the accent was not particularly Italian. Although Danzie had Italian citizenship from birth and had spent most of his adult life in Milan, he had been born and raised in Beirut.

In the half hour it took to get Danzie from West Street, the Task Force office had come alive. Antonelli and Kane had already returned, and so had some of the other men who had been in on last night's arrest. Captain Ben Marcus, the Task Force's commanding officer, stood in a corner of the wardroom near the hotplate talking with Victor Horne and two other feds from the International Group. The three agents stood shoulder to shoulder and seemed to have Marcus surrounded.

Joe set a chair next to his desk for Danzie and offered his prisoner a cup of coffee. When he went to the hotplate for it, Captain Marcus introduced him to the agents. Horne wasted no time getting to the point.

"Hey, Longo, I don't know how to say this nice," he began, "but we got an interest in this guy."

"Yeah, I heard," Joe shot back. "I do, too. My interest is I busted him. What's yours?"

Horne bristled. "I hope we're gonna be civilized about this," he said.

Joe shrugged without answering. He snapped two plastic cups into their carriers, measured out the powdered coffee, and filled the cups with water. "Haven't even had a chance to talk to the man, captain," he said, addressing himself to Marcus and ignoring the three agents. "There's no sense even talking to anyone until we find out where things stand."

Horne was ready to explode. "I told you where things stand, Longo," he almost shouted, his voice clearly audible throughout the room. "We've got a prior interest in this man. Do you understand that? Prior."

"And I asked you what kind of fucking interest," Joe repeated icily.

Horne backed down. "Look," he said, "no sense getting excited. I didn't mean to blow off at you. But we've been working this guy for years, I don't know how long . . . before I was even in the picture, and that's going back a long way. He's important to us, we don't want to lose him now. We put a lot of men on him and we keep close track of him and we can't throw all that out just because someone happened to pick him up with half an ounce of pure."

Joe picked up the two coffee cups and stepped past Horne. "Tell me something," he said. "If you keep such close track of him, how come he's sitting up in the Americana and you don't even know he's in the country until I put it out on the wire that I got him?"

Danzie was nodding his head in appreciation as Joe approached the desk. "That was very good, what you told him," he said. "They're with me all the time, I know they are. When I am home they know where I am, but when I move I move without them."

The words were both a boast and a warning. They corroborated, if corroboration were needed, Joe's low opinion of federal narcotics agents in Europe, but they also served to put him on notice that Carlo Danzie would not be an easy man to control. "We'll see," Joe said, taking a long sip of coffee and settling into his chair.

He lit a cigarette and dragged on it for a few minutes in silence, collecting his thoughts before commencing the negotiations. As soon as the talk started, Danzie wanted to know why he was under federal arrest, and Joe's explanation seemed to satisfy him.

"You don't really have a case on me, you know that," Danzie said at one point. "It was not a good arrest."

"Maybe," Joe answered noncommittally. "If you were some kind of punk street dealer I'd probably have to cut you loose. But let's be realistic about this, you know the score. I want this case, you see how it is. I'll make it so it'll stick."

"Without that piece of paper?" Danzie taunted.

Joe shook his head like it didn't matter. "I don't need a warrant," he said coolly. "I got a tip from a reliable informant, narcotics being sold on the twenty-fourth floor of the Americana Hotel. I proceeded to the hotel and placed the room under surveillance. I observed a number of male Caucasians entering and leaving the premises. I positioned myself in the corridor and when the door opened I observed—"

"Enough of this *stronzato*," Danzie interrupted. "Even if you go into court with such a story, the other officers will not back you up."

"What other officers?" Joe asked in a tone of mock innocence.

Danzie got the point and nodded. "What do you want?" he asked.

At the moment Joe didn't yet have any plans for Danzie. There were still too many questions about the man. No one knew who his connections were in America, so it wasn't clear what kind of cases he could make. "We'll work that out," Joe said. "All I've got to know now is that you'll cooperate."

Danzie, though, had no intention of cooperating. He was still counting on the people who had sent him to New York to get him out of this. But he didn't trust them enough to be sure. They were quite capable of writing off the original operation as a dead loss and letting him work his own way out of the problem they had made for him. His first instinct when he realized that everything had gone wrong was to get in touch with Scala and have the whole operation called off. But what if it hadn't been a mistake? What if Scala had set him up? Was that possible? He didn't think so but he couldn't be sure. So he decided that if Scala made a move to spring him, that would prove that it was just an accident. But in the meanwhile he wasn't going to sit around waiting to find out. He would try to go around Scala or over his head. And that meant getting in touch with Anthony Diamond, even though he had been specifically told not to.

Tony Diamond had started out as an agent in the old Bureau of Narcotics and had quickly risen until he was now deputy director of the BNDD in Washington, the second-ranking man in the entire federal drug enforcement program. Stationed in Europe for a few years in the sixties, he had been one of the control agents who operated Danzie, so that the two men had worked together before and had worked well. Once before Diamond had gotten Danzie out of a jam. It was an ugly affair that nobody could get straightened out until Diamond took charge. Then, all of a sudden, the agent who made the case and then wouldn't let go changed his mind and stepped out of the picture. Later Danzie heard that he had put a bullet in his own brain one night in a hotel room in San Remo.

"I will do what you wish," Danzie told Joe, "but first I must know that my own interests will be looked after."

The request was a reasonable one. An informant who is not allowed to circulate freely and to conduct business in his usual fashion has only a limited value. Joe immediately agreed in principle without committing himself to any specifics, and as soon as he did Danzie probed further. He had a wife and two children in Milan, he explained, and he wanted to know what could be done to protect them if anything went wrong.

"Milan's a little off my beat," Joe confessed frankly, but he did offer to arrange for some kind of federal protection for them as long as Danzie was cooperating. At this suggestion the Italian's eyes darkened and he made a wave with his left hand which seemed to be dismissing Joe and terminating the talks. For a few moments he said nothing, as though he needed the time to get his anger under control. A consummate actor, he had Joe completely convinced that this was a sensitive issue with him, an area in which his demands would have to be met.

"You are full of shit, Mr. New York City Policeman," he said at last. "I am not stupid in any case and I can see what is happening. I have eyes for a reason, you understand. Those men are not going to help you—I hear how they are talking. They will be of no help. If they tell you otherwise they are lying. And if you tell me they're telling you otherwise, then you are lying. Where my family is concerned I do not take risks. I must know they are safe or I will not work with you."

The talk went on in this vein a few minutes longer, and it was soon clear to Joe that Danzie was asking him for things he was in no position to provide. Leaving Danzie seated at the desk, Joe crossed the room and pulled Captain Marcus away from Horne and the two other feds. They conferred briefly in an office off the squad room. When Joe explained the situation, the captain's only advice was to call Danzie's bluff.

Joe returned to his prisoner and laid it out as plainly as he could. "Look, your problems are your problems. I've got my own," he said. "I wish I could help you out with your family but I can't. If that's not good enough for you, just do your time and we're even."

Danzie's eyes were locked on Joe's as the detective leaned over the desk and delivered his ultimatum. "No," Danzie said firmly, "we have no deal. I have my responsibilities."

Joe shrugged, a gesture calculated to hide his disappointment. As far as he was concerned it was now Danzie's move and there wasn't much time. It was already past nine o'clock and Joe was due in court at ten. By the time he finished testifying, Antonelli and Kane would have taken Danzie for arraignment and the chance to work something out might be irretrievably lost. "Luke, Bill," he called across the room, "take this guy downtown and have him arraigned."

On the other side of the room Antonelli and Kane rose simultaneously from their desks. Each took one last gulp from his coffee cup and walked toward the coat rack in the corner by the door. In another moment they were at Joe's desk. Antonelli reached under Danzie's arm to pull him up from the chair. *"Andiamo,"* he said.

With a quick move Danzie shook him off. "Go away," he said, snapping the words like an order. Before Antonelli could grab him again he said, "Sit down, Joe. Siamo noi due uomini giusto. Something can be done."

Joe motioned for Kane and Antonelli to leave and then sat down. "All right," he said, "so we're reasonable men. Let's hear something reasonable."

Immediately Danzie began to talk in concrete terms. For the first time since his arrest he spoke specifically about what he could offer. He gave the names of some high-powered European traffickers, whom he claimed to represent. This was followed by a brief but revealing account of the nature of their operations. Although Joe didn't recognize many of the names, he had no reason to doubt the truth of what Danzie was telling him. He knew that Danzie's story easily could be checked with international agents and he knew that Danzie knew it.

From there Danzie went on to explain in some detail how one of his European contacts had been getting narcotics into the United States. He sketched out a circuitous route from one European capital to another and named ships and ports of entry in America. "I'm telling you all this because it costs me nothing," he said. "The operation has all been changed. I mean, it is being changed at this very moment. Some of your friends," he went on, motioning in the direction of the agents across the room, "have been getting quite close to us, although to be honest with you, I doubt that they are aware of how close they have come. Tell them what I just told you and you will see that they get very interested. I am telling you all this so that you can see that I am a truthful man, someone who knows what he is talking about."

"I'll check it with them," Joe promised.

"Yes, do that please. But now listen to what I am telling you. I have come to this country to set up a new distribution system that will replace the one I have just described to you. I am not talking about one or two shipments, you understand. We are discussing a network that will be used on a regular basis. You understand that a new system will have some problems, some leaks. It is inevitable. The people I deal with will not be surprised if there are some seizures. Do you follow what I am telling you?"

Joe nodded, carefully underplaying his response to conceal his excitement. If Danzie wasn't running a game on him, it meant that he would have access to a major heroin distribution system. The fact that Danzie would try to limit that access as thoroughly as he could simply meant that it would be Joe's job to keep the pressure on. The important thing was that he was being offered an inside track. What he made of it from there would be up to him.

"Fine. Now if we understand each other, let's see what we can do about these other things," Danzie went on, speaking slowly, keeping his deep voice low in an urgent whisper. "Because none of this is going to happen unless we have satisfactory arrangements between us. I need guarantees that you cannot give me. Neither can those *federales* over there."

"I heard all that," Joe interrupted. "Just tell me what you want, we'll see what we can do."

Danzie was ready with his answer. "I want to make a phone call," he said.

Joe shoved the telephone on his desk toward Danzie but the Milanese drug dealer shook his head and scowled. "Awright, here's a dime," Joe said, motioning toward a pay phone on the far wall of the squad room. "Work out whatever you got to work out and let me know."

While Danzie walked to the phone, Joe crossed the room to Captain Marcus's office and motioned for Marcus to join him there. The captain's office was a small area created by a floor-to-ceiling partition that ran the width of the wardroom. There were three such offices side by side along the outer building wall, and Marcus's was the one in the middle. Brilliant sunlight poured in through the window, which looked out over Varick Street, stinging Joe's eyes and reminding him how little sleep he had had.

"What's up?" the captain asked, closing the door behind him and following Joe to the desk by the window.

"The guy's making a call," Joe said. "Thought you might be interested."

The captain hurried around to the front of his desk and punched one of the unlighted buttons on his telephone while Joe went to an extension phone that stood on a table in the corner of the tiny office. Both men quickly unscrewed the mouthpieces, then carefully lifted the receivers. Marcus pressed the lighted button, tapping the line into the pay phone.

There was silence on the line and then a woman's voice said, "I'm sorry to keep you waiting, Mr. Danzie." She pronounced it Dancey. "Mr. Diamond doesn't seem to be in."

"What the fuck?" Joe muttered, glancing across at the captain, who seemed as startled as he was.

Marcus shook his head and shrugged. "It's gotta be someone else," he said, unable to credit the notion that an arrested drug dealer would be calling the deputy director of the Bureau of Narcotics and Dangerous Drugs.

"You are not Mr. Diamond's secretary, are you, madam?" Danzie asked, his tone curt and intimidating.

"No, I'm—" the woman started to explain.

"Well, please be good enough to connect me with his secretary," Danzie demanded, cutting her off.

Joe and the captain listened in silence as she transferred the call. With the mouthpieces on their phones disconnected they could have talked freely, but neither knew what to say.

For almost five minutes Danzie argued with the secretary, who clearly had been instructed by her boss not to put the call through. Suddenly there was a shift in tactics and she said, "Oh, here's Mr. Diamond now. Just a moment and I'll connect you."

The line went dead and then a man's voice came on.

"Yuh?"

"Diamond? This is Carlo Danzie. I am in New York, I have been arrested."

There was a long pause and the next voice was Danzie's again.

"They want me to work for them."

"Who wants you to work for them?"

"I was arrested by some kind of a task force and for some reason it is a federal thing. Do not ask me to explain it. There are also other factors involved that I cannot discuss here," Danzie added cryptically, not yet willing to jeopardize his status as an undercover for Scala in case Scala came through for him. "I want to know what you can do for me."

There was another pause and then Diamond said, "Give me your number, I'll get back to you."

In the office Joe and Captain Marcus hung up their telephones as soon as Danzie was off the line. Diamond didn't call back for almost fifteen minutes. During that time Joe tried to get assurances from Marcus that he wouldn't let the BNDD steal his prisoner. Marcus had already stood up for him against Horne and the other feds but that didn't guarantee he would stand up against Diamond. "I don't care if he's their stool," Joe pleaded. "He can stool for them, but I locked him up. He's gonna have to work for me, too."

Marcus had a reputation as a good commander to work for and he had earned it in the only way a commander can. He backed up his men. "I'll do what I can, Joe," he promised. "But are you sure you want him?"

"Of course I want him. The guy's dynamite," Joe answered without hesitation. If anything, Danzie's call to Anthony Diamond had served to underscore for Joe the importance of the arrest he had made the night before. There was something almost scary about having your hooks into a man that well connected.

"I'm not gonna tell you what to do, Joe," the captain said from behind his desk. "But give it some thought." He was a man in his forties with a lean body and a large head. When he sat at his desk to speak to his men he often seemed more like a trusted family doctor than a boss. "The guy's no good," he went on. "I can see that just looking at him. If I was you I'd let the BNDD have him. If you hold on to him they're gonna be all over you anyway. I don't have to tell you, they can be a real bunch of fucks. It's not worth it, Joe."

The captain's advice was not something an officer could easily ignore. It came out of more than twenty years in the job, during which time Marcus must have discovered more than enough reasons to be leery of feds. But it never occurred to Joe that there may have been a specific basis to this warning, that it wasn't simply a product of general distrust. He knew he wanted Danzie and he simply wasn't listening. "I can take care of myself," he said.

Marcus nodded slowly. He had said his piece and after that he left the decision to the detective. "Okay," he said. "Just be careful."

When the phone rang they waited for Danzie to answer it, then picked up their extensions.

"Do you know the names of the guys that busted you?" Diamond began without any prelude.

"Joe Longo and four or five others. Does that matter?"

"Where are you now?"

"I'm in their office."

"Awright, put someone on."

"There's no one here, but I think they are listening on another line."

Joe and Captain Marcus exchanged smiles. Joe reconnected the mouthpiece and said, "Mr. Diamond, this is Detective Longo. What can I do for you?"

"Danzie says your guys busted him."

"That's right."

"Well, then, he must have told you he's working for us on something big. I want you to cut him loose and put him on a plane down here before everything comes completely unscrewed."

As politely as he could, Joe refused the request and Diamond immediately blew up at the other end of the line. "I don't know who the fuck you think you are, Longo," he shouted, and then went on in the same vein for what seemed an unreasonable length of time. At his best moments his speech was studded with ludicrously affected tough-guy lingo, but when he lost his temper he became almost a parody of a bad movie. He ended by saying, "I'm not asking you, I'm ordering you. Put your commander on the wire."

If everything he said before hadn't been a mistake, that certainly was. "I'm sorry, Mr. Diamond, but I don't take orders from you," Joe said, his voice perfectly level. "If you want to talk to the captain, you go right ahead. Then try the mayor or the P.C. Because I take my orders from the NYPD, and until I hear otherwise from downtown this man is my prisoner."

Joe's main purpose in lecturing Diamond was to tie Marcus's hands, for the captain couldn't back down now without losing face. Yet he hadn't really expected it to stop Anthony Diamond and was pleasantly surprised by what came next. For reasons Joe couldn't possibly understand, Diamond folded his cards without calling the bluff. Joe knew that it would have been the easiest thing in the world for Diamond to take up the matter with Marcus and then go over the captain's head to the commissioner if that proved necessary. But what he didn't know was that in the fifteen minutes between Danzie's call to Washington and Diamond's return call, the deputy director had decided to explore the possibility of using Danzie for his own purposes, employing him as an undercover to make corruption cases against the very officers who had arrested him. As Diamond saw it, the Italian *contrabandista* was like a missile in midflight. Scala had launched him when he gave him half an ounce of heroin and sent him to the Americana Hotel to await arrest. Now, although there was no calling him back, he could be retargeted.

"Look," Diamond said, "maybe we can just do this. Get on a plane and bring him down here. We'll sit down and work it out so that everybody gets something."

Joe went along for the ride when Antonelli and Kane drove Danzie to the federal courthouse in Foley Square. In the lobby they split up, Joe hurrying to the sixth-floor courtroom, where he was scheduled to testify, while the others proceeded to the office of Assistant United States Attorney Arch Russell.

Russell was expecting them. He explained that he already had been called by BNDD agents from the International Group and made a half-hearted attempt to convince Antonelli to surrender his prisoner to them. It was easy for Luke to parry his request by pointing out that Danzie was really his partner's prisoner, not his own, and therefore his hands were tied. Kane stayed neutral through the entire discussion. As a federal agent, his sympathies were naturally with the BNDD, but he was unwilling to do anything that might jeopardize his relationship with the city cops with whom he had to work every day.

"All right," Russell said when he recognized the futility of pursuing the matter any further, "let me ask you this. Does anybody know he's been busted?"

Antonelli and Kane turned to Danzie, who answered in the negative without any hesitation.

"There was no one you were supposed to see last night after they picked you up?" Russell pursued.

"No."

"And you weren't supposed to meet anyone today?"

"That is correct."

"Am I also correct in understanding that you were distributing samples?"

"Yes."

"When were the people who collected these samples supposed to get back to you?"

"It was not determined. In a day or two. Or I would get back to them."

"Then we can assume that no one is going to wonder about your absence?"

"That is correct," Danzie answered. "There are a number of things I can say if anyone should ask."

Russell said nothing for a few seconds while he made a mental check to see if there were any further questions. When he was certain there weren't, he said, "Fine," in exactly the tone a lawyer uses at the end of a cross examination. Then he toyed for a moment with a ball-point pen, clicking the point in and out about half a dozen times before tossing the pen onto a pile of papers in the center of his desk blotter. "Let me give you some advice," he said to Antonelli. "If we arraign this man, we have to take him before a magistrate in open court. That could give you some problems if anyone sees him. Now what I'd like to suggest is that the defendant waive arraignment and then we eliminate that risk. Is that acceptable to you?"

Luke Antonelli had been on the force more than twelve years and had worked with countless informants without ever once having found it necessary to take such a precaution. If there was a reason to avoid bringing a defendant into court, then he was arraigned in the judge's chambers. But, although waiving arraignment struck Luke as irregular, he could see no reason to object. Being careful never hurt. "Fine with me," he said.

Russell, who was apparently a meticulously methodical man, next secured Kane's consent before turning again to Danzie. "Are you familiar with the way an arraignment works, Mr. Danzie?" he asked.

"I believe so," Danzie answered carefully, sensing something in Russell's manner that suggested the man knew more than he was telling. It was just an intuitive feeling, but it seemed to him that Russell was pulling strings, manipulating things in a way that neither Antonelli nor Kane nor Danzie himself could understand. It was almost as though this pedantic prosecutor were playing a slow-motion shell game with the three of them, and Danzie reasoned that it would be best for him to go along with whatever Russell suggested because he might be working on instructions from Diamond or Scala.

"An arraignment is a formal proceeding," Russell went on, "during which the charges against you are read and you are asked to plead to them. Do you have counsel, Mr. Danzie?"

"No, I do not."

"Do you want counsel?"

"No."

Russell nodded appreciatively. "All right, that's fine. Now what we'd like you to do is to sign a paper in which you waive your right to be arraigned before a magistrate. Our only purpose in asking this is to save you an appearance in an open court where anyone with whom you might be dealing could recognize you. Is that clear?"

Danzie nodded.

"And is it acceptable to you?"

"Yes, it is."

Without another word, Russell picked up the ballpoint pen, slid a yellow legal pad to the front edge of his desk, and began writing. In a few minutes he stopped and passed the pad to Danzie, who read what was written, asked for a pen, and signed it. Antonelli and Kane also signed as arresting officers, and then Kane passed the pad back to Russell.

"All right," the assistant prosecutor said tersely, as though the whole proceeding were suddenly distasteful to him, "I believe our business is concluded."

Months later, after Joe Longo was dead, the purpose of Russell's stratagem became clear. Because Carlo Danzie was never arraigned, there were none of the usual court documents dealing with his arrest. When it was all over, he would be free to disappear without a trace, leaving not even a written record of the fact that he existed.

When court adjourned late Wednesday afternoon Joe Longo had not concluded his testimony. From a pay phone in the courthoue lobby he called Luke Antonelli and invited him for supper without telling him why he wanted to see him. Then he called Jeannie and told her to set another place.

Over dinner, little Marie, Joe's ten-year-old daughter, asked Luke, "Are you a policeman like my daddy?" When he said that he was, she started to giggle.

"Maybe she knows something I don't," Luke joked awkwardly. He had never met his partner's family before and he wanted to let Joe and Jeannie know that they shouldn't be embarrassed on his account.

Jeannie leaned over to her daughter and asked softly, "Is there something funny about that, honey? What is it?"

"I know," Joey piped in with a tone of considerable superiority. He was two years older than his sister.

"Well, one of you ought to tell," Joe said.

"It's his beard. She doesn't think cops have beards."

Luke had grown the beard only a few months before when he went undercover in the Caruso case, the very case on which Joe was now testifying. After the arrests were made he decided not to shave it off.

Supper passed pleasantly, with the children excusing themselves after dessert and the adults sitting over coffee until well after eight as Joe and Luke swapped police stories. When Jeannie started to clear the table, Joe said, "Cmon, there's something I want to talk to you about." He led his partner through the living room, where Joey was watching a basketball game, and upstairs. The bedrooms were the only place they could have privacy. "In here," Joe said, motioning Luke into Joey's room.

"What's up?" Luke asked. He looked for a place to sit in the cluttered room but there wasn't one.

"I know," Joe said. "I think he sleeps standing up." Then his tone changed and he said, "Look, I gotta be on the stand again tomorrow. I want you to take Danzie to Washington for me."

"Sure," Luke answered eagerly, a do-you-really-mean-it note in his voice, like a kid being offered tickets to a ball game. Getting on a plane with a prisoner and flying around at government expense was beyond anything he had ever been called on to do in twelve years on the job. It was like something out of the movies. In his mind's eye he could see himself escorting a handcuffed man up the steps of the Capitol while tourists and government officials gawked.

"Don't be in such a hurry till you hear what the score is," Joe cautioned. "You're going to see Anthony Diamond, right? Do you know who he is?"

"Yeah."

"Yeah," Joe mimicked. "You say it like he's one of the guys down at the office. Well, listen to me, he's not. He outranks you, like if you're a corporal he's a general. So he's gonna try and fuck you over. Do you think you can handle it?"

A quiet, introspective man, soft-spoken almost to the point of shyness, Luke hadn't yet convinced his partner that he could stand up under pressure. The two of them had been working together less than six months and were as unlike each other as two cops could be. So it wasn't surprising that they hadn't yet developed the close feelings of trust and responsibility that often develop between partners on the job.

"Sure," Luke said, a hint of doubt in his voice.

"The thing is," Joe went on, "you can't let who he is intimidate you. You've gotta just forget about that."

Luke laughed. "Yeah, well, thanks for reminding me," he said.

"That's okay. I didn't mean to scare you but I don't want you to run into any surprises when you get down there."

"I think I got the picture."

Joe ignored the faint coloring of sarcasm in his partner's voice. "He's gonna do a number on you," he said. "Don't forget, the feds want this guy for themselves and they must want him pretty bad if Anthony Diamond's getting mixed up in it. So if they want him that much, you just know I gotta want him worse. They're gonna give you a whole lot of bullshit that he's making some big case for them and by the time you get out of there they're gonna have you thinking you're some kind of subversive if you don't hand him over. But whatever they say, you've gotta tell them we busted him and he's gotta work for us. If he works for them, too, that's fine. But he's gotta work for us."

"No sweat."

"Look, in fact, why don't you tell them it's not your case, it's your partner's case but he couldn't come down. That way there's nothing you can do and maybe you save yourself a lot of hassle."

"All right, enough," Luke snapped, annoyed. "I'm not a fucking rookie. I can handle it. Don't worry, I won't give away any of what's yours."

Joe smiled, satisfied that he had finally provoked the reaction he wanted. "Cmon," he said, "let's see how the Knicks are doing."

Early Thursday morning Antonelli and agent Bill Kane drove Carlo Danzie to La Guardia Airport, where they boarded an eight o'clock shuttle. During the flight they spoke little, largely because Danzie, who seemed in so many respects an unflappably sophisticated man of the world, was thoroughly unnerved by the choppy flight. Twice when the plane dipped in turbulence he crossed himself.

Rain was falling in a cold drizzle when they landed at National

Airport. The three men climbed into a cab, with Danzie seated between his two captors. As the taxi inched its way across one of the Potomac River bridges, Luke lit a cigarette and tried to relax. Ahead he could already see the tip of the Washington Monument but he couldn't make himself feel like a tourist. Joe's warning last night hadn't helped, but even without it he would have realized by this time that this wasn't going to be the junket he first imagined. Whatever sense of his own importance he derived from flying to Washington with a prisoner paled beside the fact that he had been summoned by the deputy director of the BNDD. In all his years on the police force he had never even spoken to anyone with a rank higher than inspector.

As the car picked its way through the clotted traffic on Fourteenth Street, Kane reached past Danzie to tap Luke on the arm. "Hey, Luke, take a look this way," he said. "There's the Capitol."

Luke leaned over until his face was almost in Danzie's stomach. "Nice," he said, wishing he could enjoy it more, or at least think of something better to say. When he sat up he made a conscious effort to look around, reminding himself that he would feel like an idiot if he had to go home and tell his wife he hadn't seen anything. "What's that?" he asked, pointing out his own window. "Jefferson Monument?"

"Lincoln. We already passed Jefferson," Kane informed him.

"Right. Lincoln."

At Constitution Avenue Kane said, "That's the Labor Department. The Justice Department is just down the street."

A row of immense granite buildings stretched out to the right, each one of which looked like it could have held any of the New York courthouses many times over. It gave Luke a sense of the size of the government that was not calculated to ease his qualms.

"How come we didn't turn?" he asked.

"That's not where we're going."

"I thought the BNDD's part of the Justice Department?"

"It is, but we've got our own offices over on I Street."

Luke nodded. "You used to work here, huh?" he asked.

"Five years," Kane said, but it was impossible to tell from his voice whether he meant it to sound like a long time.

On the other side of Pennsylvania Avenue the scale of the city changed abruptly, and Luke was surprised to find himself suddenly in the middle of what looked like a normal city, with stores and banks and old hotels. Without any warning the cab pulled to a stop in front of a nondescript office building. Kane paid the driver and asked for a receipt. Then, hanging his identifcation badge on the outside of his jacket pocket, he walked into the building with Luke and Danzie following a few steps behind. When Luke took out his gold detective's shield, Kane told him to put it away.

It was almost eleven o'clock when Luke, Kane, and Danzie were ushered into the presence of Anthony Diamond, who turned out to be an incredibly nervous man who chain-smoked Lucky Strikes and had the disconcerting habit of pulling at the flesh just below his lower eyelids with his thumb and forefinger.

As everyone had expected, Diamond began with the pro forma plea that Danzie be turned over to his agents. Some time was wasted before Diamond could be made to realize that he was dealing with Longo's partner rather than with Longo himself. Once this was straightened out, Luke answered his request as he had answered Russell the day before. Again Kane kept out of it. Diamond surprised them both by dropping the subject quickly and asking them to leave the room so that he could confer privately with the prisoner.

"What's the idea?" Diamond snapped as soon as the door closed behind the two narcotics investigators. "How come you called me?"

"I had no choice," Danzie answered, a low note of angry resentment in his voice. "I may have been set up."

Diamond said nothing but raised his eyebrows as a signal for Danzie to proceed.

"I suppose you know I was working under cover for Paul Scala. His people used your name when they got in touch with me. Was it your operation?"

"No," Diamond said flatly. "I've been filled in on it but it's strictly his show."

This wasn't quite true. The idea of sending an undercover operator into the Tombs had originated with Scala, but when he first proposed the scheme it had been his intention to use a BNDD agent. Diamond had vetoed the plan. The chance was too great that one of the prison's fourteen hundred inmates would make him as a fed. "If you're gonna do it, you'd better use an S.E.," he had told Scala. "Someone clean, with no record and no contacts in this country. I'll have my people set it up. The only thing is you've got to keep me out of it." Scala had agreed.

Using the telephone instead of the intercom on his desk, Diamond told his secretary, "Get me Scala in New York." Then, looking up from his desk to Danzie, he said, "Now why don't you just give me the whole story?"

As quickly as he could, Danzie explained the entire incident. "A couple of months ago," he began, "three men approached me in Milan. You know, your *federales* have been giving me one headache after another, but these men said they could help me get started over here if I helped them out. Were they working for you, too?"

"No," Diamond lied. "That must have been Scala's people."

Danzie shrugged. He didn't believe Diamond but saw no reason to make anything of it. "Well," he went on, resuming his story, "at the time it didn't look very tempting. We talked about it but that was all. Then, it was perhaps a month ago, I began to have problems everywhere. Two of my people lost shipments, one of my best men was imprisoned. It was time to get out. It must have been the work of these men. They were trying to persuade me to change my mind."

"No," Diamond interrupted, "the pressure was from our people. It had no connection with anything else."

"Perhaps. It doesn't matter now. I got in touch with these men—they were in Turino by this time—and they told me to come to New York and talk to Paul Scala. And then he gave me the deal. He wanted a man whose connections could be verified, but it had to be someone who had no American record. I was given about fifteen grams and I sat in a hotel room waiting for someone to arrest me. That is the business they're in—they set people up. I was supposed to go with a policeman named Lacey. He was going to make the arrest himself or have one of his friends do it, a man named Patrone or something like that, a sergeant, I believe. But then I do not understand what happened. Instead of Patrone or Lacey, it was a policeman named Joe Longo who arrested me. He was breathing fire, I could see at once he knew nothing about any plans. And then I learn that I am going to a federal prison for holding Scala's goods. Now does that seem reasonable to you?"

"Yeah, it was a mistake," Diamond commiserated. "We'll work it all out."

A secretary's voice came over the intercom and Diamond picked up the phone. Only a few feet away, on the other side of the paneled wall behind him, Luke Antonelli was carrying a second cup of freshly brewed coffee to join Bill Kane on the huge couch in the deputy director's well-appointed outer office. As Luke sipped from the steaming cup, Anthony Diamond, Paul Scala, and Carlo Danzie were devising a scheme that would erase twelve years of his life as though they had never happened and would taint everything that lay ahead for him in the future. Two hundred miles to the north, Joe Longo sat in the witness chair in a federal courthouse testifying in the case of *The People* v. *Paul Caruso*. Half his mind was in Washington, worrying that Luke might cave in. He had no way of knowing that the real negotiations taking place on I Street concerned his own fate more than the fate of Carlo Danzie. When he stepped down from the witness stand at eleven forty-five he had less than two months to live.

Paul Scala took less than two minutes to corroborate everything Danzie had told Diamond. "It's funny," Scala said. "We had a bunch of guys up at the Americana to make sure it went okay, and they swore it went down just like it was supposed to. But then when he never showed up at the Tombs we nearly went crazy. Lacey's been running around like a madman trying to find out what happened."

"Well, it's not funny," Diamond shot back. "The man's got every right in the world to be pissed. Just spent two days in West Street for holding your shit. What were you gonna do for him?"

"I don't know, Tony. We were working on that," Scala whined. "We would have taken care of him, tell him that. They arraigned him, right?"

"No, they didn't, no thanks to you. It's been taken care of. He's as clean as before he went in."

"Thanks, Tony."

"Yeah, thanks," Diamond mimicked. "Next time you give junk to a civilian you better make sure you know what you're gonna do if it doesn't go down right. See why I didn't want to get mixed up in it? What do you know about a cop named Longo?"

"Longo!" Scala exclaimed. "That's not who busted him, is it?"

"Yeah."

"You gotta be kidding," Scala said. "The guy stepped on one of my operations a couple of months ago, we still haven't got it all straightened out."

"How'd that happen?"

"It's a long story," Scala said evasively. "What are you thinking?"

"I'm thinking, is he clean?"

Paul Scala was neither as quick nor as ruthless as Anthony Diamond. The idea of using Danzie to work under cover against Joe Longo would never have occurred to him without prompting. Although that clearly was what Diamond's question pointed to, Scala could see the drawbacks immediately. The chances of such a scheme working seemed remote, for Longo already knew that Danzie stooled for Diamond. Even the crookedest cop in the world wouldn't be stupid enough to do anything illegal with a confidential informant who worked for the deputy director of the Bureau of Narcotics and Dangerous Drugs. Besides, there was no reason to believe that Longo was crooked.

On the other hand, there were advantages to the scheme that might almost outweigh the drawbacks. The biggest one was that it would protect the Tombs operation Scala had been planning for months. Danzie had been busted with narcotics supplied by Scala and he would blow the whole story sooner than let Longo work him as a stool. The simplest solution would have been to get Longo to back off, but that didn't seem possible. Longo had his teeth into something he thought was big and there was no way he could be pried loose. The only answer was to take him out of the picture.

Quickly calculating the pros and cons, Scala saw that he had nothing to lose. "That's a good question," he said. "You want me to see what I can find out about him?"

"I already did that," Diamond answered coolly. "He's been on the Joint Task Force less than a year. Transferred in from some precinct in Queens. Our people checked him out pretty good last year before we approved the transfer and he passed all the tests. No one had anything on him. But what does that prove? Before he was in Queens he was in Narco, and as far as I'm concerned they're all a bunch of fucking thieves. So it could be he's our man. Anyway, he used to be a friend of your guy Lacey, so how clean could he be?"

"Well, maybe," Scala said evasively. "What do you think?"

"I think it's gotta be worth a try. So long as Lacey doesn't give you any problems about working on a friend of his."

Scala laughed a short, humorless laugh. "Lacey's got his own troubles," he said reassuringly. "He's so jammed up he'd make a case on his fucking dog if he had to."

Part Two
The Investigative Plan

*A creature who is half an idiot, but
who keeps a sharp look-out, and acts
prudently all his life, often enjoys
the pleasure of triumphing over men
of imagination.*

—Stendhal

Chapter 4
A Man of His Word

BEFORE PAUL SCALA and Anthony Diamond concluded their telephone conversation, Scala assigned himself the responsibility for finding out as much about Joe Longo as he could. Diamond promised to provide whatever funding the operation would need, but for the time being his job consisted simply of briefing Danzie on the new direction the operation was taking. In addition, Scala gave Diamond a phone number to pass on to Danzie, who could use it at any time of the day or night to reach one of the agents assigned to the special assistant prosecutor's office.

With all these matters amicably arranged, Diamond hung up the phone and turned to the bewildered Danzie, who had heard one side of the entire Washington-to-New York conversation and had begun asking himself all over again whether he really knew what he had gotten himself into. Two decades of constant treachery as a police informant had taught him the value of honor, for he had seen more than a few of his friends go to jail simply because they had trusted him. It was regrettable that these friends had to pay so heavily for this mistake, but it was precisely because the dishonoring of a trust cost so much that it sold so high.

When he was a young man just starting out in the rackets, Danzie had believed in a simple code. There were just two sides—the crooks and the cops—and between these two there could be no alliance. Whatever else one might do, one was loyal to one's friends and silent in the hands of the enemy. This elementary rule overrode everything else. As he grew in age and sophistication, however, Danzie convinced himself that the almost medieval code of *onore* and *omertà* was not supple enough to cover all situations. To be successful in the modern world one had to play the angles. This Danzie had done so well for so many years that he no longer could see clearly where the lines were drawn. His very life depended upon the fact that he was both a trafficker and an agent. Each role provided insurance for the other.

This dual identity gave him a unique perspective, which allowed him to see with striking clarity the validity of his original proposition. In the absence of a code of loyalty and honor, nothing would work right. Even a Carlo Danzie could not operate for long in a world of Carlo Danzies. A man who wouldn't stand up for his people could not be trusted by anyone. His own case proved it, for he was such a man himself. So were Diamond and Scala. He could work with them only because he knew them well enough not to trust them. They saw themselves as crusaders against corruption and were comfortable with cops who betrayed cops, just as that good Roman Brutus had betrayed Caesar—for the sake of a more abstract loyalty. Ah, that was the difference between a Roman and an Italian. The Romans may have admired Brutus, but the Italian Dante understood the utter immorality of such an act, for had he not assigned Brutus to the deepest circle of Hell? Brutus, Satan, and Judas. Danzie, Scala, and Diamond.

Luke Antonelli and Bill Kane replaced their coffee cups on the table against the far wall of Diamond's outer office when the secretary informed them that the deputy director was ready to see them once again. Inside, they seated themselves in the leather chairs that stood almost six feet to the front of Diamond's desk. Danzie sat in a stiffer chair by a corner of the desk, smoking a slender Italian cigarette and tapping the ashes into a heavy crystal ashtray.

"He says he'll work for you," Diamond announced perfunctorily, addressing himself to Antonelli. "But it's gotta be on his terms."

Luke nodded for Diamond to go on.

"First is no tails. It's curtains if he gets burned, so if he spots a tail all bets are off. You can trust him. If he tells you he'll deliver, he'll deliver. Two—no wires. When he sets up a deal he'll let you know, and he'll tell you when to take it. But he won't be wired when he sets it up. Three—he won't go to court for you. That goes without saying. I'm gonna need him after you guys are finished. What you do for probable cause is your business, but you keep him out of it. Clear?"

"Clear," Luke answered. "Now what do we get?"

"I was just coming to that. He's got nothing now but there are some things in the works. You take what he gives you and you leave the rest alone. One for three, is that fair?"

"Fair?" Luke asked, glancing quizzically across to Kane, who returned the look. Neither was quite sure he understood what was being said. They both knew the facts of life. An informer had to be allowed to do business or he would be of no use. As Luke later explained in an interview, "Any junk dealer that you work with as an informant is moving junk when you're working with him. It has to be. You can't waste time chasing after some churchgoing Mary. If he's selling onions, what's he gonna tell you? The only way he can know what's coming down is if he's doing business." In that sense, a working informant is more or less licensed to be in the heroin business by the authorities for whom he stools. But it is an informal arrangement. "You don't look too close at him" is the way cops express it. It is never spelled out, never made an explicit quid pro quo, and Luke wondered why Diamond was spelling it out now.

"We're talking about hundred kilos and up," Diamond explained. "For every load he gives you, he moves three. Whatdya think about it?"

"Whatdya mean, what do I think about it?" Luke shot back, uncomfortable with the direction the conversation was taking. "We'll do whatever's right. If he gives us one, it's one we wouldn't have had otherwise, right?"

Diamond smiled. "Right," he said. "Now, look, when he checked out of West Street did he get his property back?"

"What property?" Luke asked, surprised, thinking for a moment that Diamond meant the packet of heroin. "All he had was like a wallet and passport, a little bread. He got it all back. Except the passport."

"Yeah, the passport, that's what I meant," Diamond said. "Where is it?"

Kane reached into his pocket. "Got it right here," he said, handing it across the desk to the deputy director, who examined it briefly and tossed it into a drawer.

"I'm gonna hold on to this," Diamond said. "You got the guy, I'll keep the passport." He slid the drawer closed and said, "Okay, there's one other thing. This one you're really gonna like. However it comes down, he won't hand up any Italians."

Luke Antonelli shrugged. If that was supposed to cut ice with him, it didn't.

By the time Antonelli, Kane, and Danzie got back to the airport the weather had cleared and the return flight to La Guardia was smooth and uneventful. The midafternoon shuttle was half empty and the DC-9's three-abreast seating allowed them to sit together with no other passengers near. Relaxed, with the even roar of the engines providing a lulling background, Danzie spoke freely about everything from thoroughbred race horses to the international narcotics trade. Almost as though he were trying to captivate his captors, he talked on and on until the cabin attendant's voice over the loudspeaker announced that they were about to begin their descent. More than once on the short flight Luke got the distinct impression that he was attending a performance staged for his benefit.

No food or beverage is served on shuttle flights, so the three men, who had not found time for lunch in Washington, decided to grab a bite before driving back to the city. Crossing over the Grand Central Parkway on the airport ramp, Luke drove to a nearby Holiday Inn and pulled into the parking lot. An almost empty restaurant off the lobby suited them perfectly. Over glasses of draft beer they studied the menus and joked like old friends. When Danzie decided on the veal parmigiana, Luke tried in vain to dissuade him. "In America," he warned, "never eat Italian food except in an Italian restaurant."

"Or an Italian home," Danzie added.

It was a perfectly natural thing to say but it somehow had a jarring effect on Luke. In seeming to overlook the fact that the relationship between the three men at the table was not a social one, Danzie's comment suddenly jolted Antonelli back to reality. Or perhaps Danzie had not overlooked anything. Nothing this suave

Milanese did was accidental, not the slightest move was uncalculated. Luke sensed that Danzie had intended to create exactly the impression he did. With just four seemingly innocuous words he signaled that he was taking charge, that he was in command of the situation, for normally it is the detective's job to dictate the terms of his relationship with his informant. A momentary chill passed around the table and Luke found himself unable to shake off a vague apprehension that he was in over his head. It was a feeling he would have again and again over the next six weeks. As with so much else that was to happen, however, Luke wouldn't even begin to understand it on a conscious level until long after Danzie had disappeared completely.

When the food arrived the three men ate without speaking until Danzie chose to break the silence. Raising a forkful of the beige meat to eye level, he examined it minutely. "Ma che cos'è?" he suddenly asked, his rich basso projecting across the deserted dining room. "Vitello vero è giovane, ma questa cosa è molta più vecchio!"

"He says veal is supposed to be from a calf but this looks like an old cow," Luke translated for Kane. "Questo l'ho detto," he added, addressing Danzie. "But you didn't believe me. Next time you'll know.

The remainder of the meal was devoted to one of Danzie's tireless monologues. He opened with a discourse on fine restaurants, singling out the Cambio in Turino for its *fonduta* and El Tuola in Milan, where the food was not always what one wanted but where one could always feel at home. He explained that he had been fully warned about American restaurants and thus did not expect that he would be disappointed. "On the contrary," he said, timing his remark for the moment when the waitress arrived to clear the table, "the food may not be fit to eat, but the waitresses are much lovelier than in Europe."

She was a tall brunette in her early twenties with finely delicate features and a slender, small-breasted body. "In my country," Danzie said, grasping her wrist as she reached past him and gazing with insolent frankness straight into her deep brown eyes, "a woman like you would not wait on tables. She would have a lover."

"What makes you think I don't?" the waitress shot back, not in the least embarrassed, matching Danzie's insolence with her own.

"Because you work here," Danzie answered. "You may have—how do you say?—a 'boyfriend.' But a boyfriend is not a lover."

He released her wrist and she resumed the chore of clearing the table as though nothing had been said. "Buon' cameriera, buon' amante," Danzie whispered to Luke, who this time chose to dispense with the translation for Kane.

After dinner, in the car on the way back to the city, Danzie asked Luke whether he would have to go back to prison. Oddly, the question had not come up before.

"I don't think so," Antonelli answered. "But it's not up to me, it's up to Joe."

"Why Joe?"

"Because it's his case."

Danzie was silent for a moment, then said, "I would rather work with you."

At that, Bill Kane, who had been stretched out almost horizontal along the back seat, sat upright and looked intently at Luke. Although no one at the Joint Task Force talked about it, Kane and some of the other men had seen signs in recent months that everything was not right between Luke Antonelli and Joe Longo. He was understandably curious to see Luke's reaction to this suggestion that he in effect steal his partner's collar.

Kane saw nothing, yet it gave him his answer. Not even the slightest spasm of acknowledgment passed across Luke's face and he said nothing in reply. What Danzie was suggesting was impossible, didn't even deserve an answer. A cop didn't cheat on his partner. Even a guy who had never been in the country before should have known that. It was the same everywhere in the world.

When the car pulled up in front of the Task Force headquarters on Varick Street, Luke took Danzie inside while Kane, who was exhausted by the two plane rides, announced his intention to call it a night and left without reporting in. It was only six o'clock, but the clear February sky had been dark for hours and the air was beginning to sting with cold. Luke, too, found himself wishing for a speedy wrap-up to the day's work.

On the sixth floor, Luke and Danzie immediately ran into Joe, who was pacing the long stretch of corridor between the elevators and the squad room. He had taken off his jacket and tie, and the sleeves of his lightly striped body shirt were rolled up past his elbows, giving him a look of haggard impatience that was totally out of character.

"Hey, Longo, what's happening!" Luke called down the hallway as Joe strode toward him.

"What do you mean, what's happening?" Joe shouted back. "What happened?"

"I mean the Caruso thing. How'd it go?" Luke asked as Joe reached him and turned around for the walk back to the office. Paul Caruso was the drug dealer against whom Joe had testified that day.

"No sweat, they'll convict him," Joe answered matter-of-factly. "You got some reason you're not telling me what went on down there?"

"Oh, that," Luke teased. "No, no reason in particular."

"So?"

"Where's Marcus?"

"What the fuck do you want Marcus for?" Joe was losing patience rapidly. The case meant more to him than Luke could have possibly guessed at the time, although soon enough he would find out how much. Ever since he left the stand in federal court late that morning, Joe had been obsessed with worry about it. His concern focused on Luke, on whether he would be tough enough to stand up to the feds. When a guy like Anthony Diamond wanted a cop out of his way, that cop usually got out of the way. If at that moment Joe could have known how easy a time Luke had had with Diamond, he would have known for a certainty that the whole setup was wrong. Instead, when he learned that Luke had succeeded in maintaining control of Danzie, he naturally assumed that Diamond had put up a fight but that Luke had refused to back off.

Unfortunately, when Luke realized that Joe was under the impression that he had single-handedly fought off Anthony Diamond, he said nothing to set the record straight. It gave him a precious chance to look good in in the eyes of his older and more experienced partner, and he wasn't about to waste it.

"I figured I'd brief Marcus at the same time," Luke said with mock innocence. "No sense saying the same thing twice."

"Cut the shit, Luke," Joe growled. "Is the guy gonna work or not?"

"Are you gonna work?" Luke asked, turning to Danzie. They were in the office now, the three of them clustered in front of Joe's desk.

"I am a man of my word," Danzie answered, indulging his habitual flair for the epigrammatic.

"For us?" Joe asked.

"Of course for us," Luke said. "I wouldn't have brought him back if he was gonna work for them."

Joe stared at his partner coldly for a moment and then his face relaxed into the beginnings of a smile. His left hand rose slowly until his forefinger was pointing like a gun into Luke's face. There was no humor in his voice, but his eyes were laughing lightly as he said, "If you knew what was good for you, you would have stayed there yourself if you didn't bring him back."

"Well, it's all set," Luke answered quickly, then tried to change the subject. "He wants to know, does he have to go back in the joint tonight?"

Joe turned to Danzie. "No," he said. "Where do you want to go?"

"I will go to a hotel. I must get in touch with my people."

"Sure, get in touch with your people," Joe said. "You wanna go back to the Americana?"

Danzie shrugged. "I do not believe so," he said. "The hotel near the airport was very pleasant."

Chapter 5
The Caruso Taps

IN HIS TELEPHONE conversation with Anthony Diamond, Paul Scala had remarked that Joe Longo had "stepped on" one of his operations a few months before. By one of those uncanny coincidences that make life itself seem at times purposefully ironic, the incident to which Scala was referring involved the very case on which Joe was testifying on the day Danzie was taken to Washington. The story of the Caruso arrest and its aftermath is not directly related to the Danzie incident and had no direct bearing on Joe's fate. But it does throw light on the nature of Scala's operations and the role Gil Lacey played in them.

The Caruso case began late in the summer of 1971, shortly after Joe joined the Joint Task Force on Narcotics. He and his new partner had hardly had a chance to get acquainted when Luke's vacation came up in August. Luke was gone for two weeks, returning right after Labor Day to find that Joe had not been idle during his absence. The case involved a marginal drug dealer named Jason Meredith, a spaced-out speed freak who lived alone in a grubby apartment on Downing Street in Greenwich Village, just a one-block walk from the Joint Task

Force's Varick Street headquarters. Meredith himself, who was more a middleman than a true dealer, was nothing to get excited about, but Joe hoped to use the investigation of Meredith in order to get to Meredith's supplier.

The case had begun simply on a tip from one of Joe's informants. This was followed up by a brief surveillance on Meredith, which turned up nothing, in part because Joe stood out too much in a crowd. Even in old clothes and unshaven, he found it impossible to follow Meredith around the Village without being noticed. In the seedy hangouts his suspect frequented, Joe was invariably spotted as "the man" even before he got his back foot in the door.

Nevertheless, Joe was still convinced that his stool's information was good. In order to find out more, he put a tap on Meredith's phone. It wasn't a legal wire. Like many law enforcement people, Joe occasionally played it fast and loose when it came to invading the privacy of those he suspected of dealing dope. An impatient cop, always in a hurry to make a case and move on to the next, he cut corners when he felt he had to.

There has been a great deal of talk in recent years about police "corruption," and attention has been focused on everything from Christmas presents and free sandwiches at the local coffee shop to shakedowns and systematic payoff "pads." Yet undoubtedly the most pervasive form of illegal activity engaged in by law enforcement personnel above the patrol level is illegal phone tapping. Some cops say this is because a phone tap is the fastest and most efficient way to find out what a suspect is doing. Others complain that the courts have gone out of their way to make it as difficult as possible for a detective to secure a court order for a legal tap. But undoubtedly the major reason for the prevalence of illegal wiretapping is the fact that superior officers tacitly—and in some cases openly—encourage their investigators to use all means possible to get results.

When Luke was told about the tap shortly after he returned from vacation, he immediately let Joe know how he felt about it. A more conservative detective than his new partner, he didn't like to take shortcuts unless there was no other choice. "Look," he explained later in an interview, "Joe was a damned good cop—don't get me wrong. He was one of the best. But he did things like that tap on Meredith I didn't like. If it was me we'd take a couple of weeks longer but we'd get the guy right. I'm not naive, I've done things myself that aren't the way they're supposed to be done. But only when it was necessary. Joe was always in a hurry."

In this case, though, Joe's impatience hadn't produced speedy results. Jake Meredith spent so much of his life stoned that the tap proved utterly worthless during the two weeks it was in. After listening to playbacks of some of Meredith's chaotic ramblings, Luke insisted that the wire come out. "There's only one way to get this guy," he said. "A buy."

On the afternoon of September 12, Joe took Luke to see his informant, a twenty-seven-year-old chronic loser named Gregory Bates. The meeting took place at a back booth in an Irish bar in the Bronx not far from Fordham, the last place in the world they could run into anyone connected with the Village dope scene. Joe introduced Luke as "Louie Dee."

"Louie wants to hit on Jake Meredith for a coupla kees," he said.

Bates's watery brown eyes narrowed and he said nothing for a minute. Then he asked, "Is he heat or is he a friend of yours?"

"Say he's a friend," Joe answered. In the double-bang world of cops and stools, there was less chance of a slipup if Bates thought Joe really was doing a friend a favor, even though it meant he might then spread the word that Joe Longo was setting up dope deals. Sooner or later one of the shooflies from the Internal Affairs Division would hear the story and begin to wonder if it was true. More than one detective had lost his job because Internal Affairs was willing to take the word of a drug dealer who would rather perjure himself than admit that he was a stool pigeon. But these were the risks a detective had to take. The only way a cop could make sure no one was talking about him was to sit on his ass in the office.

In any case, Bates was leery. He considered the proposition less than a minute and said, "Find someone else, Longo."

Joe's whole manner changed instantly. His voice dropped a notch and the muscles in his face tightened. "It's gotta be you," he said. "You owe me and you're gonna do it."

Across the table Bates fidgeted nervously. "Whatdya mean, owe you?" he whined. "Didn't I tell you about Meredith?"

"What's told me? You gotta give me Meredith," Joe snapped, refusing to let Bates have anything to hold on to.

"He'll fucking kill me," Bates moaned, sliding sideways, trying to get out of the booth. But he wasn't quick enough.

Joe lunged forward, rising in his seat, the heel of his hand slamming past Gregory Bates's face and against the back of the bench, his thick forearm like a gate cutting off escape. Leaning over the table, his face only a few inches from Bates, he kept his voice low and menacing. "You weren't listening," he said. "I'll tell you one more fucking time but this time you gotta pay attention. I said you gotta give me Meredith. Does any part of that sound like a question to you?"

Bates looked away without answering.

Joe grabbed his face in his hand and turned it until they were eye to eye again. "Was I asking you or telling you?" he demanded.

"Hey, gimme a break," the desperate junkie pleaded. "You're gonna lock him up and he's gonna sit there with nothing to do but think. And the first name that's gonna pop into his head's gonna be mine. You're trying to get me killed."

Joe let go of Bates and settled back into his seat. When a junkie just says no you have to lean on him, but when he starts giving you reasons it means he's going to do what you want. "You won't get killed," he said. "He'll never know you set him up. We'll work it so he thinks it was Louie."

Bates said nothing but his pathetic eyes looked like they were going to cry.

"You're doing the right thing, Gregory," Luke chimed in quietly, speaking for the first time. "Ask around on the street, you'll see. The dumb guys worry about what Jake Meredith's gonna think. The smart guys worry about Joe Longo."

Two days later a frightened Gregory Bates followed Luke Antonelli past the auto-body shop on Downing Street to the narrow tenement where Jake Meredith lived. The doors to the two unrented apartments on the ground floor stood open for the convenience of the ragtag assortment of street types who used them as crash pads. Antonelli first, Bates a few steps behind, the two men climbed the dark, rotted stairs in silence, holding on to the rickety wooden banister for whatever security it provided.

Two doors opened off the landing on the third floor. Moving to the one marked B, Antonelli waited for Bates to catch up and then knocked loudly.

"Not so fucking loud, hey!" a voice called from inside. The metal disk over the peephole in the door slid back to reveal a pale gray eye looking out. "Don't stand so fucking close to the door. I can't see a fucking thing," the same voice complained.

"Hey, Jake, it's Goon," Bates said.

A skinny man in boxer shorts opened the door and studied the two men in the hallway without saying anything. He was in his late twenties and looked like he either hadn't slept for two days or had been asleep for two days straight.

"Hey, Jake, this is Louie Dee, the guy I was telling you about," Bates said.

Meredith nodded and turned away from the door. Antonelli followed him into the apartment but Bates held back. "Gotta split," he said from the doorway. "I told Louie you'd talk to him."

He pulled the door closed and scooted down the stairs, tripping as he ran. A few seconds later Luke heard the street door close after him and cursed silently.

On the sidewalk, Gregory Bates glanced to his left and saw Joe Longo standing on the corner of Downing and Varick, staring in his direction. He had promised Joe he would stay through the first meeting, just to set Meredith at ease. But when the time came he got scared and ran. Afraid to face Longo, he turned and fled in the opposite direction.

Joe watched him go without knowing what to think. As Luke's backup on the operation, he was't supposed to go in unless his partner got in trouble, but he didn't know whether Bates's sudden departure meant that something had gone wrong already. Figuring he would have heard shots by now if anything was seriously the matter, he decided to stick to the original plan. He watched the junkie disappear around the corner of Bedford Street and then refocused his concentration on the dingy brownstone.

Inside, Meredith flopped down on the unmade bed and rolled onto his side to face Luke. The fly of his dull gray shorts gaped open and he reached inside to scratch at himself. "Yeah, whatdya want?" he asked, massaging his testicles as he spoke.

"Look, if you're busy I can come back some other time," Luke said.

Meredith eyed his visitor coldly for a moment, trying to decide whether this was a guy he had to take any shit from. Then he took his hand out of his shorts and sat up on the edge of the bed.

"Goon tells me we can do business," Luke said, getting right to the point. His voice was flat and expressionless, like it didn't matter to him one way or the other.

"Can't help what people say," Meredith muttered. "Say all kinds of fucking shit, sometimes it's true, sometimes it's not."

Luke turned and reached for the door, but Meredith's voice stopped him. "What kind of business?" he asked.

"Three kees."

Meredith hesitated a moment, sizing up his visitor. "See me tonight," he said. "At The Barrel."

Over the next two weeks Luke Antonelli and Jake Meredith had over half a dozen inconclusive meetings. Most of the time they met in public places like The Barrel, a dive on the West Street waterfront favored by dope dealers, hookers, and pimps. But whenever the talk got more serious they headed back to the relative security of Meredith's filthy one-room apartment. Joe stayed on the outside, tailing them from a distance as they moved around the Village or just parking across the street when they were at Meredith's place. Once Meredith thought he spotted a tail and said, "Either I'm being followed or you are."

"It's gotta be you," Luke answered quickly. Without a word of explanation he turned away from Meredith and hurried across the street.

He discussed the situation with Joe that night and they decided to give Meredith a week to cool off. Then they sent Bates back in to let the dealer know that Louie Dee was looking elsewhere to do business. "He says he thinks you got narcs on you," Bates explained.

"Tell him he's fucking nuts," Meredith snapped back.

Three days later Luke was having a beer in a West Eighth Street bar when Jake Meredith walked in off the street and sat down next to him. "Those three shirts you wanted to order, I think they came in," he said.

"We didn't have no deal," Luke answered without looking up from the glass between his hands.

"Yeah, I know. But I didn't have the merchandise then. Now I do. If you're interested, my place tonight."

That night Meredith said, "My connection says tomorrow, like say in the afternoon. Twenty-four grand apiece. Bring the bread in the morning, you come back in the afternoon I'll have your stuff."

"Bullshit," Luke said.

"Then how you wanna work it?"

"Why fart around? I bring the green and I get the white. No sense making things complicated."

Meredith thought a moment before answering. "Don't like it," he said. "How do I know you won't rip me off?"

Luke reached down and grabbed Meredith as he lay on the bed, flinging him to the floor, where he landed like a puppet with the strings cut. Then he reached under the pillow and pulled out Meredith's forty-five automatic. He examined the gun for a moment and dropped it onto Meredith's stomach. "That's how you know, asshole. See you tomorrow."

The next morning Luke was at Meredith's door at eleven. "Fuck, man, I said afternoon," the dealer whined as he opened the door.

Luke followed him inside. "I know," he said, "but I'm not showing up with the bread unless I know it's coming down."

Meredith nodded. "Yeah, okay. My man's supposed to call me, we'll get everything worked out. You don't take any chances, do you?"

"No," Luke said. "Do you?"

After an hour of excruciating waiting, the telephone rang. "That's gotta be him," Meredith said, jumping to answer it.

The conversation was brief, with Meredith doing most of the talking. "Yeah, look, those three shirts I order come in? . . . What time? . . . Yeah, like three, three thirty. . . . Well, look, tell me three, I'll have him come back at three thirty. . . . Yeah back, he's here now. . . . Sure, no problem. He's not gonna want to sit here all afternoon anyway. . . . Tonight, five o'clock. Your place. . . . Awright, you name it. . . . Sure, okay."

He hung up the phone and turned to Luke. "Awright," he said, "say you come back at three thirty."

When Luke came out on the sidewalk at a quarter past twelve, Joe pulled the car around the corner onto Varick Street and waited while his partner walked down the block to join him. He was parked directly across the street from the Joint Task Force office. In the car, Luke explained that he was supposed to return at three thirty to make the buy. "I'll take a briefcase and if the stuff's there I'll give a yell. You just better get there before they find out I don't have their seventy-two grand."

Joe shook his head. "He doesn't have the stuff now?" he asked.

"No, it's coming at three."

"Where's your fucking brain, Antonelli?" Joe asked, laughing softly. "You want Meredith, don't you?"

Luke nodded without answering. As much as his partner's techniques bothered him from time to time, he had an almost reverential respect for Joe's instincts as a cop. Even before he heard what Joe had to say, he knew they would do it Joe's way.

"Well, you can have Meredith if you want him," Joe went on. "The guy I want is his connection. Say we go back to the office, get Wiley, Stallard, Kane, maybe a couple of other guys. We wait for the connection to show up and then we hit him right there." He paused before adding, "I want you out of it. I told Bates I'd take care of him."

Luke didn't like the idea of being left out when it came time for the collar but he could see Joe's point. If they made the arrest when Luke went in at three thirty, they would lose the connection and Meredith would know that Greg Bates had set him up. But if they did it Joe's way they would catch Meredith and his connection holding three kilos of heroin and Bates would be in the clear—at least for the time being. When the case went to trial, if it ever did, the defendants would learn that "Louie Dee" was actually a cop, but until then they would think that he was the one who had sold them out.

With the connection not expected to arrive for hours, Joe figured he had some leeway before he had to have the place under surveillance. He left the car where it was and went up to the office to brief the other men. By one thirty the four members of the team had taken their positions. Wiley was at the corner of Downing and Varick, Kane in the lobby of a building across the street from Meredith's brownstone. Joe and Stallard entered Meredith's building and climbed the stairs, Stallard proceeding all the way to the roof while Joe waited on the landing halfway between the third and fourth floors.

Jake Meredith's connection was a man named Paul Caruso. In his late forties with a long career as a hoodlum behind him, Caruso hadn't been in the junk business for long. Until his son-in-law, a decidedly sharp type who went by the name Al Roy, got him into the business, Caruso had been only a marginal figure in the underworld. Indeed, in the fall of 1971 the Joint Task Force on Narcotics had never heard of him.

They had heard of him at the elite narcotics Special Investigations Unit, however. A team of SIU detectives had been interested in Al

Roy for some time. In September they installed an illegal tap on a phone in an East Seventh Street apartment across the street from Tompkins Square Park. The apartment was rented by Roy but used by his father-in-law, who lived there with a twenty-two-year-old go-go dancer named Yvonne. The four-man team working on Roy included Detectives Philip Brinsley and Lawrence Cooper, Sergeant Arthur Schwartz, and Detective Gil Lacey, who had been assigned to SIU ever since Scala turned him around.

Lacey's involvement with Brinsley and Cooper led him into a number of heated exchanges with Paul Scala, who was eager to charge the two detectives with illegal wiretapping, a felony violation of federal law. Lacey, though, saw the issue from a cop's point of view. He was well aware that in most cases illegal wiretapping is the product of laziness or impatience rather than corrupt motives. A detective who is willing to take the time and trouble can get a court order for a wiretap whenever he needs one. The paperwork alone may involve half a day's work, and another day can be spent waiting to see a judge. But in the end the cop will get his wiretap order. Of course, many cops, unwilling to waste this much time, elect to short-circuit the system, using legal wires only when they want to be able to bring the tapes into court as evidence. In the early stages of an investigation, when they are interested merely in finding out what a suspect is up to, they cheat on the law.

Testifying under oath in 1974, Gil Lacey alluded to the thorny moral question this issue posed for corruption investigators. "I had a lot of exchanges with Special United States Attorney Paul Scala," he said. "At that time I felt . . . that to make a case against detectives that were involved with me simply on the basis of using illegal wiretaps to effect an arrest was distasteful to me and I didn't think we should do it."

The process by which each individual draws the line that separates the permissible from the impermissible is and will always be one of the great mysteries of human psychology. For Gil Lacey, busting a cop for putting in a bad wire went against the grain. But entrapment didn't. He seems never to have had qualms about approaching a fellow officer with an illegal scheme, and then coming back again and again if he was turned down. He may have begun by seeing himself as an investigator out to determine whether this or that specific cop was breaking the law, but soon he was asking simply whether the cop would be willing to engage in an illegal activity. From there, one more simple transformation utterly altered the nature of his investigations, which quickly became probes to determine whether or not a particular cop could be induced to commit a corrupt act. Like God testing Job to see whether he could be made to break faith, Lacey replaced the question, *Is he corrupt?* with the question, *Is he corruptible?* The arrogance of this procedure never seems to have dawned on him—although in fairness to him it should be said that it never dawned on Paul Scala or Anthony Diamond either.

In any case, Lacey convinced Scala to hold back on wiretapping charges against Brinsley and Cooper. According to his 1974 testimony, he told Scala that only "if the wiretaps were being utilized as a means of extortion or other illegal activities . . . should cases be made against these people." When Scala agreed to indulge his agent's scruple, Lacey knew that he had to make good by escalating the illegal tap on Caruso into an attempted shakedown. Through September he repeatedly hinted to Brinsley and Cooper that Caruso would pay good money for the conversations the detectives had on tape. Unfortunately for Lacey, neither officer expressed interest. On the other hand, they didn't turn down the idea with enough vehemence to convince Lacey that they couldn't be brought around.

As late as October sixth he was still working on the problem. That afternoon Paul Caruso parked his Ford Torino in front of Jason Meredith's brownstone on Downing Street and went inside carrying a black attaché case. Even before the street door closed behind him, Bill Kane and Jeff Stallard got on their radios and broadcast an alert. On the fourth-floor landing, Joe Longo whispered into his transmitter so as not to be heard by the man with the attaché case, whose heavy footsteps were already audible as he made his way up the stairs. He ordered Stallard to stay on the roof, from where he could cover the fire escape that led down into a littered alley behind the building. Wiley and Kane were told to come to the building entrance and await further orders.

Joe held his breath and waited. There were no corridors in the narrow building, nowhere for him to conceal himself while the man with the case climbed the stairs toward him. With his left hand Joe pulled his gun from the clip at his waist and slid it into his overcoat pocket, ready for anything.

A few feet below him the footsteps stopped and he heard the

heavy breathing of an out-of-shape middle-aged man. This was followed by the sharp report of a fist on the door. In the unnatural silence of an almost empty building on an unused street in the middle of an afternoon, Joe could hear the metal disk of the peephole on Jake Meredith's door sliding back. In a moment the door opened and closed again.

Joe waited a few seconds and then peered over the banister to the landing below. When he saw no one, he pressed the transmission button on his radio and said simply, "Let's get him."

Without waiting for Wiley and Kane, he made his way carefully down the stairs toward the third floor. Stopping five steps above the landing, he listened until he heard his two backups tiptoeing up the steps, then leaped for the door, his feet in front of him like a broad jumper stretching for distance.

The door tore from its hinges with enough force to send it halfway across the tiny room, a piece of the frame still attached where the chain lock ripped it out. Off balance but on his feet, Joe found himself facing two men who were frozen into immobility. He said nothing but kept his gun trained on the two motionless men who stared at him in shocked disbelief. A few seconds later he heard footsteps behind him and then Agent Bill Kane's voice saying, "Don't move, you're under arrest."

Gil Lacey was not a man who took defeat easily. In convincing Scala to ignore the wiretapping case on Brinsley and Cooper, he had more or less promised that he could involve the two detectives in the more serious crime of extortion. Now he would have to report that his strategy had backfired and his quarry had escaped the net. If Caruso ever had any reason to buy their tapes, that reason disappeared utterly the moment he was arrested. It was too late to buy protection—and therefore too late to sell it. After a month and a half of work, all Lacey had to show for his trouble were two narcs who had put in a bad wire. Nevertheless, he remained convinced that Brinsley and Cooper would have fallen if they had been given a chance. He had Joe Longo to thank for the fact they didn't get that chance.

Lacey didn't actually learn what had happened to Caruso until hours after the arrest. The whole day was one continuous nightmare for him, starting shortly after noon, when he and Brinsley drove to East Seventh Street to service their tap. An illegal wiretap generally is not maintained with the same care as a legal one. In a legal tap, all the tapes are carefully preserved; often the recording device is equipped with a pen register that notes the time of each conversation. When detectives install an illegal tap, however, they rarely bother with the pen register, the main purpose of which is to provide evidence of the day and time of the recorded conversation for use in court. In addition, they do not save the tapes. Instead, they simply play them back to get the information on them and then return them to the machine, so that earlier recordings are erased as later ones are made.

While Lacey waited in the car, Brinsley went to the basement of the building adjoining Caruso's, where the tap was located. In less than five minutes he returned at a dead run, his coat flapping open as he raced toward the car with two reels of tape clutched in his left hand.

"It's going down now!" he shouted as he opened the door and scrambled in behind the wheel, tossing the reels across to Lacey. In his haste he had simply pulled them from the machine, and as Lacey grabbed for them one of them slipped to the floor, unwinding as it fell. "Fucking goddamn luck," Brinsley was saying through his teeth. He pounded at the steering wheel in rage and frustration, cursing steadily and softly. Suddenly he stopped and cocked his head like an animal that hears something in the distance. Then he reached for the shift lever and slid the car into gear as his foot slammed on the accelerator.

Lacey leaned forward to retrieve the reel from the floor just as Brinsley screeched into a right-hand turn onto First Avenue. Thrown clear across the seat, he scrambled to an upright position and glared across at his partner. "What the fuck's going on?" he demanded.

"It's going down now," Brinsley repeated, barely keeping his voice under control. "A fucking month and a half and we missed it!"

"Then where the hell are we going?" Lacey asked with unanswerable logic. Brinsley didn't say anything.

Obviously, the answer was on the tape Brinsley had played in the basement. Bending forward and groping on the floor again, Lacey found the reel and managed to get the tangled tape straightened out. He twisted around and reached into the back seat for the portable recorder he kept there, almost falling again as Brinsley ran the light at Fourteenth Street and swung a left, narrowly avoiding collisions with traffic moving in both directions on Fourteenth.

"This fucking well better be worth it," Lacey said, caught up in the excitement in spite of himself. "In case we get killed before we get there, you mind telling me where we're going?"

"The barbershop," Brinsley answered. "He might still be there. Get Schwartz and Cooper, have them meet us."

The SIU team had long suspected that Caruso and his son-in-law, Al Roy, were using a fashionable midtown barbershop on Madison Avenue as their drop. Lacey nodded his comprehension and radioed for the other two members of the team. Then he went back to the job of threading the tape onto the machine as the car sped north on Madison. When he clicked it on, he was in the middle of a conversation between Caruso and Roy.

" . . . this afternoon. You have it ready?"

"Any time. You know, the barbershop."

"Okay, sure. I'll get back to you after."

"Fuck that. I don't wanna see you till you got the bread."

"That'll be tonight."

"No sweat."

The phone clicked dead and then a woman's voice was talking. It was an earlier conversation Lacey and Brinsley had heard already. Incredulous, Lacey stopped the machine and looked across at his partner. "Is that it?" he asked.

"Yeah."

"That call could have been hours ago," Lacey protested. "He's long gone by now."

Brinsley had realized the same thing already. But he couldn't stand the thought that their own carelessness had cost them the case. They should have checked the tapes more frequently, should have had the plant manned all the time. It might be weeks before Caruso made another deal, and they might never have another chance to find out about one in advance. But if the call had only been made a little while before, or if Caruso didn't go straight to the barbershop, there was still an outside chance they could catch up with him. Tightening his grip on the steering wheel, Brinsley kept his foot to the floor and closed his mind to the fact that the odds were all in favor of Caruso.

On the opposite side of the front seat, Gil Lacey was beginning to feel that things were starting to look up. So far, Brinsley hadn't taken any of his hints about running a shakedown on Caruso. He genuinely seemed to want to make a case. Now that he knew there was a chance to catch Caruso dirty, nothing would stop him. He would go charging into the barbershop, and if he found Caruso with the junk he would bust him. But unless Brinsley was luckier than he deserved to be, he was bound to come up empty. Caruso would be gone, and inside of a few hours the people in the barbershop would let him know that some narcs had been around looking for him. He and Roy would set up a new drop, only this time they would know that one of their phones was tapped and they'd be more careful about giving away its location.

Once all this had a chance to sink in, Brinsley would have to face the fact that the case was gone, probably for good. Then it would be easy to convince him he had nothing to lose by dealing with Caruso. If you can't lock a guy up, at least you could make him pay for his freedom.

Brinsley's fanatical driving got them to Fifty-third and Madison in only a little over ten minutes. Bounding from the car just as Lacey had expected he would, Brinsley raced into the barbershop. Lacey followed some thirty feet behind. There was no sign of Caruso. Two barbers and a manicurist sat idly talking in the chairs reserved for customers while a third barber was cutting the hair of an elderly man. At the back of the shop a doorway led to the toilets and a supply closet. As Brinsley headed in that direction, one of the seated barbers stood up and stepped toward him. "Do you have an appointment, sir?" he asked with complete irrelevance.

Ignoring him, the detective disappeared through the back door just as Lacey came in the front. Brinsley checked the toilets, slamming open the stalls to make sure no one was hiding in them, and then opened the door to the storage closet, knowing as he did that he wouldn't find anything.

"Awright, where'd he go?" he demanded as he stepped back into the shop.

The three barbers looked at each other while the manicurist examined her hands as though she intended to go to work on them any minute. Finally the barber in the middle of the floor asked, "Who?"

Brinsley realized it was no use, they would lie anyway. Muttering an obscenity, he pushed past the barber and stalked out the door, leaving Lacey standing there a moment with a half-apologetic look on his face.

By the time the two detectives got back to the street, Cooper and Schwartz had arrived in another unmarked car, which they parked behind Lacey's Pontiac. Exaggerating somewhat in describing the incident as a near miss, Brinsley quickly filled them in on what had happened. Clearly, there was nothing further to be done. Schwartz and Cooper returned to their car for the long ride back to the SIU office on the South Slip. Brinsley, though, was reluctant to give up so easily. The idea of just sitting around helplessly while Paul Caruso was out making a junk deal bothered him and he was ready to clutch at straws. "I'm going back to Seventh Street," he told Lacey. "Maybe we'll hear something."

Lacey shrugged and walked back to his car, taking the driver's seat this time. He knew what Brinsley was thinking and knew that it was a waste of time. If Caruso's girlfriend Yvonne knew where he was, maybe she'd mention it on the phone. Or maybe he'd call her and say something the detectives could use to locate him. It was worth a shot only because of the utter absence of anything else to do.

Pulling to the curb on the park side of East Seventh, Lacey elected to remain in the car in order to keep Caruso's building under observation. Brinsley went to the tap but didn't bother to take the tape since he intended to use the earphones.

As soon as Brinsley disappeared into the basement, Lacey reached for his two-way radio. Using the special frequency Internal Affairs had cleared for use in his undercover operations, he got in contact with Glenn Greer, the federal agent assigned to him as backup. He asked Greer to meet him behind the concrete band shell in Tompkins Square Park and told him to bring a tape recorder. Then, while he waited, he wound the Caruso tape back to the start and lit a cigarette.

"What's the deal?" Greer asked as soon as he arrived. He carried a small cassette recorder in his hand.

Lacey quickly explained why he was now confident he could get Brinsley to make a deal with Caruso.

"Then whatdya want the recorder for?" Greer asked.

"In case he doesn't," Lacey said without offering any further explanation. "You got a connector?"

From his topcoat pocket Greer produced a short length of cable with a jack at each end. Lacey connected the two recorders to each other, set his own on playback and Greer's cassette machine on record. While the half hour of conversation on the Caruso tape was being copied, he kept watch around the corner of the band shell for any sign of Brinsley. When the tape had played through, Lacey uncoupled the machines and told Greer to recopy the copy onto a reel.

"You got someone else in mind?" Greer asked. He understood

now what Lacey was planning. In case Brinsley did not fall, the second tape would allow Lacey to take his business elsewhere. He couldn't use the original because Brinsley would wonder what had happened to it, and he couldn't use a cassette recording because the police never used cassette machines on wiretaps. With the copy Greer would make for him, however, he could shop around for a cop who wanted to make some money. All he would need would be a plausible story to explain why he didn't do it himself, and that shouldn't be hard to come up with. That's the thing about crooked cops, Greer thought. In addition to being dishonest, they're stupid. They trust one another.

Sitting in the darkened basement of a remodeled brownstone on East Seventh Street waiting for a tape recorder to click on, Detective Philip Brinsley vowed he wouldn't make the same mistake again. He'd stay at the plant all night if he had to, and all the next day. When he wasn't there, Lacey or Cooper or Schwartz would be. Otherwise it didn't make any sense. You worked on a case for months, stuck your own neck out by using an illegal wire, and in the end you got nothing because no one was there to hear the one key conversation until hours after it had taken place.

As the time passed and the afternoon turned into evening and then night, Brinsley sat by the motionless machine like a visitor at the bedside of a friend in a coma. At half-past six the boiler clicked on, filling the damp basement with low mechanical noises. But the recorder didn't move until shortly after ten o'clock, when suddenly the empty take-up reel began to spin wildly. There was no tape on the machine but the phone call activated it anyway. It was an incoming call.

Yvonne's high-pitched, childlike voice said, "Yeah?"

"Evie? Al. The feds got Paul."

"Huh? How come?"

"I don't know how come. Just thought you should know."

"Is he all right, Al?"

"Sure, he's all right. Make bail in the morning. Just thought you should know, that's all."

"Yeah. Thanks, Al."

At midnight Joe Longo and Luke Antonelli were having sandwiches at the Market Diner, an all-night place on West Street that had almost official status as a police hangout. They had finished the processing and paper work on the Meredith and Caruso arrests only an hour before and were still too loose and exuberant to go home.

Gil Lacey had no trouble finding their table, for he could hear Joe's booming laugh the moment he walked into the diner. "Joe," he called, "congratulations!"

As he strode past the counter and around to the booths by the window, a dozen pairs of eyes followed him with mixed looks of curiosity and amusement. Although cops never talk about corruption to outsiders and rarely mention it even among themselves, there couldn't have been ten men in the Market Diner that night who hadn't heard stories about Gil Lacey. So they watched as his wide rolling strides carried him to the back of the diner and then looked away when Joe Longo stood up and extended his hand.

At the counter a detective leaned toward the man next to him and said, "Lacey was in the Seven-nine in Brooklyn when Joe was there." No one had asked for any explanations, but he was a friend of Joe's and felt that an explanation was called for. The man next to him answered with a noncommittal, "Yeah."

"Hey, Gil, this is Luke Antonelli. Luke . . . Gil Lacey," Joe said. "Cmon, sit down."

Luke offered his hand without standing and then slid farther into the booth to make room for Lacey. To the best of his recollection now, he is certain he had never heard of Lacey before, knew nothing of his reputation. Yet he disliked him immediately and can give no specific reason. "It was something in the way he paraded in," he says, "and maybe it was his clothes. He was a sharp dresser . . . not good sharp, but flashy. You could see he spent a lot of money on clothes and he wanted you to know it. Like I noticed when he opened his jacket that he had on these beltless slacks but he had his gun in a waist clip. Now that's gonna bunch up the fabric pretty bad, but there's nothing wrinkled about this guy. So right off that tells you this is a guy who gets his pants pressed every time he wears them."

"We used to work together in Brooklyn," Joe was saying. "Where have they got you now?" he asked Lacey.

"SIU," Lacey said.

Joe shrugged. "So you heard about the collar?" he said, not really phrasing it as a question.

"Sure did," Lacey answered playfully, throwing a jab across the table at Joe's shoulder. "You robbed us, you son of a bitch."

"Whatdya mean?"

"I mean we were on Caruso. How'd you do it . . . a wire, a stool?"

"No, it was another way," Joe answered quickly. He was being pointedly evasive, hoping Lacey would take the hint and drop the subject. He could tell Lacey wanted something because cops usually don't question each other like that. Professional curiosity is one thing, but asking a guy you haven't seen in years and a guy you never even met before how they make their cases is another. Joe figured he had to be asking for some other reason.

Instead of changing the subject, Lacey did exactly the opposite. "Can we talk?" he asked.

Both Joe and Luke knew in general what was coming, although the specifics surprised them. Lacey's proposal depended on a little-known technicality of police and courtroom procedure. An agent working on a case fills out daily report forms detailing his activities. These forms bear the code designation "BNDD-6" and are called "sixes," for short. Although they are not regarded as documentary evidence and are not subject to discovery motions by the defense, copies of them are given to defense counsel if the agent who originally filed them takes the stand during the trial.

Their value for the defense lies in the fact that they can be used to impeach the credibility of an officer's testimony. Any discrepancy between what the officer says on the stand and what he wrote in his sixes can be exploited to cast doubt on his story. For example, if Joe's report on the day of the arrest had failed to mention the seemingly trivial fact that he saw Caruso carrying a briefcase when he entered Meredith's apartment, a smart lawyer could jump all over him:

"Had you ever seen the defendant prior to the afternoon of October 6, 1971, Detective Longo?"

"No, sir."

"And yet you say that when you saw him enter an apartment building, you knew he was in possession of narcotics?"

"Yes, sir."

"Now how is that possible, Detective Longo?"

"Well, I knew from what my partner told me that narcotics would be delivered about that time. And this was a well-dressed guy carrying a briefcase and going into the apartment. He didn't look like he belonged there."

"What was the defendant wearing?"

"A dark suit."

"So you arrested him because he was wearing a dark suit?"

"No. It was because of what I told you and because he had this briefcase—"

"So it wasn't because of the dark suit?"

"No, sir."

"It was the briefcase that was the important thing?"

"Yes."

"You are telling us, then, that as an experienced police officer you knew that this was a probable way a person would transport narcotics."

"Yes, sir."

"And yet in your daily report I see no mention of this briefcase. Isn't it standard police procedure to include all important facts and observations in your reports?"

"Yes, sir."

"So that although you're telling us now that this briefcase was the most important thing you noticed about the defendant, in fact you didn't think it was important at the time, did you?"

"Yes, sir, I did."

"But not important enough to include in your report?"

"It was just a detail."

"A detail! . . . Detective Longo, did you see that briefcase at all before you entered Jason Meredith's apartment?"

Working in this way, a good defense attorney could use a tiny omission from a report to suggest that Caruso may have been merely an innocent guest in Meredith's apartment at the time of his arrest and that the detective was lying about having seen him deliver the drugs in order to make a case against someone he had arrested by accident.

For a defense attorney, the main problem with the sixes is time. In a case that is the result of a lengthy investigation, as the Meredith-Caruso case was, there can be sixty or more pages of single-spaced, typewritten data. In order to make maximum use of this material, a lawyer must know it almost by heart so that he can instantly spot the slightest discrepancy or can lead the detective into testifying to some-

thing he failed to include in his reports. In most cases, though, he is
given no time to study the sixes, which often are not delivered to him
until the detective is actually on the stand. Then he has to proceed on
a catch-as-catch-can basis, scanning them as the testimony pours in.

Lacey's proposal was so simple as to be almost elegant. If Joe
would make up a set of phony sixes, Lacey would undertake to sell
them to Caruso's lawyer, who might be willing to pay as much as ten
thousand dollars for them. The beauty of the plan was that it was
almost foolproof and wouldn't even damage the case against Caruso.
The fake sixes would do the defense no good, but the lawyer wouldn't
know that until he got the real reports when Joe testified. Then what
could he do? He would face disbarment if he reported the incident
and even if the story ever did get out, Joe could simply deny it.

When Lacey stopped speaking, Joe and Luke looked at each other without saying anything. Then Joe stood up, sweeping his own and
Luke's dinner checks from the table as he did. He turned them face up
and studied them a moment as Lacey slid from the booth to let Luke
squeeze past him. Then he took a slender roll of bills from his pocket
and pulled out a ten, which he left on the table with the checks. When
he walked out of the Market Diner with Luke, it was the last time he
would ever see Gil Lacey. Luke, though, would see him one more time.
Six months later they would meet again at Joe's funeral.

*Although Joe's rejection of Lacey's proposal in effect closed the
Caruso incident, a few postscripts must be added to our account of it.*

*First, it is important to note that Gil Lacey never filed a report in
any way alluding to his attempt to involve Joe and Luke in a plan to sell
phony sixes to Paul Caruso's lawyer—a clear indication that the offer
was in no way connected with Lacey's undercover operations but was
simply a spur-of-the-moment attempt to turn a profit on a botched investigation.*

*Second, although Paul Scala knew that Lacey and Brinsley had
been tapping Caruso's phone at the time of Caruso's arrest, he chose to
ignore a court order for the disclosure of any taps involved in the case. As
a result, Caruso was able to appeal his conviction on the grounds that he
had been the subject of an illegal wiretap which was not disclosed by the
government at the time of his first trial. When he was called to testify at
the motion for retrial, Scala defended his failure to report the tap with
the incredible explanation that he never realized that the man Longo*

arrested and the man whose phone Lacey's team had tapped were the same person. When confronted with reports on the case that would have clarified the matter for him, he denied ever having seen them—although Lacey already had testified that Scala himself had in fact written one of these reports. Fortunately for Scala, judges rarely take strong action when confronted with cases of prosecutorial misconduct. He got off with a brief admonition from the court, which chose to accept his story at face value.

Finally, a word about Detective Philip Brinsley. Even after the collapse of the Caruso case, Lacey remained convinced that Brinsley could be corrupted. With the tenacity of Victor Hugo's Inspector Javert, he kept after him until he proved his point. A few months later, Lacey, Brinsley, and a third detective arrested a drug dealer named Leon Cortez in the Bronx. As they were taking him in, Cortez offered the detectives three thousand dollars to let him go but Brinsley refused the bribe. Cortez was delivered to the station house on the Boston Post Road, where he was booked and locked up. A few hours later, Brinsley and his partner were eating at a nearby restaurant when Lacey joined them. He handed the two detectives envelopes containing three thousand dollars apiece and explained that the money was from Cortez, who had decided to become more generous and had been released. Faced with this fait accompli, the detectives took the money. Neither was the sort of man who would turn in a fellow cop, and with Cortez already free the only choice was between accepting a split or letting Lacey keep it all.

Leon Cortez, it turned out, was an undercover federal agent. Brinsley and his partner were arrested and brought up on criminal and departmental charges. Both were dismissed from the force and are presently awaiting trial.

Chapter 6
Missing Link

ALTHOUGH CARLO DANZIE had told Joe he would be staying at the Holiday Inn by La Guardia, when he left the Varick Street office on Thursday night he hailed a cab and ordered the driver to circle the block and stop at the nearest pay phone. When the first booth they came to turned out to be less than two blocks from the Joint Task Force office, he changed his mind and said, "Please, just continue the way you are going, I will make my call later."

The driver shrugged and continued north on Sixth Avenue, moving rapidly with the staggered lights, hitting each intersection just as the signal turned green. In his rearview mirror he could see his passenger checking the back window every few seconds. Nudging the accelerator closer to the floor, he picked up speed until he was running the lights on red. No one in the pack behind followed.

"Wanna make that call now?" he asked.

"Thank you," Danzie said, leaning forward to speak through the hole in the safety partition. "You are a tactful man."

"Just a job," the cabbie answered laconically.

At Thirty-eighth he pulled up by a pay phone. "Do I need a token?" Danzie asked. In many cities in Europe public telephones accept phone company tokens rather than currency.

"Just put in a dime," the cabbie said.

Danzie fished some coins from his pocket and studied them carefully before selecting the right one. From a billfold in his breast pocket he removed a slip of paper Anthony Diamond had given him in Washington. He dialed the number written on it and waited. On the fourth ring a man answered. Although he didn't recognize the voice, Danzie said, "This is Carlo Danzie. I am supposed to meet you somewhere."

"Where are you?" the man asked.

"I do not know, I am in a public telephone."

"You in a cab?"

"Yes."

"Well, come to the Lincoln Hotel. Forty-second and Tenth—just tell him Lincoln Hotel. Room twelve twenty-eight."

Danzie hung up and returned to the cab. Ten minutes later he was knocking on the door of the hotel room Paul Scala maintained for meetings with cops who couldn't afford to be seen meeting with him at his office in the courthouse. A barrel-chested man in shirt sleeves opened the door. He wore a gun in a clip at his waist but his face was smooth and pink-skinned, incongruously babyish. "Danzie?" he asked.

"Yes."

The baby-faced man stepped back to let Danzie pass, then swung the door closed after checking the corridor in both directions. "I'm Gil Lacey," he said. "You'll be working with me and an agent you'll meet tomorrow. Where are you staying? It can't be here."

"No, not here," Danzie said. "There is a hotel near the airport."

"Why there?"

"No reason in particular," Danzie answered evasively.

"Well, if it's a broad, forget about it," Lacey snapped. "We don't need complications. Anyway, it's out of the question. Too far away."

"I told the detectives I would be there," Danzie said. He liked Gil Lacey already, admired his perspicacity. For that reason he would do as he was told—especially since the restaurant at the hotel probably would be closed and the brown-haired waitress gone by the time he got there. Nevertheless, he was gratified when Lacey said, "Then I guess that's where you'd better go. We'll get you a place in town in a day or so. You're gonna need some money."

Before Danzie had a chance to appreciate how deftly Lacey had terminated the discussion of his accommodations and switched to a new subject, Lacey walked to the end table next to the bed and picked up a bulging white business envelope. He removed a sheet of paper from the envelope, folded it twice, and slid it into his pants pocket. Then he handed the envelope to Danzie. "Count it," he ordered.

Quickly leafing through the wad of bills with his thick, short-fingered hands, Danzie counted five thousand dollars in fifties and hundreds. "Five thousand," he announced, discarding the envelope and putting the money in his pocket. "Do I give you a receipt?"

"No," Lacey said. "If you have to spend it on them, spend it on them. And if you need more, let us know. But try them with this first. Okay?"

"Yes."

"If you have any expenses, use your own money and keep track of it. You'll be reimbursed later on. Any questions?"

"Yes," Danzie said, eager to cut through the evasions and get some clear-cut instructions. "Will it be necessary for me to carry a transmitter?"

"Later," Lacey answered without hesitation. "For the time being just kind of suck them along, do what you have to. You'll know when the time's right. Did you say they know you're out by the airport?"

Lacey's disconcerting habit of changing subjects from one sentence to the next kept Danzie off balance. "Yes," he said, at a loss to know why they were back to this again.

"Well, when you get there call and give me your room number," Lacey said. "We'll set up a plant in the next room."

Danzie nodded. He liked the idea of starting out with a listening device operating from outside his own room. It was much less risky than being wired yourself, where there was always the chance that something might happen to give it away. Sooner or later he knew it would have to come to that—Lacey had told him so already. But the longer he could put it off the better. Of course, a recorder on a room was much less effective than a recorder on a person, since it allowed them to monitor conversations only in one place. But that was their problem, not his. "Who should I work on?" he asked. "Just Longo?"

Lacey lit a cigarette and dragged on it thoughtfully for a moment, taking the time to harden his own mind before answering. Even for a practiced double agent, the kind of explicitness Danzie wanted was not easy to provide. At first, each new case is almost an abstraction, an "investigation," a search for incriminating facts. Later it becomes an "operation," an elaborate trap baited to draw the quarry into it, tightly sprung to lock closed when the bait is taken. But in between there is always the moment when the reality of what is happening overrides the euphemisms and the self-deceptions. It is at this moment, this single moment in the whole process, that the double agent must face the fact of what he has become. Even if it lasts for less time than it takes to suck the smoke out of a cigarette and blow it back into the air, the short stab of pain that accompanies it lingers for . . . How long? Long enough to remember teaming with Joe in Brooklyn? Sunday dinners at his house? Jeannie and the kids?

"Yeah," Lacey said, his voice deliberately cold. "He's the one they're interested in, mainly. The partner doesn't matter, but it might be easier to work on him. He's less experienced, probably not so cagey. So you might want to work through him. If you get him dirty, then you've got Longo. You'll have to see how it goes."

"There's another man, too," Danzie said, questioningly.

Lacey seemed surprised. "Who's that?" he asked.

"His name is Kane. He was with Antonelli when they took me to Washington."

Lacey laughed. "No," he said. "You leave Kane out of it. This is a federal investigation and he's a fed. They don't make cases against themselves."

Then he laughed again.

"I don't know where he gets it," Joe said.

Jeannie laughed. "Where does he get anything?" she asked. "He's the image of you and you know it."

Joe did know it. At twelve, Joey had his father's black hair, straight nose, and clear green eyes. Skinnier then Joe remembered himself at that age, he was a tall boy who carried himself without awkwardness. Already he promised to be a physical match for his father when he filled out. From the moment he had started junior high in September he had become passionately addicted to basketball, yet whenever anyone asked him what he wanted to be he always said a priest.

"Well, maybe," Joe said, speaking to Jeannie but looking straight across the table at his son. "Some things he got from me, but the priests are all on your side of the family."

The boy took the teasing well, secure in the knowledge that his father took a secret pride in the idea of having a son in the priesthood. They were close but not the way Joey would have liked it, because his father was away so much. Sometimes he would hear him come in in the middle of the night, and then he and Mom would be talking— quiet, laughing talk, his father's voice rapid and excited, his mother questioning, caught up, sharing it. Sometimes he could even make out snatches of what they were saying, and at those times he thought that being a policeman like his father was the best thing in the world to be. But when he got up in the morning his father might be gone already, and he knew how his mother had her heart set against it. So he had begun to say that he wanted to be a priest, for in his naive and idealistic mind there was a clear connection between the two vocations that he couldn't put into words but that lay perhaps in the taking of confessions, the call to correct and minister to the sinful and the wicked.

It was a treat having his father home in the evening. When Joe called earlier and said he'd be home by nine, Joey begged for permission to wait to eat with him. So Marie, who was only ten, had to eat by herself. After supper she schemed to wait up for Daddy, but then fell asleep in her pajamas on the gold carpet in front of the television set. Jeannie left her there so that Joe could carry her to bed when he got in. He kissed her and talked to her, even though she was too sleepy to understand, and when he came back downstairs to the kitchen Jeannie had dinner on the table for her two men.

The clock radio was playing softly. Still half asleep, Joe rolled toward Jeannie's side of the bed and realized that she was gone. Her robe lay across the foot of the bed and the hiss of the shower sounded dully under the music. A snatch of giggling laughter drifted up from the kitchen and through the bedroom door, which meant the kids were up already.

It was a perfect Friday morning, bright and warm-looking with sunlight thick as butter across the bedroom floor. Naked at the window, he looked out over the backyard and was almost surprised to see the bare trees and the thin crust of old snow on the grass. He felt fresh and strong and eager, like he had slept through to April and half expected to see spring blossoms. The jury had the Caruso case, Danzie was being given the weekend to try to set something up, and nothing else called for his attention.

Except Jeannie and the kids. He promised himself a short day at the office and a weekend at home. They were growing up so fast, he thought, vowing to make himself as much a part of it as he could. He had missed too much already. And Jeannie, too—how much of her had he missed? Why did it have to be one or the other, home or the job? It didn't, he told himself, feeling optimistic, in control, ready to make everything right. He knew that he was just one step away from making the biggest case of his career, maybe the biggest ever, and it gave him a sense of potency and command that made everything else seem possible.

Turning from the window, he took his plaid wool robe from the needlepoint chair and slipped it over his shoulders. The news had come on the radio and he stopped at the bathroom door to listen with amused curiosity as the announcer detailed the latest development in the story of Clifford Irving and Howard Hughes. And the woman, a baroness or whatever she was. In a way, none of it seemed real. And yet the greeds and passions weren't strange to Joe Longo. They were the same ones he saw on the job every day of the year. For sheer romance, he concluded, the delicate intricacies of the underworld were infinitely more fascinating than the shoddy gambits of a fancy hoax-ster and his glamorous playmate.

The announcer seemed almost to have reached the same con-clusion. Without missing a beat he went on to the next story, holding Joe where he stood, one hand clutching his bathrobe closed, the other on the bathroom door.

"In an early hours raid in the Bronx, narcotics detectives last night seized just under a million dollars in cash and arrested three men. The raid was conducted by New York City policemen and feder-al agents attached to the Joint Task Force on Narcotics. According to a Police Department spokesman, the arrests came as the culmination of a lengthy investigation. Arrested were reputed gangland figure Larry Sciarra, known as Larry Boston, and two associates whose names have not yet been released. Shortly after two o'clock this morn-ing, narcotics agents spotted Boston and his associates driving in the Van Ness section of the Bronx. A search of their car disclosed a suit-case containing approximately nine hundred and sixty-seven thousand dollars. A spokesman from the federal prosecutor's office said that it was his belief that the money was apparently the payoff for approximately two hundred pounds of pure heroin. No narcotics were seized in the raid.

"The Police Department also announced today the funeral arrangements for Patrolmen Gregory Foster and Rocco Laurie, gunned down last night by the Black Liberation Army. . ."

Joe turned down the radio and reached for the phone. "Paula, it's Joe. Is Luke there?" he asked urgently when a woman's voice answered on the second ring. He had met his partner's wife only once.

"He's not here," she answered flatly, her words clipped but toneless. Once or twice Luke said things that hinted his marriage was in trouble, but he hadn't indicated any desire to talk about it, and Joe didn't feel he knew him well enough to pry.

"Is he at the office?" he asked.

"At the office," she repeated, paused to let Joe say good-bye, and hung up.

Eager to get to Varick Street and learn the whole story, Joe dressed without showering and quickly told Jeannie what he had heard on the radio. Even though it wasn't his case, he wanted to be in on the excitement at the office and to learn the details. When something that big went down, it affected every case every narcotics cop was working on.

"If you're leaving right now," Jeannie asked, "why don't you take the kids to school?"

"Okay," he said. "I'll just have a cup of coffee. If they can be ready by then, I'll take them."

The children jumped delightedly at his offer and raced upstairs to get dressed. Marie was in the fifth grade at a parochial school about five miles out on the Island, and Joey was in his first year of junior high at the same school. It wouldn't take him more than fifteen minutes out of his way, and on this morning in particular it seemed worth it.

Over coffee, though, he found himself starting to think like a detective again. Quickly getting impatient, he drank the cup still steaming and paced the kitchen floor while he waited. He had worked on Larry Boston himself a number of years ago but nothing much came of it. It was when he was in SIU, nineteen sixty-eight or nine, and remembering the case brought back unpleasant thoughts. His team had a productive tap on Boston's phone that all of a sudden stopped producing, and Joe had wondered at the time whether someone had sold out the wire. Then one day he was tailing Boston, paired with a detective named Ernie Blake. It was winter and a light snow was falling. Joe and Blake were switching off with two other cars so that Boston wouldn't be able to spot them as they followed him around Queens and the Island. Blake was driving. Then they got bogged down in traffic on Northern Boulevard, unable to move because a tanker truck in the eastbound lane knifed in ahead of the car in front of them but couldn't get through both lanes of westbound traffic. Boston was three or four cars ahead, at the light at the corner of Main Street in Flushing.

"We're gonna lose him," Blake said. "I can't see him."

"Don't sweat it," Joe tried to reassure him. "If he takes a right I'll see him, and if he goes straight we'll catch up as soon as we get out of this."

Blake fidgeted another half minute and then said, "I gotta see where he is."

Suddenly, before Joe could stop him, he bolted from the car and ran down the center of the boulevard, cutting in to go around the cab of the tanker. He was out of sight for only a few seconds, and when he got back to the car he said, "He's still there."

"Yeah, well he won't be for long," Joe snapped. "That was a fucking dumb move. Did he see you?"

"No, I don't think so," Blake answered.

When the traffic started to move again, Joe and Ernie quickly reestablished visual contact with Boston's car. At 112th Street his silver Imperial took a left. Joe radioed the information back to the other cars and had Blake continue west on Northern Boulevard. A few minutes later the radio crackled with the news that Boston was back on Northern Boulevard, this time heading east. He had simply circled the block. The tail continued as Boston drove aimlessly through Queens and then led his pursuers back to his house in Astoria. Wherever he had been going, apparently he changed his mind.

Joe was in a rage but said nothing until the whole team was back in the office. He told Blake he wanted to talk to him in the locker room, and when they were alone there he let his partner know what he thought of his work. A stocky, taciturn man in his mid forties, a few inches shorter than Joe but about the same weight, Blake listened without answering as Joe's anger mounted.

"That was a dumb fucking move, Ernie," Joe repeated belligerently. "You probably blew the whole goddam case."

"I blew it?" Blake spat back. "If we did it your way we would've lost him."

"Come off it, Ernie," Joe challenged. "You should have just put on the fucking dome light and siren."

Even before the words were out, Blake jumped for him and they brawled in the locker room. Joe flung his attacker back, sending him crashing into the green steel lockers, the noise like a car wreck echoing through the empty room.

Blake pulled himself to his feet and charged again. They were still wrestling when four other men from the team raced down the row of lockers, vaulted the low wooden bench, and pulled them apart, grabbing Joe first because he had his back to them, and then Blake.

Shaking himself free from the men who were holding him, Joe walked away from Blake, who stopped struggling against the two detectives who held his arms. At the door Joe stopped to face the five men in the locker room. "This is between me and Ernie," he announced sharply. "Y'understand?"

Joe never told anyone about the incident, but apparently someone did because word of the fight quickly got back to the captain, who called them into his office a few days later. "What's this I hear about you two guys fighting?" he asked, addressing the question to neither one in particular.

"It was nothing," Joe answered quickly.

The captain looked to Blake, who didn't offer to add anything to Joe's explanation.

"I don't call it nothing when two of my men are going at each other in the locker room," the captain said sternly to Joe. "Is there something about this case I don't know?"

Joe didn't answer.

"Okay," the captain said, standing up and walking around his desk. "I don't want you two working together. Effective now, you get yourselves two new partners."

Blake turned and walked from the room. From that moment he

never spoke to Joe again until Joe transferred out of SIU at the end of 1970. And Joe never learned whether there was any basis for his fleeting moment of suspicion. Now it was all water over the dam as far as he was concerned.

He checked his watch and called impatiently for the kids, who hurried downstairs into the kitchen. In a moment they were all piled into the car and on their way, Marie and Joey both jabbering for his attention while his mind was elsewhere. He dropped them off and watched absently while Joey ran off into the yard to join a group of boys. Marie trudged up the walk by herself, stopping at the school door to turn and wave. He waved back, then pulled the car around and headed for the city, his mind clear now to think things through. There was just one question, but he didn't have the answer.

No matter how he tried, he couldn't understand why Larry Boston was busted with a million dollars and no junk. Boston had to have been on his way to the deal, at least a couple of hundred pounds. But they hit him before the deal went down. It didn't make any sense.

In December of 1972, nine months after Joe Longo died, the Police Department discovered that almost five hundred pounds of heroin and cocaine, valued at over seventy-two million dollars, had been stolen from the Police Department Property Clerk's Office. Investigators speculated that the million dollars found in Larry Boston's car had been slated to purchase a portion of the stolen narcotics. Detective Ernie Blake, who retired from the Force on the day Joe Longo was buried, was later publicly accused of having masterminded the thefts. The Property Clerk's logbooks revealed that the missing drugs had been signed out in nine separate batches. Six of the logbook entries pertaining to these transactions bore the apparently forged signature of Joe Longo.

How were millions and millions of dollars' worth of narcotics stolen right from under the Police Department's noses? Why was Joe Longo's name used to cover up the thefts? Was there a connection between Joe and Larry Boston? Was Joe's death related to the Property Clerk thefts?

Until now, no one has answered these questions. The Property Clerk Ripoff is far and away the biggest robbery in the history of crime. To this day it has never been solved. But perhaps now it is possible to speculate that there is a missing link that ties together all the unexplained facts about Joe's life and death. That missing link is Carlo Danzie.

Instead of driving straight to Varick Street, Joe cut off the Long Island Expressway at the Grand Central Parkway and headed toward La Guardia Airport. Leaving the parkway before the airport exit, he circled down Ditmars Boulevard to the Holiday Inn. In the lobby, he rang Carlo Danzie's room number and told Danzie he was on the way up.

Two minutes later, the door to Danzie's room swung open. Danzie was standing in front of him, barefoot in a gray wool dressing gown with matching satin trim. Joe noticed the crisp, astringent smell of good cologne and the momentary look of annoyance that crossed Danzie's face and quickly gave way to a broad smile. "Come in, come in, Joe," his voice boomed into the corridor. "You will excuse my dress, but I did not expect you."

"Something came up," Joe said, stepping past Danzie and surveying the room. "You gotta come to the office."

The bed was unmade and a woman's clothes lay on a straight chair by the window, a bright paisley blouse over the back, a skirt and underwear across the seat. The bathroom door was closed. Danzie saw where Joe was looking but said nothing. He was not a man who made explanations.

"Yes, of course," he said, padding across the thin carpet to the closet. Like a man accustomed to the presence of servants, he removed his robe and hung it carefully on a hanger. Totally naked, he contemplated the contents of the closet and then selected a slate-gray suit from the row of clothes that crowded the closet like a rack in a department store. Four pieces of matched lightweight luggage stood on the closet floor.

"Where'd that come from?" Joe asked.

"Venice," Danzie said, carrying the suit, still on its hanger, across the room. For a middle-aged man with no clothes on, he moved with surprising dignity. "Are you ever in Italy?" he asked, the prelude of an offer to set Joe up with his tailor.

"That's not what I meant," Joe said, not particularly to cut him off but because he wanted his question answered. "You didn't have any luggage at the Americana. Where'd all this stuff come from?"

From a dresser drawer, Danzie removed a pair of printed silk boxer shorts and stepped into them. Then he sat on the bed to pull on a pair of cashmere socks. "My belongings were misplaced in transit," he said without looking up. "The airline delivered them last night."

Simply out of habit, Joe made a mental note to check with the airline, although it didn't seem particularly important. Unfortunately, he quickly forgot about it and never followed up. If he had, he would have learned that Danzie was lying—lying, in the first instance, about the clothes, but also about what else? If his belongings, as he called them, were already stored somewhere in New York when he was arrested Tuesday night, then he hadn't just flown in that afternoon. When had he come? And on what business? None of the events of the last six weeks of Joe's life would have happened if he had asked these questions.

Danzie's shirts were custom-made, and the Venetian tailor who had done the suit was obviously a craftsman of considerable discretion. "I ask because if you are in Venice you may wish the name of my *disegnatore*," he said, deliberately choosing that word in preference to the humbler *sarto*, tailor. It was his first tentative probe of Joe's character, but it produced nothing.

"Who's in there?" Joe demanded, pointing toward the closed bathroom door.

"Just a friend."

"Let's have a look at her."

"I would be happy to oblige," Danzie answered lightly, "but unfortunately the young lady has no clothes on."

"If that bothers her, maybe she shouldn't have taken them off," Joe said. With his thumb he gestured toward the clothes on the chair, instructing Danzie to hand them in to her.

Before Danzie could move, the bathroom door clicked open and a woman in her early twenties stepped into the room. She was wearing a thin linen bath towel that barely reached down to the top of her long, slender legs. "Satisfied?" she asked, cocking her head insolently, her soft brown hair falling suggestively to the side.

Joe resisted the temptation to answer in kind. "Pleased to meet you," he said, laughing.

She pursed her lips and shrugged, as though she were accepting an apology. The look of defiance melted from her face and she met Joe's laugh with a soft smile.

The Varick Street office was more crowded than Joe had ever seen it. Reporters clustered in the hallways, looking for anyone who would be willing to make a statement. Camera crews from all six television

stations milled about, socializing with each other and guarding their
bulky equipment.

Joe saw the crowd as soon as the elevator doors opened. Realizing
that he would have to find another way into the office, he punched the
Door Close button and rode down to four, then led Danzie past the
locker room to a staircase in a service corridor. They walked up to six
and entered the squad room through a back door. Except for an elderly sound man from one of the television news crews, the squad room
was free of newsmen.

Joe shook the man gently. "Let's get going, Pop. Reveille," he
said, gesturing toward the door with his thumb.

The old man looked up at him dumbly. The wire dangling from
the earpiece in his ear gave his sleepy face the look of an old and
battered ragdoll whose stuffing is starting to come out. He pushed
himself up from the desk and shuffled off in the direction of the door
to the front corridor.

"Sit here," Joe told Danzie. "You can get yourself some coffee if
you want, but don't leave the room unless you want your picture in the
papers. I'll be back in a minute."

He crossed to Captain Marcus's office, knocked once, and
stepped in. Marcus was alone in the small cubicle, seated behind his
desk. He was on the phone, listening while the person on the other end
did most of the talking. It was barely nine o'clock and he already
looked like he had put in a long day. His shirt was open at the neck
and his sleeves were badly wrinkled from having been rolled up and
down a dozen times through the long night. His limp necktie mean-
dered across the blotter on his desk like a hair floating in soup. "We're
working on it," he said into the phone at one point. A little later he
said, "What do you want me to say? I can't tell you what I don't
know." Then he hung up.

He stood slowly, using his hands like an old man, and walked
around the desk to a plain wood table that stood along the side wall.
In the center of it a space had been cleared among the papers and
coffee cups for a green imitation-leather suitcase. "Look at this, will
you," he growled, flipping the two locks and flinging back the lid.

From side to side the suitcase was so tightly crammed with neatly
bundled bills that a small man would have had trouble lifting it.

Joe's first reaction on seeing such an immense quantity of money
was the usual moment of shock, which almost instantly gave way to a

cool indifference, as though the money couldn't possibly be real. As a narcotics cop he had busted more than his share of wise guys with large amounts of cash. But he had never seen anything like this. He had grabbed couriers with thick brown envelopes stuffed with money, and once he nailed a dealer with fifty grand in a briefcase. Now he was looking at almost twenty times that much.

The captain slammed the two-suiter closed and snapped the locks, turning to face Joe with a look of weary disgust on his face, as though the suitcase contained the evidence in a brutal hatchet murder instead of a narcotics raid.

"Fives, tens, twenties, and fifties," he said. "There's not a hundred in there. Nine hundred and sixty-seven thousand, five hundred and fifty dollars. And do you know what they're saying already? Where's the other thirty-two and a half?"

He walked quickly to his desk and shook a cigarette from the crumpled pack on the blotter. Without lighting it, he turned to face Joe again and went on talking. "Goddamn it, I spent five years in Internal Affairs. Five years! It's rotten work, Joe, I don't have to tell you. I never knew a good man there who liked it, but look, it had to be done. I don't want to make excuses, you know how I feel about it. As far as I'm concerned, there's nothing lower than a wrong cop. I've said it a hundred times and I still say it. But it's getting so I don't know anymore."

He paused to light his cigarette and then went on with his monologue, almost as though he were talking to himself.

"It used to be we'd get a squeal on a cop and we'd look into it," he said. "It doesn't matter to me if you believe this or not, Joe, but I'm telling you, deep down I wanted to find out the guy was right. That's the truth. Every time I had to say a guy's no good, it hurt. He was one of our own and it hurt every time. But, Christ, I don't know what's happening anymore. The guys who were there when I was there are all gone now. And all the new ones think is crooked cop, crooked cop, crooked cop. They keep score the way we keep score on wise guys, and if a guy turns out to be clean, do you think they say, Hey, that's nice, he passed the test? Nah, they say, He got away with it this time but we'll catch up with him one of these days."

Marcus stopped talking, as though he suddenly realized he was being overheard. He unbuttoned his cuffs and rolled up his sleeves, the cigarette dangling from the corner of his mouth until his hand was free to take it. "They got here at five o'clock," he said, looking straight at Joe now, his eyes watering from the smoke. "Can you believe that? Boston couldn't get a lawyer here as fast as they showed up. We should have had the Chivas Regal out, we should have been celebrating. We get Larry Boston and nine hundred and sixty-seven thousand dollars! God, that's gotta hurt him bad. I mean, we broke up a deal that has to be over a hundred kilos. Even before it has a chance to sink in, these fucks show up and start asking where's the other thirty grand. Right away, if it's not round numbers it's gotta be a bad cop. The whole fucking thing makes me sick."

Joe said nothing when Marcus stopped. He had never heard the captain like this and he felt that anything he said now would be an intrusion. Besides, he was embarrassed about what he had been thinking when he walked in. He had wanted to ask if the radio report was true that there was no dope seized in the raid. He wanted to know why they busted Boston before the deal went down. But he knew the captain must have asked himself that already. It was probably part of what was torturing him right now.

"You know, there's another thing," Marcus said, almost as though he had read Joe's mind. "You've gotta ask yourself, Where's the junk? Those bastards in the three-piece suits are asking that right now. They've got all my detectives over there on Broome Street and that's what they want to know. Where's the junk and where's the other thirty grand? That's what's got the P.C. worried. How's the whole thing make us look? If a hundred kees comes into the country somebody's gotta know about it. But this time, nothing."

"Don't sweat it," Joe said reassuringly. "We'll hit the streets, ask some questions, squeeze a couple of guys. Somebody's gotta know, right?"

Marcus smiled. "Right," he said, trying to echo Joe's optimistic tone. "What about that guy from the other side you busted? This sounds like the kind of league he plays in."

Joe nodded judiciously. "That's not a bad idea," he said with impish seriousness. "Why didn't I think of it?"

"Well, just get right on it," Marcus ordered. "Bring him in and see what he knows. There's not gonna be much fun around here until somebody finds out what Larry Boston was buying with his million dollars."

Joe left the captain's office and went back to his desk for Danzie. In order to avoid having to run the journalistic gauntlet in the corridor, he led Danzie through an interior door into the next office. Moving room by room, they crossed all the way to the extreme south end of the building, where they darted across the corridor to a stairwell. Removing his shield case from his inside jacket pocket, Joe flipped it open and tucked it into his breast pocket with the gold shield hanging on the outside. Then he and Danzie took the stairs up one flight and emerged into the wide corridor, where they were met by a uniformed patrolman on guard duty.

Passing the guard, who scrutinized his shield but said nothing, he proceeded with Danzie to the interrogation area, a set of small rooms separated by narrow observation alcoves. Luke Antonelli, Bill Kane, and two other detectives were in the alcove adjoining the room where Larry Boston was being questioned, watching through one-way glass and listening over a small speaker like the voice box of an intercom. An inspector from Narcotics was conducting the interrogation.

Luke quickly filled in his partner, talking candidly despite Danzie's presence. The inspector was doing the questioning, he explained, because all the arresting officers had been hauled over to Broome Street for a grilling by Internal Affairs. From the moment he was arrested, Boston had been playing it completely dumb, Luke added unnecessarily, for Boston's gravelly voice could be heard repeatedly insisting, "I'm telling ya, I don't know nothing about it. I stop to make a phone call and I seen this suitcase in the phone booth. So I pick it up. Someone musta just left it there. So I figure I'll take it to the police station. Then there's cops all over me."

"Someone left a million bucks in a phone booth?" the inspector challenged, incredulous.

"I don't know," Boston said. "I didn't open it. If that's what you say is in it, I guess so."

It was such a ludicrous defense that the four narcotics investigators laughed lightly. Even Danzie smiled.

"Do you know that guy?" Joe asked, motioning Danzie to approach the window.

Danzie stepped to the glass and carefully studied the man on the other side for over a minute. A wiry, narrow-faced man in his late forties, with greased hair and a chin dotted with graying stubble, Larry

Boston was seated directly facing the one-way window. His facial muscles sagged with fatigue but his dark eyes smoldered with inexhaustible malice as he stared straight past the questioner.

"No," Danzie said, turning to face Joe. "I have never seen him before."

"You don't know who he is?"

"I know who he is," Danzie corrected, "but that is not what you asked. He is Boston."

"That's right, and he was busted with a million bucks last night. What do you know about that?"

He didn't really expect to learn anything, but he figured it was worth a try. If Danzie was as well connected as he was supposed to be, then he might know something if there was a million-dollar deal in the works. In any case, bringing him in at least served to remind him that he wasn't a free man just because he had been cut loose.

As Joe had expected, Danzie just shrugged. Then, with a quick motion of his head, he signaled for Joe to step around to his other side and then turned his back on the other detectives in the room. Speaking softly so as not to be overheard, he said, "That man had fifty thousand dollars of my money. It is part of what your people have now."

Joe looked straight into his informant's gray eyes. "What was it for?" he demanded, hissing the words to keep his voice low.

Danzie removed a gold cigarette case from his breast pocket, slid a cigarette from it, and replaced the case. Holding the tip of the cigarette between his teeth as he lit it with a matching gold lighter, he puffed lightly before answering. He smoked in the old European style, handling the cigarette with thumb and forefinger.

"What was it for?" he repeated, turning the question into its own answer. "It was for business."

"Yeah, I know business," Joe growled, an unmistakable note of anger and impatience creeping into his voice. "What I want to know is where the stuff's coming from."

"If I knew, I would tell you," Danzie answered, speaking louder now, his voice audible to the others. "I'm trying to be, how do you say, level. I tell you he had my money so you can see I hide nothing from you. But that is all I will tell you."

Chapter 7
"Some Other Consideration"

AFTER TAKING DANZIE back to his hotel early Friday afternoon, Joe drove straight to his son's school, parked in the teachers' lot, and hurried to the gym. He walked in and stopped by the door, letting his eyes adjust to the dim light and then watching without being noticed. After a few minutes he heard a piping teenage voice say, "Hey, Joey, isn't that your father?"

Joey turned but Joe motioned for him to stay with the game. There were only seven boys but they played a four-man game with Joey, who was the tallest and the quickest of the group, playing offense for whichever team had the ball. With his father watching, though, he refused to shoot. Twice he drove in for lay-ups, only to make flashy underhand passes to his surprised teammates when he got in under the net. For as long as he could remember, his father had been telling him he had to be a team player, the kind who never took a low percentage shot if he could find an open man, the kind who hit to the opposite field to move up the runners, the kind who always ran out his pass patterns.

Joe watched and laughed to himself, thinking that perhaps he had overdone the lesson. He took off his jacket and shoes, unclipped his gun, and folded the jacket around it. Putting the shoes on top, he deposited the clothes on the floor where he could keep an eye on them and jogged across the court to join the game.

He played for almost half an hour, an intense reckless game with more showboating than skill on all sides. Except for his son, the boys all called him Joe. Three of them were on the baseball team he had coached last spring and was looking forward to coaching again. This year Joey would be on it.

Promptly at four o'clock the coach appeared from the locker room. A fat, balding man in a gray sweatsuit, he tooted on his whistle and bellowed, "Nice practice, kids. Hit the showers!" Joe watched, sweating and out of breath, as the boys walked slowly from the court. "Hey, Joey, I'll wait for you here," he called.

While Joey showered and dressed, Joe passed the time talking with the coach. To be polite, he asked about his son's progress, but he put no stock in the answers of a man who did his coaching from an office in the locker room underneath the gym. They talked briefly about some of the other boys but soon ran out of things to say.

When Joey came back, he had two of the boys with him. He had offered them a ride home, and they all piled into Joe's car. On the way, Joe suggested that they stop to eat. Over hamburgers at a fast-food restaurant in Douglaston one of the boys asked Joe if it was true that he had been a major league baseball player.

"Who told you that? Joey? No, I was just in the minors."

"What happened?" the boy asked with the innocent insensitivity that children can always get away with.

"You gotta be real good to play in the majors," Joe said. "I didn't make it."

"You broke your leg!" Joey objected defensively.

"Yeah, that's true," Joe shrugged. "But Ted Williams broke his elbow. If you're good enough it shouldn't stop you."

After dropping the other kids off, Joe and his son drove home. It was dark when they pulled into the driveway beside the house, almost six o'clock. "Hey, Joey, don't tell your mother we stopped to eat," Joe whispered conspiratorially. The boy laughed and bolted from the car, racing happily for the back door. As Joe crossed the gravel driveway after him, already he could hear his son's voice from inside the house.

He stopped at the kitchen door to let the boy finish his story.

When he walked in, Jeannie said, "Congratulations. I hear you made the team."

"Did you really, Daddy?" Marie asked from the table, a half-eaten bowl of tomato soup in front of her.

"No," Joe answered seriously, pulling up a chair and sitting next to her. "Mommy was just joking. I picked Joey up at practice, that's all. I played a little, too."

She was going through a stage when she didn't take teasing well, so he had to explain the joke to her or she would become upset when she realized they were kidding.

Joey went to wash up for supper, and then, while the kids were eating, Joe talked Jeannie into going out dancing. "We haven't done it in a long time," he said, "and I feel like celebrating." What he didn't tell her was that he wanted to get out to take his mind off the things that were bothering him. He knew Danzie hadn't told him everything about his connection with Larry Boston and realized that unless he kept active he would brood about it until he had no choice but to go to see Danzie and force some answers out of him. "Call Grace, see if she can sit," he said.

In the end, the only sitter they could get on such short notice was Joe's sister-in-law, his brother's wife, who had to drive out from Brooklyn after her own kids were asleep and couldn't get to the house until after nine. "Don't hurry back on my account," she said when she walked in the door. "I told Sal I'd sleep over if you were late."

"We won't be," Jeannie promised. "At least I don't think so. Joe won't tell me where we're going."

In the car he still wouldn't let her in on the secret, but when she realized they were heading out on the Island she guessed. In a red wool dress that clung to her slender-hipped, full-breasted body and set off her long red-blonde hair, she slid across the seat to be next to her husband and relaxed in pleasant anticipation. A half hour later they had ordered dinner and were already dancing to the six-piece band at Carmello's, a restaurant in Huntington where they had been going ever since before the children were born. She felt a dozen years younger than she was and looked it. Both fine dancers, she and Joe were hardly off the mirror-smooth floor except to eat.

After dinner the bandleader, a Jewish saxophonist who had been at Carmello's for as long as Joe and Jeannie had been going there, stopped by their table to talk. He stayed for almost half an hour, the whole of the break between sets. When his musicians had all returned to the bandstand, he excused himself to join them.

"We've got a special treat for you tonight, ladies and gentlemen," he announced after the first number. "We've got a very special guest out there I'd like you to meet, an old and dear friend of mine, Joe Longo. Stand up, Joe."

There was a tinkling of polite applause. With a shrug and a sheepish grin for Jeannie, Joe stood up and made a few perfunctory bows that were little more than nods of his head. "I'll kill him," he whispered as he sat down, laughing.

"Hey, cmon, folks, we're not gonna let him off that easy. Some of you may not know it, but it just so happens that Joe is not only one of New York's finest, he's also one of New York's finest singers. Whatdya say we give him a nice welcome, maybe he'll do a couple of songs for us?"

The applause was louder and more friendly. Some of the regulars at Carmello's, who had heard Joe sing before, shouted encouragement. Joe stood up again, smiling. "Honest, I had no idea," he whispered to Jeannie. "If I'd have known he was gonna do this ..."

The sentence trailed off, unfinished. He always pretended it embarrassed him to be called on to sing, and Jeannie, who saw through him perfectly, pretended to accept his apology. She knew him well enough to know that he didn't need to be told that his rich, warm voice thrilled her. Even if there had been a hundred people in the room, she alone would have heard in his singing the tenderness, the gentleness, the muted note of vulnerability that a man can hide from everyone except his own woman.

When he got to the bandstand, the leader handed him a microphone and the piano player gave him an eight-bar intro for "This Can't Be Love." He sang in a loose, easy baritone, pleasant but not perfectly trained, so that once or twice he felt the song was getting away from him. At first his singing was a bit stiff and mechanical, his approach to the song copied from the Sinatra arrangement. But gradually, as he wove through the clever, cutting Lorenz Hart lyric, the musicians picked up on him and he grew in confidence, leading them with his voice and letting the sharp, incisive melody carry him along.

The crowd responded warmly, and for his next number he chose "By the Time I Get to Phoenix," singing unaccompanied until the piano and guitar joined him. At the table, Jeannie's eyes misted with pride and sadness, for the song had a special meaning to her. The man in the lyric, driving through to morning, was Joe. The woman waking in an empty bed, wondering, was her.

He sang for over half an hour, mixing the numbers well, ranging from "Satin Doll" and "I Cover the Waterfront" to a flashy version of "How High the Moon" with a good jazz feel, letting the bandleader take long intricate breaks on sax in the up numbers, working mostly with the piano and guitar on the ballads. He felt comfortable on the stage, detached and free and completely self-possessed, for his singing was something he felt he could pride himself on without vanity. He had been taking voice lessons once a week for almost two years now, missing more than half of them because he couldn't get away from the job.

He closed with another song sung specially for Jeannie. As the pianist fingered his way carefully through the first chorus, Joe walked to the piano and began to sing, his voice surging powerfully, rich and responsive, filling the hushed room. As he sang, everything fell into place and he could hear himself delivering the tender lyric with the supple precision he always strove for in his singing yet achieved only when a song was suddenly no longer a performance but an intimate message of love.

> *Cara Mia, why must we say good-bye?*
> *Each time we part, my heart wants to die.*
> *My darling, hear my prayer, Cara Mia fair . . .*
> *I'll be your love till the end of time.*
> *Cara Mia mine say those words divine*
> *I'll be your love till the end of time.*

Saturday morning Carlo Danzie was waiting in the lobby when Joe pulled up at the front entrance of the Holiday Inn. Danzie pushed through the revolving door and stepped to the car, his face grim with displeasure.

"Get in," Joe said. "We got some things to straighten out."

As soon as Danzie was seated, Joe circled out of the drive and back toward the highway. Cutting easily into the light traffic on the Grand Central Parkway, he headed east, away from the city. They drove for about twenty minutes without exchanging any words. By the time Danzie broke the silence they were on the Van Wyck Expressway only a few minutes from Kennedy Airport.

"You must understand, Joe," he said, making a deliberate effort to start off with a show of patience. "I cannot work if there is so much interference."

"You're doing just fine," Joe answered. He pulled to a stop near the freight terminal at the edge of the Airport complex. "Listen, Carlo," he went on, "I don't call it cooperating when you got fifty grand out with Larry Boston and I don't get told till after he's busted. If you're working for me, then I gotta know everything that's happening. Those are the only rules I play by. If you're holding out, then you're not doing your job. And in that case I gotta forget that we got an arrangement and you gotta do your time."

They argued back and forth for some time, Danzie insisting that he be allowed to work on his own terms, free of supervision, Joe reminding him that he was still technically in custody. "I wanna know where you are and what you're doing every minute," he said. At one point Danzie got out of the car and stood by the side of the road, for all the world like a petulant girl offended by her boyfriend's advances. He stood in the brisk February wind that whirled over the open spaces of the airport long enough to smoke two of his black cigarettes before he returned to the car.

"It is not something I can do," he announced with an air of utter finality, his deep voice booming the ultimatum and then modulating quickly into a more conversational tone as he went on speaking. "I would like to trust you, Joe," he said. "I feel I can trust you. But it is necessary to me that I can move without interference. I must know that you will not do something that will put me in danger."

Joe wasn't budging either. "We're not gonna have you tailed, if that's what you mean," he said. "I just gotta know where you can be reached if we need you."

"When there is something for you to hear, I will call you," Danzie countered impatiently. "There will be no necessity for you to call me."

The argument went on in the same vein for another ten minutes. At one point Danzie asked to be cut loose from the whole arrangement. "I cannot work that way," he said flatly. "It will not be. If it is impossible for you to permit me to do it my way, then we must stop here."

Joe turned the key in the ignition and put the car in gear. "Fine with me," he said, calling his informant's bluff. "You don't wanna work, you know what's gotta happen."

"Perhaps," Danzie answered softly. "But perhaps we can arrange for some other consideration."

The phone was ringing when Luke Antonelli got home from church late Sunday morning. He unlocked the door, and his eight-year-old son Rickey rushed past him and answered it on the kitchen extension. In a moment he called, "Daddy, it's for you."

Luke picked up the extension in the hall off the kitchen. "I got it, Rickey," he said. "Hang up. Yeah?"

"Luke, this is Carlo Danzie. I must meet with you."

"Sure, right away," Luke said. "Where are you?" It bothered him that Danzie had his home phone number but he figured that Joe must have had his reasons for giving it to him.

"No, it does not have to be now," Danzie said. "But it must be today."

"Tonight okay?"

"Of course."

"At your hotel?"

"No, I am no longer there," Danzie said.

Luke's voice hid his surprise. "Where are you?" he asked. "In the city?"

Danzie paused for a moment to get the geography straight in his mind. "Yes," he said, "the city."

"Okay," Luke said. He named an Italian restaurant on Third Avenue in the mid Fifties, and after getting an assurance from Danzie that he would be able to find the place, they agreed on nine thirty that evening for the meeting.

"Until tonight, then," Danzie said, and then added, almost as though it were an afterthought, "There is one other thing, Luke. I would like to see you alone. Do not bring Joe."

After church every Sunday, Joe, Jeannie, and the kids drove to

Brooklyn for dinner with Joe's parents. Two huge restaurant-size pots stood on the stove, heating the water for pasta. Of Mamma Longo's six boys, four still lived close enough to make the pilgrimage every week, and they made it without fail. They came in part for Mamma, who would tolerate no excuse for absence, but also because they wanted to be there, knowing that Sundays were really what held the family together. This was true even for Sal and Chris and Lou, who worked with each other every day in their father's plumbing contracting business, but it was especially true for Joe, who rarely saw his brothers between one Sunday and the next.

Counting the children, there might be as many as twenty people in the small frame house, filling it with noise and laughter. The smaller children ate at bridge tables and tv trays in the small sitting room off the kitchen while the grown-ups sat around the long dining room table, which every Saturday night Mamma Longo covered with an ancient ivory linen cloth on top of which she spread the delicate lacework tablecloth her own grandmother had crocheted for her as a wedding gift almost half a century before. It had arrived from Italy in a slatted wooden box specially made for it by the village carpenter, and the letter inside demanded a pledge from the new bride that she would pass it on to her grandchildren. The box was long since gone, and the letter, too, but Mamma Longo couldn't spread the cloth without remembering the moment she had unpacked it and wondering which of her granddaughters would be the first to marry. She liked to tease little Marie, the youngest of the girls, about it. In the evening, as the families gathered their belongings to go home, she might say, "Wait, Maria, I will put the cloth in a box for you to take. Mark my words, Little Monkey, you will be married before your cousins." The joke had started before Marie was old enough to understand it, but now it made her blush and giggle and run to the car ahead of the others.

On this particular Sunday the telephone rang while the four daughters-in-law were still in the kitchen helping Mamma. The men sat in the living room, Pappa with a glass of Chianti and a short, thick cigar. The phone rang four times, but Pappa didn't even look toward it because on Sundays he was the *patrono* and didn't lift a finger. Mamma came from the kitchen to answer it, wiping her hands on her apron.

"Mrs. Longo? This is Luke Antonelli. Io lavoro con Joe. Mi dispiace disturbare il suo pranzo. Ma devo parlare con Joe. Lui è la?"

"Ma certo. Io lo chiamo," Mamma answered pleasantly. "Non mangiamo ancora. Momento, per favore."

She called Joe to the telephone. The cord was long enough to let him take the call in the hallway off the living room. There was no door he could close, but just stepping out of the room made his business less of an intrusion on the others.

"Joe? Listen, Danzie just called. You didn't give him my number, did you?"

"Yeah, I did. What'd he want?"

"He said he wants to see me tonight."

"Yeah?"

"He said I shouldn't bring you. Dyou think it's okay?"

"Sure, why not?" Joe said. He knew Danzie was up to something but he wanted to put Luke at ease. "Where you meeting him?"

"La Pentola, nine thirty."

"Okay, I'll be around the corner."

As soon as he said it, Joe realized he had made a mistake. "Maybe you just oughta meet us there," Luke suggested nervously.

Joe laughed. "Hey, Luke, you're a big boy now," he said. "If I'm there, how the hell are we gonna find out what it is he doesn't wanna tell me?"

"Okay, okay," Luke answered impatiently. It annoyed him when Joe treated him that way, teasing him like a rookie. For a few seconds no one said anything. Then Luke asked, "Whatdya think he wants?"

"How the . . . How'm I supposed to know? Go see him, you'll find out."

He hung up the phone and returned to the living room. The others had moved to the table and his mother was backing through the kitchen door with a gigantic tureen of minestrone. "Il tuo compagno," she said, "lui mi sembra un simpaticone."

"Yeah, Mamma," Joe answered, taking his place at the table. "He's a very nice boy."

La Pentola is a well-appointed Italian restaurant in midtown Manhattan specializing in elegant service at stiff prices. Too expensive and sedate for the singles crowd that has taken over Third Avenue north of Bloomingdale's, it caters largely to Madison and Park Avenue businessmen and those out-of-towners who stay at the East Side hotels.

Dimly lit, with widely spaced tables in the large main dining room, it turned out to be a perfect place for meeting an informant. As soon as he walked in at nine o'clock, Luke realized that he had been worrying unnecessarily all afternoon and evening. He had suggested the restaurant on the spur of the moment, unable to come up with the name of another place that would be both suitable and easy to find. When he hung up the phone, though, he began to think he had made a mistake in arranging a meeting in a public place, but it was already too late to change the plans since there was no way for him to reach Danzie.

Selecting a table in the far corner, he told the maître d' that he would be joined by another man in a half hour. Then he surveyed the dining room to reassure himself that none of the other patrons represented a threat. A few tables away two men in blazers and turtleneck sweaters were arguing softly about some radio station's advertising rates, their words occasionally loud enough to be heard. Beyond them, toward the middle of the room, two couples of middle-aged men and young, elegantly dressed women with impressive breasts lingered over brandy and coffee, the men smoking cigars the waiter had brought them. A couple of guys from Scarsdale double-dating with their mistresses, Luke thought. What's this city coming to? Then he dismissed them from his mind and surveyed the rest of the room. Only four other tables were occupied, none of them by anyone who looked wrong. Besides, Danzie had said once that his connection was in Brooklyn.

"Would you care for a cocktail, signore?" a waiter suddenly asked. He had approached the table while Luke was looking the other way.

"Uh, no, no thank you," Luke answered.

"Some wine perhaps? While you wait?"

"No."

As if offended, the waiter turned abruptly to leave but Luke called him back. "Yknow what, let me have a cup of coffee," he said self-consciously. He rarely drank and knew that when Danzie showed up he would probably have to.

"Coffee?" the waiter asked incredulously.

"Yes."

"American coffee?" The heavy emphasis on the first word underlined the waiter's scorn.

"Yes."

The waiter stalked off and returned with the coffee in less than a minute. Although he drank it black, Luke stirred absently at the steaming cup with his spoon until it cooled enough to let him sip at it. The fact that he didn't know what to expect from Danzie was making him nervous and he checked his watch every few minutes, annoyed with himself for accepting Danzie's terms in excluding Joe, and annoyed with Joe for going along with it. *Fuck that,* he kept trying to tell himself, *if it doesn't bother Joe why should it bother me?*

Precisely at nine thirty the maître d' reappeared, leading Carlo Danzie. Stopping a few yards from the table, Danzie conferred with the host in Italian, obviously ordering elaborately but speaking too softly for Luke to hear. When he finished he stepped to the table and offered his hand to Luke, who stood to greet him.

Within minutes a waiter appeared with a bottle of Bardolino, which he set on the table but did not offer to pour—apparently on Danzie's specific instructions. When he left he took Luke's coffee cup with him and returned a few moments later with a magnificent antipasto, which also was not served. As soon as he withdrew, Danzie poured the wine into two glasses and passed one across the table to Luke. Then he served the antipasto, selecting carefully to get a proper mixture of greens, anchovies, and olives onto each plate. All the while he kept up a running monologue in both English and Italian, switching at random from one language to the other, prompted more by whim than by anything Luke could detect in either the subject matter or the limits of his English vocabulary.

He spoke mostly about New York, having formed some very decided opinions about the city and its inhabitants in the few days since his arrival. Obviously he was stalling, taking his time before he worked his way around to whatever it was that prompted his urgent request for this meeting. Luke let him go on, but when a half hour had passed and a bottle of white wine replaced the half-finished Bardolino, he decided it was time to make Danzie get to the point.

Recalling the incident later, Luke explained, "I really liked hearing the guy talk, and frankly I could have listened to him all night. I mean, I never met a guy like that before and I guess I was a little bit

awed by him, if that's the word. If you're in the job any length of time
you're gonna meet a lot of wise guys with the cashmere coats and the
fifty-dollar socks, so it wasn't that. He was . . . the only way I can
describe it is to say he was really a classy guy. Really. Smart as hell and
he always had things to say. So cutting him off wasn't an easy thing to
do. But I could see he was doing some kind of number on me and I
wanted him to remember who was who and that I was in control of the
situation."

"Hey, look," Luke said, pushing his wine glass toward the center
of the table, "how'd you make out with your people in Brooklyn?"

Danzie pursed his mouth. "You are an impatient man, my
friend," he said. "You Americans are all impatient. Forgive my
thoughtlessness but I forget that I have taken you away from your
family."

He paused and Luke nodded for him to go on.

"You have a little boy?" the informant unexpectedly asked.

Luke stiffened defensively. "What's that got to do with this?" he
demanded. "You been checking up on me?"

"He answered the telephone," Danzie shot back with an air of
offended innocence. "I mention the child only to show that I understand your impatience. I will come to my point." He paused again, this
time to sip on the wine and light a cigarette, passing the box across to
Luke. "I too have a family and am impatient to be home," he went on.
"But I have business that I must do before I return to my native
Milano. Why do I tell you this? So that you will recognize that I have
no wish to draw out this thing I have told you I will do for you. Do
you understand me?"

Luke shrugged and took a shallow drag on the pungent black
cigarette. "Go on," he said, his head swimming from the smoke.

"Yes, of course. I am having difficulties, that is what I want you
to know. I am becoming concerned that these people in Brooklyn will
not be ready as quickly as I was led to expect. Immediately I thought
I must tell Luke. I know the *polizia*. I know you are impatient people.
It is the same everywhere. You have captains and chiefs and they become vexed with you when things do not happen quickly enough, am
I correct?"

He hesitated barely half a beat, then went on, his right hand tapping against his breast pocket over his heart. "So I say, these two men

are my friends. That is to say, I acknowledge that we are not friends but circumstances have happened that we must work together and trust each other. We are like friends in the regard that we can help one another, is it not so? And when I find that my business will take longer than I was led to expect, I ask myself how I can expect you to trust me. And I think, you have wives, you have families, I must show my good faith so that you will not become impatient."

From his breast pocket he withdrew a white business envelope, which he first set on the table directly in front of himself and then moved to his left, putting it a few inches from the edge of the table, halfway between himself and Luke.

Antonelli looked from the envelope to Danzie, caught off guard by the unexpectedness of Danzie's offer. It wasn't the first time someone had tried to lay money on him, and his usual response was simply to make it clear that he wasn't interested. But something in the way Danzie did it confused and frightened him, for he couldn't help but notice the almost uncanny tact that had told Danzie not to try handing it across to him. "If that's what I think it is, put it away," he said.

Danzie started to say something but Luke cut him off. "I said put it away," he repeated, his voice firm now. "It's not necessary and it's not expected. You do what you have to do, that's all. If it takes time, it takes time."

Danzie retrieved the envelope and slid it back into his pocket. "I meant no offense," he said. "I will have them bring the dinner now."

Before he left New York sometime in February or March of 1972, Carlo Danzie submitted a report of his activities to Special Assistant United States Prosecutor Paul Scala. Studded with the pedantries of legalistic jargon, this report undoubtedly was authored by Scala himself or someone in Scala's office, although it may well have been based on information supplied by Danzie.

The author of the report, whoever it may have been, alludes to Danzie's February 6 meeting with Luke Antonelli at La Pentola but makes no mention of the unsuccessful attempt to bribe the detective. If the report is to be believed, at the end of the meal Danzie handed Antonelli a hundred-dollar bill and asked him to take care of the tab. Antonelli then paid the waiter and kept the change. The dinner cost somewhere between thirty and forty dollars.

Luke vehemently denies this story. "It's nothing but horseshit," he says. "Just Danzie's way to get a free dinner off the government and pick up a little change. Besides, at the time it happened he hadn't been able to get to first base with me or Joe, so he had to tell them something. And this is what he told them. Later, when they arrested me and Joe, they hardly mentioned it at all, so I guess they knew it was a bullshit thing. Scala brought it up once, but the fact is I didn't even stick around for dinner that night. I told him that and after a couple of minutes he dropped it and I never heard about it again.

"The way it happened is I got out of there right after Danzie tried to lay that envelope on me. If they wanted, they could have checked that out with the waiters in case somebody remembered. Don't forget, this was, like, only a month, month and a half after it happened, so somebody would have remembered. What it comes down to is I had a cup of coffee and a glass of wine and a little bit of the salad that he paid for. Hell, Joe and I were having beers at the Taft by ten thirty or eleven, so you know I couldn't have stuck around there to eat. But that was years ago, and Joe's dead now, so who's gonna tell them that?

"I know it bothers me more than it should, because it's just nickel-and-dime stuff, but what I keep thinking is that they've still got it in their files. For all the mistakes I made, this is one thing I didn't do, but it's his word against mine. In fact it's not even that, because I'm willing to bet they don't have what I told them in those files and they never asked the waiters. So it's just his word. And years from now anyone in the world can look it up and they'll think I was the kind of bum who sells himself out for a free meal and pocket money."

"How'd it go?" Joe asked as the car door opened.

"He tried to lay some bread on me," Luke answered.

Joe smiled. "Yeah, I figured it'd be something like that," he said lightly. "He tried it on me yesterday."

Luke exploded with unexpected anger. "Jesus Christ, Joe," he shouted, "why the fuck didn't you tell me?"

"What for? There was nothing to tell."

"Nothing to tell? I don't believe this. What are we talking about? You know the guy's gonna make a move on me and you don't warn me?"

Joe shrugged. "Hey, Luke, you're a big boy now," he said, using the same words that had exasperated his partner earlier that day.

Luke reached for the door handle but stopped himself before he could open the door. By temperament he was the sort of man who prefers to walk away from an argument rather than to have it out, but he didn't want to do anything to make himself look foolish. "I've had it up to here with this shit," he said. "We're supposed to be partners, that's all. We're supposed to look after each other. What if I'd done the wrong thing?"

Joe smiled disarmingly. "Cmon, Luke, do I look like Jiminy Cricket?" he said, reaching out to touch his partner on the arm. He knew Luke had a valid point. No one ever knew what another man would do caught off guard in a moment of weakness. Cops always warned each other about the wise guys who were quick with the envelopes. At least that way a man would know what to expect, and if he made the wrong decision it wouldn't be because the temptation hit him before he knew what was coming. But in this case Joe had had his own reasons for keeping silent. He didn't like the way Luke depended upon him for guidance and was willing to jeopardize their precarious friendship to drive the lesson home. Besides, he suspected that if Luke had known what was coming, he wouldn't have gone to meet Danzie. "I knew you weren't gonna do the wrong thing," he said. "Now you know it, too. Whatdya say we get a couple of beers?"

They drove across to the West Side and went into the bar at the Hotel Taft. After a few minutes each of them was able to relax somewhat and Luke broke what was left of the ice by asking, "Did he really try it on you yesterday?"

Joe nodded. " 'Look, Joe,' " he quoted, dropping his voice a whole octave and doing a passable imitation of Danzie's accent and inflection, " 'perhaps we can arrange some other consideration.' "

"Is that what he said?"

"Yeah, 'some other consideration.' I told him to blow it out his ass, so I guess he figured he'd have a go at you."

Luke muttered an obscenity, but Joe tried to shrug off the incident. "Forget about it," he said. "He's entitled to try. At least now he knows where we stand, so that's outta the way. What else'd he say?"

Luke explained that Danzie was expecting some delay, and then the two detectives tried to analyze the situation. Neither believed the story about the "difficulties" Danzie claimed to be experiencing with

his Brooklyn connection. In fact, they took his behavior over the
weekend as an indication of exactly the opposite. "I think that weasel's
got something coming down pretty soon," Joe concluded. "It's gotta
be something big, something he can't see his way to hand up, so he's
trying to get us off his back. Did he tell you he wants to move out of
that hotel at La Guardia?"

"Yeah, he moved already."

"See? He doesn't want us to know where he is, he says nothing's
happening, he tried to buy us off the case. It all adds up, right?"

Luke agreed. Except for one fleeting moment a week later, neither
he nor Joe ever suspected the real nature of Danzie's mission. Everything pointed to a big narcotics deal and they were going to be right
in the middle of it. In hindsight there were a dozen things that could
have tipped them off—things like Danzie's luggage, his curiosity about
why he was under federal arrest, the unusual arrangement for waiving
arraignment, the fact that Anthony Diamond had been willing to let
two city cops operate one of his prized informants. But there were also
a hundred things that blinded them to the reality.

The most important was the promise of hundred kilo cases. International agents had vouched for Danzie's credentials as a top-level
trafficker, and in a sense so had Anthony Diamond in Washington.
Despite their combined experience of almost thirty years on the job,
neither Joe nor Luke had ever been into anything this big and they
knew that they probably never would be again. In fact, Joe even told
Jeannie at about this time that he was thinking of getting out of
Narcotics after the Danzie case. Maybe it was time to think of something quieter, closer to home, like the D.A.'s squad in Queens. But his
real reason for considering a transfer was something he didn't mention. He liked the idea of going out a hero.

Chapter 8
The Passport Gambit

AFTER DANZIE'S MEETING with Luke at La Pentola on Sunday, an entire week passed without a word from the informant. For the first three days, neither Joe nor Luke was disturbed by his disappearance, which might mean either that there was nothing for him to report or nothing that he chose to report. In any case, there wasn't much the two detectives could do about the situation.

By Thursday, though, Joe was running out of patience. When Luke got to the office in the morning, his partner was already there. The number of dead butts in the ashtray on Joe's desk gave an indication of how long he had been waiting, even though it was still well before nine. His camel overcoat lay across a corner of the desk.

"Where we going?" Luke asked.

Joe snuffed out his cigarette and reached for the coat. "Grab two coffees," he said. "We're gonna find that sonofabitch."

The problem was that they didn't have a place to start. Danzie had given them the names of some of his contacts in Brooklyn, and if it became necessary Joe would be willing to send out feelers through

121

some stools connected to those organizations. But it was still too soon for that. Until he was certain Danzie was dealing behind his back, he wouldn't do anything to jeopardize Danzie's cover as an informant.

That left the Holiday Inn at La Guardia as the only lead they had, and it wasn't a good one. Danzie wasn't the sort of man who left a forwarding address. But if he had taken a cab when he checked out it might be possible to trace him through the cabbie's trip sheet. Besides, he didn't travel light and he might have had his luggage sent for.

They drove out in Joe's car, the two styrofoam coffee cups balanced on the dash. As soon as they identified themselves and told the desk clerk what they wanted, he sent for the manager, who quickly ushered them into his office behind the front desk.

"Now how can I help you, gentlemen?" the manager asked as he lowered himself into his leather-cushioned swivel chair. A shallow-chested, potbellied man in his mid fifties, he reached for a pipe from the two-tiered rack at the side of his desk.

"We're looking for a man who was here last week," Joe said. "He probably checked out either Saturday or Sunday. Carlo Danzie."

"Ah, yes. I remember Mr. Danzie. A European gentleman, am I correct?"

"That's the guy."

"He checked out Saturday. What did he do?"

Joe ignored the question. "How come you remember him so well?" he asked.

The manager didn't say anything for a few seconds, as though the question gave him some difficulty. He lit his pipe and puffed on it enough to get it going, quickly filling the room with unpleasantly sweet smoke. Pipe smokers, Joe had found, were always the toughest people to interrogate because they were invariably well practiced at using the pipe to stall until they knew precisely what they wanted to say. "I try to make it my business to know the guests," the manager answered at last.

Both Joe and Luke sensed that he was hiding something. On a hunch Luke said, "Hey, Joe, that broad you saw in his room Saturday morning—what'd you say she looked like?"

"Tall, nice body. Brown hair. Why?"

"You have a woman answering that description working in the restaurant?" Luke asked, turning to the manager.

"We did, yes," the manager answered coldly.

"Did, huh? What happened, you fired her?"

"Not really. It was more. . ." His voice trailed off.

"Never mind," Joe said. "Just give me her name and address."

The manager reached for a card file and began to sort through it.

"How did Danzie leave?" Joe asked.

"Excuse me?"

"Did he take a cab or what?"

"Oh. I couldn't tell you that. Perhaps the bell captain could."

Joe stood up but the manager stopped him. "I'll send for him," he said quickly, reaching for the telephone. He dialed one number and asked the captain to come to his office. Then he resumed his search through the file drawer.

Barely a minute later an elderly man in a braided uniform stepped into the office. "You wanted to see me, Mr. Flood?" he asked. He spoke with a heavy German accent.

"These two gentlemen are police officers, Hugo. They want to ask you some questions."

"About one of the guests," Joe added quickly, noticing the frightened look that momentarily crossed the old man's face. "Were you on duty Saturday?"

"Of course."

"Hugo works every day," the manager cut in to explain. "He lives by himself and—"

"Do you remember a man named Carlo Danzie?" Joe interrupted. "He's an Italian man, about five foot nine or ten."

"I remember Mr. Danzie, yes."

"And he checked out on Saturday?"

"That is correct, Saturday."

"He had a lot of luggage. Did he take it with him?"

"Yes, sir, he did."

"How did he go, by cab?"

"No, sir, another gentleman called for him."

Joe and Luke exchanged glances. "In a car?" Joe asked.

"Yes, sir."

"Do you remember what kind of car?"

"No, it doesn't seem to me I do. It was red, I remember that."

"Do you remember what this man looked like?"

"Younger, a much younger man. Heavy, I would say. Not fat, but big."

The old man gestured with his hands in front of his shoulders. He was describing Gil Lacey, but it could have been anyone. Joe and Luke, of course, assumed it was someone from one of the Brooklyn organizations and didn't pursue it further since there would be no way to trace where he had taken Danzie. Dismissing the bell captain they got the waitress's name and address from the manager and drove back to Manhattan to find her.

"Oh, it's you," Mickie Lang said as she opened the door, puzzled that a cop should want to question her and even more surprised that he should turn out to have a familiar face. "And you," she added in the same tone, recognizing Luke from the lunch with Danzie at the airport exactly a week before. She lived in a large, overfurnished apartment on Charles Street at the west edge of Greenwich Village. "Are you guys really cops?" she asked as Joe and Luke stepped past her and crossed the entrance foyer into the cluttered, high-ceilinged living room.

Joe flipped out his gold shield and showed it to her. "I'm Detective Joe Longo and this is Detective Luke Antonelli," he said. "We'd like to ask you some questions about Carlo Danzie."

She laughed and leaned back against the front door to close it. She was wearing blue jeans and a plaid wool shirt that was much too large for her but still somehow managed to suggest the smooth, lean lines of the slender body underneath. The long sleeves had to be rolled back once at the cuffs or her hands would have disappeared entirely.

"Sure," she said in the light, mocking tone Luke remembered. "But what if I want to ask some questions, too? Who goes first?"

"We will, if you don't mind, lady," Joe said.

"Mickie," she corrected. "Then you'd better sit down, it might take awhile."

With her eyes she indicated an old thick-armed sofa whose heavy stolidity suggested a man's taste despite the still-bright floral print of the upholstery. Behind it stood a baby grand piano with the sounding board raised. Mickie sat in the square stuffed chair facing the sofa, perching lightly on the cushion with her bare feet curled under her. When she leaned forward to slide a cigarette from the pack on the glass table in front of the chair, her shirt fell away just enough to provide a momentary glimpse of her small but well-shaped breasts.

"Okay," she said, smiling confidently at the two detectives, "let's hear the questions."

"When's the last time you saw Carlo Danzie?" Joe began.

The smile instantly gave way to a look of almost defensive seriousness. "That's not a question about him, that's a question about me," she protested firmly. "I don't want to answer questions about me."

"I understand that," Joe apologized, "but we're looking for him and maybe you can help."

He expected her to ask what Danzie had done, because everyone always asked that about a wanted man. When she didn't, his first thought was that Danzie had somehow let her know the nature of his business, but later he realized he was wrong. Privacy was a fetish with her and she neither knew nor cared about what Danzie had done, nor why the police wanted him. That was his business and theirs, just as her meetings with Danzie were her business. Because the cops were the ones in the room with her at the moment she would tell them what they wanted to know—not because they were cops nor because she felt no loyalty to Danzie, but simply because they must have had reasons of their own for asking, reasons that were none of her concern.

"I will if I can," she said, "but you'll have to tell me how."

Joe hesitated a moment, trying to phrase the question in such a way that her finicky scruples would let her answer it. "Do you know where he's been since he left the hotel on Saturday?" he asked at last.

"I know some places he's been but I don't know where he's staying. I guess that's not much help."

"Maybe it is," Joe answered encouragingly. "What are the places?"

"A hotel on Waverly Street."

"When was this?"

"Monday night."

"And since then?"

"Last night, too," she added.

"So he's still in town," Joe said, more to himself than to her. It was something he had been worried about. "Do you know how to get in touch with him?"

"No."

"Will he be getting in touch with you again?"

She smiled for the first time since the questioning started but otherwise didn't answer. It was one of her rules never to count on what a man would do, so she wouldn't have been surprised if she never heard from him again.

"If he does, will you let us know?" Joe asked, fishing a card from his breast pocket and passing it across to her. She made no move to reach for it, so he set it on the glass table between them.

"I'll have to think about it," she said.

Joe thought he knew what she was thinking. "We don't want to arrest him," he explained. "We just want to talk to him."

She shrugged as though that didn't matter. "I'll have to think about it," she repeated.

At about seven thirty Monday morning, the fourteenth of February, Carlo Danzie called Joe Longo at home. "I must meet with you tonight," he said.

"Where are you?"

"That is of no consequence," Danzie answered. "You will understand everything tonight."

They arranged a meeting for nine o'clock at Little John's, a steak-and-beer restaurant on Second Avenue that catered mostly to a young clientele. It was Danzie's choice.

"What was that all about?" Jeannie asked.

"Danzie's back."

She wasn't particularly glad to hear it but she smiled anyway, for Joe's sake. "See? I told you it would all work out," she said.

In fact, that hadn't been what she said at all. Over the last four days Joe had been depressed and disappointed about Danzie's vanishing act, for he was beginning to be convinced that he had let his prize informant slip away. And she had said, "Don't worry about it, it'll work out. If he's gone, he's gone. There'll be other cases just as good."

That wasn't the kind of reassurance he had wanted, for he had been counting heavily on the Danzie case. Now, even before he could resign himself to the loss, Danzie's sudden phone call revived his hopes. Like the time a couple of years ago when he found his old high school first baseman's glove that he had given up for lost, he realized that it wasn't the thing itself that mattered. It was the ideas the thing allowed you to start thinking all over again. Danzie, he felt certain, held the key to his future just as surely as that limp and frayed mitt held the key to his past. With Danzie back it was possible to think again the ambitious thoughts of headline cases that had come to seem a trifle silly and irrelevant when all he had was the name of an uncooperative informant who might just as well have not existed for all the good he was doing.

He gulped down his coffee and held out the mug for a second cup. Realistically, he knew, Danzie's reappearance could mean that a deal had just been completed, so that Danzie now felt free to reestablish contact. It could mean more of the same runaround. The difference would be that this time he and Luke wouldn't let Danzie get away. They would tail him if he wouldn't tell them where he was staying, keep close track of him, maybe tap his phone. If he wanted to stay in business he would have to hand up something big.

The Diplomat is a fashionable apartment house on Forty-sixth Street near the East River. Only a two-minute walk from United Nations Plaza, it is heavily populated by U.N. personnel, as are most of the other hotels and apartments in the vicinity. As a result, the neighborhood has an international flavor unmatched anywhere else in the world. On a bright, springlike morning in mid February the street suddenly became alive with African women parading their babies in huge "prams," turbaned men with shiny leather briefcases, Eastern Europeans talking in clusters at the streetcorners.

Carlo Danzie strolled up First Avenue, his eyes scanning the long row of flagpoles that stretched along the promenade north of the United Nations glass tower. Briefly he tried to calculate how many of the flags he could recognize but gave up when he reached Forty-sixth Street. Turning left, he hurried to the entrance of the Diplomat, quickening his pace as he neared his temporary home. His night of lovemaking in a Greenwich Village hotel had invigorated him and raised his spirits. After breakfast with Mickie in a Sixth Avenue coffee shop they had gone their separate ways, she back to the musician with whom she lived on Charles Street and he to the suite of government rooms Anthony Diamond had secured for him at the Diplomat.

The long walk from the Village to the East Side had consumed the better part of Danzie's morning. Along the way he had stopped at a public telephone and made a call to Joe Longo in which he set up a rendezvous for nine o'clock at Little John's, the restaurant where

Mickie was now working. Then he had browsed through the flower district in the west Twenties before selecting a bunch of long-stemmed daisies and a bouquet of brilliant anemones. At a tobacconist's a dozen blocks farther along he had bought two boxes of Jamaican cigars after failing to convince the storekeeper to sell him the Cuban *claros* he had been told they kept in stock. By the time he greeted the doorman at the Diplomat it was after ten o'clock.

"Good morning," Gil Lacey purred sarcastically as soon as Danzie unlocked the door and stepped into the sixteenth-floor apartment. "Nice of you to drop by."

Lacey had been sharing the apartment in the Diplomat ever since Danzie moved in Saturday afternoon, although neither man understood the necessity for the arrangement. Apparently it had something to do with the fact that the apartment, rented by the federal government and maintained as a safe house for undercover agents, could not be turned over to a civilian employee. For the most part it was used by FBI and CIA agents on assignments involving infiltration and surveillance of the diplomatic community, but somehow Anthony Diamond had got wind of the fact that it was vacant and put in a request for it. When Danzie moved in, the security measures ordinarily employed whenever the apartment changed hands automatically went into effect, although in this case they were completely unnecessary. A lease bearing Danzie's name and dated February 5, 1972, was inserted in the landlord's files, where it replaced the phony lease of the last agent who stayed there. The phone listing, too, was changed to Danzie's name, and phone company records now gave the installation date as Monday, February 7. It was all very elaborate for a stool pigeon trying to trap a pair of cops, but the capability to do it came with the apartment, and it wasn't very often that Anthony Diamond got a chance to play at big-league espionage.

"For your wife, living with you may be adequate," Danzie joked in response to Lacey's sarcasm. "For me, it is not."

In the kitchen he unwrapped the flowers and set them in two vases, which he carried back to the living room. Unwrapping the cigars, he opened one of the boxes and held it out toward Lacey.

"You gotta be kidding, first thing in the morning," Lacey snapped. "Those things are worse than drinking before breakfast," he said, getting up and heading for the kitchen with a coffee mug in his hand. The striped shirt he had worn last night lay crumpled at the foot of the couch and he was wearing a sleeveless T-shirt.

"A man should not sleep so late, that is your problem," Danzie called after him. "It causes you to lose such a fine part of the day."

Lacey returned with a fresh cup of steaming coffee, pausing at the kitchen door to watch as Danzie settled into the Eames chair and commenced the elaborate ritual of lighting his cigar. First he selected one from the box, his hand hovering over the row of identical cigars as hesitantly as if they weren't all his already. With a small pocketknife he carefully cut an eighth of an inch from the end, then gently rolled the cigar in his fingers to gauge its moistness. Before lighting it he puffed through it a few times to refresh the stale air trapped in the leaves.

"It's like the Japs with their tea!" Lacey scoffed. "You beat anything I ever saw."

For a week now he had been hiding his annoyance at the assignment, but his original feeling of warm regard for Danzie had long since given way to cranky petulance. "We're the fucking Odd Couple, that's what we are," he had complained to Paul Scala, but Scala had neither the authority to change the arrangement nor the sense of humor to appreciate the aptness of Lacey's comparison.

"You must not concern yourself with me, it will all be over soon," Danzie said reassuringly, as though he were reading Lacey's mind. "I am meeting Longo tonight."

Lacey brightened. "Yeah? And you're gonna lay it on him?"

"About the passport?" Danzie asked, not understanding the idiom. At a meeting in Scala's hotel room, which Diamond had come up from Washington to attend, it had been decided that Danzie would tell his two marks that he needed to leave the country to complete the drug deal but had no passport. He would ask for their help. There was a chance that even if Joe and Luke wouldn't take money straight out, they would not be above accepting payment in return for a favor.

"Yeah," Lacey answered brittlely, "the passport. What the fuck do you think we've been talking about?"

Danzie nodded. "I will tell them I must go back to Italy," he said, like an arrogant schoolchild repeating an obvious point for an irksome and demanding teacher. "I will tell them I must straighten out my affairs."

"And that you'll pay them if they get your passport," Lacey prompted.

"Yes."

"And you think that'll work?" Lacey asked.

It was difficult for Danzie to tell whether the remark was a question or a taunt. Unsure of how to respond, he said merely, "I will do what has to be done."

Lacey smiled broadly, a cold smile that perfectly expressed his utter detachment. "You do that, Carlo," he said, with only the faintest trace of a sneer in his voice. "But I'll give you odds right now this thing isn't going to work."

"If not this, then it will be something else," Danzie answered. "I am not a man to boast, but I assure you they will not say no to me forever."

Lacey considered a moment before answering. "I'll tell you what your mistake is right now, Carlo," he said. "You think you can handle Joe because you're smarter than he is. But I'm not so sure you are."

Danzie exhaled a dense cloud of white smoke that hung in the still air of the room like a cartoon balloon by his head. "You are not a tactful man, but you are quite correct," he said. "I acknowledge that I am not dealing with a fool. But Longo is a greedy man. Not for money, but that is to our advantage because such greed makes a man careful. Longo's greed is for the glory, and in that way he is worse than a fool. I can handle him because he is vain and I have no vanity."

Lacey shrugged. "Come off it, Carlo," he snorted. "You're right about Joe but you're dead wrong about yourself. The only difference between you and him is that one of you is gonna come out of this thing okay and one of you is gonna get wiped out. But I'm not taking any bets."

Danzie didn't answer. Turning in his chair until he could reach the vase he had set on the low parquet table to his right, he adjusted the anemones.

"I have taken the liberty of ordering," Carlo Danzie announced as the two detectives slid into the chairs pulled out for them by the officious maître d'. Even as he spoke, the cocktail waitress arrived with three glasses of Campari on ice. As she reached over Joe's shoulder, he glanced up and was surprised to see Mickie Lang, although he immediately realized that he shouldn't have been. Danzie, after all, had picked the restaurant.

As with everything else where Danzie was involved, it was impossible to tell what kind of games were being played. Had Mickie told her lover that Joe and Luke had been asking about him? Had he invited them to the restaurant where she now worked in order to show her off, to advertise the fact that he knew they had found her and that he didn't care? Or was the explanation as simple as wanting to get laid after dinner? Joe didn't have the answer, and Mickie, in any case, gave no sign of recognition as Joe looked into her eyes and then looked away. But because he couldn't be sure of what had shown on his face and didn't want to compromise the girl, he knew he had to say something. He waited until she was gone and then asked, "Isn't that the girl I saw in your room at the hotel?"

"You have an excellent memory," Danzie answered. "But of course she has a memorable face. In America one looks for different things in women. To be beautiful an American woman must be, how do you say, 'narrow.' "

"Thin?" Joe suggested. "Slender?"

"No, not thin. Slender, that is the word. Yes, an American woman must be slender. In Italy one is wise to avoid the slender women, they are all schemers. But it is not women we have met to discuss, is it, my friends?"

"Some other time, maybe," Joe said.

"Although what could be of more interest for men to discuss among themselves?" Danzie went on. "Especially when the news I bring is not good. I am having still more difficulties."

"What is it this time?" Joe asked warily, expecting another runaround.

"It is my people at home. We have an arrangement for making contact but they have stopped returning my calls. It causes me some concern."

It was easy to see why. "Do you think they know you were busted?" Joe asked, going right for the most dangerous possibility. If Danzie's contacts in Europe knew he had been arrested and turned around, then he was finished as a middleman in the drug business. It also might mean that there was a leak somewhere in either the Joint Task Force or the International Group.

"It is my hope that they do not," Danzie answered with surprising blandness, considering that it could cost him his life if they did. "The people in Brooklyn are eager for the transaction, but until my affairs in Europe can be arranged there can be no deal. I am sorry to have to tell you this because, you understand, we want the same thing, is it not so? I must ask you to show patience."

In substance, his speech was a copy of what he had said to Luke one week earlier, with the addition of the new problems in Italy. And what followed was an exact replay. From his breast pocket he removed the same envelope. Only this time, before Danzie could get it to the table, Joe leaped to his feet, his chair skittering back until it crashed loudly to the floor.

"Get up," he barked, his hands on the table as he leaned forward until he was almost face to face with Danzie. Behind him a busboy scurried up to straighten the chair but stopped abruptly a few feet away, sensing that the big man who had knocked over the chair and who now towered over the table was in command of the situation.

Danzie didn't move.

"Get up," Joe repeated, his deep voice slicing sharply through the quiet dining room.

"I do not understand," was all Danzie could manage to say.

Luke watched apprehensively from a point halfway between the two antagonists, his own anger at Danzie's repetition of the offer for the moment giving way to a sort of embarrassed confusion as he realized Joe was making a scene but was unsure of what his partner intended to do.

"You don't understand, huh?" Joe snarled, lowering his voice to a brutal whisper. "Look, Danzie, you tried it on me and you tried it on Luke and both times you got the same answer. Now I wanna know how come you have so much trouble understanding. Get up!"

While Danzie kept his seat, staring defiantly back at Joe without saying anything, Luke realized intuitively that his partner wanted him to intercede, as though Joe had been cuing him for a variation on the old good guy–bad guy routine. "Take it easy, Joe," he said. "What're you gonna do?"

"I'm gonna find out if something's the matter with this guy," Longo answered, not taking his eyes off Danzie. "Whatdya say," he went on, addressing Danzie now, "you and me go back to the men's room and strip down. Cmon."

"Sit down, Joe," Luke pleaded. "What's that gonna prove?"

"It's gonna prove whether he's wired or he just doesn't understand English," Joe shot back.

"Pardon me, sir," a small voice asked hesitantly from slightly behind Joe, "is anything the matter?"

Joe wheeled around and found himself towering over the maître d', who until that moment had been standing beside the awestruck busboy, knowing he had to do something but afraid to try. As he spoke he pulled his sheaf of menus from under his arm and held it in front of his belly like a shy girl clutching her pocketbook.

"Is anything the matter?" Joe mimicked. "No, there's nothing the matter that I can't handle."

He turned back to the table, as much to dismiss the embarrassed young headwaiter as to address Danzie again. But as soon as he did, he thought better of whatever he had planned to say and sat down. Later, when it turned out that Danzie was indeed an undercover operative, Joe never once alluded to the near fight in Little John's, even though he and Luke spent countless hours obsessively analyzing and reanalyzing the entire Danzie case, trying to understand how they had let themselves be trapped, trying to see if they had missed any clues that could have alerted them that they were being set up.

"I never knew if he was serious about wanting to frisk Danzie that night," Luke explained later. "At the time I thought he wasn't, because Joe wasn't the kind of guy who got exercised about things like that. He didn't take it like an insult, the way some cops did. He always figured a guy was entitled to try, and then it was up to the cop whether he takes it or not. He told me once he never made a bribery collar in his life and I could understand that. I was the same way myself, so are most cops I think. But the day after that thing in the restaurant we talked about taking the money in order to get a bribery rap we could hold over Danzie, just to keep him in line. It was Joe who suggested it, and I thought right then, Christ, this case means a hell of a lot to him. Because that wasn't the sort of thing he would normally do. A bribery charge is a whore's trick, that was one thing we both agreed on, but he was willing to do it if it gave him a little leverage with this guy.

"In any case, the thing is that no matter how often we went over the whole thing Joe never mentioned that business about frisking Danzie. So at the time I thought it was just a bluff to let Danzie know we didn't want to hear that kind of talk. It never dawned on me that he really thought Danzie was trying to set us up. But since then I've been thinking maybe he did mean it and if I hadn't stopped him he would have found out Danzie was wired and he'd be alive today. It would be like him not to mention it, because he knew I'd blame myself for everything that happened. And in a way I do."

Nothing about the whole Danzie operation made sense. In retrospect, it is difficult to see how it could have worked and impossible to understand how its planners imagined it would. The very idea of trying to entice two experienced cops into accepting a payoff from a man they knew to be an informant for the deputy director of the Bureau of Narcotics and Dangerous Drugs is outlandish on the face of it.

And even more outlandish when one considers that Joe Longo's background had been exhaustively examined only a few months earlier, when he applied for assignment to the Joint Task Force. His record was found to be spotlessly clean. On the other hand, perhaps Joe's honesty was a factor that worked for them. If he had been as crooked as they later tried to say he was, then he would never have let himself take so much as a free cup of coffee from a stool pigeon who had Diamond's private phone number. But he was an ambitious cop, and it just might be that Danzie's impeccable credentials as a topflight international drug dealer and the promise of a string of hundred kilo cases would so blind Joe that he would fail to see their ill-concealed trap.

In 1974, Senator Henry M. Jackson's Permanent Subcommittee on Investigations conducted a limited but revealing inquiry into the federal government's role in the events leading to the death of Detective Joe Longo. In his testimony before the Jackson subcommittee, Anthony Diamond, the deputy director of the BNDD, tried to brush aside the notion that Longo was merely a target of opportunity, the random victim of a flagrant entrapment. Employing a startlingly inapt euphemism, Diamond explained that Detective Longo was "the subject of an investigative plan." In reality, however, there was neither an investigation nor a plan, for the repeated attempts to induce Joe to accept a bribe scarcely qualify as an "investigation" of his conduct and the series of blunders in this particular case could be described as a "plan" only by a person given to either metaphor or self-delusion.

Nevertheless, by whatever name one calls it, by the early evening of Monday, February 14, Carlo Danzie's machinations on behalf of the BNDD and the Southern District of New York had produced absolutely nothing. On three separate occasions he had tried to give money to Longo and Antonelli, the last time with near disastrous results. Having narrowly escaped a search that would have revealed any transmitting devices on his person, Danzie must have recognized the heavy risk involved in yet a fourth attempt. And the two federal agents who listened in on the conversation as Joe, Luke, and Danzie ate the steaks Danzie had ordered must have felt they were wasting their time. With Longo already suspicious that Danzie was trying to set him up, it was inconceivable that the Milanese spy would choose this moment for his next move in a game he was clearly losing. Yet that is precisely what Danzie did.

With his fork in his left hand, Carlo Danzie jabbed at a small, blood-red piece of meat and gestured with it as he spoke, the fork describing tiny circles in front of his mouth. "If my people would call me," he said, returning to a subject that had been dropped almost an hour before, "I would learn the nature of my difficulties. But they do not, and there is an ocean between us."

"Maybe there's someone else you could deal with," Luke suggested helpfully. It didn't matter much where Danzie got his drugs—that was a problem for the Italian police. What mattered was getting a crack at the importers in Brooklyn, whom Danzie described as "eager for the transaction."

"No," Danzie answered after considering the suggestion for a few seconds. "There is a Lebanese syndicate in Beirut and I have been in contact from time to time with a Corsican in Toronto. But it would not be possible. It would be necessary for me to be there."

Joe swallowed the bait. "Maybe it could be arranged," he said tentatively, merely offering the possibility as something to be explored. He guessed that the Corsican in Toronto was probably Emile Sabiani, long known to be one of the chief contact points between the Corsican underworld in Marseilles and buyers in Montreal, New York, and Miami. And the Lebanese syndicate was probably the organization that Lucky Luciano had put together in the early fifties, when he turned Beirut into a major transshipment point for unprocessed morphine. With contacts like these, there was no limit to the amount of intelligence Danzie could supply.

Danzie cocked his head quizzically, as though his problem suddenly had been solved in a way that was so obvious he had looked right past it before. Then his eyes darkened with disappointment and he said, "No, it cannot be done. I am not able to leave your country. I have no passport."

"Whatdya mean, you don't have a passport?"

"They took it away from me."

"Who did?"

"Anthony Diamond. When I was in Washington."

Joe glanced across to Luke, who confirmed what Danzie had just said with an apologetic nod. It was the first Joe had heard of it.

"Look, maybe it's no problem," Joe said, trying to think his way through the situation. "I'll check it with my captain and we'll try and get the damn thing back, that's all."

"Can you do such a thing?" Danzie asked, his voice slyly complimentary, expressing at once his awareness of the difficulties and his confidence in Joe's ability to get it done.

"I'll let you know tomorrow," Joe answered. "All I've gotta do is sell him on the idea that you're too smart to skip out on us."

Danzie nodded in appreciation. "Yes," he agreed, "you understand how it is with a man such as myself. I have made my adjustments and I can be of value to all people. But with Interpol looking for me I would be of value to no one. I would return."

He ended the speech with two loud slaps of the fingers of his right hand against the palm of his left hand. A waiter hurried to the table. "If this can be arranged, we have cause to celebrate," Danzie announced. "Three whiskeys, please. Your best, with the lemon peel and little ice."

As the waiter retreated to the bar, Danzie leaned forward over the table and put his heavy hand on Joe's arm. "You must listen to me now, my friend," he said softly, earnestly. "There will be some risk in what we are planning. It may be that you are correct, that my people in Milan have learned of my arrest. If this is so, it would be better for me if I did not go. But I must find out, so I will take that chance. They can only kill me, is it not so?"

He laughed lightly, a laugh that sounded brave and frightened at the same time. It was the best performance of his life, and Joe listened, too absorbed to try keeping ahead of him, taking it in as it unfolded but not anticipating the direction in which Danzie was going.

"And for you, my friend," Danzie went on, interrupting himself when the waiter reappeared. "Here, let us drink to the success of our enterprise. And for you, my friend, there is also a danger. If things go badly and I am unable to return, the blame will be yours. Even if your captain approves the arrangement, he will not accept responsibility. I know how such men are. This is why I must tell you now, although I know your feelings on this matter, that it would mean much to me if I could repay you for your confidence. I see that you are taking a chance for me and I am not a man to permit that."

This time there was no anger in Joe's voice when he answered. "It's not necessary," he said. "You see the Corsican or the Lebanese or whatever, do what you have to do, and I'll take care of this end."

"Yes, yes, I know," Danzie replied quickly, "but I would be less than honest if I did not tell you this would be worth a great deal to me."

Danzie spoke excitedly, and for a moment the thought passed through Joe's mind that he had no intention of returning. But what did that matter? In New York he was without contacts, as useless as if he had been on the moon.

"No," Joe said firmly, "you don't owe us anything. We'll get you the passport and you do what you have to."

"If that is how it must be," Danzie answered with a tone of resigned finality.

"That is how it must be. To the success of our enterprise."

The three men raised their glasses and drank.

At first it wasn't clear whether Carlo Danzie knew he was being followed or routinely took such precautions. He hailed a cab on Second Avenue in front of Little John's and headed south until Forty-fifth Street, where he turned right, and then right again onto Third. Joe and Luke, who had been parked about a block north of the restaurant, followed easily, laying well back in the thin late night traffic.

At Forty-first Street Danzie's cab turned west again. Twice he circled the block between Third and Lexington, so that now there could be no doubt that he knew he had picked up a tail. Luke, who was driving Joe's car, glanced across to his partner for instructions.

"Stay with him," Joe said. "Sooner or later he's gotta go somewhere."

For another twenty minutes Danzie's cab zigzagged aimlessly through the midtown area, finally pulling to the curb at the Thirty-fifth Street entrance to the Russell Hotel just west of Fifth. Joe and Luke watched from a position about seventy-five yards back as Danzie paid the driver and entered the building through the revolving door.

"I don't get it," Luke said, studying the dingy entranceway.

"What's he staying in a place like that for?"

Joe shrugged. "Beats me," he said, but the words were hardly out of his mouth before he figured it out. "The building runs through the block," he said, flinging open the door and bounding into the street. "Take the other side."

While Luke circled the block, Joe crossed the street and moved up to a restaurant doorway just across from the revolving doors at the Russell. He didn't even try to guess what Danzie would do, whether he would leave by the Thirty-fourth Street exit or double back. After ten minutes had passed, he started wondering whether Danzie had left from the south side, drawing Luke after him. In another five minutes he had his answer.

Carlo Danzie strode briskly to the sidewalk and scanned the deserted street in both directions. Satisfied that the car that had been following him was no longer in sight, he walked quickly to Sixth Avenue, where he crossed to the north side of Thirty-fifth and then continued up the avenue. Joe waited until he was out of sight and then jogged after him, slowing as he reached the corner. Half expecting to find Danzie leaning against the corner building waiting for him, he stopped and stuck his head out past the building line just far enough to see the sidewalk ahead. Danzie was almost to Thirty-sixth Street, still walking rapidly and not looking back.

Joe took that moment to dash across Sixth Avenue, where he could follow Danzie from the other side of the street with less chance of being seen. Matching his pace to Danzie's, his longer strides quickly closed the north-south space between them until he was only a few yards behind, on the shabby side of the most schizophrenic avenue in New York. The east side, where Danzie was, is fronted almost entirely with stately granite office towers, but the west side, from below Thirtieth Street up past Forty-second, consists of a ragtag assortment of two- and three-story buildings in prewar brick, with rundown Irish bars, ripoff gadget stores with eight-dollar transistor radios on display behind the wire-mesh burglar screens in their windows, and even a pawnshop or two.

Danzie kept walking, coatless in the freezing February night, with Joe doggedly behind him through the Forties and then past Fiftieth, Fifty-first, and Fifty-second. There he stopped, as though he were considering something. Across the avenue in front of him stood the Hilton Hotel, its taxi port set back behind the pavement under the cantilevered façade. Turning his head, he checked the traffic on the avenue, which at that hour consisted mostly of private cars and occupied cabs. If he was thinking of hailing a taxi he didn't stand much of a chance, since empty cabs cruise mainly on the southbound avenues."

Crossing the avenue, he headed for the hotel, where three taxis waited, their rooflights lit, their engines idling. Joe moved closer until he was almost to the corner. If Danzie took a cab, he would have to get another one to follow. He watched as Danzie waved off the doorman and rapped lightly on the window of the first cab in the line. From his pocket he took a roll of bills, peeled off one and passed it to the cabbie, then proceeded to the second taxi, where he did the same thing. Joe immediately realized what was happening and broke into a run for the taxi port. He dashed across Fifty-second and down the circular drive just as Danzie climbed into the last cab. Breathless, he watched impotently as all three taxis drove off.

"Cab, sir?" the doorman asked mechanically. "There should be one along any minute."

Luke Antonelli waited by the south entrance of the hotel for a little over half an hour before running out of patience. He realized, of course, that Danzie might well have doubled back and left the same way he came in, which would have drawn Joe after him. Gunning the engine, he raced around the block to see whether his partner was still in position and to suggest that if Danzie was still inside they should check to see if he was registered there, as unlikely as that seemed.

There was no sign of Joe on Thirty-fifth Street, which meant that he must have followed Danzie either on foot or in a cab. If it was a cab, there was nothing for Luke to do except wait for Joe to contact him by radio. In the meanwhile he decided to cruise the neighborhood on the off chance that he might spot them. For about a quarter of an hour he zigzagged the streets east and west of Sixth Avenue and was about to quit when he saw Joe walking south in the direction of the hotel.

"Need a lift?" he called as he pulled to the curb.

Joe climbed in without saying anything, the lumbering movements of his powerful body communicating through an almost physical language that Danzie had gotten away from him and that he was in no mood for jokes.

"Forget it," Luke said, "we're no worse off than we were an hour ago. Let's get something to eat."

"We just ate."

"Yeah, well, a cup of coffee or something. Whatdya say?"

"You get something," Joe countered. "Drop me off on Charles Street."

Luke was puzzled for a moment, until he remembered that Mickie Lang lived on Charles Street. "You think she knows where he went?" he asked. "I'll go with you."

"Forget it," Joe snapped. "Go get your coffee, I'll see you tomorrow."

Luke didn't give him an argument. Obediently swinging a left on Thirty-ninth, he cut across to Seventh Avenue, where he turned left again, heading south. Five minutes later he rolled to a stop in front of Mickie Lang's brownstone. "Sure you don't want me to stick around?" he asked, knowing what the answer would be.

"For what?" Joe said lightly, noticing the faint trace of hurt in his partner's voice. "I'm just jerking myself off, right? She doesn't know anything, no sense both of us wasting our time."

"You sure?"

"Yeah, I'm sure. See you in the morning."

Joe waited on the sidewalk until Luke rounded the corner onto Bleecker Street. The inner hallway door in Mickie's brownstone had a defective lock, so he let himself in and climbed the two flights to her apartment. There was no answer when he knocked. His watch said twelve thirty and he figured that the restaurant probably didn't close much before one. Since he had no way of knowing she would be coming home when she got off, he decided he'd give her only until one thirty. Sitting on the staircase above her landing, he lit a cigarette and settled in to wait.

The time passed quickly as his mind alternately raced through the complicated possibilities of the Danzie case and idled in a kind of numb fatigue. He was perfectly aware that finding where Danzie was staying was not the important thing. It was merely a psychological victory he needed at that moment, a feeling that he had some measure of control over the activities of a man who till then had been calling all the shots, coming and going as he pleased, disappearing when it suited him, and so far delivering nothing.

But of course it would be a meaningless victory, because what mattered most at this point was not holding on to Danzie but getting permission to let him go. He lit another cigarette and rehearsed what he would say to Captain Marcus in the morning, how he would convince him to allow Danzie to leave the country.

The downstairs door opened and a woman's footsteps mounted the stairs. By the time Mickie Lang reached the landing, Joe was waiting by her door. She was looking down as she crossed to the door, searching through the change purse of her wallet for her key. Almost bumping into him, she jumped back and barely managed to stifle a scream, which came out instead as a short yelp of terror. In the dim light of the gray hallway a few panicky seconds passed before it registered in her mind that the man lurking by her door wasn't a stranger.

She let out a long slow breath that hissed through her teeth and said, "Jesus Christ, don't ever do that again!"

"Sorry, I didn't mean to scare you," Joe said. "What do you live in a place like this for?"

"I'm saving my money," she snapped with an icy sarcasm his tactless question fully deserved. "I suppose you want to come in?"

"Uh-huh."

She unlocked the door and stepped into the entrance hall, Joe following after her and closing the door behind him. Under her coat she still wore her waitress's uniform, a short red tunic with yellowed white trim and dark stockings that almost glowed on her long, slender legs.

"Let me guess," she said coyly. "You have some more questions about Mr. Danzie."

"No, the same questions."

"Well, sit down. I'll give you the same answers."

"You move like a dancer," Joe said, watching appreciatively as she wandered meaninglessly about the living room, ritualistically rearranging stray magazines before gathering up maybe half a dozen dirty coffee cups. Each step she took was carefully articulated, a precise and fluid movement of her hips and legs. There was no ass-wiggling obviousness, but her walk was sexy to the point of suggestiveness. As she moved about the room she seemed almost to be darting among the furniture like a bright fish in a tank.

"I am," she said. "Do you want some coffee?"

Joe nodded. "I thought you were going to call me if you heard from him."

"No, what I said was I'd think about it," she answered flatly, walking away from Joe toward the kitchen as she spoke. "Why don't you come in here, we can talk?"

The kitchen was a small, square room with a vintage gas stove on cast-iron legs and a tiny refrigerator that growled ominously every few minutes as it turned itself off and on. All the surfaces were spotlessly neat but Joe suspected that was because no one ever did any cooking there. He pulled a straight armless chair from under the table and sat down while she spooned coffee into a paper cone.

"And you decided not to?" he asked.

"Um-hum. Can't we talk about something else?"

"Not until we get this straightened out," he said.

"You wanted to find him and you found him. What difference does it make?"

"It makes a difference because I thought you were on the level when you said you didn't know how to get in touch with him. Now I don't know."

She turned abruptly from the stove, where the water was just coming to a boil, and looked directly at Joe, staring down at him for a long while before speaking. Her eyes moved nervously about his face, like the hands of a blind man groping for recognition. "If I lied that's my business," she said at last, almost spitting the words. "I think you'd better go."

She walked from the kitchen and Joe followed. "What time did you get off work?" he asked.

"Around twelve thirty."

"And it took you an hour to get here?"

"I had to—" She stopped in mid sentence.

"Change your clothes?"

"That wasn't what I was going to say," she answered belligerently, but it had been, until she realized she was still wearing her uniform.

"Where did you meet him?"

"I didn't."

"Are you going to?"

"Maybe."

"Here?"

"I said you'd better go."

"And I said I'm not going until I get this straightened out," Joe answered doggedly, matching her determination with his own.

She started to respond but quickly caught herself. A quizzical expression crossed her face and she said, "No, you didn't say that."

"I didn't?"

"I don't think so."

There were a few seconds of silence during which they stared across at each other, three feet of space between them. Then they both laughed.

Mickie said, "Honest, I didn't know where he is, he's not coming here and I'm not seeing him later. It's late and I want to go to bed."

Joe didn't answer.

"You don't believe me, do you?" she asked plaintively. She spoke softly and her voice had the flutelike clarity of a girl's, making Joe wonder if she did it on purpose or if she always sounded like that and he just hadn't noticed it before.

"Not really," he said.

She smiled again, the same ambiguous smile he had seen on the landing when she came in. "Suit yourself," she said. "I'm going to bed."

She turned and disappeared down a short corridor that led to the bedroom. Joe went to the couch, from where he could see into the bedroom through the door she hadn't closed. She was out of his line of sight, but in the near total silence that is as rare in New York City as true darkness it seemed to him he could hear the incredibly sensuous sounds of a woman undressing, the soft gossamer fabrics drawn across warm skin. He could hear a closet door open and close and then she walked past the doorway in a pink and gold robe or dressing gown. A few seconds later she reappeared in the doorway again, hesitated a moment, and then came down the corridor toward him, backlit from the bedroom. Her feet were bare and she wore a silver and turquoise bracelet that he hadn't noticed before on her left wrist.

"You're really going to stay, aren't you?" she asked, really meaning it as a question.

Joe said, "You left the water boiling in the kitchen."

Under her delicate Oriental robe she wore her nakedness as only the most exquisitely dressed women can wear clothes.

From Charles Street it is just a short walk to Varick, which is the southward continuation of Seventh Avenue. As he passed Downing

Street Joe glanced to his left, trying to see the front of the peeling brownstone where only a few months before he had arrested Jason Meredith and Peter Caruso. That trial was over now, ending with Caruso's conviction, but remembering the three-kilo case gave him no satisfaction at that moment.

At the doorway of Two-oh-one Joe slid his shield from his pocket and flashed it to the patrolman on duty in the lobby, who nodded a desultory greeting. Taking the elevator upstairs, he went straight to the squad room. It was quiet and dark, deserted except for two detectives eating sandwiches at a corner desk. The window behind them was still black an hour before the late winter sunrise, and the gooseneck lamp on the desk illuminated their corner with the gross intensity of a Goya night. Hunched forward to keep their sandwiches above the waxed paper wrappings unfolded on the desk, the two detectives looked up at the sound of Joe's footsteps like nocturnal scavengers caught in a sudden searchlight.

"Want a sandwich?" one of them called. "We got plenty."

Joe tossed his coat on his desk and took a few steps in the direction of Captain Marcus's office. "Thanks, I ate," he said. "Any chance the captain's around?"

With an elaborate gesture the detective extended his arm and checked his watch. "Hey, Joe, the little hand's on the five. You gotta be kidding," he said.

"Yeah, that's what I figured. What about Verlon?"

Hal Verlon, a federal agent, shared the leadership of the Joint Task Force with Captain Marcus. On paper both Verlon and Marcus had equal command authority over all the men in the unit, but in reality the feds ran the show. Nevertheless, the police officers invariably reported to Marcus and ignored Verlon.

"Verlon?" the detective asked. "Look, I'm only the *schwartze* around here. You'll have to come back during business hours."

Joe laughed. "How come you can never find a boss when you need one?" he said.

"I don't know, I never needed one," the detective answered. "Seriously, though, if you need to see someone, Looie went down to the diner about a half hour ago, said he was coming back."

Looie was Lieutenant Francis O'Neill, a forty-eight-year-old detective who had been one of the first men chosen for the Joint Task Force. Never much of a street cop even in his early years in uniform, he always struck the men who worked with him as the sort of guy who wiggles his way up to an inspector's rating and a desk job in Headquarters. But somehow it didn't turn out that way for him and he had more or less resigned himself to the fact that he was locked into the Detective Bureau until he put in for his pension.

Joe wasn't sure whether he wanted to talk to O'Neill or wait for the captain in the morning. He felt tired and drained after the long day that had started with Danzie's phone call in the morning. The emotional ups and downs were like nothing he had ever experienced before and he wondered if he was losing his perspective. His sudden elation at finding that his informant was still on the scene now seemed as remote as if it had happened weeks ago, as did the hours of anxious anticipation, the disappointment when he got to the restaurant and realized that Mickie Lang knew Danzie's whereabouts and had failed to call, the anger over the attempted payoff, and then the frustration and humiliation of losing Danzie in the middle of a city Joe knew as intimately as he knew his own family, a city in which Danzie was a stranger.

But slicing through those dim, weary memories, like the sound of a siren heard in one's sleep and woven into all the mind's other processes, was the note of bright hope Danzie had sounded with his vague references to a Corsican in Toronto and a Lebanese syndicate in Beirut.

"Yeah, okay," Joe said. "I'm gonna sack out for a couple of minutes. When Looie gets back tell him where I am."

About an hour later he was awakened by the pressure of a hand on his bare shoulder.

"You wanted to see me, Joe?" Lieutenant O'Neill asked. He had small hands for a man.

Joe sat up on the cot and scraped the back of his hand hard across his forehead and over his eyes, massaged the knotted muscles in his neck, and then tried blinking himself into wakefulness. "What time is it?" he asked thickly.

"Quarter past six."

"Jesus Christ. Yeah, I just wanted to talk to you about something, see what you think."

As briefly as he could, he explained the situation to the lieutenant, going all the way back to the arrest in the Americana and ending, fifteen minutes later, with Danzie's request for his passport and permission to leave the country. O'Neill listened intently, fascinated by the account. Like everyone else in the Joint Task Force, he knew that Joe and Luke were operating an informant so powerful that the top-ranking officers of the BNDD in Washington had an interest in the case. But many of the details were new to him. As he listened to Joe's story, O'Neill imagined he already could hear the smugly self-right-eous comments the other cops in the group would be making if they knew that Longo's hotshot stool pigeon hadn't produced anything but pigeon shit.

"Okay, but what do you want from me?" O'Neill asked, genuine-ly not understanding. "I can't get you the passport."

"No, I know. I just wanted you to know what the story is, back me up with Marcus in case he doesn't want to go for it."

O'Neill shrugged. "He'll go for it," he said. "I guess you don't really know him or you wouldn't be asking that."

"Thanks, Loo, that's what I wanted to hear," Joe said, then hesitated a moment, unsure of whether he should continue. "Look," he said at last, "there's another thing, too. The guy's been making some funny sounds lately. I think he wants to lay some bread on me."

O'Neill turned away. "If he does that—" he said, but Joe didn't let him finish the sentence.

"I know all that," he said. "But the way it is now, all we got him on is that possession thing that won't hold up, and I think he knows it. So I was thinking that if he tried it again, I've got half a mind to take it. Then I hold it and if he doesn't come through I stick him with a bribery."

"I see your point," O'Neill said cautiously. "But if that's what you're thinking, what do you want from me? Before you do a thing like that, you'd better talk it over with your captain."

"Yeah," Joe answered absently, his mind already elsewhere.

"No," Captain Marcus said levelly. "I don't need guarantees, that's not what I'm asking you. I just want you to tell me you don't think the guy's gonna skip."

"That's what I *am* telling you," Joe repeated. "Do you want me to put it in writing or something?"

Marcus raised his left hand, palm forward in warning. "Okay, back off, Longo," he said. "I'm not gonna do something like this just because you want it, so stay cool and convince me."

Joe nodded apologetically. "Yeah, but look, it comes down to this," he said. "He might be bluffing, and if we tell him we're gonna put him back in the joint maybe he'll come through with something. But I don't think he is. I think he's telling the truth, he's tapped out. So we got two choices. We can lock him up for that fucking half ounce, but you know as well as I do he can walk away from that. It's a bum case. Or we can let him split back to the old country. To me that's no fucking choice at all."

"And he'll put a deal together and then fly back here to hand it up?" Marcus asked, the skepticism in his voice so apparent it came across like sarcasm.

"I'm not saying he will, I'm saying it's a chance we gotta take," Joe answered. When the captain didn't say anything Joe took the opportunity away from him. "Look, captain," he said, "you gotta go with how you feel on a thing like this. The guy tells me he'll come back and I think he will."

"You think he will," Marcus said icily. "Hey, Joe, this isn't fucking General MacArthur we're talking about, you know."

"All right. Say I don't think he will, what goddamn bit of difference does it make? We've got nothing to lose."

"Maybe you've got nothing to lose, but I'm the one that's gonna have to take the heat when that weasel runs and hides and I gotta explain why I said it's okay for a junk dealer to go home."

Joe had been waiting for just such an opening and was ready for it when it came. He was counting on the fact that although the captain tried to talk like a boss, tried to think the way they thought downtown, he never could pull it off because at bottom he was still a cop. "Anyone asks you that, send him to me," Joe said, "because I know what I'd tell him."

Marcus smiled for the first time all morning. "I'll tell him myself," he said. "Did you say Diamond's got the passport? You gonna ask him for it?"

"Go smoother if you do it," Joe said.

"Good enough. Get back to me tomorrow morning, I'll have it for you."

Good news always made him restless, the way uncertainty affected other men. He tried reading the paper, and then watching television, but it didn't work. After a while he was walking around the living room like a child on a rainy afternoon. Finally he gave up and went to the kitchen.

"Forget dinner," he said. "Whatdya say we go out?"

Jeannie wasn't surprised. The first thing he had done when he came home was to tell her that Danzie had asked for his passport last night and that Captain Marcus had given his approval. She was as happy with the news as Joe, only for her own reasons.

"I guess I was hoping that Danzie would go away for good," she said later. "I don't know why, but I never liked any of it. I think it was because I'm really very different from Joe, I don't believe in getting excited about something before it happens. In fact, I don't even like to think about it. So when Joe got so carried away about this case, about all the wonderful things that were going to happen, I got just plain scared. He was so certain about the whole thing, he was going to make the biggest case in history, he was going to be Sonny Grosso and Eddie Egan and Kojak and Columbo all rolled up in one. And I thought, No, things like that don't happen. He's going to get hurt by this. But he wouldn't listen and I knew I was wasting my time, so I just kept quiet and hoped for the best. I don't really know what it was like for him, but for me it was like a dream that you're not certain if it's a dream or a nightmare. And I remember thinking . . . this was about a year after he died and I was sitting in the bedroom and I couldn't help myself, I just said out loud, Oh, Joey, you were so naive. After all the crying I did, that's what really broke my heart the most, that he was so naive. He was a tough guy and he was smart and he knew all the angles—that's how he liked to picture himself, and in a way I think he really was all those things. But in the end he did just what they wanted. He went along with them the way your dog goes with you when you have to take him somewhere to put him to sleep."

Chapter 9
The Split

JOE WALKED INTO the captain's office with his coat still on. Hal Verlon, the highest-ranking federal officer in the Joint Task Force, sat in the straight-backed armless chair directly in front of Marcus's desk, his immense legs and his huge body flowing around the edges of the puny stick of furniture like something soft that had been left to melt there overnight.

"When you're free, captain," Joe said, hesitating by the door.

"No, no, cmon in, Joe," Marcus answered from behind his desk. "We were more or less expecting you."

Whatever Verlon's presence meant, Joe knew it couldn't be good. The feds had never been happy about letting him operate Danzie, but up to now they had laid back. "I just wanted to know what happened with that thing we talked about," he began, being purposefully vague until he knew what Verlon's involvement was.

"Sit down, Joe," Marcus said. When Joe made no move for the chair next to Verlon, the captain went on anyway. "The thing is this," he said. "Danzie can't have his passport. It's too much of a risk."

149

"What fucking risk?" Joe demanded, making no effort to hide his anger but fighting to master it before he said anything else. He thought it had all been settled yesterday, so that his first reaction was a combination of shock and disappointment confusedly mixed with the rage of betrayal.

"Look, Joe," Marcus said in his most fatherly tone, "we don't know enough about this guy to trust him on a thing like this. If he goes away maybe we lose him for good."

"So we lose him. What good's he doing us?"

Marcus looked to Verlon, whose smooth, expressionless face offered no answers. "There's more to it than that," he said softly, trying to placate his detective, perhaps even trying to warn him. "Take my word for it, Joe."

Before he could say anything else, Verlon cut in, looking up at Joe with his small close-set eyes. "We told you from the start, Longo, we had an interest in this man. But you wanted a chance and they gave it to you. You blew it and now they got their own plans for him. He can't leave the country."

Joe studied the fat man's face before answering. Then, his voice a stinging hiss of contempt, he said, "Hey, I'm tired of playing games. If the guy can't work for me I gotta lock him up. Then where are their goddamn plans?"

Verlon said, "Suit yourself."

Marcus said, "Joe, be reasonable about it, you don't want to make trouble for yourself. It didn't work out, so let's just forget it."

"You gotta be kidding."

"I'm not kidding. Now back off," Marcus answered, his voice firm. "You know I'd help you if I could, but my hands are tied. I can't get the passport for you, that's all there is to it."

"Who can?" Joe asked, throwing the question at Marcus like an insult he was immediately sorry for. "I mean, let me talk to Diamond," he said. "Maybe we can work something out."

"Believe me, Joe," Marcus pleaded, "he won't talk to you. It's final. Just forget about it, whatdya say?"

"Yeah, I'll forget about it," Joe snarled. "In a pig's ass I'll forget about it."

He turned and walked away from the captain's desk, two long strides carrying him to the door, which he pulled violently open, then slammed behind him as he left. In the squad room, half a dozen pairs of eyes gave him the mixed looks of pity and admiration men in the ranks always reserve for those who have done combat with superior officers.

"Way to go, Joe," someone called from across the room.

Joe smiled in acknowledgment, and the anger drained from him. There was no point in getting worked up about the bosses. He knew what he had to do and was going to do it.

DANZIE: Sit down, sit down, my friend. Luke, it is good to see you. Three Campari, please. You have news for me?

LONGO: Yeah, some news. We're fucked.

DANZIE: I do not understand.

LONGO: Fucked. You don't understand fucked? It means no passport, you don't go.

DANZIE: But this cannot be, you must be joking with me. Luke, is he joking?

ANTONELLI: Yeah, sure, he's joking.

[No one says anything for about thirty seconds. Then Danzie speaks, apparently to the waiter.]

DANZIE: Thank you.

[Another silence, lasting almost a minute.]

DANZIE: This cannot be. I was of the opinion . . .

LONGO: Yeah, I was of the opinion, too. Yesterday the captain said okay, but today they say no go.

DANZIE: The captain?

LONGO: No, the feds.

DANZIE : Ah, so that is how it is. They do not want you to make this case, Joe.

LONGO : What're you talking about?

DANZIE : The . . . the government *polizia*, the . . . the "feds" . . . they want the big cases. The big cases are not for a policeman from the city. It is a pity but that is how it is.

LONGO : Yeah, maybe. . . Ah, look, I don't know about that. The thing is you can't go, we're gonna have to work out something else.

DANZIE : Perhaps . . .

LONGO : No perhaps. You're gonna have to get in touch with your people.

DANZIE : But it is impossible, my friend. Do you not think I wish it could be done?

LONGO : It can be done. You don't want to go to jail, you figure out how to do it.

DANZIE : My friend, I understand your feelings and so I will overlook that you have no . . . no justification—yes, justification—you have no justification to talk to me this way. I have been honest with you, have I not? And you have been honest with me. But my people do not return my calls. I cannot, you know, go through the telephone wires. I have only these two telephone numbers and it is a person of no consequence who answers. *Pronto? Pronto.* This is Carlo. And I give him my number. Then I wait. Does he give them my message? Yes, no, how can I know? I am here.

ANTONELLI: Isn't there someone else you could call, find out what's going on?

DANZIE: Luke, Joe, believe me, I have tried. Do you think I do not think the same thing myself? I have friends. But they have been able to learn nothing. I give you my assurance, there is nothing I can do.

LONGO: What the fuck's this? Who ordered this?

DANZIE: This, it is . . . it is what you see. I had no thought that you would be bringing me such news. Come, we must eat.

LONGO: Take it away.

DANZIE: No, no. Put it down, be quick. . . . A man must live nevertheless, eh, Joe? . . . No, I will do that. Go away. . . . Tell me, Joe, will I have to go back to prison?

[There is no audible reply. Perhaps Longo answers with a gesture.]

DANZIE: If that is how it is, then I tell you this very moment, they do not stop us so easily. . . . Did you ever see the great Pelé? I imagine not, you Americans. . . But that is neither here nor there. I mention him only to make a point. The man is a genius. Yes, a genius. And why do I call him that, a football player? Let me tell you why. Because he is a man of many resources.

LONGO: Carlo, you're too much.

DANZIE: No, no, listen to me, my friend. In Milano last year—or perhaps it was not last year, it is of no importance—I saw the great Pelé. There remained only one minute, two minutes in the contest. Pelé advanced the ball toward the goal, traveling at a great speed, believe me, a great speed. In front of him, left, right, two men. They block his path. And his own men, one feels it sitting there, they are of no use. If the goal is to be scored it is a matter of his resources, do you see that? He moves toward the center, straight on goal, between the two men. They come together and then quick, like a lizard, he is around them. He stops, he moves slowly, now he is like a tiger moving toward the goal. After so much speed, he is moving carefully, in a way that is frightening to watch. His body shifts with feints this way and that, and one feels almost a pity for the goalkeeper. His own men move toward the goal, but still one senses that they will only get in the way. He moves in a circle now, away from where I am sitting, toward the far side of the arena. Do you see how it is, his path forms an arc that ends in the goal? And he moves faster and faster, so rapidly, and the goalkeeper comes forward to meet him, and then he moves sideways. That is to say, in a horizontal way. He is off the ground, his feet are up here, and his head is on this side, and the ball shoots from him like a bullet from a gun. Do you see what I am telling you? A man of many resources.

LONGO: Yeah, okay, Carlo. You're a man of many resources. Which is terrific because I'm tapped out. You get on the phone or do whatever you have to do with all your resources, and you get me something pretty damn fast—

DANZIE: Or I must go to prison?

LONGO: That's the way it looks.

DANZIE: Do not be in such a hurry, my friend. You can understand, I do not wish to go to prison. And you do not wish me to go to prison.

LONGO: What I wish has got nothing to do with it. If I've gotta lock you up, I will. You know that.

DANZIE: Yes, of course. I am not so foolish to think that you would not arrest me. Our friendship would not . . . our friendship, after all, it is only a small thing. You have your necessities, I understand that. But still, you do not want me in prison because I am no good to you in prison, is it not so? Then I say, listen to what I am going to suggest.

LONGO: I'm listening.

DANZIE: Here, give me your glass. . . . Now, our problem is simple. I have no passport. But you, Joe, you are a man of the world, you have been a policeman for many years. Get me a passport and I will go.

LONGO: What?

DANZIE: Get me a passport. You know how these things are done, you have connections everywhere. I will pay whatever it costs. How much is it? Ten thousand? Fifteen? I will pay twenty-five, there will be something in it for you.

LONGO: Hey, Carlo, this isn't fucking Casablanca, you know, and I'm not Sidney Greenstreet. Who the hell do you think you're talking to?

DANZIE: Perhaps you are right.

[There is a silence lasting slightly under a minute.]

DANZIE: You are not eating, Joe. These little obstacles can be overcome. . . . Ah, well, then, perhaps you would like a cigar? . . . Luke?

ANTONELLI: Nah.

DANZIE: They are not the *cubanos* I am accustomed to, but I offer them to you anyway. Your country has strange politics. . . . What? . . . Ah, no, no. There is no problem. Just bring us some brandy. . . . No, no, I assure you . . . Joe, let me ask you something. Two nights ago you followed me, is it not so?

ANTONELLI: What's that got to do with anything?

LONGO: Yeah, we followed you.

DANZIE: Ah, good. I assumed it was you but I wanted to assure myself. You did not follow me very long?

LONGO: Fairly long.

DANZIE: Do not be so vain, my friend. I tell you, you did not follow me very long. Do you think I do not know?

LONGO: Okay, so what's the point?

DANZIE: The point, as you say, is that you let these people have their way with you!

LONGO: Keep it down.

DANZIE: They do not want you to make this case because . . . Because of what? Jealousy? Yes, I suppose so. They take it away from you. And you allow this to happen because you are so . . . so *misero* that you do not see what any man of imagination would see. But Carlo Danzie does not go to prison just because these *federales* say there will be no passport.

LONGO: That's what I've been trying to tell you, Carlo, so let's just cut out the bullshit, and if there's something you can do, do it. I don't care how you do it, Carlo, but unless you put me on to a big shipment, you're going in.

DANZIE: Yes, yes, just listen to yourself, my friend. Did you not just tell me that when you followed me you did not follow me for long? You do not know where I am living, that is what I am trying to tell you. I am free to leave at any time. This is the reality, this is the truth. Why are we talking like such fools? They say you are not to let me go. Could you stop me?

LONGO: Get to the point.

DANZIE: Could you stop me?

LONGO: No.

DANZIE: That is correct, my friend. I come as I please, I go as I please.

LONGO: Don't try it, Carlo. It's crazy. If you skip, I've gotta report it and you'd be a fugitive.

DANZIE: Because they say so?

LONGO: Because they say so.

DANZIE: Joe, I am laughing at you, you are such a fool. I tell you I can do nothing here and you tell me I cannot go. So what will be the result? You think you will lock me up? Even if such a thing were to happen, what good would it do you? And I assure you it will not happen. Your Mr. Diamond in Washington, I have worked for him before and I will work for him again. How do you think it happens that he has my passport?

LONGO: What are you talking about?

DANZIE: When I am in Washington he demands my passport. It gives him, you understand, a control. He thinks I cannot leave America without it. But why does he want this control if I am working for you? Do you ask yourself that?

LONGO: Yeah, I asked myself.

DANZIE: Then ask yourself, did he foresee such a thing, that my people would not return my calls, that I would have to return to my homeland?

LONGO: What the fuck are you getting at, Carlo?

DANZIE: They did not want you to have this case, Joe! They have made it so you will get nothing. And then when you lock me up they will release me. I will go back to working for them. I will get my passport and I will go. Only I will go for them. And you, fool that you are, you will get nothing.

LONGO: All right, Carlo. *[There is a long silence, lasting over a minute.]* All right, goddamn it, get to the fucking point.

DANZIE : I will go. One week, two weeks, I will return.*[There is a silence.]* And you will give me that much time, you will not report that I have, how do you say, flown?

LONGO: Two weeks. No more.

DANZIE: And what if they ask? They will, they are not fools.

LONGO: Look, we got daily reports. I'll put down I saw you, I'll put down you're working.

DANZIE: Ah! You will see, Joe, I am a man of my word.

ANTONELLI: Where are you gonna be?

DANZIE: I will be moving about, of course. I understand that through Detroit it is easy to leave the country. I will go to Milano and find out what is the difficulty with my people. Here, do you have a pencil? . . . Good. This is my telephone number in Milano, it is my home. If it goes well in Milano I will come back. If not, I will go to Beirut and make the necessary arrangements. My wife, she can tell you how to reach me in Beirut. I have family there, too, you understand. Do you anticipate difficulties?

LONGO: I'll handle it here. You just take care of business over there.

DANZIE: That is good. Now, listen, my friend. It embarrasses me to talk about this matter again but I am sensible of the fact that you are taking a big risk. You anticipate no difficulties but I cannot be so sure for myself. I may have been betrayed, and I may be going to my death in Milano. If it is so, I have no need of this. But you will have much trouble here when they find my body in the Fiume Lambro and you have been telling your chief that you have been talking to me. But I am a man of honor, Joe. I cannot permit you to take such a risk unless I can prove to you my good faith. I insist—

LONGO: Just put it down. Put it on the table.

ANTONELLI: Joe—

LONGO: It's okay, Luke. Now you listen to me, Carlo. You get on the first plane you can get on and you set this thing up. Then you get back here. When the deal goes down we take your buyers.

Then you and me are square. But until then I'm holding this for you. *Capisce?*
DANZIE: It is yours, Joe. It is for you and Luke.
LONGO: I'm holding it for you, Carlo.

When Joe Longo walked out of Little John's restaurant on Thursday, February 17, his fifteen-year career as a police officer was effectively over. The microphone under Danzie's shirt had picked up the entire conversation, transmitting it to the Plymouth parked on Second Avenue, where agents Glenn Greer and Ramon Barrera monitored the recording as it was being made. Both of them would have liked it better if Danzie had been more explicit when he handed over the envelope, but even without an overt reference to a specific amount of money, they were confident they had a solid case against Longo and Antonelli.

Later, Paul Scala claimed that in addition to monitoring the conversation in Little John's on the seventeenth, Greer and Barrera had also overheard the meeting between Joe, Luke, and Danzie in the same restaurant on Monday the fourteenth. According to Paul Scala, the two agents were prepared to testify that they were in the restaurant that evening at a table close enough to hear what was said by the two detectives and their informant. Not surprisingly, their version—or at least what Scala claimed their version would be, for Joe's death made it unnecessary for them ever to give testimony in the matter—differed significantly from Joe's and Luke's recollection. In essence, Scala claimed that Greer and Barrera had heard Longo tell Danzie that he would get him his passport for twenty-five thousand dollars or would permit him to leave the country without a passport for four thousand.

It is not difficult to decide which of these two versions of the February 14 meeting makes more sense. In the first place, Joe and Luke carefully noted all the strangers present whenever they met Danzie in public. Detectives are trained to check out their surroundings whenever they have to deal with informants, and years of experience in the job had given Joe a sixth sense for spotting faces that didn't belong. "We checked when we went in and it was all couples," Joe later told his lawyer. "Except there were these two women, older women, by themselves up toward the front. Besides, the place was too noisy. There's no way anyone could have heard what we were saying—except, you know, when I was yelling at him. But when we were talking—no way."

Even more important is the fact that the conversation Greer and

Barrera are said to have overheard does not jibe with the one they record-
ed on tape three days later. In the Thursday meeting, Joe reacts in-
dignantly when Danzie suggests he obtain an illegal passport and it is
Danzie who mentions the figure of twenty-five thousand dollars. If on
Monday Joe had demanded twenty-five thousand dollars for getting
Danzie his own passport, it does not make sense that Danzie would quote
the same figure when asking Joe to buy him a fake passport on the black
market. "How much is it? Ten thousand? Fifteen? I will pay twenty-five,
there will be something in it for you," he said on Thursday. Obviously, he
was fishing for the appropriate price, a clear indication that he had never
heard Joe make the demand Scala's agents purportedly overheard.

Furthermore, in the recorded Thursday conversation, it was Danzie
who first suggested the possibility of leaving the country without a
passport. Indeed, he beats around the bush for quite some time before
getting to the point, taking the trouble first to convince Joe and Luke that
they would be powerless to stop him from going in any case. Surely
Danzie would not have found it necessary to speak in this way if he was
merely accepting an offer Joe had made earlier in the week.

And finally, the entire account of the overheard conversation simply
does not make sense in terms of police procedure. Danzie knew before
the Monday meeting that he would be telling Joe and Luke that his con-
tacts in Europe had deserted him and that he could not consummate a
deal unless he could return to Milan to straighten out the situation. Until
that time Danzie had offered Joe and Luke money more or less as a
gratuity, and on each occasion the offer had been rejected. Here, for the
first time, he was going to be able to give them a rationale for taking the
envelope. This time he was going to couch his attempted bribe in terms
of a quid pro quo—*the money as payment for the risk they ran in cover-*
ing for him while he was out of the country. Here, then, was the moment
of truth for Paul Scala's so-called investigative plan.

It is therefore inconceivable that Danzie was not wired at this
crucial meeting. In order to accept Scala's version of the Monday meet-
ing, one must be willing to believe that at the most critical point in the
entire "investigation," Paul Scala let his agents rely solely upon their
ability to get within hearing range of a conversation in a crowded
restaurant.

Simple common sense dictates that the Monday meeting must have
been covered in exactly the same way as the Thursday meeting. Greer
and Barrera were not *in Little John's in a position to overhear anything.*

They were in their car on Second Avenue, just as they were three days later, listening to what was being said inside through the monitoring equipment on their tape recorder. But, unfortunately for the "investigators" and their "plan," Joe and Luke did not say what their prosecutors wanted to hear. And so the tapes were erased or filed in a bottom drawer, to be replaced by a bogus account of an overheard conversation.

It must be remembered that Joe and Luke learned that their conversation had been "overheard" only from Paul Scala. The agents themselves never testified to this effect and probably never would have, even if Joe had lived to call Scala's bluff. In all likelihood, Scala never intended them to. He was simply using an old cop's trick, one that Joe recognized immediately. Hadn't Joe done the same thing himself to Danzie on the morning after Danzie's arrest, when he outlined the testimony he would give if Danzie tried to fight the case on the grounds that the arrest lacked probable cause?

Now he was in the same position himself. "It's nothing but bullshit," he told his lawyer. "I know it, Scala knows it, and he knows that I know it. But do you think that changes anything? Believe me, it doesn't. I know, I've seen it happen a thousand times."

"I still think we oughta do something with the money," Luke said softly, speaking straight at the windshield, not looking across at his partner.

Sensing Joe's glowering stare almost as though it had touched him physically, Luke glanced sideways, then averted his eyes again. "Watch where you're driving," he said.

"Christ, Luke, sometimes you're so fucking much like a little old lady it scares me," Joe muttered, finally beginning to give voice to something that had been building up inside him for three days now. "You drove me up the wall the whole goddamn weekend and now you're starting to sweat I'll run into a lamppost or something. What the hell's the matter with you?"

"Nothing."

"You know, it's not like we stuck up a bank."

"I know that."

The car was moving slowly in the congealed Monday morning traffic, stuttering forward in intermittent leaps as the two detectives made their way to work. For a few minutes no one spoke.

"How many times do I have to tell you?" Joe said at last. "There's nothing we can do with the money. Tell me what to do and I'll do it."

"I don't know. I just don't like driving around with it. It makes me nervous." He paused, then added, "I never did anything like this before."

"And you think I did?"

"That isn't what I meant. How do I know?" Luke stammered awkwardly. "I mean, maybe ... Who was that guy you said you talked to about it?"

"I didn't say."

"Was it O'Neill?"

"What makes you think that?" Joe asked, holding his voice level so it wouldn't tell Luke whether he had guessed right or not.

"I was thinking it was last Monday night, right? After I dropped you off? And Looie's always hanging around at night."

"Well, what if it was?"

"I don't know. What did you tell him?"

"I told you already," Joe answered, exasperated. "I told him I had half a mind to take the bread if he offered it again."

"Did you tell him what for?"

"No, I told him I wanted to buy a cabin cruiser. Of course I told him, what the fuck do you think!"

Luke pondered awhile. Then he said, "Yeah, okay, that's good. But, Christ, what if something happens? Don't you think somebody ought to know the way it went down? Maybe you should let him know. Tell him you took it and you're holding it."

The personal pronoun registered in the back of Joe's mind but he decided to let it pass for the time being. They would be at the office in a few minutes and he had enough to do to keep him busy all day— busy and away from Luke. "Look," he said, "I told you what that was. He says it's okay but he doesn't wanna know about it. So if I come back and tell him flat out it happened, he's gonna tell somebody and then where are we? This way he knows but he doesn't know."

"Yeah, well what the fuck good is that gonna do us?" Luke demanded with a show of impatience that startled Joe. "What you're telling me is he doesn't wanna get mixed up in it. Which is fine if nothing happens, but if anything goes wrong he never heard about it."

"Fuck that, he's a stand-up guy," Joe answered without any conviction. "Anyway, what's gonna go wrong?"

"A thousand things. That's what I keep trying to tell you."

"Like what?"

"Like I don't see how you can trust Carlo, for one."

Joe shrugged. "Where do you get I trust him? The guy's a fucking stool pigeon. What does trusting got to do with it?"

"Okay, right," Luke said, using his left hand like a conductor to orchestrate his chain of logic. "So say he gets jammed up again. Like they could bust him trying to sneak out of the country, right? It's not impossible, you know. And he's got nothing going, nothing to give them. So he says, Hey, you know Joe Longo in New York? I laid some bread on him."

This time Joe couldn't let it pass. He stared across at his partner with an intense look of distrust. He wasn't quite sure what he wanted to say, and in his momentary uncertainty he almost missed the turn on to Seventh Avenue. At the last moment he cut sharply to the left, tires squealing, a horn exploding in protest from behind. Then he drove the few blocks to Varick and pulled to the curb in front of Two-oh-one before he spoke.

"Hold it right there, Luke, there's something we gotta get straight," he said as Luke reached for the door handle, then turned to face him. For the first time in days their eyes met, but it was an unequal contest. Joe's eyes were a hard, cold green as they narrowed in on his partner's face, reading it carefully for signs of fear and weakness. "Who'd Danzie give the money to?" he asked.

The corners of Luke's mouth twitched once. "He gave it to you," he said.

Joe shook his head and slid a cigarette between his lips but didn't light it. "He gave it to us," he said, speaking so softly that his deep baritone whisper was unmistakably menacing.

"Yeah," Luke agreed timidly. "Yeah, I mean he gave it to you, right, but it was for us. Sure."

"Are you sure, Luke?"

"Cmon, Joe, what is this?"

"You know goddamn well what it is," Joe exploded, his anger in the open now. "Three days now I've been carrying all the weight and you know it. And you're acting like a scared rabbit. We aren't exactly brothers, I realize that, but I always figured I could trust you."

Luke started to say something but stopped himself.

"I'd still like to think I can, Luke. But you talk like a guy that's getting ready to jump ship."

"Hey, I didn't mean anything, Joe."

"Yeah, I know you didn't. But maybe you'd handle yourself a little better if you didn't have to spend so much time sweating how deep you're into this thing."

With a sudden movement he leaned forward, his right hand stretching across the seat and up under the dash where it groped blindly for a moment until it found Danzie's thick envelope in the hiding place where he had taped it. The two Band-Aids he had used to fasten it dangled incongruously, advertising, if either of them had been able to see it at that moment, the makeshift quality that had characterized all their moves.

"Half this trouble is yours," he said, counting out the money—four thousand dollars—and then recounting it into halves.

A block and a half away, two of the federal agents who had been tailing Joe and Luke ever since they took the money from Danzie were watching through binoculars. They could see the bills in Joe's hand.

"Now you know where you stand," Joe said, handing half of the money to his partner.

Luke said nothing. He accepted the thin wad of bills, folded it once, and slid it into his pocket.

Joe was smiling. "Besides," he laughed, "nothing's gonna go wrong. What was it you said Danzie said in Washington? He wouldn't hand up any Italians?"

As Joe stuffed the remaining bills back into the envelope and slipped it into his breast pocket, the two federal agents were already jotting the time and place of the split in their pocket memo books.

For two weeks Joe and Luke heard nothing from Carlo Danzie. Both of them filed periodic reports about fictitious meetings with their informant, but, except for brief discussions to coordinate their lies, they never mentioned the case at all. Two weeks, of course, should barely have been enough time to start getting nervous, since they had promised Danzie he could have that long. But once he was gone, time started to move in funny ways for the two detectives.

"Joe tried to hide it," Luke recalls, "but I could tell he was impatient right from the start. Like when you're waiting for someone you know is gonna be late. He had this way when things bothered him, he'd just run around like crazy all the time. I don't mean crazy, really, but active—the way we talk about an active cop. When a guy in the job tells you someone's an active cop it means that's a person that really breaks his ass, makes cases, a guy who's all over the place. Now Joe was like that all the time. But when something was eating at him it was twice as much. He was a whole fucking squad all by himself.

"I remember we took that Friday off, the day after that business with Danzie in the restaurant. And then there was the weekend. But Sunday he calls me from his mother's house about this case we're working on. So I met him and we went to see these guys. It doesn't matter who, they were guys we were working on. We were setting up a buy I was gonna make. And from then on it was, believe me, it was nonstop. We made the buy, we made, God, I don't know how many cases. Just in those two weeks. I almost felt like saying to him, Christ, Joe, if you don't ease up there's not gonna be any traffic left by the time Carlo gets back.

"Well, that was Joe. Impatient, you know what I mean? And I was just the opposite. If it wasn't for Joe I don't think I could have done a thing. I mean I was just plain scared, or maybe confused is a better word. Like I had no idea where we stood and I couldn't see how the whole thing was gonna end. To be perfectly frank, it wasn't the money that bothered me, not after the first few days. I had myself so I was one hundred percent convinced there was no way that could hurt us. It was just something we had to do to set the guy up, anybody could see that. Because if you don't believe that, you gotta believe we were stupid enough to take four gees off a stool that works for Anthony Diamond. And nobody was ever that stupid.

"So if it wasn't the money, what was it? Well, the reports had a lot to do with it. In the back of my mind I guess I knew Carlo wasn't coming back. So how long were we gonna keep jerking ourselves off, writing down that we're seeing him, he's making promises, all the bullshit things we're putting in those damn reports? The whole thing was such a mess, at least that's how it looked to me. And I can't handle that kind of situation. With Joe, he's in his element, he liked things complicated. But with me, like I said, if it wasn't for him I would have been about paralyzed.

"Then, on this Thursday [March 2]—I remember it because it was exactly two weeks to the day from when we saw Carlo that last time —Marcus calls me into his office, says we're not getting anywhere with Danzie and we gotta bring him in. Well, I know there's no way we can bring him, but I can't tell the captain that. I try telling him it's Joe's case and he should talk to Joe about it. But he's not listening. So I tell him we'll do what we can but we don't know where Danzie's living—which was the truth, I mean even when we had him it was the truth—and we'll have to wait for him to get in touch with us.

"Now I don't have to tell you, that talk with Marcus just about destroyed me. And at the time I couldn't figure out why he wanted to tell it to me instead of Joe, since he knew perfectly well it was Joe's case. But of course I understand it now. They just wanted to shake us up, and they must've figured I'd be easier to shake than Joe. In a way they were right, too, because I did get all excited, and I did get on Joe and we put in a couple of calls to Milan and all that. And maybe everything that happened afterwards wouldn't have happened if I was a little cooler. But in a way they were wrong, because when the whole thing was over they did shake the shit out of me but at least I came through it. I came through it and Joe didn't.

"I don't know, maybe that doesn't tell you anything. But if you thought about it at all, even for just a minute, and if you had any idea what Joe was like, then I think you could figure out what this thing was gonna do to him. When they fuck over a guy like me they mess up my life, they throw me out of the job—sure. But Joe was a guy who had all his chips down on every bet, so there was no way he could come out of a thing like this. When they set him up they killed him, it's as simple as that. And if you ask me, I think they knew it. I think they knew all along how it had to end. I really believe that."

The first weekend in March was filled with that almost unbearable tension that is possible only when nothing is happening. Curiously, at this stage the pressure affected Joe more than it did Luke, who readily admits that he would have been perfectly satisfied just then if Carlo Danzie had stayed in Milan or Beirut forever.

Joe, though, still wanted the case—wanted it all the more desperately for all the chances he had taken. He knew his partner was right in fearing that if Danzie got picked up trying to sneak back into the country, he might try to buy his way out of trouble by turning state's evidence on the two cops he had "bribed" in New York. Then it would all be over—not just the case, but everything. It would be the end of the job, possibly even jail. Because in the overheated atmosphere of the early seventies, when police corruption was the most explosive political issue in New York and men like Frank Serpico were selling their stories to the movies, who would believe a couple of cops who claimed that they took money from a drug trafficker in order to get a better grip on him? Especially when those cops were filing fraudulent reports to cover the fact that they had given the arrested drug dealer permission to leave the country.

For four agonizing days Joe lived with the realization that an informant about whom he knew practically nothing could destroy him utterly, could obliterate his career and bring disgrace on himself and his family if his reading of the situation told him that was his best shot.

But, given the risk, what were the choices? Luke wanted Joe to tell Captain Marcus straight out that they had lost contact with Danzie. He should ask for more time and then leave it up to the captain. Whether Marcus went along with the request or not, Joe and Luke would be off the hook. The trouble with that idea, as far as Joe was concerned, was that Marcus, who didn't seem to have much confidence in Danzie as an informant, wouldn't approve. He'd write the whole thing off by putting out a fugitive warrant, and once Danzie learned that he was wanted, he'd never return. He would simply disappear, and with him would go the last chance to make the hundred kilo collars he had been promising for over a month.

The gamble, then, was glory or disgrace—and the choice was Joe's. Or at least he thought it was, sweating it as he had sweated no other decision in his life. The irony, of course, in a story so filled with ironies that virtually nothing is what it seems to be and the actors all play many roles—the irony is that the choice had already been made and Joe didn't know it. While he was figuring the odds on whether or not Danzie would betray him, it never dawned on him that Danzie had betrayed him already, had betrayed him from the start—indeed, had had no motive during their entire relationship other than entrapment and betrayal.

At his mother's house Sunday afternoon Joe was moody and withdrawn, and on the drive home he evaded Jeannie's questions about what was troubling him. He pulled to a stop in the driveway and sat motionless behind the wheel as Joey and Marie tumbled from the back seat and raced for the kitchen door, their hard-soled Sunday shoes crunching the gravel and then clattering up the steps.

"Aren't you coming in?" Jeannie asked, not moving from her place beside him on the front seat.

"I think I'll go for a drive," he said.

The children waited at the door for someone to unlock it.

"Would it help to talk about it?" she asked. "I can send the kids next door. We'll have the house to ourselves."

Her voice was soft and coaxing, but the problem concerned him so intimately that he couldn't let her in on the decision. "They're waiting for you," he said with deliberate coldness, forcing himself to send her away. "Maybe later."

He watched until they were all in the house and then backed the car into the street. Without knowing why, he retraced the path he had taken on the morning he picked up Danzie at the Holiday Inn near La Guardia. Again he took the expressways from one airport to the other, and when he found himself approaching Kennedy he pulled off on the seldom used side road that led to the north terminal. He stopped at exactly the spot where Danzie had made his first veiled reference to "some other consideration," and there he went over the whole thing for what felt like the thousandth time.

This time, though, conflicting streams of thought wove back and forth in his consciousness like a radio picking up two stations at once. For the first time in a dozen years he thought about those ten uncomfortable months he had spent working for his father after he got out of the army. Suddenly it puzzled him that his brothers took to it so naturally while he was unable to fit in at all. Surely this indicated some fault in his character, some pride or vanity that unsuited him for the place in the business his father had been saving for him from the hour he was born.

No, that wasn't it, he told himself in his own defense. If Pappa every so often let something slip that hinted at his disappointment, at least Mamma didn't feel that way at all. She was unmistakably proud of the fact that her last-born wore a suit to work and didn't have the smell of pipe calking on his hands. Of all her sons, Joe, her baby, was her hero. He had been the biggest and the handsomest and the smartest child at Saint Vincent de Paul's, the best athlete in the whole archdiocese. And when it troubled her that her son wanted nothing more than to play ball after he finished high school, the priest had put her mind at ease by promising that he would be another Joe DiMaggio. Then she could accept it, because it promised so much more than her husband's dreams of someday handing a share of the business over to him.

Not that she had any complaints about her husband's business, for he had done well by his family. But it wasn't for this, to have a grandson in the plumbing business, that her own parents had sold the farm at Portomaggiore and moved to America.

So she could understand why Joe couldn't be content to be just another cop, any more than he could be just another plumber, just another one of the Longo boys. And so could Jeannie understand— although perhaps understand was too strong a word. She accepted the kind of man her husband was, had learned to live with his restlessness and his ambition, and gave this side of him her support though not her sympathy.

And the children—what did he owe them in this decision? Joey, who liked telling the other boys that his daddy was a detective, and Marie? On more than one occasion Joe had risked his life on the job and never once had he hesitated for even a fraction of a second because of thoughts of them. It never occurred to him that perhaps he hadn't the right to let himself get shot, and he never asked what would happen to them afterward. If it had to be that his children would get only the memories of a hero's funeral and the benefits of a line-of-duty pension, then it would have to be.

But this was different because the stakes were so much higher than death. If he was wrong on Danzie it would mean the worst kind of disgrace he could imagine, and they would have to live with the fact that their father was branded a crooked cop. Could he chance it on their account?

Even before he could answer the question, if indeed it could ever be answered, he interrupted himself with a new thought. Danzie wouldn't come back if it was just going to be more promises. Ever since he had been arrested in February he had done nothing but string them along with all his talk about the "difficulties" he was having. So if he came back now it meant he was ready to go to work. Unless he had something solid to deliver, he would stay where he was.

But what about the kids?

It wouldn't come to that, Joe reassured himself. It was going to work out.

Chapter 10
Stakeout

Joe PUSHED THROUGH the door into the Joint Task Force squad room and stopped just on the other side, his green eyes quickly scanning from desk to desk. "Luke," he called, motioning with his left hand for his partner to join him in the corridor.

"Yeah, what's up?" Antonelli asked boyishly, responding to the look of pure satisfaction on Joe's face.

"He's back, that's what up," Joe answered.

It was Friday, March 10, three weeks and one day after the final meeting with Danzie at Little John's.

"No shit. What'd he say?"

"Didn't say anything. I was on Seventh around Times Square and I saw him on the other side of Broadway. By the time I could get out of the car and get over there he was gone. I think he went down Forty-third."

Antonelli's face dropped. On Monday they had called Milan and a woman answered at the number Danzie had given them. She said she would give him the message. The next night Danzie had called Joe at home.

"I am sorry I could not return your call," he had said. "I was in Genoa on our business. I arrived just this moment and my wife informs me you have been trying to contact me. Are there difficulties?"

"Yeah, I think so," Joe had said. "I'm getting a lot of heat here. You gotta come back."

"But that is impossible," Danzie had protested. "The arrangements are incomplete. I require only until the weekend."

"Can't do it, Carlo. There's only so long I can hold them off."

"I will return on Monday," Danzie had persisted. "I am making arrangements to ship two hundred and fifty of those watches our friends wanted to buy. When I see you I will give you all the information you require for your transaction with them."

Involuntarily, Joe had gasped at the number. "American watches or European?" he had asked.

"American. Two hundred and fifty American watches."

Of course. Two hundred fifty kilos was too much to hope for, impossible really. No one dealt that big. But two hundred fifty pounds was still over a hundred ten kilos, which would make it easily the biggest seizure since the French Connection case.

Pressing the heel of his hand against his eyeballs to ease the pressure he suddenly felt there, Joe had said, "Look, Carlo, I'll tell you how it is. Things are falling apart at this end. I can't keep telling them I'm seeing you because they're gonna tell me I've got to bring you in. I'll stall them off as long as I can but I can't promise anything. Take care of what you have to and get back here. Tomorrow if you can, Thursday, Friday at the latest. By next week the whole thing's gonna blow up."

"I am not meeting the man with the watches until Sunday."

"Make it tonight, tomorrow. Call him, tell him whatever you have to, but make it sooner."

"He is a cautious man, Joe," Danzie had explained. "If there is pressure he will withdraw."

There was no denying the validity of Danzie's argument. Anything that didn't smell right—too much urgency or not enough, a telltale impatience or an equally telltale lack of it—would scare off a top-level narcotics dealer as surely as a footstep spooks a deer.

"That's your problem, Carlo," Joe had said, his voice cold and commanding. "You'll know how to handle it. Just make the fucking deal, that's all. Make it and make it fast." Then he hung up the phone.

That was on Tuesday. Now, three days later, Danzie had returned.

"I don't get it," Luke was saying. "Did he set up the deal or didn't he?"

"Can't tell you what I don't know," Joe answered with the air of casualness he always adopted to conceal his own doubts. "I don't know what he's up to, but I don't figure he came back just so we could lock him up."

"Yeah?" Luke challenged. "Then how come he didn't get in touch with you?"

"Maybe his plane just landed."

"In Times Square?"

The door to the squad room swung open, catching Antonelli in the back.

"You okay?" Jeff Stallard asked, grabbing the door on the backswing and sidling into the corridor. He was the young detective who had been in the squad room when the tip from Patrigno came in and he had gone along to make the collar in the Americana.

"Sure, my fault," Luke apologized, turning back to Joe, who pointedly said nothing.

"My interrupting something?" Stallard asked lightly.

There was an awkward moment of silence and then Joe said, "Next time knock when you wanna come out."

Stallard laughed and walked down the corridor to the elevator. When the doors slid closed behind him, Luke said, "So what do we do now?"

Joe parried the question with one of his own. "You still got that present I gave you?" he asked.

"In the car. Why?"

"Gimme the keys, I gotta go somewhere."

Luke groped in his pocket for the keys, handing them to his partner but not releasing his hold on them for a few seconds. "It's under the spare tire," he said. "What're you gonna do?"

"What do you think I'm gonna do? I'm gonna find him."

"Yeah, okay." Then he added, as an afterthought, "I'll go with you."

Joe turned toward the elevators, rejecting the offer. "You make me nervous," he said.

Taking the steps two at a time, Joe bounded to the third-floor landing and paused a moment to get his breath before knocking. He waited, listening at the door, then knocked again. From inside he could hear footsteps scraping across the uncarpeted living room toward him.

"Who is it?" a man's voice asked as the door opened.

He was tall, over six feet, with a bony, angular face and deep-set dark eyes that threw back the glaring light of the naked bulb in the landing fixture. His long hair was uncombed and he wore the plaid wool shirt Mickie Lang had been wearing the day Joe and Luke came to question her.

"Yes?" the tall man asked, the faintest trace of a drawl discernible in the way he stretched out the syllable. His left hand, which had been gripping the door frame at shoulder level, dropped to his side and he stepped back a tiny quarter step, either to invite Joe in or to put some distance between them. Joe couldn't tell which.

"I'm looking for Mickie Lang," he said.

The man said nothing, but he turned his head slightly so that the light from the bulb no longer caught his eyes.

"Is she here?"

"No."

"But she does live here?"

"Yes." His voice betrayed annoyance at the questioning.

"When do you expect her?"

"I don't know. She—" He broke off in mid sentence, seemed about to say something else, then decided against it.

"Do you know where I can find her?" Joe asked. When there was no immediate answer, he added, "It's important."

The man seemed to be considering the situation. He looked at Joe fixedly, sizing him up. Finally he asked, "Who are you?"

Without even thinking about it, Joe rejected the opportunity to identify himself as a cop. "Joe Longo," he said.

The man considered the name a moment, trying to gauge whether it meant anything to him. When he decided it didn't, his left hand, which had been hanging loosely by his side, came up again to twist nervously at a shirt button on his chest, the way a girl twirls her hair between her fingers. He was still standing half behind the door, the knuckles of his right hand gripping it backhanded just inches from his face. He cocked his head slightly to the side until his cheek rested against his fingers. "She's at unemployment," he said. "Do you want to come in?"

"No thanks. I'll find her."

The man nodded slowly. "Do you know where it is?" he asked.

"I can find it."

Joe turned to leave but stopped at the top step as he saw the man step back from the door and swing it open.

"My name is Roy," he called. "Are you sure you don't want to come in? You can wait here."

Joe hurried down the steps without answering. When he reached street level he heard the apartment door close above him.

Three-quarters of the wide, low-ceilinged room were filled with row after row of gray folding chairs. Mickie Lang sat slightly toward the front, close to the bank of desks where applicants were interviewed. Around her was a swarm of bored and tired-looking people, sullenly waiting for their names to be called.

Joe threaded his way to her and waited until she noticed him standing over her.

"Joe!" she exclaimed. "How did you—?"

"Cmon," he cut her off. "We've gotta talk."

"I can't. I'll lose my place."

He didn't say anything.

"You met Roy?" she asked, only half phrasing it as a question. There was no other way he could have found her.

"I met Roy."

She nodded, registering the fact but unable to infer any judgment from his intonation. "I've been here over an hour," she said. "Can't it wait?"

"No."

She rose slowly, in unconcealed protest, pushing past him into a small clearing that was all that was left of what earlier that morning had been an aisle down the center of the room. He followed her to the door and then down the three flights of steep stairs to Thirty-fourth Street. "Where to?" she asked on the sidewalk.

"Here's good enough," he said coldly. "Where's Danzie?"

Her voice expressed her surprise. "Is that what this is all about?" she snapped. "I haven't seen him in weeks."

"But you heard from him?"

"Not a word. Really."

Joe didn't say anything.

"Don't believe me if you don't want," she said bitterly. "I'm going back upstairs."

As she turned away from him, he reached for her slender arm and caught it, spinning her upper body back until she faced him. But her feet seemed rooted in the pavement and her hips pivoted only slightly, for she had committed herself to walking away from him. He realized it immediately and let go.

"I've got to find him," he said.

Now she turned to face him, moved by the urgency in his voice. She looked straight into his clear green eyes and saw something there that overrode her resentment and compelled her to answer him. "I don't know where he's staying and I never did," she said. "That's the truth. But he gave me a phone number before he went away. Maybe it's still good. Do you want it?"

"Please."

"It's from before he went away," she repeated, apologizing in advance in case it should turn out to be worthless.

For a few seconds she fished through her pockets for an address book, but when she realized she didn't have it with her she recited the number from memory, half expecting a comment from Joe. If he noticed, though, he gave no sign that it meant anything to him.

He repeated the number once but didn't write it down. "Take care," he said, trying to put some warmth in his voice.

She watched as he walked away from her, down Thirty-fourth toward Herald Square. "Bastard," she said softly, when he was too far away to hear.

Christina James worked on the eighth floor of the telephone company's windowless office tower on Tenth Avenue. Forty-three years old, she dyed her hair a different color every month, trying always to find the brilliant red it had been when she was half that age.

Hardly a detective in Manhattan didn't know Christina, who liked cops and made it her personal policy to pass out information that telephone company policy said couldn't be circulated without a court order or, at the very least, a mass of paper work.

"What's the chance of getting a favor in a hurry?" Joe asked, the brusque words combining with the bantering tone to give the precise combination that was so necessary for Christina's fantasies.

"Anything for you, Joe," she answered coyly. "What is it?" She looked up from her desk and smiled garishly. Her lips were thin and painted like a puppet's.

"I've got a number, I wanna know where it is."

"Nothing easier. Unlisted, I suppose?"

"I guess so."

She took down the number on a tiny desk pad and sauntered across the wide office to a set of swinging doors that led to a file room. Joe rested a hip on the corner of her desk and slid a cigarette from his pocket while he waited. He had to borrow an ashtray from a neighboring desk.

Ten minutes passed before Christina returned with the two-by-five slip of paper still in her hand. When she put it down on the desk Joe could see there was nothing written on it except the number he had given her.

"What's the problem?" he asked.

"There's no problem," she said evasively, looking down at the scrap of paper and adjusting it on her blotter. She picked up a pen. "You don't know who this phone's listed to?" she asked.

"Yeah, I think I do. You sure there's no problem?"

"No, of course not," she said, still looking down. "Could you give me the party's name?"

For a moment he felt the automatic racing of his pulses that he always felt when something happened the way it wasn't supposed to. For as long as he had been on the job, you told Christina what you wanted to know and she came back with the answer. "Carlo Danzie," he said. "D-a-n-z-i-e."

She nodded and wrote. "I'll just be another minute," she said, standing again. "Sorry, Joe."

"Take your time."

This time she was gone almost twenty minutes. Then she pushed through the double doors from the filing room and paused for a moment to smooth her skirt before walking back to Joe. "I'm sorry," she said. "There was a mix-up in the files."

Her casual explanation cooled Joe's smouldering nerves—although later, of course, he began to wonder whether she had been telling the truth, even trying to warn him. "No problem," he said, straining to be pleasant. "What've you got?"

"Four eighty-five East Forty-sixth Street. Apartment Sixteen D."

Some neighborhood, he thought, mentally locating the address on his internal map of the city. He didn't know the building by number but he accurately identified it as one of the exclusive apartment houses near the U.N. "Thanks," he said. "Be seeing you."

"Joe," she called after him, her voice soft and tentative, as though she wasn't sure she wanted him to hear her.

"Yeah?" He turned to face her.

She hesitated, seemed to stammer. "Uh, nothing. Just take care of yourself, that's all."

He smiled awkwardly, not understanding. "Sure," he said. "You know me."

She nodded. "Just take care of yourself," she repeated as he reached for the door. "And don't be such a stranger."

For the second time in six months, Joe called Juan Piedra. He and Joe had worked together on a number of occasions when Joe was in the Special Investigations Unit, but when Joe transferred out at the end of 1970 he cut all ties with the men who remained in the unit.

But in the late summer of 1971, when Joe wanted to put a cheater on Jake Meredith, he had called "Johnny." A wizard with electronics, Piedra had his own private warehouse of the latest surveillance hardware in the basement of the brownstone he shared with two families of cousins on the Upper East Side. Not only did he use it himself for the hot wires he maintained on practically all his cases, but he loaned it out liberally to other narcotics investigators—both cops and agents.

Piedra, incidentally, had one of the most unusual careers in Police Department history. A Nicaraguan by birth, he dropped out of a pre-law program at City College to join the Police Force, then was pulled from the Academy before graduation and given a special assignment as an infiltrator of the tiny Spanish-speaking radical movement at Columbia University. Posing as a transfer student from the University of Managua, he quickly established his credibility as a staunch Castroite and rose to a leadership position in the movement. His contacts soon extended down from Morningside Heights into Harlem and Spanish Harlem, where he was well known and trusted in militant black circles and in the Puerto Rican separatist movement.

He stayed under cover for about a year and a half, then was sent back to the Academy to complete his training as a police officer. In a remarkably short time he was appointed to the Detective Bureau, winning his gold shield at the unprecedented age of twenty-three. By the middle of 1967 he had worked his way onto the elite Special Investigations Unit, the youngest man in an all-star outfit that boasted some of New York's most famous detectives. Eddie Egan and Sonny Grosso, who had made the French Connection case, were still there, although they would be leaving before the end of the year. And the others were all cut from the same mold—old-school detectives, freewheeling, independent, knowledgeable, and tough. Joe Longo and Dave McGibbon, Ernie Blake and Russ Vernon, were the most active cops on the scene, and soon Piedra was working with them.

Then, somewhere along the line, he got turned around. There are no reliable accounts of how it happened or when. According to one rumor, he was caught holding on to a considerable portion of the fruits of a two-hundred-pound coke bust. But reliable insiders speculate that he was actually an undercover operative for the Internal Affairs Division from the moment he was appointed to the Detective Bureau—a contention that is given some support by the unusual pattern of his career and by the fact that such a role would not have been inconsistent with what is known about him. His premature removal from the Academy cut him off from the normal avenues of socialization which, for better or worse, elevate loyalty to fellow cops into the most binding commandment in the police officer's catechism. What is more, his first police experience was as an infiltrator and double agent who had to develop friendships for the purpose of betraying them. Not all men are capable of such activity, but those who are may be capable of doing it again. Thus Piedra may well have lacked the normal resistance to the idea of joining a squad of detectives in order to spy on his fellow officers.

In any case, it is now known that by 1974 Juan Piedra was working for Internal Affairs, either as a matter of choice or necessity. Whether he was already playing a double role in March of 1972 must remain an open question. But if he was, it would explain how the Internal Affairs Division of the Police Department learned almost immediately that Joe Longo had installed an illegal wiretap in the basement of 485 East Forty-sixth Street.

"Any time," Juan Piedra said lightly in response to Joe's thanks. They were standing on First Avenue as the early waves of the

Friday evening rush-hour traffic washed past them. "You need anyone to help you with the plant?" he asked.

"I can handle it," Joe said, already impatient to be rid of Piedra. Over the long weekend ahead there were going to be times when he would be glad enough for someone to talk to, but it was still too early for that.

"Okay," Piedra said. "You know how to reach me." He turned to walk away, then stopped himself. "You still with the same partner?"

"Why?"

"The guy who made you take out the wire we put in last summer?"

"He didn't make me take it out," Joe snapped defensively. "We weren't getting shit on it."

Piedra shrugged. "No skin off my ass, Joe," he said. "Take care."

Joe watched Johnny drive off, then hurried around the corner onto Forty-sixth and into the Diplomat, past the doorman, who stifled an instinct to nod a greeting. Only a few hours earlier Joe had given him ten bucks for access to the phone pairs in the basement.

Walking to the elevator at the far end of the ornate and richly furnished lobby, Joe punched one of the lower floor buttons at random and rode up alone. On the way up he noticed that the numbering started in the European style with the first floor above the lobby and that there was no thirteenth floor. He got out when the door opened and walked down the carpeted corridor until he reached apartment D. A few yards past it was a heavy steel door leading to a fire stair. He pushed through it and walked directly to the window on the landing, which he lowered enough to look through and get his bearings. Then, satisfied that he would be able to locate the D apartment line from the street, he retraced his steps back through the lobby.

Out on Forty-sixth Street, he stopped long enough to calculate the best place for him to position himself. From Forty-sixth he would be able to watch both the main entrance and the garage entrance almost forty yards to the west. But Danzie's windows were on the east face of the building, overlooking First Avenue. Unless he stood directly on the corner, where he would be in plain view, it wouldn't be possible to keep both entrances and the windows in sight.

Quickly assessing the possibilities, he decided that the windows were more important than the garage entrance, which Danzie probably wouldn't use in any case. With no one to help him on the stakeout, he had to be prepared for the fact that Danzie might be able to slip in unnoticed, during a moment of inattention. But it was already turning dark, so he knew that even if he missed Danzie at the door, he could watch for a light in the window to tell him if anyone was inside the apartment.

Joe hurried to his car, which he had left on the west side of First a few yards down from Forty-sixth. He took the Police Department card from the dashboard and slipped it into the glove compartment, then started the engine and circled the block quickly. The east side of the avenue would give him a better angle of vision and it was easier to drive around the block than to try cutting straight across four lanes of clotted traffic. Ten minutes later he killed the engine and settled in for what he knew was going to be a long wait. Counting up from the first floor and across from the fire stairs window, he located Danzie's apartment, then lit a cigarette and tried to clear his mind.

As the cold darkness of an early March night lowered onto the city, Danzie's windows slowly blackened until at full nightfall they were the only unlit panes on the top three floors. From where Joe was sitting he could just barely see around the corner to the main lobby entrance at street level, but he had a good view of the windows and was satisfied with the vantage point he had chosen. If he had had to say, he would have put the chances of Danzie's actually showing up at no better than fifty-fifty, but figuring like that never did any good. You did what you had to do, which in this case meant staking out a longshot. If he had known anyplace else to look for Danzie, he would have gone there—but he didn't.

As he waited, the traffic thinned out and picked up speed, taxis moving swiftly with the staggered lights, private cars ambling the avenue with lackadaisical carelessness. Toward midnight the volume increased again as cars lined the even-numbered streets to his left, waiting for the lights to give them permission to pour on to the avenue. Once a cruiser, moving slowly, pulled alongside. The cop in the passenger seat studied Joe brazenly, trying to decide if this was worth stopping for. Joe nodded and smiled but succeeded only in provoking the cop to turn and say something to his partner. When the patrol car pulled to a full stop Joe slid his gold detective's shield from his pocket and held it up in the open window. The blue-and-white cruiser drove on.

Joe watched it go. Then, noticing the cold for the first time, he rolled up the window and started the engine, which idled roughly for a few minutes as it labored to catch the right rhythm. He found himself wondering whether the cruiser would come back and made a mental bet with himself that it wouldn't. Almost against his will, a chain of associations dragged through his mind and he found himself asking the same question about Carlo Danzie. Would he come back?

Not to New York—that had been last week's question, but the chance glimpse of him earlier this morning in Times Square settled that. If, in fact, it was Danzie he had seen. He had had the man in sight for only a few seconds and at a considerable distance. It could have been just an anonymous New Yorker transformed by Joe's imagination into the Milanese dope dealer he wanted to see. Was his mind playing tricks on him? No—that thick black hair, those rolling bearlike strides, that fleetingly seen figure shouldering its way through the Times Square crowd, coatless in the March cold—it had to be Danzie, had to be because Joe insisted on it. Danzie was in New York, no two ways about it. But would he come back to the Diplomat? The fact that the phone was still listed in his name didn't necessarily mean anything.

And what was he up to? Joe couldn't be sure, but it had all the earmarks of a double bang. That was the way with stool pigeons and always would be. They stalled for time and tried to maneuver for room. Like the time Terry Dupuis said he needed three days to go to Toledo and set up a deal. But the next day Joe saw him in a shooting gallery off Lenox. Or the time Joe and McGibbon actually put Bobby Lopes on a plane to the coast and then decided to stick around the airport on a hunch that paid off when Lopes got off the plane just before the doors closed. They tailed him and broke up a deal that Lopes told them wouldn't go down until after he got back from L.A.

Now Danzie was probably playing the same game. Says he'll be back on Monday but slips in on Friday. The deal goes down, say, over the weekend, and by Monday, when Joe starts looking for him, it's all wrapped up and he's gone. Or maybe he's not gone. Maybe he calls with the same horseshit story, some more of his jerkoff "difficulties." Either way, the fact that he said he'd be back Monday and was back already pointed to one thing. It was going down before Monday.

The bitch of it was that Danzie was probably too cute to use the same apartment. When he left he knew that Joe had no idea where he had been staying, but he also knew that the girl had his phone number and that Joe knew how to get to the girl. Which meant that Joe could find out about the apartment at the Diplomat if he wanted to. A man as cagey as Danzie probably wouldn't want to take that chance. *Give him credit,* Joe thought with a mixture of self-pity and admiration. *He's got me tapping a phone no one's gonna use and staking out an empty apartment.*

He smiled bitterly to himself and began the tedious process of reliving the month and a half he had already put in on the Danzie case, the chances he had taken, the fights he had had with the bosses just to keep control of the guy. He felt first a tightening in his throat and chest, and then an almost physical sickness in his gut that told him he had been played for a sucker. Somewhere, probably right now, the deal he had staked his hopes on was going down while he was powerless to stop it. For some reason the comparison that came to his mind was the scene in *Mr. Roberts* where Henry Fonda hears that the war just ended in Europe and he's suddenly afraid the one in the Pacific will also end without him.

The sharp hiss of a street sweeper brought Joe back from his reverie. In the predawn stillness he watched the high, boxlike truck roll toward him in his rearview mirror, its giant front brushes churning the debris. Its driver veered around Joe's car, the only one on the avenue, and glared down through the open window with an unmistakably communicative expression on his sleepy gray face. It seemed to Joe an unnatural hour for cleaning the streets but he understood why his presence there was offensive to the sweeper, who must have expected the streets to be his alone at this hour. For a moment Joe felt like an intruder, but then a slow, rolling wave of melancholy sentimentality washed over him, for it is always easy, toward morning, to imagine that there is a bond of brotherhood joining all those who work for the city before it gets up, who clean it and police it and carry it its food, the night clerks and night cooks and night haulers, the five-in-the-morning hookers and the cops on twelve-to-eight.

Brotherhood or not, the machine lumbered indifferently away, leaving a slick path around Joe's car like a worm trail on dry earth. Because its departure seemed to mark a measuring point in an otherwise vacant expanse of time, Joe felt entitled to check his watch. *Twenty past six,* he thought, articulating the words in his mind and nodding as though his watch had confirmed something he was already thinking. It was a time now to be alert, to keep the building entrance and the apartment windows both in view. The sun would be coming up over the East River, lighting the whole front of the tower, so that if Danzie came in now he wouldn't have to turn on the lights. And it was a good time for him to come in, Joe thought, his hopes reviving. At a certain point in the night he had known Carlo wouldn't show, but had stayed anyway. Now he could feel that the possibility had distinctly returned.

At seven o'clock a team of six black men in coveralls began running flags up the poles in the U.N. plaza. They worked quickly, in two-man teams, one man holding the cardboard box with the folded flags at waist level while the other attached the clips and worked the lanyards. Like butterflies struggling from their cramped cocoons, each crumpled flag rose clear of its box before shaking itself free in the morning breeze. In less than twenty minutes the men were gone, having accomplished with their brief and furtive ceremony a total transformation of the terraced plaza.

Drawing his eyes from the flags in his rearview mirror, Joe forced himself to concentrate on the front door of the Diplomat. He decided he would wait until eight o'clock and then call Mickie Lang on the chance that Carlo had spent the night with her. Not likely, but it was worth checking. He counted on being able to tell if she was lying.

The phone rang only once, and when Jeannie picked it up in the kitchen the first thing she said was, "Joe?"

He laughed. "Who'd you expect?" he asked. It was a joke between them to hide the fact that they both knew that she half expected the same thing every cop's wife expects when the phone rings in an empty house in the morning.

"You're okay," she said, not as a question.

"Sure. Just wanted to check in."

"Okay," she said flatly, her sense of relief already giving way to annoyance.

"The kids up?" he asked.

"Joey is. I heard him in the bathroom."

The mention of Joey reminded him of something and there was a moment of awkward silence as he tried to remember what it was. "Just wanted to check in," he repeated foolishly, simply to have something to say.

"Will you be home this afternoon?" Jeannie asked.

"If I can."

"I suppose you forgot about Joey," she said. "You were supposed to take him to get his suit."

"I didn't forget," he said, but he had. "I'll be there as soon as I can."

She knew what that meant. "It'll have to be altered," she said, "and Easter's just three weeks. You know how slow they are this time of year, Joe."

"You wanna take him, take him," he said, cutting her off. "I said I'll try to be there, what else can I tell you?"

"Nothing else," she answered, keeping her anger under control. "He doesn't have a suit that fits, that's all."

"So you take him."

He hadn't called for a fight, so when she didn't say anything he said, "I'm sorry, Jeannie. It can't be helped."

Her anger vanished instantly and she said, "I'm sorry, too, Joe. If we're out when you come home, try and get some sleep."

He held the receiver to his ear and waited until she hung up. Then he clicked the lever in the phone cradle and the dial tone returned immediately. He dropped in the dime he had been holding in his hand and dialed Mickie Lang's number.

She answered the phone herself, her voice thick and sleepy but turning to ice the moment she recognized Joe. But he believed her when she said she hadn't heard from Danzie. Even before he left the phone booth it was clear to him that he could never call her again.

He walked slowly back to the car and settled into the front seat. Somehow, in that moment of aching fatigue, he jumbled the two phone calls in his mind and felt an uncontrollable shiver run down his back that he couldn't quite recognize as loneliness. Yet he felt inexpressibly cut off from everyone, frustrated, bitter, and desperately without any control over a situation that was supposed to have been the most beautiful case he had ever made.

He sat in utter passivity, letting the hours pile up, unmarked except for the twisted cigarette butts that collected in the dashboard ashtray. Mickie Lang had rolled onto her stomach but couldn't get back to sleep after she hung up the phone. On Long Island Jeannie had showered and dressed and taken Joey to a shop in Bay Ridge where they picked out the Easter suit that he wouldn't be allowed to save for Easter. He had to wear it on Good Friday to his father's funeral.

Chapter 11
The Plant

LIKE A MAN lost in the desert who must carefully limit his intake of water when he is found, Joe didn't want to allow himself more than a few hours of sleep. After almost sixty-five hours alone on a fruitless stakeout, he was weary beyond anything he had ever felt in his life. His clothes clung to his body like tightly wrapped bandages and his head ached with a stinging numbness that wasn't helped any by his bitter awareness that Carlo Danzie had outmaneuvered him.

By Sunday, in fact, he had known, without consciously admitting it to himself, that Danzie wasn't going to show, but by that time he didn't have left even enough strength of will to give up. So he sat through another agonizing night, telling himself that if Carlo had been too cagey to use the apartment at the Diplomat before the deal went down, perhaps he would get careless after it was all over. At that point Joe would have settled for a chance just to get his hands on that double-crossing weasel of a dope dealer.

The sun rose brilliantly on Monday morning, glowing at first like peach neon before it cleared the Brooklyn skyline. Soon First Avenue was a harsh pattern of vivid light and sharp angular shadows that seemed to dance like a pinwheel in front of Joe's throbbingly sore eyeballs. For a few more hours he sat, kept awake only by his tiredness itself, which was as sharp as pain, and by his anger. At any moment he expected to see, ahead of him on First Avenue or moving eastward on Forty-sixth, the big-chested bold walk of Carlo Danzie. Leaning sideways in the seat, he studied himself for a moment in the rearview mirror, taking a grim amusement from the scene that unfolded before his imagination. Unshaven, his hair thick and clotted on his head, his handsome features swollen into a lumpish puffiness, he would accost the impeccably Continental Danzie right there in the lobby while the alarmed doormen gaped helplessly. He would take him in without listening to a single syllable of his horseshit excuses, and lock him up. Then he would get some sleep.

By noon, though, Joe couldn't stick it out any longer. Without actually deciding to leave, he reached for the ignition key as automatically as he had reached for the cigarette lighter a hundred times over the weekend. The motor shivered on and he snapped the transmission into drive, then pulled out from the curb and cut recklessly across the avenue. At Forty-sixth he didn't even indulge himself in one last look back at the Diplomat, one last check. He turned west on Forty-seventh, then south on Second. It took all his concentration just to get to Varick Street.

At five o'clock Joe rolled over and snapped off the alarm clock on the floor next to his cot. Four and a half hours of almost deathlike sleep had been more than enough and he felt surprisingly refreshed and clear-headed. Only when he tried to get up did his body remind him that it would take somewhat longer for his bones and muscles to recover. His back and shoulders were painfully stiff and both legs ached where he had broken them playing ball.

For twenty minutes Joe stood under a steaming jet of hot water in the shower just off the bunk room, trying to wash the last traces of the weekend from his body. He wrapped a towel around his waist and shaved at the sink, then combed his thick black hair straight back and blotted it with the towel. At his locker he put on fresh underwear and a clean pair of slacks. He always kept a few spare shirts in his desk, so he had to go up to the office to finish dressing.

As he pushed through the swinging door into the squad room he was greeted by a chorus of good-natured jibes. He hadn't seen so many men in the office at one time since they picked up Larry Boston with a million bucks in his car and he wondered what was up.

"Didn't think you'd make it, Joe," Jeff Stallard said. "The way you looked when you came in, we wrote you up as a D.O.A."

"What's her name, Joe? You can tell us," another detective chimed in.

"Where the fuck have you been?" Luke Antonelli asked, the sharp edge of his concern blunted by the general levity in the room.

Joe ignored his partner's question, not wanting to explain until they were alone. "Hey, what's the matter, didn't any of you guys ever have a heavy weekend before?" he said lightly. "What the hell's everyone doing here? We having a party or something?"

A few of the men exchanged puzzled glances and then Bill Kane held up three fingers and said, "How many fingers do you see, Joe?"

"Three."

"Not bad. Do you know where you are?"

"Bellevue."

"Right again. Now let's try a tough one. What day is it?"

"How many guesses do I get?"

"Seven."

"Monday."

Kane shrugged elaborately. "Then we're having a party," he said. "Arch Russell, remember?"

Russell, an assistant prosecutor in the narcotics section of the U.S. attorney's office, was retiring to go into private practice after nine years in the Southern District. The other lawyers in the office were throwing a party for him at Lüchow's on Fourteenth Street and had invited the agents from the Bureau of Narcotics and the members of the Joint Task Force, both agents and cops, to chip in. It was Russell who had induced Luke to waive arraignment on Carlo Danzie the morning after Danzie's arrest.

"Slipped my mind," Joe said. "What time?"

"Eight, but we figured we'd all head over to Puglia's first, scare up some eats."

Leo Wiley, one of the agents, said, "You're coming, aren't you? You look like you could use something."

"Yeah, what he could use is a shirt," Stallard squealed, laughing as he spoke. "It's not that kind of a party."

Joe joined in the laughter and walked to his desk, where he took an old shirt with faded narrow blue stripes from the bottom drawer. The small wardrobe he kept in the office consisted mostly of old clothes he had stopped wearing. "Why don't you guys go ahead, I'll catch up," he said.

Luke said, "I'll ride over with Joe."

When the others had all gone, Luke followed Joe to the staircase and down to the fourth floor. He watched while Joe combed his hair and pulled a necktie from his locker and began knotting it, using the small mirror on the locker door. "What is it, a secret or something?" he finally exploded, exasperated by his partner's silence.

Joe turned to face him. "No," he said flatly. "I just figured you were out of it, that's all."

"What the fuck is that supposed to mean?"

"It means—" He stopped himself in mid sentence, realizing he was being unfair. It had been his decision not to let Luke help him on the stakeout and there was no sense adding now to the distance between them. "It doesn't mean anything, Luke," he said, reaching a hand for the other man's shoulder. It was the only form of apology he would make. "There's not that much to tell," he said.

He knotted the tie quickly and slipped a sport jacket over his broad shoulders, the movement reminding him that the stiffness was still there. "Look at that," he said, indicating where the buttons on the jacket pulled at his waist. "Fucking thing's been hanging here so long it shrunk."

He turned and walked back to the bunk room, talking as he went. "I found out where he was staying," he said. "It's over by the U.N., one of those big apartments on First."

"How'd you find that?"

"The girl."

"So she did know," Luke laughed. "The bitch."

"No, she had a phone number," Joe said. He picked up the wrinkled jacket he had worn over the weekend and went through the pockets, transferring the contents to the jacket he was wearing. In addition to his shield case, his memo book, and a couple of ballpoint pens, there was a white envelope containing the four thousand dollars Danzie had given him. "Anyway, I found the apartment but I didn't find him," he said, gesturing with the envelope, which he then slipped into his breast pocket.

"So, what do you figure?" Luke asked, trying to forget what he had just seen. The mere sight of that envelope was enough to make him feel uneasy, and the loose and casual way Joe handled it actually frightened him.

"I don't figure anything," Joe said. "We got fucked every way there is, that's all."

"You think he's gone again?"

"No, he'll be back," Joe answered with a tone of assurance that his partner found incomprehensible under the circumstances. "But not till after he moves whatever he's got to move. That's his big mistake."

Luke was incredulous. "His mistake?" he challenged. "The guy's making us look like a couple of assholes."

Joe smiled sardonically. "That's the mistake," he said, then added, "Look, I still got, uh, we still got a couple of shots at him he doesn't know about."

Luke wasn't sure he wanted to hear about it.

"First is he hasn't called yet," Joe explained. "Which means it hasn't gone down, which means we still got a chance to catch up with him. See what I mean? As long as we don't hear from him we're still in the ball game. I got a cheater on his phone, maybe we'll find out what he's up to."

"You got what?" Luke almost shouted.

"You heard me," Joe said. He had deliberately tried to bring up the subject as offhandedly as possible, knowing how his partner felt about it. "And the second thing is," he went on without letting Luke make an objection, "if he does move the stuff, if he does call, then I got something of his and this time he's going in for it."

He tapped the breast pocket that held the envelope as he spoke.

Luke shook his head slowly in numbed disbelief. He had thought that the whole thing was done with, and now his partner was carrying the money around in his pocket and had put in a hot wire on top of everything else. "You never give up, do you?" he said, but it wasn't clear from the way he said it that it was meant as a compliment.

The food and liquor were plentiful but the party fell something short of success. As usual at these affairs, the guests—or rather, the hosts, since everyone but Arch Russell had pitched in a few dollars—

split into factions, with the cops, the agents, and the lawyers each congregating separately.

The cops, who had come as a group from Little Italy, didn't arrive until almost nine but most of them made up the lost time quickly. Joe, though, had to stick to ginger ale. Never much of a drinker, he had had a huge dinner after his long weekend fast and immediately began to feel drowsy. With only a few hours of sleep after three days of wakefulness, he knew that even a glass of wine would wipe him out.

At around eleven o'clock, he said goodnight to his fellow detectives and crossed the room to where Russell was standing in the center of a circle of lawyers from the U.S. attorney's office. Russell graciously broke off from his friends to accept Joe's congratulations and to thank him for coming.

As Joe walked to the front of the restaurant, Luke fell in step beside him. "I'll drive you home," he volunteered. "You look like you could use it."

"Okay," Joe said. "Just gotta make one stop."

As the door to Fourteenth Street closed behind him, two federal agents set their drinks on the bar and crossed to the same exit. It could have been a coincidence, but Arch Russell, the only one at the party who noticed, didn't think so. "You get a feeling for these things," he said later. "As soon as I saw it I knew they were in trouble."

The doorman looked away as Joe and Luke walked past him to the staircase at the back of the lobby. "What's with him?" Luke whispered nervously as Joe pulled at the heavy steel fire door.

"Nothing," Joe answered, but he had the same feeling himself. He tried to tell himself that it was only that funny way people always act whenever they run into a working cop. But as he led the way down the dingy concrete stairs, an inarticulate premonition formed in the back of his mind and a violent shiver ran the length of his body as though his nerves were trying to shake off the feeling the way a dog shakes water from its back. Another door at the bottom opened onto the main corridor. He pushed it forward and hesitated a moment to get his bearings, then stepped clear. "Cmon," he said unnecessarily, heading in the direction of the service elevators at the end of the corridor.

To his right was the laundry room, dark and quiet at this hour, the round windows of the coin machines catching the light from the naked bulb in the corridor like enormous cat's eyes. Ahead, on the same wall, was the superintendent's office, and beyond that a branch corridor to the boiler room. The phone pairs were in a culvert off this corridor, along with the gas and electric meters.

Walking rapidly, with Luke now beside him, Joe passed the superintendent's office and stopped abruptly one step beyond it. Out of the corner of his eye he had noticed that the door was slightly ajar. Behind it he had seen, fleetingly, the shape of a man seated at the desk. Even before he had time to ask himself why a super would be in his office at midnight, he realized it was all over. He turned back to the door and a voice behind it boomed his name.

"Longo!"

About half a dozen men suddenly appeared in the corridor from doorways to his left and right, doorways that he hadn't even known were there. Turning from side to side like an animal at bay, he recognized only one of them, a detective attached to the Manhattan D.A.'s squad. The others were strangers. Expressionless, without hand or body gesture of any sort, they moved toward him, closing in menacingly.

Beside him, Luke stood motionless, understanding it all with a nightmarish clarity and paralyzed by what he understood. In the barest fraction of a second, two thoughts flashed through Joe's mind and disappeared, like the bright stab of a signal beacon revolving in the dark. First came the instinct to run a bluff, to talk his way out of it. Automatically, his shoulders set and a smile flickered across his face, and if he could have held it there he would have thought of something to say. But it was useless and he knew it. Then he wondered whether they would reach for their guns if he made a move.

With a decisiveness that surprised him as he looked back on it a few days later, Joe turned toward the office door and slapped at it violently with the meaty side of his fist. It flew open, slamming into the wall with a loud jangling sound as Joe stepped through the doorway and stood there, legs apart, body square to the man behind the desk. It was a gesture of defiance and self-assertion, and in that instant he felt as he had felt on a thousand earlier occasions when he was the cop charging through a suspect's door to take command.

Over the next two weeks it would be this one moment that would return again and again to haunt his mind as he came gradually to lose his appreciation for the grandeur of the gesture and to see only the sickening futility of it. All his life he had been a powerful and forceful

man, had prided himself on his ability to dominate every situation.
Now he was left only this empty shadow of an act.

Even before the echo of the crashing door had faded from the
damp cement walls, he knew what the man behind the desk was going
to say, knew it because he had said it himself a thousand times to a
thousand trapped men. Had said the same thing, though not in the
same words, for he had never busted a cop.

"I'm Darlan, Internal Affairs," the man said. "I'll take your
weapons and your shields."

They held Joe and Luke in the basement all night, questioning
them in relays, not letting up.

"I never saw any fucking wiretap," Luke protested at one point,
stopping them for a moment as they realized they had made a mistake.
They should have let Joe and Luke get to the machine before taking
them, for now there was no way to tie Antonelli to the illegal wire.

A few minutes later, though, they were back with the same questions, and this time they were ready for him.

"Then what were you doing down here?"

"I came with my partner."

"To service a tap?"

"I came with my partner."

"What for?"

Luke didn't answer.

The inspector suddenly turned fatherly. "Do you know you can
get five years in federal prison for illegal wiretapping?" he asked, as
though he were offering helpful information.

Luke said, "I want to talk to a lawyer."

The inspector ignored his request. "Whose phone were you tapping?" he asked, the harshness back in his voice.

And so it went. They traded off. First one team worked on Joe
while the other worked on Luke. Then they switched. For hours the
two Joint Task Force detectives and their seven captors stayed in the
tiny eight-by-ten superintendent's office, only Joe and Luke sitting, the
others hovering over them, their faces glinting with sweat in the smoky
room like moons seen through clouds. The drone of their voices became unbearable, and soon Joe and Luke each lost track of what the
other was saying even though they were only a few feet apart.

For the most part, Luke refused to answer their questions or put them off with evasions. Some he truthfully couldn't answer because his partner had left him so much in the dark about recent developments. Others he ducked because he didn't want to say anything about Joe's activities until he knew what Joe was telling them. He felt trapped and victimized, innocent but with no hope of convincing anyone of his innocence.

Through the questioning Joe was more belligerent than his partner but also more cooperative. The hypocrisy of the whole thing outraged him. Like most cops, he looked at illegal wiretapping less as a crime than as a technical violation of procedure. *But the bosses could treat it as a crime when they wanted to.* Most of the time they ignored it, because the results were to their liking. They read reports filled with ridiculous stories about impossible surveillances or imaginary informants and then handed them back with sly compliments. "That was a good piece of detective work, Longo," they would say, never once asking about the blatant reality barely concealed between the lines. Now, all of a sudden, they were appalled to learn that such things went on. It was like being in a game where the umpires had two rule books and wouldn't tell you which one you were playing under.

"Let's go over it again," one of the federal agents said. He was a man in his fifties who puffed on mentholated cigarettes whenever someone else was doing the talking. "When did you put in the tap?"

"Friday."

"You and your partner?"

"I told you, just me. He didn't know about it."

A few hours earlier he had said the same thing to the IAD team, and the inspector had said, "You're lying, Longo. You put it in with that Spanish guy." Apparently the federal agents didn't know about the Spanish guy yet, because they let Joe's answer pass. In any case, Joe never implicated Juan Piedra. To the end he stuck to the story that he had installed the tap by himself.

"Then what was he doing here?" the agent pursued, indicating Luke.

"Ask him yourself."

"Don't be cute, you're in a lot of trouble, Longo. Whose phone you tapping?"

"I told you, Carlo Danzie."

"Who's that?"

"A stool."

"A dealer?"

"A stool and a dealer."

"You were moving junk for him, weren't you, Longo?"

"Bullshit," Joe said. It was obvious they were just fishing.

"Well, what was it? You were shaking him down, is that it?"

"He's a stool and I'm working him."

"Don't play games, Longo. It's all over, can't you see that?"

"I'm not fucking blind."

"Then you might as well tell us."

"He's a stool," Joe said, speaking with the exaggerated slowness of exasperation. "He wasn't doing what he was supposed to. He knew things he wasn't telling me. So I put in the wire. How many times do I have to explain it?"

"Till you get it right."

"Go fuck yourself."

The other agent stepped in, a younger man with watery blue eyes and curly sand-colored hair. "Where is this guy?" he asked. It was a new question no one had asked before.

"Danzie?"

"If that's his name."

"I don't know."

"What do you mean you don't know?"

"I haven't seen him since Friday."

The agent seemed surprised. He glanced at his partner, then looked back at Joe. "You saw him Friday?" he asked.

"Yeah."

"Don't bullshit me, Longo," the agent snapped. "He's out of the country, isn't he?"

The question hit Joe like an electric shock and he sat bolt upright in his chair. It was a strange and alarming question that made him wonder what they knew. For the first time he realized that all these men weren't here simply because a cop had put a cheater on a phone. "No," he answered without any hesitation.

"He's in Italy, isn't he?"

"No."

"But he went to Italy."

"Are you telling me or asking me?"

"I'm asking you."

"I don't know if he went anywhere. I told you, I don't know where he is."

"You know he went to Italy," the agent snarled.

Joe smiled derisively. "Make sense," he said. "Why the fuck would I tap his phone if he was in Italy?"

The first agent, the older one, shouldered his partner aside and bent low until his face was just level with Joe's. "You let him go to Italy, didn't you, Longo?"

"I didn't let him do anything. I don't even know where the fuck he is."

"He paid you to let him go, didn't he, Longo?"

The question exploded inside Joe like a bullet tearing into flesh. The room fell suddenly quiet and Joe could hear the squeak of shoes as Luke's interrogators turned to listen. At his breast he could feel Danzie's envelope like a hot coal in his pocket. He didn't think he'd be able to answer the question but he heard himself saying "No."

For a few seconds there was absolute stillness, and then the tempo picked up again, the agent firing his questions rapidly, not even taking the time to phrase them as questions.

"He paid you to let him go."

"No."

"You and your partner."

"No."

"He gave you four thousand dollars to let him go, Longo."

"No."

"Isn't that right?"

"No."

The agent stood up straight and took half a step backward. "Longo," he said softly, the words hanging in the air with the thick perfumy smoke of his cigarette, "Carlo Danzie is a special employee of the Bureau of Narcotics and Dangerous Drugs. Now do you want to tell us about it?"

Austere and elegant, the massive federal courthouse in Foley Square stands atop a set of block-long granite stairs. Whether by accident or design, the steps are too wide to be taken comfortably one at a time except at a run. A grown man of average size must reduce his stride in order to get both feet on each step, like a toddler trying to negotiate a world too large for him.

Ten columns, each over two feet thick, rise to support the classical façade. Behind them, a set of heavy iron and glass doors remains closed until the court opens for business in the morning. At seven fifteen the lobby is deserted except for a uniformed security guard lounging backward in a folding chair by the elevators, his ankles resting on the lip of a shiny chrome cigarette receptacle. Two agents pounding at the door startle him out of his end-of-the-tour reverie and he jumps awkwardly to his feet, catching the chair and then folding it against the wall before answering the knock.

At the door both agents flash identification. Technically, the two men with them are not prisoners, for there has been no arrest. But they are treated as prisoners, nudged through the door with just enough force to get the message across. The security guard closes it behind them and it clangs with a hollow ringing sound that inescapably suggests the snap of cellblock gates. In the cavernous lobby the echo of the door surrounds them, but only the two men between the agents seem to notice it.

Joe and Luke were taken to the office of the special prosecutor on the fourteenth floor. One agent remained with them in the carpeted reception area outside Paul Scala's office while the other went off down the corridor in search of something. In less than five minutes he returned. "Come with me," he said.

"Me?" Luke asked. It hadn't been clear.

"Yeah. Come with me."

With his partner gone, Joe was alone with the sandy-haired agent. For about five minutes they stood without speaking. Then the agent said, "Wait here," and walked from the room. After ten minutes by himself, Joe realized that he was in for a long wait and sat down in a chair next to the secretary's desk. There was a short couch, more like a love seat, on the opposite wall but he took the straight chair instead.

For an hour and a half he was left alone with his fear and his fatigue and his despair. Once, an agent Joe hadn't seen before came in to deposit some papers on the secretary's desk. He wore a BNDD identity card on the outside of his breast pocket and as he shuffled papers on the desk he kept glancing up at Joe. Was it just curiosity or had he been sent in to make an identification? But in what connection?

Confusedly sorting through a thousand faces he had seen over the last few months, Joe tried for a match but came up empty. Had the man been in Little John's—that table by the front, two guys? No, they were older, weren't they? Yes, older. But what about the hotel? Or Little John's that first time? And weren't there agents in a car at the Americana the night Danzie was arrested?

He realized it was no use and looked away, alarmed and sickened at how quickly they had made him start thinking like a criminal. He had used the same trick himself, sending guys around to look at a suspect, making him think he's being fingered, making him torture himself wondering where this guy might know him from, what he might say. But the thing of it was, it worked, and that was what Joe found so frightening. It worked even on someone like Joe, who knew it was a trick.

"Okay if I use the phone?" he asked, just to have something to say, to make himself feel like this was a normal thing, a guy waiting to talk to another guy in his office.

"No," the agent answered flatly, destroying Joe's pretense with a single word.

"Hey, look," Joe protested. "I know I got a right—"

"It's not that," the agent said, cutting him off and walking around the desk toward the door. "Switchboard's not on yet."

He disappeared into the corridor, closing the door behind him, leaving Joe alone with his humiliation. *It's not that. It's not that. That. That.* Like some unnameable deformity. Like an eyeless socket in your head.

"It's about time, isn't it, Longo?" Paul Scala asked from behind his desk.

Scala hadn't come in through the reception area, so Joe glanced around the office looking for the other door. When he found it, some chain of association suddenly made him remember Luke and he wondered what they had done with his partner.

"It's about time," Scala repeated, but Joe still didn't understand what the question meant. A lumpish man with a round face and surprisingly soft features, Scala sat behind his desk with the composure of a mandarin. Except for the telephone and a transparent cube that held a ballpoint pen, his desk was bare. The desk itself was starkly modern, more like a table, and the rest of the office matched it in conveying a feeling of antiseptic purity. At Police Headquarters they all went in the opposite direction, leaning toward heavy oak furniture, old stuff suggesting tradition and values, wood paneling on the walls, leather on the chairs.

Behind Scala a window looked out past Chinatown and Little Italy to the river, and on the wall to his left—the one with the door in it, the door he must have come in by (had he questioned Luke yet?)— hung a huge painting, if you could call it that. The canvas was covered with a vibrant nightmare orange, shading slightly to peach at the edges to show that it hadn't simply been dipped in paint.

Joe still didn't say anything, although it was clear he was expected to.

"You're in a lot of trouble, Longo," Scala said levelly after letting the silence wear itself out. "If you want to do yourself some good you'll tell me about it."

"There's nothing to tell that you don't know already," Joe said.

Scala cocked an eyebrow. So that's how you want it, he seemed to be saying. "I don't have to tell you, Longo, there's an easy way and a hard way," he said out loud. "You're smart, you should know what to do."

"I don't even know what the fuck you're talking about," Joe shot back, finally relieving the smallest portion of his anger and frustration. "I mean, am I under arrest or what?"

"No, you're not under arrest."

"What about my gun and my shield?"

Scala smiled superciliously. "You fucking cops are all alike," he said. "It's the first thing you ask. Why is that?"

"If I told you you wouldn't understand. What about it?"

"It's up to you."

For another half hour the questioning continued as a wry and courtly game of wits. At around ten o'clock one of the agents who had been in the basement the night before came into the office and slid a chair to within a few feet of Joe. Then things started to heat up. Scala's voice grew increasingly loud and shrill, his questioning took on the sharp edge of accusation even though Joe was not uncooperative. He admitted putting in the tap, admitted taking the money. But he refused to back down from his insistence that there was no shakedown and no bribe. His own voice grew louder too. When Scala said, "You were moving dope for him, weren't you, Longo?" Joe leaped to his feet. "You're full of shit!" he screamed.

No one said anything, and after a few seconds Joe sank quietly back into his seat, overcome by the futility of trying to defend himself. They knew everything that had happened between him and Danzie. Explaining wouldn't do any good because they already knew and they were deliberately twisting it. They could make it come out any way they wanted. They had all the answers and their version made sense. The truth was the truth, but it didn't make sense.

Scala was nodding his head slowly. "You want to go to jail, don't you, Longo?" he said sadly. "I thought you were smart but you're acting like a dumb fucking cop. How many years you got?"

"Fifteen."

It was a relief to have a question where nothing was at stake. It relaxed him momentarily, and as he let down his guard a wave of desperate anxiety washed over him. Tension had been damming it back but he had slept only five hours in as many days and had no mental reserves left to help him regain his equilibrium once it was gone.

"Fifteen," Scala repeated. "Five to go for a full pension. Not a bad life, is it, Longo?"

Joe didn't answer.

"You got a wife, right? And a kid?"

"Yeah."

"Two kids?"

"Yeah, two kids."

"They in school, is that right?"

It was a stupid question and Joe ignored it. Obviously Scala had studied the file on him, knew how old Joey and Marie were.

"Parochial school, isn't it? That costs money."

"That's my business."

"Yeah, I'll bet it is," Scala sneered. "But after school it's college. Nowadays that's for girls, too. That pension's gonna come in handy."

Joe raised a finger in warning. "I take care of my family," he said, "and I don't need your fucking advice. Just say what you gotta say and leave them out of it."

Scala leaped to his feet and darted quickly around the desk. He stood over Joe, the soft features of his round face flushed pink with either genuine anger or a superb imitation. "Don't tell me what to say, Longo, don't you dare tell me what to fucking say!" he shrieked, his voice suddenly, inexplicably, hysterically shrill. "You know what you are? You're a whore, Longo, and you've always been a whore. You've been a whore for fifteen years and we knew what you were. So don't come to me now crying about your family. You should've thought of them before you changed sides. What is it with you? Did you think you could get away with it forever?"

The cold, astringent smell of Scala's cologne stung Joe's senses like ammonia. There was no point in saying anything, so Joe just waited, rendered powerless by the indignity of having to let a man like Scala treat him this way.

"Hey, why don't you do yourself some good, Joe," the agent purred helpfully as Scala made his way back to the chair behind his desk. "You're in a lot of trouble and you're not helping yourself any."

"What are you talking about?" Joe asked. He knew the answer of course, for in the back of his mind he had been wondering how long it would take them to get around to it. And he knew, too, what his answer would be. Like most cops, he held loyalty to his fellow officers as an unquestionable canon of honor. When you ran into a wrong guy in the job you stayed clear of him, that was all. You looked the other way, you didn't forget he was a cop. You didn't judge him because you knew what the temptations were. It was a world full of desperate men, addicts and pushers and stools, users who'd rat on their pushers for the price of a fix, dealers who kept themselves in business by selling out the guys they bought from, stools who'd hand up their connections to get you off their backs and then hand you up to the shooflies for the same reason. If you didn't take it on the chin you'd get it up the ass, either way, banged and double-banged. In the last analysis that was why you had to be the exception, why all cops had to be. In the vast, pulsing spider web of betrayal, cops had to stand together, had to have each other to trust.

"You know what I'm talking about, Joe," the agent answered soothingly. "We got a job to do, right? No one likes it but it's gotta be done. And you're in a position to help us. It's that simple, Joe. It's that simple. If you help us, we can help you. Just think about it."

"There's nothing to think about."

From the other side of the desk Paul Scala's voice cut in irritating-ly. "Don't be so sure, Longo," he said. "There's jail to think about, there's you'll be outta the job to think about. There's your pension to think about."

"Hey, now don't get us wrong, Joe," the agent interrupted smoothly. "We're not making any promises. You just do what you can and we'll do what we can. I mean, it's not like we're asking you to tell us a bunch of stories about this guy, that guy, whoever you're working with. We just want you to keep your eyes open, that's all. If you see anything we should know about, you let us know. We don't want you to set anybody up, nothing like that. We don't work that way."

Joe raked his hand through his hair and snorted a short humorless laugh. "You're so full of shit," he said. "Whatdya mean you don't set anybody up? What the fuck do you think this was?"

"It wasn't a setup, Joe," the agent answered softly, in the tone of a man speaking candidly. "You knew what you were doing."

Christ, that was true. It took the last fight out of him, if there was any left, and he started to say things he knew he didn't mean. But he had to get out of that office, had to get some sleep.

"You mean that about no setups?" he asked.

"Sure."

"Because if that's what it is, I'm not—"

"Of course."

"I don't know. I gotta think about it."

"That's all we want you to do. Just think about it. Get some rest, you'll see."

No one said anything for a long while.

"Is that it? Can I go?" Joe asked, hardly able to believe they would just let him walk away.

"Yeah. Just let us know what you decide."

Scala remained seated but the agent stood as Joe did. Joe didn't notice him reaching for anything but when he held his hand out there was something in it.

"You'll be needing these," the agent said.

He handed Joe his shield. And his gun.

Chapter 12
Point Blank

A BOVE THE WHINE of the vacuum cleaner, Jeannie heard the car pull into the driveway and crunch to a stop. When the car door slammed, she was already on her way downstairs, her mind racing with a thousand ways she could express her indignation. He hadn't been home since Friday, not a word since Sunday. No job was worth that. Or if it was, she wanted to hear him tell her to her face.

As the kitchen door opened, her words—she doesn't even remember what they were going to be—froze in her throat and she knew something was terribly wrong. She had seen him many times when he had pushed himself to the point of exhaustion, pale and hollow-eyed. But she had never seen him like this. He looked like he had aged a dozen years since the last time she saw him, and she gasped involuntarily.

He even walked like an old man, with small tired steps.

"Joe, what's wrong?" she asked, her voice sharp with alarm.

"Nothing, I'm okay," he muttered as he shuffled past her toward the stairs. "I've gotta get some sleep."

She hesitated a moment, baffled. "Did someone get hurt?" she asked. "Is it Luke?"

"Everybody's okay," he said without even turning. "I'll tell you later."

She watched him go painfully up the stairs, then hurried after him and helped him to bed. He didn't say anything and she knew better than to ask questions. For a few moments she stood over the bed and watched him sleep, but soon the unanswered questions hammering at her mind drove her away. She was sure someone had been killed and she selfishly thanked God it wasn't Joe.

Downstairs she realized it had to be something else. If someone had been shot it would have been on the radio, she would have heard. She poured herself a cup of coffee and paced the kitchen as she sipped on it. As the afternoon slowly passed, something like the anger she had felt before he came home began slowly creeping back. She wanted to go upstairs and shake him awake, she wanted to demand that he tell her what was happening, not later, not when he felt better, but now. Then she remembered how he had looked when he walked past her as though he couldn't even see her and she knew she wouldn't be able to do it.

The phone went off like a fire alarm, so startling she had to catch her breath before she could answer it. She raised it to her ear carefully, not knowing what to expect.

"Hello?"

"Jeannie, is Joe there?" It was Luke's voice.

"He's asleep, Luke."

"Yeah, okay. Would you have him call me when he gets up."

He sounded like he was in a hurry to get off the line.

"Luke," she called, trying to catch him.

There was a pause and she imagined he was deciding whether to hang up. Then he said, "Yeah?"

"Luke, what's happening?" she pleaded.

Luke hesitated before answering. "What did Joe tell you?" he asked.

"He didn't tell me anything. What's happening, Luke?" When there was no answer she said, "Don't I have a right to know?" As soon as the words were out, she realized she had phrased it as a question when she didn't mean it as a question at all.

"Sure you do, Jeannie," Luke said. "He'll tell you."

"Luke—"

"I can't," he said and hung up.

She cried for less than a minute and then took a deep breath to stop the tears. It's probably nothing, she told herself, some case they were on didn't work out. Good, it served them right. If they wanted to run themselves into the ground, if they thought it was so important they couldn't even take time out to come home, then she wasn't going to let herself get upset because some stupid dope peddler got away. They were little kids running away from home and when they got back you were supposed to forget about it, like everything was normal. Okay. She made up her mind to forget about it.

But she couldn't. He was still asleep upstairs when the children burst in through the kitchen door. "Daddy's home," Joey shouted. The screen door banged shut.

She quieted them, told them Daddy had worked very hard and was taking a nap. She felt like he had somehow made her lie to her children for him.

"Is he going to have supper with us?" Marie asked.

"Yes, honey. He'll be up in a little while and we'll all have supper. Just be kind of quiet so he can rest a little."

At five thirty she heard footsteps and then the shower. Out of stubbornness she waited downstairs for him to come to her. When she heard his bare feet on the carpeted stairs she turned to face him.

He stood at the kitchen door, his thick black hair glistening with water, his broad powerful body filling the doorway. But the smooth white skin of his chest somehow suggested the vulnerability that she felt only she knew in him, and as he buttoned his shirt she noticed that his fingers stumbled awkwardly. The four-day growth of beard was gone and his face looked almost pink from scrubbing, but beneath the color she could see a gray ashenness. In spite of herself she smiled at him, the way a mother smiles encouragement at a sick child, and he smiled back mechanically, bravely, just with his lips. His green eyes gleamed feverishly.

"I'll bet you didn't eat either," she said. "Sit down, I'll get you something."

"Where are the kids?" he asked.

"Joey's at Tommie's and I think Marie's next door. They'll be home any minute."

She though he'd be eager to see them because that was always the first thing he wanted when work had kept him away. He always had to make it up to them. "Have they eaten?" he asked.

"No, Marie made me promise she wouldn't have to have supper till you got up. Do you want me to call them?" she asked, completely misunderstanding what he wanted.

"Call them," he said, stammering, "call, call over there, see if Alba or Irene can give them supper. I want to talk to you." ·

Jeannie started to protest but he cut her off.

"I know," he said. "Please. I've gotta talk to you."

He listened in pained silence at the kitchen table as she made the calls. Then she poured two cups of coffee and sat near him, in the chair where Joey usually sat.

He took a few short, hissing sips of the steaming coffee and looked at her for a long time without saying anything, not so much rehearsing what he wanted to say as preparing himself for it. Then, when he was ready, he began talking, his voice low and expressionless, as though he were reading from a script he had read too many times. He didn't start from the beginning because she knew all that, knew about the tip from Pete Patrigno and the arrest at the Americana, Luke's trip to Washington and the promise of hundred-kilo cases. So he began his story with the Saturday meeting at which Danzie had hinted to him about "some other consideration." It took almost half an hour to tell—the envelope offered to Luke, Danzie's "difficulties" in Italy, Captain Marcus's promise to get the passport, and Hal Verlon saying there would be no passport. The last meeting with Danzie. The envelope. The wiretap.

Jeannie listened, almost hypnotized by his flat, toneless voice, not understanding until the very end what the problem was, too innocent and candid to comprehend the intrigue, the tortuous purpose behind each of Carlo Danzie's acts. She was misled, too, by the dull, methodical way Joe told the story, and half expected it would end simply with Danzie's disappearance in Italy.

Then Joe said, "They arrested me."

Her mind jumped as though someone had touched an electrode to her brain. She wanted to say, *You mean him—they arrested him,* but an instinct told her she had not misunderstood and she said nothing.

"Monday night," he went on. "They kept us there all night, me and Luke. They say he bribed us to let him go. They say . . . "

His voice trailed off and his hand reached over the table for hers. She took it and held it, because it was the only way she knew to tell him what she wanted to say.

Late that night Joe returned Luke's call but they discovered quickly that there was nothing they could say to each other. Luke wanted some kind of guidance and kept repeating, "What are we gonna do? What do you think we should do?" to which Joe could only answer, "There's nothing to do. We'll do what they tell us, that's all." He wanted to hang up the phone but stayed on because he knew that if it hadn't been for him, Luke wouldn't have been in trouble.

Plaintively, Luke asked, "Are you going in tomorrow?"

The question caught Joe by surprise. The idea of going to the office seemed so unrelated to everything that had happened, so incongruous next to the sickening certainty that his career was over and it was only a matter of days until he was suspended and then thrown off the Force in disgrace. But they had given him back his shield and gun, so he knew that that was what he was supposed to do.

"Yeah, I guess so," he said. "I can't sit around here driving myself crazy, that's for sure."

"Yeah, me too," Luke echoed.

There was a long silence marked only by the low irregular static on the line. Joe wondered if his phone was tapped.

"I'll talk to you tomorrow," he said. "I can't even think straight yet."

"Yeah, okay."

"Luke?"

"Yeah."

"I'm sorry about this." He meant it as an apology.

"Yeah, me too," Luke answered, generously not taking it that way.

If he had thought about it, it would have been obvious to Joe why they wanted him to keep working for the time being. They weren't really interested in prosecuting him—Scala had made that clear already. They wanted to turn him around and leave him in place as an undercover agent. If they suspended him, even temporarily, everybody would know he was in a jam and when he went back to work they would know how he had gotten out of it. Then he would be useless to them.

He didn't think about any of this because he hadn't even for a moment seriously considered the possibility of doing what they wanted. He was giving them no choice but to bring charges against him. Hauling him into court would be a defeat for them but they would have to do it because only in that way could they make it clear to those who came after him that they meant business. If the next detective they trapped knew that Longo was doing five or ten years in a federal prison, it would help him make the right decision.

During a moment of weakness Tuesday morning he had told Scala he would think about the offer and would get back to him with his answer. But even as he said it he had known that his answer would be—indeed, already was—no. He knew it meant jail but there was nothing he could do about it.

Strangely, for a man who had been a fighter all his life, the idea of fighting them never occurred to him. Jeannie had urged him to fight it out on Tuesday evening, when he told her about it, and Luke raised the issue again on Wednesday. "Maybe we oughta get a lawyer, see if there's anything we can do," Antonelli suggested.

But Joe, convinced of his moral innocence, was no less convinced of his legal guilt. "The fucking money's right here," he said, tapping his breast pocket. "I had it on me all the time and they didn't even ask about it. Not once, didn't ask where it was, didn't mention it. That ought to tell you where we stand. If you know a lawyer that can change that, call him up, we'll go see him."

"There's gotta be something we can do," Luke pleaded.

Joe's eyes flashed with suspicion. "There is," he snapped, "but I'm not gonna do it. What you do is your business."

It wasn't the kind of statement Luke could answer, so he said nothing. Deeply hurt, he let the tense silence speak for itself. He had known the moment the agents appeared in the basement of the Diplomat that the trap had been set for Joe and that he himself had merely stumbled into it. Then, when they took him to the Federal Courthouse in the morning, he was questioned by two agents but not by Paul Scala. They didn't even offer him a deal the way Scala offered one to Joe. They just said at one point that it would go easier for him if he told them anything he knew. But he didn't know anything and the subject was dropped.

They also told him they knew Danzie had given him a hundred-dollar bill to pay the check at La Pentola and that he had kept the change. "That's a fucking lie and you know it," Luke shot back angrily, the only time in his whole long ordeal that he let himself answer their charges. "If he told you that, he's lying," he went on. "You guys like to think you're cops. Why don't you act like it for once? Go ask the waiter, ask the cashier. I left before he even finished his fucking dinner."

And that subject, too, was dropped.

Now he was in an impossible position. If his actions over the next two weeks seem those of a weak man, easily led, this is only in part because he let himself be dominated by his partner's more dominant personality. He knew that he could have taken a stronger line, could have defended himself forcefully. His defense, though, would have to be an attack on Joe, who had put in the wiretap himself, had accepted the envelope from Danzie, and even now still held the money. But if that was the only way for him to beat the case, then he wanted no part of it.

So he left his fate in his partner's hands. It was probably the most painful decision of his life, and undoubtedly the most courageous. If Joe made a deal, both of them would walk free and if Joe stonewalled they would both go to jail. Somewhere in the middle was the possibility that Joe would lay it all out for them exactly the way it happened, would in effect testify against himself and for Luke. But that decision had to be Joe's.

It meant putting up with so much pain and bitterness, it meant swallowing his pride and not answering his partner's suspicious and self-righteous innuendoes. There were times when he wanted to grab Joe and scream to his face, *Can't you see what I'm doing? Don't you know that you got me into this? And have I asked you once, even once, to get me out of it?*

But he never said it, and perhaps the most melancholy part of this whole tragic affair is the fact that over the last two weeks of his life Joe Longo, sinking deeper and deeper into morbid suspiciousness, grew to distrust the one man who was standing by him. They had never been close, the way police partners often are, and Luke knew it. He knew it when Joe insisted on splitting the money, and again when Joe took it back without explanation. He knew it when Joe didn't ask for his help on the long weekend stakeout. But on Monday, March 13, shortly before midnight, in a basement below Carlo Danzie's apartment, they became close. Luke could have walked away but chose not to. He would stand by his partner.

Even if his partner didn't see it or understand.

Wednesday evening both Joe and Luke were called at home and told to meet Paul Scala at noon at the La Guardia Airport Holiday Inn. The significance of the location didn't escape either of them. It was Scala's lightly veiled way of saying that he knew they had met Danzie there. Further, it suggested the possibility that the room was bugged and that Scala had at his fingertips every word that had ever passed between the two detectives and the double agent.

Joe spent a restless, sleepless night desperately trying to reconstruct all his conversations with Danzie. Starting with his black memo book and a clean sheet of paper, he methodically wrote down all the dates on which he had seen Danzie. Then he filled in the locations and put an L in the margin next to those occasions on which Luke had been with him.

At first it was easy to remember what had been said and he quickly filled the page with scrambled notes about the general purport of each meeting. Then he read it all back and was sickened by what he saw. The notes laid it all out so that even an idiot could see the pattern. How had he missed it? How had he failed to see he was being set up?

Because you just don't think of things like that. Because you would have to be crazy to think that way.

He stopped himself cold and tried to get back to what he had to do. It didn't matter now how it happened. What mattered was what Scala would say in the morning, and he had to be ready, had to know every last word that had been said. Not just the things they had talked about but the words themselves, words that could be taken out of context, played back, made to sound worse than reality.

There was so much to go over and no place to start as his mind jumped wildly with uncontrollable associations. At Kennedy, in the car at Kennedy Airport, did they have that? Did they have a tape of Danzie's vague allusion to "some other consideration" and Joe's vehement answer? No, they wouldn't have that. He was undoubtedly wired, had to be wired, but they wouldn't have that tape. It was erased or buried in a file somewhere, along with all the other tapes where Joe said no to him.

Without consciously directing his mind to the incident, he suddenly called back from memory the way it had all started. In front of him as he fought to regain his balance after plunging into the room at the Americana was Carlo Danzie in shirt sleeves, ignoring his shouted order to stop, moving across the room, trying to hide the junk behind the television.

But every dealer in the world knows that a hotel room is a public place. When he checks into a hotel room carrying junk, the first thing he does is always the same. He stashes it somewhere in the room— under the bed, taped behind the nightstand, in the back of a close . That's his defense because the police can't prove possession unless they can prove it wasn't in the room when he checked in.

So Danzie must have wanted them to find it. The setup hadn't started after Danzie was caught but before. Of course—that was what they said, wasn't it? "Carlo Danzie is a special employee of the Bureau of Narcotics and Dangerous Drugs." It just hadn't sunk in before. For the first time he realized that the call from Patrigno had been part of the trap.

Oh, God, Pete! They had known each other since Brooklyn. Who would have believed it? *No one, no one. How could you be expected to think like that? You had to be crazy to think like that.*

But that was the way it was. You had to be crazy, you had to trust no one. Then you'd be right.

He crumpled the paper in disgust and stood up. It was already past two and Jeannie had long since gone to bed. He reached forward to snap off the desk lamp, then, in the dark, lifted the white-wood chair back into place. For a few moments he stood in the living room, uncertain of what he wanted to do, aware that he hadn't found any of the answers he had been looking for when he sat down at the tidy, too small desk Jeannie used for writing letters and paying the bills. Then he walked to the window, but the deserted street seemed cold and uncomforting. Across the way stood three houses, their windows dark, the trees behind them bare, still a few weeks shy of budding into leaf.

He turned and picked his way carefully to the stairs, hardly able to hear his own footsteps on the carpet even in the blanketing silence of his house. Upstairs he undressed noiselessly and slid into bed beside his wife. As she moved unconsciously to him, he tried to relax, to empty his mind of everything but her.

Instead, the whole thing started coming back again in random pieces. Beside him, he could hear Jeannie breathing in the slow, shallow, sensuous rhythm of sleep, inexpressibly far away. Nearer, right in his ear, inside his head, he heard the rumbling bass of Carlo Danzie's voice, a meaningless jumble of phrases that came back to him unbidden.

I am not talking about one or two shipments, you understand. We are discussing a network that will be used on a regular basis.

We want the same things, is it not so?

The people in Brooklyn are eager for the transaction.

. . . a Lebanese syndicate in Beirut . . . a Corsican in Toronto.

I am a man of my word.

When there is something for you to hear, I will call you. There will be no necessity for you to call me.

I am a man of my word.

Perhaps we can arrange for some other consideration.

In Italy one is wise to avoid the slender women, they are all schemers.

They do not want you to make this case, Joe.

The people in Brooklyn are eager for the transaction.

. . . a Lebanese syndicate in Beirut . . . a Corsican in Toronto.

Your Mr. Diamond in Washington, I have worked for him before and I will work for him again.

You will understand everything tonight.

The people in Brooklyn are eager for the transaction

I am a man of my word.

It is yours, Joe. It is for you and Luke.

An agent they had never seen before was waiting for them in the lobby. "This way," he said without introducing himself and without asking if they were Longo and Antonelli.

He led them to the elevator, stepped aside when the door opened, and then followed them in. He punched the six button and they rode up in silence. When the doors opened on the sixth floor he waited for them to get out, then stepped past them and repeated, "This way." They followed him down the corridor to the left.

Danzie had stayed on the fourth floor, so at least they weren't using the same room. As if that mattered.

At six twenty-seven the agent stopped abruptly and knocked twice, his movements so sharp and mechanical that it sounded like a code knock, which it wasn't.

Paul Scala opened the door. He said only, "Gentlemen," and stepped back to invite them in. Then he closed the door after them, leaving the agent in the hallway where he had been standing when he knocked. His work done, he probably went off to wait in Scala's car, but it wouldn't have been surprising if he simply stood where he was left, like a vacuum cleaner someone forgot to put away.

Except for the prints on the wall, which were different scenes but from the same lot, the room was an exact duplicate of the one Carlo Danzie had stayed in. The hotel probably only had three different rooms, although it would quote six different rates. Years ago, when he was in Mounted, the night manager at the Taft had explained the way it worked, and what it came down to was the sixteen-dollar room and the eighteen-dollar room were the same room. It probably still worked the same way, only now there were no sixteen-dollar rooms.

It's funny, the things you think of.

"Antonelli, I met you in Washington. You must be Longo," a sharp piercing voice said suddenly. Joe turned to face it and saw a man he hadn't really noticed on his first quick scan of the room. Seated with his back to the writing table set against the far wall, wearing a dark, pin-striped suit and a narrow tie, he had one finger cocked in Joe's direction.

No one said so, but Joe knew this had to be Anthony Diamond.

"Sit down," Diamond said, lowering his hand now that he was sure Joe had seen it. "Mr. Scala tells me you boys have been doing some thinking."

"Mr. Scala doesn't know what I'm thinking," Joe answered.

Face to face with the enemy, he handled himself as he always had. He was tough, cocky, self-assured, and he would be to the very end. It was when he was alone, or alone with Luke, that he knew himself to be defeated. But in front of them his voice sounded like it still had some fight in it.

"Well, maybe you oughta do some thinking," Diamond snarled, his voice sharp and insolent.

Joe shrugged. "About what?" he asked with incredible non-chalance. He and Diamond both knew it was a bluff but that didn't matter because as long as he could still bluff it meant they hadn't broken him yet.

"A lot," Diamond said. "Want me to spell it out for you?"

Joe just stared angrily straight into Diamond's cold eyes.

Diamond rose slowly and with the back of his heel shoved the chair in under the desk. For a moment he stared back at Joe, his face gray with contempt. Then he turned to the window and looked out, motionless, as though he drew strength from the Grand Central Parkway.

"A guy like you, Longo, likes to play dumb," he began. "But I don't think you're dumb. So I'm gonna lay it out for you, and if it turns out you still can't understand, then you got no one to blame but yourself. Okay, now let's say we go back to square one. See, what I'm trying to do, Longo, is I'm trying to make it easy for you. I wanna make sure you understand."

He turned from the window and went on talking, his nervous hands making small gestures in front of his chest.

"Now square one, Longo, that's where it says we got a big drug problem in this country. Okay. Now why do we have this drug problem? Well, there's a lotta reasons, but right up at the top is this one. We got a bunch of whores working narcotics. Top to bottom. A bunch of two-dollar whores that are supposed to be cops. . . . I don't have to tell you, you know it better than I do, Longo."

He paused just long enough to shrug his shoulders. "It's the way it is. I didn't believe it myself when I started but that's what it is. It's a fucking nightmare. We got ourselves a Police Force that's walking around with their skirts up to here, their pussies sticking out. A bunch of fucking whores.

"Okay. So you gotta know a thing like this just can't go on, right? So we look around, we make up a list, who's turning tricks, who's running the whorehouse. Then we get ourselves a guy we can work with and we put out the word. We let people know there's a guy sitting in his hotel room that wants a screwing. And what do you think happens? The madam hears about it, there's a phone call, and pretty soon the whores show up. They take him dancing, they take him drinking, they go to dinner. This isn't a couple of quickies we're talking about, this is a couple of pros. And before long they figure they've got him by the nuts. At least that's what they think, because they think they're smart. But they're not smart, they're whores, and a whore thinks with her pussy. She wants this, or this."

In quick succession, his right hand, fingers cupped, gestured a jerkoff, then a payoff, the thumb massaging the fingertips.

"So how smart's a whore gonna be? But they tell him, Mister, you've been fucked. And now it's gonna cost you. If you wanna go home we can help you out. For twenty-five grand we'll get you a passport. You don't need that? Okay. Just slip us four, we'll let you go."

Joe leaped to his feet. "That's a goddamn lie and you know it," he said.

Diamond cut him off. "Don't tell me what I know, Longo. I'm telling you."

Paul Scala said, "We had men at the next table, Longo."

He had been standing by the door, satisfied to be forgotten. But when he spoke, Joe turned to face him, then thought better of it. Scala was leaning against the wall, arms folded almost languidly across his chest. If he meant to look imposing, the effect was almost exactly the opposite, so Joe turned away to deal with Diamond, who was harder and more formidable.

"There was no one at the next table," Joe said flatly, stating a fact, even though at the moment he couldn't quite remember. If they would give him a few seconds to think he could reconstruct exactly who was in the dining room but he didn't have to. He knew for a certainty that Scala and Diamond didn't have a man there.

"There were two men," Diamond said, emphasizing the number.

"Horseshit. Danzie was wired."

A small smile flickered across Diamond's face. It said, *I say we had two men at the next table. Prove we didn't.*

Joe threw up his hands. "So what's the fucking point?" he asked. "You wanna say it happened that way, you can say it. If I'm supposed to be surprised, I'm not."

Scala spoke again, his voice measured and condescending. "We're not trying to surprise you, Joe. We just want you to know where you stand."

Diamond said, "I think Antonelli here understands. Don't you, Antonelli?"

Luke didn't want to answer and Joe didn't want him to. "What's that got to do with it?" Joe demanded. "Are you talking to me or aren't you?"

Diamond bristled, irritated that his attempt to drive a wedge between the two partners had been countered so easily. "I'm talking to anyone who doesn't wanna go to jail," he said.

He knew what it meant when Joe didn't answer. Jail scared the shit out of him like it scared the shit out of all cops Diamond had ever met. Deep down, Diamond was convinced that all cops were thieves, except that way back the punks who couldn't stand the thought of jail signed up for the cops and the ones who knew they could take it if they had to went the other way. That was what made his job so easy. You just had to mention jail to a cop and you found out what he was made of.

Before he could say anything, Joe heard the door click open and turned to see Scala leaning out. Then Scala pulled his head in, leaving the door ajar for the agent who stepped through it a few seconds later. "I don't think he wants to talk in front of Longo," the special prosecutor purred. He motioned with his thumb and a nod of his head at Luke.

The insult was too much for Luke to take after all he had been through. "Cmon, Joe, let's get the fuck outta here," he said, standing and taking a step toward the door. "If they wanna arrest us they know where to find us."

The agent at the door took a step forward but Scala held up a hand to stop him, then turned to Joe and said, "Is that how you want it, Longo?"

Joe shook his head slowly. "It's okay, Luke," he said, his voice barely audible.

The agent advanced another step and reached for Luke's elbow, but Luke shook him off and walked resolutely to the door. Then he stopped and turned to look back at Joe, trying to make his eyes say, *Don't worry about me.* But what Joe saw was that he was scared.

"It's a shame, isn't it, Longo," Diamond said as soon as Luke was gone.

"What is?"

"If it was just you, you could be a tough guy all you want. But you're taking that poor schnook with you."

Joe turned to Scala. "You said," he said, but his voice was so soft he could hardly hear it himself. "I . . . you said I just have to keep my eyes open?" he asked.

"That's right."

"Do I have to stay with the Task Force?"

He didn't know if he could do it if it involved any of the men he knew. He didn't think he could do it in any case but at least he had to ask.

"Could be," Scala said. "We had some other things in mind."

"Like what?"

Scala threw a glance to Diamond as though he wasn't quite sure how much they had agreed to say at this point. Taking the cue, Diamond said, "Sit down, Longo," and motioned to a chair next to the television set. He waited until Joe was seated, then pulled the chair from under the writing table and straddled it, its back only a few inches from Joe's knees. Meanwhile, Scala had come around behind Diamond. He stood at the writing table, leaning back slightly with his buttocks on the lip of the table, his round face hanging in midair a foot above the deputy director's head.

"You know Bob Mackenzie?" Diamond began.

The question, if it was a question, caught Joe off balance, like hearing your name called in a place you've never been before. He hadn't so much as tried to guess what they were going to ask him to do, but if he had tried he never would have guessed that it involved Bob Mackenzie. If he hadn't known it before, there was no mistaking now that these guys were high rollers.

"I know who he is," he lied, instinctively ducking whatever the question implied.

"You know him," Diamond corrected.

"Yeah, I know him. It's . . . " He gestured with his hands, then decided against explaining. "I know him."

Bob Mackenzie was district attorney of Queens County and a political comer. Joe first met him in 1971, when he was in the one-oh-eight in Queens. It was one of those fluke things that, as best as he could remember, came about because Jeannie worked with Mackenzie's wife on some kind of parents' organization. The two couples became friendly enough to go out to dinner maybe half a dozen times, but neither was ever at the other's house. Once Mackenzie offered Joe a transfer to the Queens D.A.'s squad, but it was said casually, over cocktails, not the sort of statement you could take a man up on.

Since then Joe had thought about Mackenzie's offer from time to time. With fifteen years in the job, it was time to start thinking about what he was going to do after he had put in his twenty. He had never given much thought to politics, but when he did he found that it appealed to his image of himself as a guy who makes things happen. Working it out in the privacy of his fantasies, keeping it to himself as he always did, he evolved a scenario in which he would stay with the Task Force another year at most, then transfer to the D.A.'s squad in Queens. In a couple of years he would be ready to put in his papers and Mackenzie would be ready to run for the Senate or even the governorship. They would make a hell of a good team, Mackenzie up front, Joe behind the scenes, mastering the intricate and gregarious world of political manipulation.

But none of it was to be. Anthony Diamond, with his arms crossed on the back of his chair and his head thrust forward over them, would see to that. His sharp, small-featured face hung in front of Joe's eyes like a disembodied apparition. With the malign cleverness of a nightmare that steals a thousand details from reality so that you can't make it go away by waking up, he had insinuated himself, with his probing questions about Bob Mackenzie, into the most secret corners of Joe's privacy. It took fully a minute for the enormity of what had just happened to sink in, but when it did, it hit with an impact that felt more like terror than anything Joe had ever known before. A convulsive shudder ran the length of his body and for that moment he actually believed that they had the power to tap his mind.

"He wants you to work for him," Diamond was saying.

It wouldn't help to lie or evade, they knew everything. "We talked about it last year," Joe said. "I don't know if he still does."

Diamond's eyes narrowed. "There's a telephone over there," he said. "You get him on the wire, Longo, and you work it out."

Scala said, "You've gotta do it if you want to help yourself, Joe. There's a lot of wrong stuff going down out there and we need a man on the inside."

Unable to answer, to say anything, Joe just shook his head dumbly. He felt almost physically sickened by the way Scala tried to make it sound like they were asking him to accept a daring and attrac-

tive assignment. *A man on the inside.* As though he would be volunteering to infiltrate behind enemy lines. Except that Mackenzie was his
friend not his enemy, had asked for his help, trusted him at least to the
extent that trust was implicit in the offer of a job.

"Think about it, Joe," Scala said softly, stepping forward almost
in front of Diamond. "You're in too much trouble to make the wrong
decision now. If you need a couple of days to think it over, that's
okay."

Joe nodded.

With his left arm, Diamond shoved Scala to the side and thrust
his finger, pointed like a gun, in front of Joe's face. Just four days ago
no one, not even the commissioner, could have done that without getting his arm torn off. But now it was no contest. Diamond's eyes
burned in on his and his voice was like splintered ice.

"But if you gotta think about it, Longo," he said, "here's what I
want you to think about. No matter how you cut it, you only got three
choices. You can work with us, you can go to jail, or you can blow
your brains out. Take your pick."

Something in Joe's mind clicked, as though Diamond's words
clarified something that had been confusing him. He slapped
Diamond's hand to the side and stood up. "You are a fucking
animal," he said, choosing the word because it was the strongest way
he knew to express his contempt. Not hatred, not anymore, but contempt, the contempt he had seen once, in a film, on the face of a tiger
shot once straight through both shoulders, unable to move, twisting its
neck painfully so that it could stare directly into the camera as the
hunters moved in for the point-blank kill.

Something else, too, was beginning to become clear. Not with the
sharpness with which he suddenly saw who Diamond and Scala were.
It was less sudden and less intelligible, the feeling a man gets when he
is beginning to understand. He wasn't even sure what it was he understood, but it was about what he had to do. It was about himself.

Chapter 13
Advice of Counsel

THIS TIME JEANNIE didn't cry.

She listened in silent fury as Joe recounted his meeting with Diamond and Scala. As her anger mounted, she realized it wasn't all directed at them. She was angry with Joe, too, for she never would have believed before this that he could let himself be defeated, could let himself accept defeat. Ever since Tuesday night, when he told her the whole story, she had done nothing but brood about it, had gone over it so many times that she actually felt as though she had lived through it herself. And still she couldn't see what he had done wrong.

Broke a regulation perhaps. He should have reported it when Danzie tried to give him money, he should have reported it when he took it. But he didn't. Was that a crime? Was that any reason to treat him like a criminal? It wasn't fair, and she couldn't understand why Joe accepted it.

She knew he had finished talking only because she didn't hear his voice any longer. They were sitting opposite each other at the kitchen table in the dim light of the late afternoon. The low sun, setting at the

217

front of the house, washed in through the living room windows and spread across the carpet like syrup on a plate, stopping well short of the kitchen. Why are we sitting here, she thought, when it's so much brighter in the living room? But in a few minutes the light would be gone there, too, so she didn't suggest moving.

His eyes begged her to say something, so she said, "Joe, this is just ridiculous. I can't believe you're just letting this happen."

"Letting it happen?" he protested weakly, using her words, but with despair in place of bitterness. It hurt to have her turn on him, but it was what he had wanted her to say. He needed her anger because just then he had none of his own.

"Yes, letting it happen," she said sharply. "You know you didn't do anything wrong, at least not what they say."

"I took the money," he answered.

"But why did you take it?"

"What does that matter?"

"Of course it matters. Did you explain it, did you try to tell them?"

"I did, I tried to, but—"

"But what? They didn't believe you?"

His shoulders shook with a kind of low sobbing laugh. "Of course they believe me," he said. "But that's got nothing to do with it. They know why I took it. They've known all along. It's the way they set it up."

"But if they believe you—"

He cut her off. "Jeannie, when you want a guy you get him," he explained. "I've told you that a hundred times. Only now it's me, don't you see that? The whole thing was to get me to take that envelope and I took it. What else is there to say?"

He knew how the system worked and that you couldn't beat it. In all his years in Narco he had never flaked a guy but he knew detectives who had and he knew why he didn't do it. It wasn't because it was wrong but because a good detective could make cases without cheating. Usually the guys who would lay stuff on a dealer they couldn't catch dirty did it because they were too lazy to make the case the right way. But if that was what they had to do, then it was what they had to do. What it came down to was that when a cop knew you were dealing and knew he was going to get you, then one way or the other you were going to be busted. Sooner or later you'd make a mistake, or

if he had to he'd make you make the mistake, but in the end it came
to the same thing. It was an ugly system but it was the only system
there could be. At least Joe thought so up to now, had used it because
it gave him the power to operate, and had never questioned it.

Now it was too late to start asking questions. That was all right
for Jeannie, who couldn't get it out of her mind that it wasn't fair. But
fair had nothing to do with it. The fact was Diamond and Scala had
him cold and, fair or not, there wasn't a thing he could do about it.

"I don't know," she said sharply, standing up from the table and
walking away from him. "Maybe you're right, maybe there's nothing
to say. But it's not like you, Joe, to give up. If that's the only thing you
can think of to do, then do it. Just roll over and let them walk all over
you, let them do whatever they want to you. You understand these
things, I don't."

She spoke with a cold anger Joe had never heard in her before.
"What do you want me to do?" he pleaded. "It's easy for you to say
don't give up but there's nothing to give up. I don't have any choice."

"Of course you do," she said, standing directly in front of him,
her feet planted wide apart on the linoleum floor, her body suddenly
like iron.

He looked up into her eyes and then looked away, a wave of self-
pity washing over him. "Yeah," he laughed sardonically, "I could
shoot myself."

"What are you talking about?" she demanded angrily.

"That's what Diamond said."

"What is?" She was suddenly frightened.

He hadn't told her about the three choices Diamond had given
him because he knew how she would take it. But now he had to tell
her, had perhaps alluded to it on purpose in order to make himself
have to tell her.

"He said that if I didn't work with them I could go to jail or I
could blow my brains out."

For an instant she thought she would scream. It may have been
just a remnant of the Old World superstitions she had learned from
her mother, but that kind of talk filled her with a gut-deep dread, like
when you wake up cold and panicky from a nightmare in which something terrible is happening to the children. Then she took a deep
breath and said, "This has gone far enough, Joe. I don't know who
these men are, but a human being doesn't treat another person that

way. There's got to be something we can do. I want you to call a
lawyer."

"What good'll that do?" he asked.

"I don't know," she said, "but if you don't go to a lawyer I will."

Joe had known John Meglio since he was working narcotics in
Brooklyn and Meglio was in the Brooklyn D.A.'s office. Ironically,
that was also where he had met Pete Patrigno, who was in the D.A.'s
squad there at the time.

Over the years Joe and John had kept in contact, even though Joe
was no longer in Brooklyn and John had left the district attorney's
office, at first for a Bar Association fellowship in Los Angeles and then
for private practice back in New York. Three or four times a year,
when Joe knew he would be working late, he would call John at his
office and they would go out to dinner together, where they could
reminisce about the Brooklyn days over a plate of linguine and a bottle
of Verdicchio. It was a strange friendship, warm and close, but based
entirely on the past. In a way, each of them saw something of himself
in the other, something of his more youthful self that he wasn't quite
sure he had been able to preserve. For they were both dedicated men
who had somehow managed to hold on to the passionate enthusiasm
they had brought to their work when it was all fresh and new.

It was a little past six when Joe called Meglio's office. The secretary said he wasn't in and hadn't been in all day. He was home sick
and she wasn't sure if he would be in on Friday.

Joe called him at home. "I've gotta see you," he said. "Are you
gonna be in tomorrow?"

"I think so," Meglio answered, "but I'll have to see how I feel in
the morning. Why?"

"I've gotta see you," Joe repeated, obviously not wanting to say
more on the phone. "It's a personal thing."

"If I can be there I will," John promised. "Call me again in the
morning."

Joe woke up from a night of restless sleep cursing his stupidity.
During his brief conversation with John Meglio the night before, the
suspicion that his telephone might be tapped had once again passed
through his mind. By morning he was certain of it. That meant they

knew he was talking to a lawyer and probably would increase the pressure to get him to crack.

He went down to breakfast determined not to do anything that would let Joey and Marie sense that he was troubled. But on his way into the kitchen his eye was caught by the white wall phone next to the stove. Taking his usual place at the table between the children, he listened distractedly to Joey's effusive predictions about the basketball playoffs, but after a few minutes realized that he was unable to follow what the boy was saying. Confused, he threw out a few observations of his own and then felt all his nerves tighten as it dawned on him that he probably wasn't making any sense.

He glanced nervously over his shoulder to where Jeannie was stirring the scrambled eggs at the stove, then repeated the gesture half a minute later and again only a few seconds after that. At first he thought he was looking at her, impatient for her to come to the table. But after she had served the eggs and taken her seat opposite him, he caught himself looking in that direction again and realized that he hadn't been looking at her at all, but at the telephone. Like a parasite in the bowels of his own home, it sucked at his consciousness, draining away even the pretense of composure. At any moment he expected it to ring, expected a cold and unfamiliar voice to tell him to meet Anthony Diamond at noon.

He tried to think whether he knew anyone around the courthouse who would tell him whether there was an order for a wiretap on his phone, but he didn't know whom he could trust or what courthouse to try. Scala worked in the Southern District but Joe's home was in the Eastern. He had friends in both places, except that a cop in a jam doesn't have friends. They turn away from him the way football players walk away from a man injured on the field.

Besides, Diamond would have thought already what Joe was thinking now. He wouldn't have risked going into a courthouse where Joe had friends. He and Scala were too cagey to take the chance that there wasn't somewhere in the vast law enforcement system one person with enough guts to get to Joe and say, *Joe listen forget I ever told you but I just saw an order for a tap on your phone I don't know what it means but I thought you should know.*

If there was irony in the fact that they would probably use a cheater, it was an irony that escaped Joe entirely. What galled him instead, as he waited for the phone to ring, convinced that it would, was the fact that they could use his telephone but that he couldn't.

"If you want a ride to school, cmon, I'm going now," he announced suddenly, cutting Marie off in the middle of something she was asking her mother. Joey, his breakfast half finished, looked at him uncomprehendingly and then turned to his mother for help. When she nodded permission, he bounded from the table and ran upstairs for his books.

Little Marie sat motionless, a look of hopeless confusion on her face. She said nothing but her eyes filled.

Joe stood up and walked from the table, intending to ignore her. Instead, he turned. "What's the matter with you?" he demanded roughly.

"She's not ready to go, Joe," Jeannie said. "She's not dressed."

He hesitated a moment and then, almost out of a compulsion to make things worse, to lash out, he said, "Why couldn't she tell me that?"

Jeannie said only, "Please, Joe."

"Please what? She can answer a question, can't she?" he asked cruelly.

"Don't take it out on her," Jeannie pleaded. "You can see that she's upset."

Of course he could see it, could even, really for the first time, feel it. Over the past two months how many whispered conversations had they had in the bedroom about her, the two of them trying to understand their little girl's sudden moodiness? It was just a phase, they had agreed, exhorting each other to greater shows of patience. Once Joe had said, "The trouble with us is we're spoiled," by which he meant that neither of the kids had ever been the fragile sort.

Yet recognizing the problem had never helped him understand it, for he had always been incapable of understanding weakness. If he succeeded in masking his secret intolerance, it was perhaps only because he took his wife's word for it that this was what he had to do. It came, then, almost as a shock to see suddenly inside her despair, to hear his own words replayed in his mind as though through her ears. If he could have he would have said something to make up to her for his cruelty, but instead he heard himself say, "It's no big deal. She was going to take the bus anyway."

Then he turned and hurried out the back door, knowing even as he did that he was fleeing from his own child because of something of himself he had seen in her.

"It was very important to Joe that people liked him," Jeannie said in an interview. "I know everyone wants to be liked, but with him it was almost an obsession. I don't mean to sound like he was sick about it or anything like that, but sometimes he did carry it too far.

"I remember once I took him to meet this friend of mine. She was a couple of years younger than we were, a very attractive woman. So Joe and I went over to her house and she and Joe hit it off right away. They were just kidding around, you know, the way people do, and at one point she said something about Joe's clothes. He was just wearing a sport jacket and slacks but everything he wore always looked good on him and she commented on it. It was obvious it was a dig at her own husband— at least it was obvious to Joe and me. I don't remember if she said, 'Why don't you dress like that?' or something to that effect, but that was the gist of it. And we could see he didn't take it quite right.

"Well, a couple of days later she was at our house and Joe came home. She said something to the effect that 'My husband doesn't like you.' It was really part of the same kidding, like she was saying her husband was jealous. But it upset Joe. He didn't show it at the time but later that night he asked me if I knew why Ted didn't like him. And for a couple of days he kept coming back to it.

"I tried to tell him how silly the whole thing was. I mean, these were people we hardly knew. But Joe just couldn't stand the idea that there was someone who didn't like him. It preyed on his mind.

"Now, I don't know if all this means anything, but it's the way he was. What people thought of him meant an awful lot to him, more than it should have, really. And that may have had something to do with what happened. He was a strong man in so many ways, strong in his opinions, in what he believed in. That was his nature, I don't know how else to say it. But there was this one weakness, and it was what they used to destroy him."

"Joe called me at home late Friday morning and he said he had to see me," John Meglio recalls. "I said, 'Look, Joe, if I could have gone in I would have. Won't it keep till Monday?' And he said no, it had to be right away. But then when I told him he could come out to the house it turned out he couldn't make it that afternoon so we ended up arranging it for Saturday.

"Around one o'clock Saturday afternoon the doorbell rang and there was Joe and he had Luke Antonelli with him. It really threw me because it wasn't what I was expecting at all. I had met Luke once a number of months before. Joe and I had gone out for supper and then we stopped off at his office and he introduced me to all the guys who were there. I remember he threw his arm around Luke's shoulder and he said, 'And this is my partner, or at least he will be as long as he lasts.'

"At the time Luke didn't have the beard, so it must have been before he went under cover to make the buy in the Meredith case because that's when he grew it. In other words, it must have been around August of seventy-one, which was very shortly after Joe joined the Task Force. I guess he was very excited about being there and was more or less showing off all his new buddies to me. He was like that.

"Anyway, I recognized Luke even with the beard, but to tell you the truth I hardly recognized Joe. He looked terrible. He was drawn and tense—the kind of nervousness you can actually see in a person the minute you look at him. The whole look of his face was different. And he was pale, the color of this paper.

"I was just wearing a bathrobe because I had no idea he'd be bringing anyone. So I asked them in and offered them coffee or beer or a drink, but they didn't want anything. Then I excused myself and I went into the bedroom to get dressed. The bedroom's right down the hall from the living room and I could hear that neither of them said a word to the other one, which gives a good idea of what the atmosphere was like.

"When I came back to the living room Luke was sitting on the sofa and Joe was standing in the middle of the room. I said, 'Okay, now what's the problem? What can I do for you?' Luke looked at Joe and Joe didn't say anything. He walked right across the room to where I have this old console radio in the corner and he turned it on.

"Now of course I knew what that meant. It's a thing you do to defeat a bug because the microphones can't distinguish one kind of sound from another. But I was too flabbergasted to say anything. Luke, though, just looked at him for a minute and then he said, 'Jesus Christ, Joe,' and went over and turned the radio off.

"I don't know whether Joe was thinking that someone had

bugged my house or that I was going to be recording what he said, but whatever it was, he didn't say anything. He just stared at the radio for a few seconds and then he went and sat down. He took out his memo book and leafed through it until he found the right place to start. Then he told me the whole story. He had it all down in that memo book, except that every once in a while Luke would correct him on some little detail or add something that Joe left out. But other than that, Joe talked without interruption, using his notes from the book.

"Of course, there were some things in there that he got wrong, that he and Luke both got wrong because no one knew anything about them until after Joe was dead. For example, he didn't know anything about Gil Lacey's involvement, the fact that Lacey was working for Scala and was Scala's intermediary with Danzie. And he didn't know a thing about Danzie's original mission, which was to get into the Tombs. So, naturally, he assumed that the whole thing had been set up to get him, that he had been the target from the beginning.

"Up until that point I hadn't said a word, because when a man comes to you and he's in trouble it's important to let him tell it in his own way. But I had to ask him if he had any idea why they would want to get him, because if I was going to defend him it was something I had to know.

"Joe said, 'I think because they thought they could use me to get at Bob Mackenzie.'

"Luke seemed very surprised. Apparently it was the first he had heard about the Mackenzie business. So Joe explained what it was they wanted him to do and then—I remember it very distinctly, I think these are his exact words—he said, 'You see what it is, John. Luke's got nothing to do with any of this. Frankly, they don't even want him, it's me they want. But they're squeezing him to put more pressure on me.'

"And then Luke said, 'Joe, you do whatever you've got to do.'

"So Joe turned to me and he said, 'Well? What do you think?'

"And I said, 'It stinks.'

"And he said, 'I know it stinks but I'm asking you as a lawyer what do you think.'

"I told him I thought they had a weak case, because of the entrapment issue and a lot of other things. And he said, 'Yeah, really? How much time you think I'll get?'

"Now that was the last thing in the world I had expected him to say, because just listening to him, without even taking notes or going into it very deeply, I could see a thousand and one ways to fight the case. First of all, as I just said, there was the entrapment. Flagrant, no two ways about it. I realize that's not an area where we have very good case law, but even back then—this was seventy-two—the courts had already started looking at entrapment cases a little more closely. Just off the top of my head I could think of at least two or three cases where there had been reversals under circumstances far less flagrant than what we had here.

"And in the second place, it seemed to me that the wiretap case against Luke was almost nonexistent. He hadn't installed the tap, he never serviced it, and he went to the basement that night only because he was giving his partner a ride home. And as far as Joe was concerned, his case afforded a perfect opportunity to turn the tables on them and put the whole double-standard system on trial. Personally, I'm opposed to illegal wiretapping and always have been. I was opposed to it even when I was a prosecutor. But bringing charges against the cop who uses illegal taps isn't the right way to put a stop to it. It only compounds one injustice with another. What has to be attacked is the system where the superior officers wink at the practice and tacitly encourage it most of the time, except that every once in a while the Internal Affairs Division singles out one particular individual for prosecution. If you stop to think about it, when you put those two things together it adds up to a form of blackmail, a way of keeping people in line. Because what you've got is a system where every cop is under terrific pressure to do things that will compromise himself.

"Now, those are just a few of the main lines a defense could have taken. In addition, there's a very real rights question here. Luke repeatedly asked for an opportunity to consult with counsel and was told he couldn't. And Joe certainly was never told that he could refuse to answer their questions. Now to a layman this may seem silly, because these are cops who should have known what their rights were. But you have to remember they were questioned by superior officers who had the authority within the Police Department to give them orders. You have to remember that they were never formally arrested or charged with any crimes. There's no question but that procedures like this would not be allowed in dealing with a civilian. A civilian is arrested and arraigned, and then the police talk to him about making some kind of deal in exchange for information. They don't give him back his weapon and send him back on the street and in effect toy with him for a week or two while he thinks things over.

"Look at the hypocrisy involved. If this man is a criminal—or rather, accused of a crime, since there is supposedly a presumption of innocence—how can they justify giving him his gun and his shield and permitting him to function as a police officer? He should be suspended at once. But, of course, they're not interested in protecting the public —because that's what we're talking about here, isn't it? Their only interest is in exerting the maximum pressure on him. And they know, from experience and from simple human nature, that it's infinitely harder for him to say no to them if he's still got his freedom, his gun, and his shield. Everyone knows that. If a man won't break under torture, then stop torturing him, let his senses recover, and then ask him if he wants you to start in again. By the same token, if a man won't do what you want in order to gain his freedom, then give him his freedom and let him think it over. The longer he stays out, the harder it becomes to turn himself in. This is what I mean when I talk about toying with a man instead of proceeding in the way the law says you should.

"Or consider the question of the right to counsel, which I've alluded to already. Now this Sixth Amendment area is what some people might consider a 'technical' defense. But in a sense it really gets at the heart of the matter because it goes straight to the issue of whether a policeman accused of a crime has the same rights as any other citizen. Obviously, as it stands now the answer is no, that he doesn't have any rights at all. And this is a very frightening situation. It starts with men like Paul Scala and Anthony Diamond using what I might call extra-Constitutional means to prosecute police officers, but before long they're looking outside the Police Department. They're looking at judges and district attorneys and other elected officials. And when that happens—and it was happening already, that's what the Mackenzie thing was about—then what we've got is a bunch of self-appointed Robespierres, a Committee of Public Safety that metes out vigilante justice to its political enemies.

"Of course, I didn't go into all of this with Joe and Luke. But I did tell them that I thought they had a strong position for making a defense. I also told them that it wouldn't be possible for me to represent both of them because of the potential conflict of interests. At first Luke said he didn't care about that but I explained that it was out of the question. As a lawyer I'd have to be free to advise my client to do what was best for his own interests, regardless of whether or not he was going to take my advice. And of course I couldn't do that if what I was advising one client was inimical to the best interests of another client.

"I could see that talking about this was making both Joe and Luke very uncomfortable. Luke, I would say, was embarrassed by the whole thing. At least that's the closest I can come to putting it into words. He kept saying, 'Look, I'm not interested in that,' and 'Joe and me are in this together.' But Joe's reaction was something else entirely. He didn't say a word and he seemed to be just staring across the room. Except that I could see he was looking at Luke out of the corner of his eye, as though he were watching for him to make a wrong move. It was very unpleasant, because I always knew Joe as a very open guy, very trusting of his friends. And when a man like that starts to get suspicious, it's a very sad thing.

"Sad and dangerous. But of course the danger never struck me at the time. It should have, I suppose, but you just don't think of things like that.

"In any case, I asked Luke if there was any attorney he had in mind and he asked me to recommend someone. So I called a man I knew, a very good attorney, and asked if he could come over. It turned out he had plans for the afternoon but he said he could come on Sunday. Well, that was okay with Joe and Luke so we settled on a time that we would all get together on Sunday.

"Then, just as they were leaving, Joe turned to me and he said, 'John, what should I do about the money?'

"At first I didn't know what he meant. I guess I thought he was referring to my fee, although it was a funny way to say it. But then he said, 'Should we hold on to it or give it back to them or what?'

"Frankly, I was shocked. I don't think that's too strong a word for it. I said, 'You mean you've still got it?'

"In all the years I've been practicing law I never heard of such a thing. It would be like arresting a man after a bank robbery and letting him keep the money.

"But Joe just said, 'Yeah.'

" 'Why didn't you give it back to them?' I said.

"He said, 'I thought about it but I wasn't sure it'd be the right thing to do. I had it on me that night, you know.'

"I had known that—he had mentioned it. That was part of the reason I had assumed he had given it back to them. But I just couldn't believe they hadn't even asked for it. I don't mean that I thought he was lying but I was just so surprised I couldn't help myself. I turned to Luke and I said, 'Do you mean to tell me they never asked you for the money?'

"And he said, 'That's right. I kind of thought Joe would give it to them, too.'

"So Joe said, 'I don't know what I was thinking. I guess I was afraid they'd just stick it in a drawer somewhere and say I never gave it to them, and then I'd really be up Shit Creek. I guess I should have anyway, shouldn't I?'

"I just said, 'Well, it doesn't matter now.' But it was too bad he hadn't done it. Because the whole bribery case, of course, depends on their contention that Joe and Luke took the money for their own use. Now obviously, a cop who takes a bribe doesn't carry the money around with him. He sticks it in a mattress or something. And he certainly doesn't have it on him two weeks later. So if he had returned it that night it would have been exculpatory, but now all it would mean was that he was making restitution. There would be only his word for it that he had kept the money intact in order to make a bribery charge on Danzie.

"But of course that's precisely why they didn't ask him where the money was, which would have been the normal thing to do. You see, they knew why he took the money and they knew he was looking for Danzie. That's why they didn't search him and that's why they didn't ask about it. In that way they could make it look like he kept it for himself.

"Obviously, I didn't say any of this to Joe. He was upset enough, and he didn't need me telling him he had made a mistake. So I just said it didn't matter and the way it ended up was that he gave me the money to hold in the original envelope Danzie had given him.

"And that was the first meeting, really the only one I ever had with Joe. It was the last time I ever saw him. I remember when they left I went to the window and I watched the two of them walk down the street to Joe's car. And I thought, Jesus Christ, what they had done to him. He looked so stooped and old. It broke my heart to see him. And if he hadn't just been at my house and if someone had called me over to the window and said, 'Look, there goes Joe Longo up the street,' I would have looked at him and I would have said, 'No, that's not Joe Longo.' "

The Sunday appointment with John Meglio was the first of a series Joe broke that week. Luke Antonelli arrived promptly at eleven, followed a few minutes later by George Wilson, the lawyer who would be handling Luke's defense. Meglio poured three cups of coffee from the large pot on the sideboard and suggested that they start filling Wilson in on the case.

"If it's all right with you, I'd rather not talk till Joe gets here," Luke said apologetically. "He should be here any minute."

When half an hour had passed and he still hadn't arrived, John tried calling him at home. He got Jeannie, who said that Joe wasn't in and that she didn't know where he was. Playing it carefully because he didn't know how much Joe had told her, John identified himself and said, "Joe and I were supposed to get together this morning and he's not here. Do you know if he's on his way?"

She said, "I'm sorry, I don't, John."

"Okay, no problem. Just have him give me a call when he gets home."

Jeannie hung up the phone. "That was John Meglio," she said. "He says you were supposed to meet him this morning."

Joe nodded but didn't say anything.

"Didn't you see him yesterday?" she asked.

"I told you I did."

"No, you said you were going to but you never said you did. Did you?"

She had been angry all night because he hadn't said a word about his meeting with the lawyer, had in fact walked away from her when she tried to question him about it.

"Yes."

"Well, what did he say?"

"He didn't say anything."

"But he wants to see you again?"

"Yeah."

"Well, don't you think you had better go?"

"What the hell for?"

His passivity was as frightening as it was exasperating, as though he already had seen the foreordained outcome. All she could say was, "Because he wouldn't want to see you if he didn't think he could help."

When that got no response she said, "And because he's a friend and you said you'd be there."

In the end she had her way, at least to the extent of getting Joe to promise he would keep the appointment. "Call him, so he'll know you're coming," she said, but Joe promised to call from a pay phone along the way. Knowing how frightened he had become of the telephone in the last few days, she didn't push it.

Whether he was lying to her or whether he meant to keep the appointment when he left the house, neither John nor Jeannie can guess. But by the time he called John he had decided not to go. When John's phone rang, Luke said, "That's Joe."

"John?"

"Yeah, where are you?"

"I had some things to do, I got tied up," Joe lied.

"Well, the others are already here. How long till you can get here?" John asked.

Instead of answering, Joe asked, "What's Luke been telling you?"

"He hasn't been telling us anything," Meglio answered impatiently. "He didn't want to say anything till you got here."

"He says it's my fault, doesn't he?"

"No, he doesn't say that. You're the one who's been saying that, you said it yesterday."

Joe ignored the last words as though he hadn't heard them. "He's probably telling you I took the money and I got him into this," Joe snarled, his voice twisted with inexplicable bitterness.

"Well, didn't you?"

"No. We split it," Joe hissed, like a malevolent child telling someone else's secret.

"You what?"

"We split it. Ask him, he'll tell you," Joe said, his voice suddenly cold and distant. Then he added, "Unless he doesn't remember that."

There were a few seconds of silence while John groped for the right thing to say. He didn't believe Joe's statement about splitting the money, assumed it was just an irrational accusation. So quickly that he barely had time to realize the implication, half a dozen examples of his friend's erratic behavior flashed through his mind—turning on the radio yesterday, attacking Luke today, pretending he hadn't been home when the fact that he called back less than five minutes later proved that he had been. It wasn't clear what it all added up to, but it was clear that one wrong word might start Joe off on another round of crazy suspicions.

"Well, that's something we've got to talk about," John said. "When you get here we'll straighten it all out."

"Ask him yourself, you don't need me for that," Joe answered angrily.

There was a click and then the line seemed dead. "Do you want me to ask him now? Hold on, I'll ask him," John said quickly, afraid that it was already too late, that Joe had hung up. An instinct told him to keep talking, to keep his friend on the line, and he heard himself going on with words he can't remember now. Then there was a dial tone in his ear and he stopped, stunned.

Jeannie stood in the doorway, opening the door just to her shoulder. "You should have called, Luke," she said. "I don't know when he'll be back."

"That's okay, I just thought if he was in . . . " He let the sentence trail off, unfinished. Then he said, "Do you mind if I wait for him? It's kind of important."

She forced a laugh and stepped back from the door. "Of course. I wasn't even thinking."

He walked into the kitchen and closed the door behind him. She said, "Do you want a cup of coffee? There's some cake unless the kids finished it."

"Just coffee. You don't know where he went?"

"No." She picked up the percolator and shook it to gauge how much was left. "This is from this morning," she said. "I'll make fresh."

"Don't bother, it's what I'm used to," Luke said.

He sat at the kitchen table and waited while she poured two cups and joined him. After a few seconds he said, "He's home, isn't he?"

"Yes," she confessed, after only the slightest hesitation.

Luke smiled thinly, thanking her for her honesty. "Do you know why he doesn't want to see me?" he asked. Somehow they both sensed that a barrier had fallen and they could talk to each other freely. They needed each other's help if they were to get through this and get Joe through it.

"He doesn't want to talk to anyone," she said. "He's very upset."

"Oh."

"Were you at the lawyer's this afternoon?"

"Yeah, I just left there."

"Was Joe there?"

"No. Wasn't he here?"

"He went out, he said he was going. He got back about five o'clock."

"Oh. Well, he wasn't there."

She nodded. "He doesn't tell me anything anymore. He doesn't say anything." She took a sip from her coffee and asked Luke for a cigarette. Then she said, "What did he say?"

"John? He thinks we have a good chance. So does Wilson."

"Who's Wilson?"

"The other lawyer. John said he couldn't represent both of us."

"I see. Does Joe know that's what they think?"

He took a deep breath and let it out slowly. "I don't know, Jeannie. I don't know what he knows. John said yesterday he thought we had a good case but I don't know if Joe was listening. Do you think it would help if I told him?"

She nodded.

"Where is he? Upstairs?"

She nodded again.

He knocked twice at the bedroom door and then opened it. Joe was in a chair by the window, facing him.

"Joe?"

"Yeah?"

"Jeannie said it'd be all right if I came up."

There was no answer.

"Mind if I turn on a light?"

There was no answer.

Luke walked across the dark room and sat on the corner of the bed barely two feet from his partner. "I just came from John's. He says he thinks we have a good chance of beating this thing."

"And you believe him?"

"Sure."

"Well, maybe you have a chance, I don't know. Does anyone know we split the money?"

"Just John and Wilson."

"Who's Wilson?"

"The other lawyer."

"Oh. Well, they can't tell and I won't. You'll be okay."

"They said they thought we could both beat it."

"They're full of shit, they're all full of shit. They're just trying to string us along."

"I don't know, Joe. They said there were a lot of grounds, they said—"

Joe cut him off. "They're still full of shit. There's only one way to beat it and that's if I work for them."

"Is that what you want to do?" Luke asked, his voice registering not so much anger as disappointment.

"No. And I'm not going to either."

There was a childish petulance in the way Joe said it that made Luke hesitate. Then he said, "John thinks you should just tell them that and then we'll see what they do."

"I'll tell you what they'll do. They'll put me away, no two ways about it."

"John says they must know they've got a weak case and maybe they're bluffing."

"What the fuck does he know? He doesn't know the way they operate. I do. And I'm telling you it doesn't matter what kind of case they have, they're gonna lock me up. Did I tell you, Joey wants to be a priest."

"You always said you didn't want him to be."

"No, it'd be nice. I don't think we have any priests in the family."

"If that's what he wants."

"He's okay, he'll be okay, but I don't know about Marie. She's so scared all the time, every little thing frightens her."

"She'll be okay. Some kids go through it, that's all. When Billy was in first grade—no, kindergarten—he had the same thing. Like starting school was too much for him. You just looked at him the wrong way and he started bawling."

"Yeah?"

"Yeah, but he's over it now."

"Really?"

"Yeah."

"How come you never mentioned it?"

"I didn't know you then."

There was a long pause. Then Joe said, "Still, it's a rotten thing."

"Not really."

"Sure it is. Being scared, it's rotten. Even if you get over it, it's rotten. You ever been scared?"

"Sure." In the silence, Luke could hear Joe's unstated question so he said, "I was scared shitless the other night when all those guys came out of the walls."

"Yeah, me too. Could you tell?"

"I don't know. You were acting pretty tough with them."

"But could you tell I was scared?"

"Yeah, I could tell."

There was a kind of lightness in the conversation, which had suddenly turned into the sort of talk cops share late at night over beers in a dingy bar around the corner from the station house.

Luke said, "The way you hit that fucking door I knew you had to be as scared as I was."

Joe's rich baritone rumbled with suppressed laughter. "You better believe it," he said. Then the laugh came, loud, from deep inside him, tumbling out of control, growing like an ovation that starts slowly in one corner of a stadium and spreads, multiplies, fills the air. His body shook with it and he could hardly catch his breath, but still it came, drawing the air from his lungs like fire. Luke, too, felt the sudden release of tension and joined Joe's laughter, adding a higher, more trilling sound, like the way Glenn Miller used to play the clarinets over the saxes.

"You better believe it," Joe said again when he caught his breath. "I was never so scared in my whole fucking life."

"Yeah."

"They told me I should blow my brains out."

"It figures. Fuck em," Luke said, not catching the sudden shift in his partner's mood.

"It's better than jail."

"You're crazy. Besides, we're not going to jail."

"Yeah," Joe said. "That's what I mean."

Chapter 14
Palm Sunday

JOE LONGO SPENT the last week of his life alone. From his wife and from Luke Antonelli we get conflicting pictures of, on the one hand, a withdrawn and broken man, and on the other, a detective racing against time to solve his biggest case. At home he took his meals in silence and had almost no contact with his family. He spent a few hours in front of the television with the children, answered them when they spoke to him, but otherwise acted as though he were in a darkened theater sitting among strangers. For the most part, though, he spent his evenings alone in the bedroom, either pacing the floor like a somnambulist or sitting in the chair where Luke had found him Sunday night.

He didn't talk to Jeannie at all, seemed not even to be listening when she tried to tell him that his family would stand by him whatever happened. "We'll explain it to them," she said. "They're strong, they'll understand. You brought them up right, Joe. They know their father wouldn't do anything wrong."

It was no use but she kept trying. Each night she left him alone for an hour or more, then climbed the stairs to sit with him, to talk, to turn on the lights so that in his loneliness at least it wouldn't be dark. She knew that his world was irrevocably shattered, regardless of the outcome. He had given his life to the job. That was what all cops called it—the "job"—a word they used as a kind of private password, an ironic bit of self-mockery that only they (and their families) understood, because it wasn't a job at all but was more like a calling. And he had given his life to it, had surrendered himself so completely to the unfathomable passions of being a detective that he could never make up for all the meals missed at home, all the promises broken. At heart he was a family man who ached inwardly because he couldn't give enough of himself to his children, who couldn't let a Sunday go by without visiting his parents. Was it any wonder, then, that he blamed himself, even at times hated whatever it was in himself that drew him to the job with such compulsive fascination? Like a jealous bride who poisons her husband's intimacy with his sisters, his brothers, his bachelor friends, the job demanded all of him. Now it was thanking him with a kick in the groin.

Even if he won, could he go back to it without bitterness? Could he go back to it at all? He probably didn't know it himself, but Jeannie knew why it didn't matter to him that she and Luke and John Meglio held out the hope of vindication. Because even if a jury and a court of law believed him, even if they declared that he hadn't broken faith with the job, they could never change the fact that the job had broken faith with him.

Twice during the week, on Tuesday evening and again on Thursday, Luke came by the house to talk to Jeannie and to commune with Joe in the darkened bedroom. It was from Luke that she learned that in the daytime he was a different man. Each morning he left for work as he always had, but until Luke told her otherwise Jeannie suspected that he wasn't going to the office at all. In her mind's eye she could picture him sitting motionless behind the wheel of his car somewhere, letting the hours slip by until it was time to go home again at night.

"No," Luke told her, "he comes in. In fact, you wouldn't believe it. He's all over the place, it's like nothing's changed. Most of the time when he goes out he doesn't take me with him, but a couple of times he did. And do you know what he's doing? He's trying to find out who Carlo Danzie is."

What did he hope to discover? Luke, who was closer to the case

and to Joe than anyone else at this time, explained in an interview that
Joe never really accepted the claim that Carlo Danzie was simply an
undercover agent of the Bureau of Narcotics and Dangerous Drugs. "I
wish he told me what his thinking was or what he was trying to prove,"
Luke said, "but the best I can piece it together is this. You have to
remember that for almost two months we were both convinced that
Danzie was moving big loads. Then they told us he was working for
the BNDD. Now I remember it really bothered Joe that they had
suckered him like that. It's one thing to be working with a guy and
then instead of handing up the shipment he blows the whistle on you.
But it's ten times worse if there never was any shipment to begin with.
It galled Joe that he stuck his neck out to make this case and there
never was any case and never had been.

"Well, anyway, the best I can figure is that Joe got it into his head
that they still weren't being straight with us. Whether it was just a
guess or a hunch or he was jerking himself off, or whatever it was, I
don't know, but he had this idea that even if Danzie was working for
them he was still working for himself. And the funny thing is, of
course, he was right. I mean, Carlo was no agent and he wasn't doing
anyone any favors. So it must have been that they were letting him
move dope in exchange for him doing a number on us. Which, when
you stop to think about it is pretty disgusting, although for Carlo, of
course, it's great. Let's face it, you've got to let a stool do business, but
at least he's got to hand someone up. Except in Carlo's case. He had
it worked out so the only people he had to hand up were cops.

"So what Joe was probably thinking was he'd find out how it
worked and then when they stuck it to us he'd stick it to them even
worse. He wasn't gonna go down without taking some of them with
him. I don't know for sure that that's what he had in mind, but it'd be
just like him. I mean, can you imagine the stink if it got out that they
let this guy deal drugs in order to set up a couple of cops?

"So that's what he was doing, he was pushing all the buttons he
could trying to get a line on Carlo. See, we didn't even know who his
connections were in Brooklyn, which isn't to say we didn't have some
pretty good ideas. But that was the thing he had to find out.

"Let me give you a couple of examples. Like I said, most of the
time those last two weeks Joe didn't take me with him, didn't tell me
what he was doing. But a couple of times he did. One of the things is
he was meeting with one of the guys from the International Group.

That's the feds that handle dope deals from the other side. They got offices on Church Street. I don't wanna tell you the guy's name because he was really trying to help Joe and I don't want to get him in trouble.

"Actually, when you look back at it that's a laugh. I mean there wasn't really a damn thing he could do for Joe. But I'll give him credit, he did try, which most of them didn't—and I don't mean only the feds but the guys in the job, too. There's one thing about this job and that's when you get in a jam you find out who your friends are. What you find out is you don't have any.

"But this guy, he met Joe a couple . . . two, three times. They met at a bar uptown where nobody'd see them. Like Washington Heights, somewhere up there. And Joe would pump him about Danzie, who he moved with in Europe, what kind of business he was running, that kind of stuff. Then, what the guy didn't know, he'd go back to the office, make inquiries, and then he'd feed it back to Joe the next time they met.

"Now, practically speaking, that's a roundabout way to go but it was the only way Joe had. Say he finds out that in Italy Danzie's dealing with X or Y or Z. Well, that gives him a name, something to go on. Then he runs around for three solid days plugging that name in with all of his own people—dealers, stools, cops, anyone who might tell him, Yeah, X, he's the guy that made a big shipment to So-and-so in Brooklyn back in sixty-seven. He goes down to BCI on Broome Street checking old cases. What he's hoping to do is piece together a network of who Danzie might know. Then those are the guys he's gonna lean on—Find Danzie for me, either hand him up or I'll be all over you.

"That was his approach. Believe me, he came down pretty hard, shook a lot of people's trees that last couple of weeks. In fact, you know there are some people think he was killed. Frankly, I don't believe that for a minute, cause I was there. But if you saw the way he was pushing guys around, guys that aren't used to being pushed around, you could understand why people would come to that conclusion. Because there were a lot of people he scared.

"Like there was one time we were driving downtown, I guess it was Mulberry Street, and all of a sudden Joe sees somebody. It could be that the guy was out on the sidewalk but I kinda remember it that he was in a restaurant and Joe saw him through the window. Whichever it was, he jumps out of the car and the next thing I know he's dragging the guy back with him. Shoving him. And this isn't some spade junk dealer up in Harlem. This is a guy wears white-on-white shirts, he's got two bodyguards, he's got more lawyers than Nixon. And Joe shoves him in the back seat like the way they throw hookers in the wagon.

"Then he starts in with the questions. 'Where's Carlo Danzie?'

"Well, either the guy doesn't know or he's playing dumb, and in any case he's pissed, so he says he never heard of him. And this gets Joe mad. He starts making threats. 'You're finished, you won't be able to operate in this fucking city.' And at one point I remember he says, 'You tell So-and-so'—and he names this guy who's the head of one of the biggest families out on the Island, who also happens to be this guy's boss—'You tell him he better find Carlo Danzie by this weekend. You tell him if Danzie doesn't turn himself in to me, Sands Point ain't gonna be fit to live in.'

"Well, the guy's kind of scared, because a cop doesn't talk to people like him that way unless he doesn't care what happens. He says, 'For Chrissakes, I can't give him a message like that, are you crazy or something?'

"Joe says, 'Try me.'

"So at this point what else can the guy do? He says, 'Okay, Joe, I'll do what I can. You must want this guy pretty bad. What'd he do, kill a cop or something?'

"And Joe says, 'Yeah, that's just about it. Now get the fuck outta here, you got a message to deliver.' "

"There's very little I can tell you about that last week because I was kept pretty much in the dark myself," John Meglio says. "Luke saw Joe on Sunday and then called me at the office Monday morning. Then I called Joe at home Monday night. At first Jeannie said he wasn't in, but I told her I knew what the score was and I had to talk to him. After a few minutes he came on the line.

"He was kind of apologetic about not keeping our Sunday appointment. He admitted he had been home when I called but said he just hadn't felt up to going out. I tried to tell him that there was no reason to be so down about it, and that if we put our heads together and really worked on it we stood every chance in the world of beating this thing. Whether he believed me or whether he just wanted to get me off the line I don't know, but he agreed to come see me in my office the next day, which was Tuesday.

"I don't have to tell you, he didn't show up. When I called him that night it was the same thing all over again. Jeannie said he wasn't in and I told her quite frankly that I didn't believe her. Then she said, 'Just a minute,' and put down the phone. I waited about five minutes but I couldn't hear anything. Then she came back and said he wouldn't come to the phone. There was nothing either of us could do.

"Then, on Friday, he called me. It was a strange call, very brief. He just said, 'John, I want you to know, I got another lawyer.'

"Well, I was shocked. And to be honest with you, my feelings were hurt. I asked him who it was and he told me. But I don't think it would be proper for me to give his name. I can say this, though. I was very surprised that he would have gone to this person. In the first place, I don't think he and Joe knew each other at all. In the second place, he was Irish. Not that Joe had anything against Irish people, but the point is he wasn't Italian. Normally that was a big thing to Joe— most of his friends were Italian.

"Besides, there was another reason I was surprised. This particular lawyer had been quite a good attorney with an excellent reputation, but he was getting along in years, he had a drinking problem that was more or less common knowledge, and he was either semiretired or didn't have much of a practice left.

"I asked Joe what they were going to do but he wouldn't tell me. So I just told him that if he changed his mind or if there was any way he wanted me to help out, to feel free to call.

"And that was the last time I ever talked to him.

"I never did find out for sure how Joe came to this man, but I've always had a suspicion that it might have been through Gil Lacey. Which, of course, would have been very ironic but it makes perfect sense. Lacey had a reputation as a wheeler-dealer, a fast mover, the kind of guy who would be able to tell you what to do if you got in trouble. So it wouldn't surprise me if Joe got in touch with Lacey and Lacey gave him the name of a lawyer to go see.

"Of course, this is all guesses on my part. But what's not a guess is what the lawyer told Joe to do. He told him he didn't stand a chance and that if he took a plea maybe he'd get a suspended sentence. And you don't have to be a genius to see that that's just what Lacey would have wanted him to say. He certainly didn't want Joe going to court and possibly opening up the whole can of worms.

"But regardless of whether it was through Lacey or not, the point is that the man told him to take a plea. How do I know that? Because he told me. It was at the funeral parlor, and just about everyone Joe ever knew was there. Everyone from the Task Force was there and all the guys, with one or two exceptions, from the Special Investigations Unit that he used to be in. There were guys from his old Mounted unit in Central Park and even some actors from *The French Connection* who were friends of Sonny's and had gotten to know Joe because Joe had a bit part in the picture. And there, off in a corner—by the front door, really—was this lawyer. I recognized him but I don't think he knew who I was, so I went over and introduced myself.

"And that's when he told me. He said, 'They had him dead, I told him that. I told him he had a good record, if he took a plea he probably wouldn't do worse than five years suspended.'

"Then he asked me, 'Is that the widow over there?'

"I took him over to where Jeannie was sitting so he could pay his condolences. She was sitting on one of those benches they have by the wall talking to Sonny.

"I'll never forget it. I introduced him to her and he said, 'It's a terrible tragedy, Mrs. Longo. I guess your husband got his hand caught in the cookie jar.'

"If it hadn't been for where we were and the fact that he was an old man, I think Sonny would have hit him. He went white just like that, but then he got a hold of himself and he took Jeannie away."

"Thursday—this was a week to the day after the time we went to Scala and Diamond in the hotel—we were supposed to meet them again," Luke remembers. "It's funny but I can't recall how that came about. Whether it was that they called Joe or they called me or however it was, we were supposed to meet them and tell them what we were going to do.

"But then at the last minute we didn't go. Joe just said fuck em and that was that. We didn't show up. I can't say I was sorry either, although in a way I kind of wanted to have the whole thing over and done with. We had more or less agreed we were gonna tell them we weren't going to work, so we both figured they were going to lock us up. But for all the good we were doing ourselves we might as well have been locked up. You know how it is. You get so screwed up in your head you're no good to anyone, so that if you're gonna have to do time you might as well be doing it and getting credit for it.

"Still, it's a hard thing to do. Yknow, I think that first night, when they got us in the basement, if they'd have just took our shields and guns away and booked us that would have been the end of it. We would have done what we had to do, we'd probably both be out by now, and Joe would be alive. But they don't make it simple like that. First they take away your shield and your gun and then they give them back. It's like the way, did you ever see in the movies when the Japs have this prisoner somewhere in the jungle and he's dying of thirst? When he asks them for water they don't tell him no. They hold out the canteen and then they spill it on the ground.

"Well, this is the same thing. They dangle that bait in front of you, your gun and your shield. They let you go home. So you can see what Joe was going through, and me too, only with me it wasn't so bad because I made up my mind I was sticking with Joe. Which isn't to brag on my part about what a stand-up guy I am but just to tell you the way it was. Actually, what it did was it put all the weight on Joe's shoulders. But the point I'm trying to make is you walk out of there, like out of the courthouse that Tuesday morning after we were busted, and you say to yourself, *Fuck this, I'm not working for those bastards. I might as well go right back in and tell them.*

"But how can you do that? You just got out of there. So you figure you'll go home and get some sleep and then you'll tell them. What's the rush? And when you wake up you feel like shit and you can't get yourself to make that call. I'll take a shower, I'll get myself something to eat, get myself together, right? So then I call Joe and of course neither of us is in any hurry to go to jail so we say we'll talk it over at the office in the morning. And it just goes on like that. I remember when Joe told me he wasn't gonna work—this was before we saw John or anything—I said, 'Well, that's it, then. I guess we better tell them.'

"And he said, 'They're not gonna forget about us.'

"Well, I thought for sure that when he saw them that first Thursday he was going to tell them. Only he didn't. He was still stalling for time, I guess because of the stuff he was doing about trying to get a line on Danzie. Maybe he was getting somewhere and he figured he needed more time, or maybe he needed more time because he wasn't getting anywhere. Or maybe he was just gonna string them along for as long as he could till they had enough and they locked him up. He just wasn't gonna lock himself up, that's all.

"Well, whatever it was, a whole week passed and we were supposed to see them but we didn't. So naturally they called. They used to call us at home, which was very aggravating, even though I don't think they did it just to get on our nerves. It was more a thing where they didn't want anyone at the office to know we were talking to them. But regardless of that, they called both of us Thursday night and they set up a meeting for the next Monday.

"I wish I could remember where that meeting was supposed to be. I remember it was a bookstore. We were supposed to go to this bookstore and go back to the manager's office and there'd be someone there. Real spy stuff. If it was somebody else's nuts they had in the wringer we probably would have thought it was funny. The bookstore was somewhere in Greenwich Village or just east of there but . . .

"I tried to find it once only I couldn't remember the exact address and there must be a dozen bookstores around there.

"Anyway, Friday at work Joe and I sort of agreed that this was gonna be it. He said, 'I'll talk to you over the weekend.'

"He didn't call Saturday, and Sunday I knew he always went to his mother's—especially this Sunday because it was Palm Sunday. Well, anyway, late in the afternoon the doorbell rings and it's Joe. My wife answered the door—we were still married then. Since all this happened we've gotten . . . we're divorced. Okay, so she answers the door, and I don't have to tell you Joe didn't stand too good with her just then. She blamed him for everything. She used to say to me, 'You know you had twelve years and until you got mixed up with him you never had any trouble.'

"Fortunately I got there before she had a chance to say anything to him. We went into the living room and we turned on the television so we could talk without the kids hearing or my father, who was living with us at the time. So we talked and we decided that what we were gonna do was just hand them our shields and our guns and tell them that was our answer and that it was their move.

"But the thing was while we were talking we were sitting down and getting up and walking around, and it just so happens I look out the window and there's Joe's car out in the street. I saw it just after he pulled up, but the way the light was I couldn't see in. But by this time the street lights had come on and I could see Jeannie sitting in the front seat and the kids in the back.

"I told him, 'Have them come in,' but he didn't want to. It had been maybe forty-five minutes to an hour they had been sitting there. So I said, "Look, do we have anything else to talk about?' and he said, 'Yeah.' So I said, 'Well, let them go home, this is crazy. I'll give you a ride home later.'

"Then later we figured that since we were going to see them to-gether in the morning it made more sense for him to take my car home and then pick me up.

"Which is how we came to be driving my car that day."

Joe got up early Monday morning. He was showered and dressed before Jeannie came downstairs. She found him in the kitchen, the coffee already made, a cup by his hand. He was standing by the stove, cracking eggs into a frying pan awash with bacon grease. Strips of bacon, crisp to the point of crumbling, lay jumbled on a plate, glisten-ing with hot fat like a freshly painted wall.

She smiled and offered to help but he declined.

"You should put the bacon on a paper towel," she said.

"Put yours on a paper towel," he answered lightly. "Leave mine alone."

He carried the frying pan to the table and slid all four eggs out onto his own plate, then cut carefully between the yolks and trans-ferred her portion, slightly smaller, to her plate. He made his own breakfast infrequently, but whenever he did he always fried the eggs in the bacon fat because it gave them more flavor. She disapproved, in part because it was unhealthy and in part because she just didn't share his fondness for greasy food.

"Big day," he said, sitting down and reaching for the salt.

"I know."

She would have said more but was afraid. For almost two weeks he had been so forbiddingly unapproachable that she couldn't bring herself to seize the opportunity now that he was suddenly more himself. He seemed almost willing to talk and perhaps would have if she hadn't been too timid to press the matter.

"Yeah," he said, more to himself than to her.

They talked about inconsequential things, their conversation broken up by long silences that felt as natural as words. Then he stood up and said, "I gotta go upstairs a minute."

Tiptoeing up the stairs so as not to wake the kids, who wouldn't be getting up for another half hour, he went to the bedroom and closed the door behind him. From the closet he took the black leather attaché case Jeannie had given him when he was promoted to the Detective Bureau. It was a gift he had teased her about many times and sometimes he would tell the story to other cops as an illustration of how police wives don't understand the nature of their husbands' work. He rarely took it to the office, except when he was due to testify in court. Then he would carefully pack it with all his notes and records from the case so that he could show up at the courthouse looking as sleek and professional as any lawyer.

Although he wouldn't admit it to Jeannie, it had become over the years one of the few possessions that he really treasured. The leather was unscratched, as perfect as the day she gave it to him.

He put the attaché case on the unmade bed, snapped open the two locks and raised the lid all the way back. In a bureau drawer he found notes from some of his active cases, in the back of the closet he found a two-inch pile of old papers. Proceeding methodically, he rounded up all the records he had of his fifteen years as a cop and laid them on the bed in two small piles. Then he packed them neatly into the bottom of the case. He didn't use the accordion folder in the lid, which already held a three-page note he had written some time earlier.

Back at the closet again, he took his two guns, his Colt thirty-eight Police Special service revolver and his snub-nosed off-duty gun, from the locked case on the top shelf. He snapped the snub-nose in its waist clip over his belt at the small of his back and put the service revolver in his briefcase on top of the papers.

He put on his jacket and from the breast pocket removed his gold shield in its worn leather case. How long did he hold it in his hand, feeling the heft of the heavy metal, the worn smoothness of the cracked leather as soft and pliable as velvet? Did he open it to study for one last time the intricate casting of the bright gold?

The shield went into the attaché case beside the gun, the two locks clicked closed.

He tiptoed to the top of the stairs, then stopped as though listening for something. Setting the attaché case down, he walked back to

Marie's room and opened the door soundlessly. She was sleeping on her side, her long black hair—she had her father's hair—strewn on the pillow, her eyelids fluttering open. "Daddy?" she asked, sleepy voiced. Her eyes closed again and she smiled in her sleep as she felt him sit on the bed beside her.

He watched his little girl sleep until he knew he couldn't wait any longer. Then he bent to her and kissed her on the lips, a long, tender kiss that ached with love and regret.

He rose slowly, reluctantly, but then hurried from the room, unable even to look back at her again as he closed the door. It was fully five minutes before he could bring himself to open the door to Joey's room. So much of his son reminded him of himself that for a moment he felt almost as if he had just stepped back twenty-five years into his own room in the old house in Brooklyn. The pennants on the walls, the clutter, the carefully oiled first baseman's glove on the dresser all year round, not just during the baseball season—even Joey himself, whose shy, awkward smile Joe recognized as the same smile he saw every Sunday in the old pictures on the credenza in his mother's living room.

He reached down to brush the hair from his son's forehead, then let his hand rest on the boy's head the way in Sunday school he used to picture the aged Isaac, who looked like his own father, laying his hand upon the head of Jacob, his youngest, to bestow a blessing in his old age. But there were no words for Joe to say, there was no benediction, no counsel for him to impart.

He turned and walked from the bed but couldn't bring himself to leave the room. At the dresser he folded back a sweatshirt that hung half out of an open drawer, then straightened a stack of schoolbooks and hefted the mitt. At the desk he lingered long enough to read an unfinished homework assignment of sentence completions in American history. When he got to the one that said, "Henry Ford's most important contribution to modern society was the automobile," he took a pencil from the desk and lightly lettered in "assembly line" over the word "automobile."

The last two weeks had so filled him with bitterness that he had not had much to say to his son and now it was too late.

He stopped at the door for one more look at the boy. "Take care, Joey," he whispered.

He picked up his briefcase at the top of the stairs and carried it down to the kitchen, where Jeannie was waiting for him. When she saw the leather case she knew what was in it.

"It'll work out," she said. With the tips of her fingers she smoothed the collar of his shirt and then kissed him, yielding to him as he held her tight.

Then they stood awkwardly, a few inches apart. When he made no move to leave she said, "The kids will be up in a minute. Do you have to leave so early?"

"I'm picking up Luke."

She walked with him to the door. Then he was gone, down the three steps and across the yard to Luke's car in the driveway. She called his name and when he turned she ran after him, her peach and silver robe blown against her body in the cold and windy morning.

"You'll see," she said, her voice trembling and earnest, "it'll work out. It will."

Then she kissed him again, but this time it was like kissing stone.

Although Joe left home before seven thirty, he didn't get to Luke's house until after nine. Luke, who was at the window, came out before Joe could get out of the car. He walked around to the driver's side, opened the door, and asked for the keys. The brown paper bag in his hand held his two guns.

He put the bag in the trunk and slammed the hatch down. Then he opened the trunk again, unfolded the bag, and added his gold detective's shield. He noticed Joe's black leather briefcase next to the spare tire and knew without asking what was in it. *A briefcase and a fucking brown paper bag,* he thought. *That's all that's left of twenty-eight years.*

Joe slid to the passenger side and Luke climbed in behind the wheel. They drove for almost fifteen minutes without speaking, both men grim and sorrowful. Then Joe started to talk, a long rambling speech filled with apologies. Half listening, half lost in his own sad thoughts, Luke drove on.

"I remember that by the time we got to the Williamsburg Bridge I was a wreck," Luke says. "I was so nervous my hands were shaking. Literally shaking. I think that was when it really hit me for the first time. My shield and my weapons, they were already locked in the trunk and this was the end. For two weeks I knew I was going to have to face this, but that's not the same as when you realize it's not some-where down the road anymore. Now it was just another hour or so and then all of a sudden I wouldn't be a cop anymore. I had thirteen years and never got even one civilian complaint. But for all I knew I was gonna be in jail that night. And even if it wasn't that, I'd be out of a job, thirty-five years old, no skills, and no pension. I mean, we had planned our future around that pension.

"And then look how it worked out. No future and no pension.

"Well, anyway, like I was saying, by the time we got to the bridge my hands were shaking. I drove down below Canal Street and then I got all lost in that construction they had in the plaza there. I don't think I knew where I was going at all. There's like a rotary just below where the Manhattan Bridge comes in and I know I went completely around it twice. And all the time Joe's talking, he's saying, 'It's all my fault,' and 'I got you into this, I wish I could get you out of it.' And he's telling me he could get me out of it if he worked for them but he just can't do it.

"And then all of a sudden he said something that absolutely floored me. He said, 'Don't worry, Luke. I know where I can get my hands on ten thousand dollars. We'll get ourselves the best lawyers and we'll fight this thing all the way.' "

The car pulled to a halt at the curb opposite the foot of Mott Street. The two men talked for about five minutes but Luke couldn't get his partner to say anything further about the money.

"I wanted to know where he was gonna find that kind of money. Him and Jeannie weren't exactly savers, you know. I'm sure they had something put aside but, yknow, none of us save very much money. We just count on that pension.

"So I guess I was a little upset because, let's face it, unless you got some rich relatives, where the fuck could you get that kind of money? But it didn't bother me too much because at that point I really didn't believe him. Then he said, 'Cmon, let's get back to Brooklyn.' "

The car slid out into the midmorning traffic and made its way slowly up Bowery to Delancey and back onto the Williamsburg Bridge. Luke drove slowly, smoking cigarette after cigarette and let-ting Joe direct him through a maze of broken streets. Except for giving directions, Joe didn't say anything after the stop at Confucius Plaza. He sat stiffly upright and looked straight ahead, refusing to look to either side as they drove down streets where he had played as a child.

The course he charted zigzagged erratically, lefts and rights in a seemingly random sequence, so that on more than one occasion Luke noticed that they were on a street familiar from but a moment before.

Somewhere in the middle of the Williamsburg section of Brooklyn something changed. "Take the next left," Joe said, the firmness in his voice hinting that he had made a decision and was now directing the car toward some specific destination. After a few more turns he said, "Pull over just past the intersection."

Without a word of explanation, he climbed heavily from the car, walked back to the intersection, and disappeared around the corner.

"I had no idea where we were, I mean it wasn't a part of the city I knew. He went down the street and then I lost him. For a minute I thought maybe I should go with him but I just had this feeling like it wasn't any of my business. So I just sat there. The one street sign I could see said Hope Street but I don't know Hope and what. John Meglio knows, though. I went out with him in the car later on and we drove all the way down Hope Street till we found it."

In less than five minutes Joe returned, his massive athlete's body swaying in the stiff wind as he walked. As soon as he was in the car Luke said, "Diamond said twelve o'clock. We'd better get going, don't you think?"

Joe said, "Fuck him, let him wait."

"I looked over at him and he looked worse than ever. I mean, the week before he had been a wreck, but that morning, from the time he picked me up, I was kind of surprised at how good he was taking it. But when he said let him wait, he didn't say it like *Fuck him let him wait*. I mean, that's what he said, those were the words he used, but he said it like, Let's just wait a couple of minutes, not yet.

"I said, 'You okay?'

"He said, 'Yeah.'

"So I said, 'Cmon, let me take you home.'

"But he didn't want that. He said, 'I don't want Jeannie to see me like this,' so I guess he knew how bad he looked. Well, anyway, we sat there a few minutes and then he started giving directions again."

Soon the dull-green Plymouth was moving quickly down a broad avenue, once again heading for the bridge. Just before it reached the up ramp Joe said, "Do me a favor."

"Sure."

"Call my brother Sal, tell him I want to see him."

He told Luke to pull off the avenue into Williamsburg, then directed him past Spanish stores and two-story frame houses surfaced in asbestos tile, past vacant lots and bright brick brownstones, west on Fourth Street, past Driggs, then right on Bedford, right on Seventh, past the bulky gray back of Saint Vincent de Paul Church, where the priest once told Joe's mother that some day her son would be another Joe DiMaggio.

"Take a right here and pull up," Joe said.

The car pulled to the curb at a bus stop on Driggs Avenue down about twenty yards from the mouth of the subway station. Getting Sal's number from Joe, Luke crossed to the tiny store at the corner directly across from the subway. It consisted of one small square room with a counter to one side and pinball machines and public telephones along the opposite wall. He got change from the counterman and dialed the number.

A woman's voice answered.

"Teresa? This is Luke Antonelli, I'm your brother-in-law's partner. He asked me to call, he said he wanted to see Sal."

There were children squealing in the background. Teresa said, "Sal's at work, Joe knows that."

For a moment neither Joe's partner nor his sister-in-law knew what to say. Then Teresa said, "How come he had you call? Is he all right?"

Luke hung up the phone and hurried from the store, a vague presentiment growing at the back of his mind. When he got to the street and saw that Joe was still in the car, he slowed his pace, momentarily reassured. Then suddenly he broke into a run, his eyes locked on the window through which he could see his partner slumped in the seat, his head resting on the back cushion.

When he got to the passenger door he didn't even open it. He saw at once that Joe was dead, knew it as certainly as if he had felt his lifeless pulse. He looked away so quickly he didn't even see the small bright splotch of blood that gleamed on the dashboard, pumped there in one violent thrust when the bullet sliced into a corner of his heart.

He raced back to the candy store, confused. "What precinct am I in?" he shouted, a question so irrelevant that later he couldn't understand why he had asked it. He got his answer and dialed 911. "My partner's been shot," he screamed into the phone, "corner of Driggs and Seventh."

Alone in the suddenly empty store, he closed his eyes and held his hand over them to blot out everything. Then he walked out to the sidewalk and staggered unconsciously around the edges of the crowd that had collected there. He hesitated a moment, listening to the urgent, curious whispers of the men on the sidewalk as though he were no more a part of what had happened across the street than they were. Then, his head down so that he wouldn't have to see the car, he crossed to it and stood by the trunk, legs apart at parade rest, waiting for the sirens he already could hear crying toward him.

Part Three

Of Accidental Judgments, Casual Slaughters

by Sonny Grosso

And let me speak to the yet unknowing world
How these things came about. So shall you hear
Of carnal, bloody, and unnatural acts;
Of accidental judgments, casual slaughters;
Of deaths put on by cunning and forced cause.
                                        —Hamlet

Chapter 15
Good Friday

I WAS WORKING in the Sixth Detective District when Joe died. The Sixth D.D. includes the Twenty-fifth, the Twenty-eighth, and the Thirty-second Precincts, all of which are located in an old and vicious part of Harlem where dope and rundown tenements combine to create one of the highest incidences of violent crime anywhere in the country. At the time, my partner, Randy Jurgensen, and I had just spent two of the most frustrating months of our careers trying to get a lead on a pack of depraved gunmen who called themselves revolutionaries and were trying to prove it by killing cops. While Joe was working on Carlo Danzie, a couple of these Black Liberation Army assassins walked up behind Patrolmen Gregory Foster and Rocco Laurie on a quiet street in the East Village and shot them in the back. Both the cops died, and the butchers who did it disappeared without a trace. Needless to say, everyone working on the case was as tense as you can get without snapping. When a cop is killed, nobody gets any rest until the case is closed.

When a cop is killed. I wrote these words automatically, without even thinking, because I was trying to remember how we all felt when we were working on the Foster-Laurie investigation. And I'm going to leave that sentence the way I wrote it because that's the way it's supposed to be, and in fact the way it almost always is. But that isn't the way it was with Joe.

Sure, there were differences. Foster and Laurie were gunned down on the job, whereas Joe apparently killed himself. But in a case like Joe's, "apparently" shouldn't be good enough. A quick look at the obvious facts tells you that Joe was in a jam, that he was under tremendous pressure, that he must have cracked. His partner was out of the car less than five minutes, and when he got back Joe was dead, shot once through the heart, his own gun on the floor between his feet, one shot fired. Obviously suicide. That's what they said at the time and, to be perfectly honest, that's what we all thought.

At least that's what we thought until we started looking behind all those obvious facts. Then we started finding things that didn't fit. When I say we, I mean Joe's friend and lawyer, John Meglio, and myself. Unfortunately, the Police Department had officially closed its mind about Joe and didn't want to hear another word about him. As soon as Internal Affairs let everyone know that he was under investigation at the time of his death, the Department washed its hands of him. Internal Affairs was saying he was a crooked cop, so the sooner he was buried and forgotten, the better everyone at Headquarters would feel.

Now it's probably too late ever to know the real truth about what happened to Joe. Maybe they were right, maybe he did kill himself. It wouldn't be hard to believe—Diamond and Scala certainly pushed him hard enough in that direction. But what if he didn't? What if all the things that don't fit in add up to murder? I don't know. No one does. Maybe if the Department had cared enough at the time, it would have checked out all the facts, the way it would have done for anyone else. But years have passed now, things have been hidden and covered up, people have died or have forgotten things they might have remembered then. I wish I knew what the answer is, but I don't. All I can do is tell you what John and I found out.

I got to the Three-two sometime early Monday afternoon and I knew the minute I pushed open that warped wooden door that something was wrong. The sergeant behind the desk turned away, pretending he hadn't seen me, and a small bunch of patrolmen who had apparently been talking together broke off and headed away in different directions. Three people at the complaint desk, small, elderly black women with stories about being robbed at knifepoint or cheated in a store, stories about missing husbands or no electricity, chattered on in the strange silence until they realized no one was listening. Then they stopped and looked around in frightened old-lady confusion.

Out of the corner of my eye I saw the captain tap my brother-in-law Mike Treanor on the shoulder and gesture in my direction. Then the captain also turned away and Mike pushed his heavy frame up from where he was sitting behind the switchboard and started to walk toward me.

The first thing I thought was that it was something about my mother. I had seen her just the day before and she seemed fine, but she mentioned something about a cold.

It was taking Mike forever to get across that wide gray wood floor, and his big Irish face hung in front of me like a headlight down the highway that doesn't seem to be getting any closer. Then he was standing next to me and he said, "Sonny, Joe's dead."

For a second I was sure I was going to be sick. The next thing I remember, I was sitting on the complainant's bench along the wall opposite the desk, crammed in between Mike on one side and a long line of black faces who were staring at me with sullen curiosity. God knew, they had seen enough trouble in their lifetimes to keep a whole precinct busy. It didn't seem to surprise them that The Man had his own grief to deal with. Faces like those gave sympathy grudgingly, but they gave it.

"I thought it was going to be Momma," I said. I knew I should have felt some kind of relief that it wasn't, but I didn't feel anything like relief.

Mike put his arm around my shoulder and I asked him how it happened. He said he didn't know.

"Shot?" I asked.

"I think so," Mike said softly. "In Brooklyn, sometime this morning. We tried to get you on the radio but—"

"Does Jeannie know?"

"I think so."

I closed my eyes. If Jeannie knew, that meant it was definite.

Sometimes when a cop is killed the wrong name goes out on the wire, but they never notify the widow until it's certain.

"Who was with him?" I asked.

Mike said, "There wasn't anything about his partner."

"Did they get the guy that did it?"

Mike didn't say anything.

It took a long time for the meaning of his silence to sink in. When it did, I wanted to cry but couldn't in front of all those people. So I sat there, while next to me on the bench a black man with bloodshot eyes rocked back and forth like an old Jew praying.

The drive out to Joe's house was the longest ride I've ever taken. His brother Sal, who must have been looking out the window, opened the door even before I had a chance to knock. The house was filled with quiet, subdued voices in half a dozen different conversations, but the only one I noticed was Jeannie. She seemed to be practically running toward me, and in a moment my arms were around her and she was crying uncontrollably against my chest. She was saying something but her voice was so choked that it was hard to make out the words.

She said, "What are they going to do without a father?" and, "What are we going to do, Sonny, we're all alone?" and a lot of other things, some of which I didn't understand. I realized that they must have told her what they told my brother-in-law Mike but that she wasn't able to accept it. She was sobbing that Joe had been murdered and that the Department was protecting someone by saying he had killed himself. She was obviously beside herself, making crazy accusations I don't want to repeat about who she thought killed him.

I knew she didn't mean the things she was saying, but the loss itself was so cruel and sudden that the horrible insult of suicide was more than she could face and so she had to defend herself by closing her mind to it.

"Jeannie, where are the kids?" I asked. I wanted to make her stop talking that way.

She forced herself to stop crying and said, "Marie's upstairs with my mother."

"And Joey?"

Either the mention of his name or just the fact of having to think about the children shook her loose from her self-control. The tears came again, and all I could make out from what she said was that Joey wasn't home from school yet.

"Do you want me to tell him?" I asked.

"Please, Sonny," she sobbed.

I didn't want to do it, but it was obvious that she couldn't handle it herself and I thought it would be less painful for me than for one of Joey's uncles.

Finally we stepped away from the door and walked into the living room. I recognized three of Joe's brothers and their wives. They were clustered around his mother, ministering to her, talking to her in low voices. In a corner by himself stood Joe's father, on his face the bitterness of a man from the Old World who feels it as almost a shame that he has outlived his lastborn son.

A woman—I think it was someone I had met once before, a neighbor—came out of the kitchen with a coffee pot and a dozen cups on a tray. Jeannie led me over to where her mother and father were sitting by themselves on two kitchen chairs. Her father was a short, athletically built man who still looked as young as when I first met him a dozen years before. He let go of his wife's hand and stood to greet me. We shook hands and then embraced. "Sonny and Joe were like brothers," Jeannie said in a strange voice. I think she was telling it to her father, but somehow it came out as though she were announcing it to the whole room.

No one said anything and there was a long silence. Then Joe's brother Sal broke off from the group around Mamma Longo and walked back to the window by the front door. I wanted to ask him to let me know the minute he saw Joey because I had made up my mind to meet him outside before he had a chance to walk into the house and see everyone sitting there.

Just then the back door slammed with a sound that shot through the quiet house like an explosion. Someone gasped and Mamma Longo crossed herself and buried her face in her hands, but other than that no one moved or made a sound. By the time I could get myself together and move toward the kitchen to head him off, Joey had stepped through the doorway into the living room. He started to say something, but the words froze in his throat and his eyes darted around the room taking in all those familiar faces like he had never seen them before. I was walking toward him and in my heart I was crying for him, I was saying, *Jesus, Joe, look at what you did.* But the boy's poor frightened eyes didn't even see me, wouldn't stop moving, couldn't stop searching the room for the face he wouldn't see.

As far as the Police Department was concerned, it was like Joe Longo never existed. No one from the job got in touch with Jeannie about funeral arrangements and no plans were made to have anyone represent the Department at the funeral. They had made up their minds that he was a crooked cop and were willing to see him put in the ground without any acknowledgment on their part that for almost fifteen years he had worn the same shield they wore and had served it well.

On Thursday, when he still hadn't heard anything about the Department's plans, Captain Marcus called the Chief of Detectives office. When he told them why he was calling, the only person he could get through to was an aide to one of the deputy chief inspectors. "One of my men died this week and the funeral's tomorrow," he said. "I haven't heard a word yet and I was wondering what the Department's planning to do."

"You mean Longo?" the aide asked.

"That's right."

"The Department's not planning anything. If any of your men want to go, they can go. On their own time, that's all."

"No," Marcus said, "that's not all. I don't know what Longo did and I doubt if anyone else does. But we're not burying him like he wasn't one of us."

The aide said, "Well, I can't help you there. The decision here is no official participation."

Marcus hung up the phone and in longhand wrote out an order detailing all members of the Joint Task Force to attend the funeral as representatives of the unit with which Joe was serving when he died. A half hour after the order went up on the bulletin board in the squad room, a superior officer from the Internal Affairs Division called back to tell Marcus it had to come down. "We're not having an inspector's funeral for Longo," the deputy said. "The Department cannot officially involve itself."

In a command situation, loyalty is a two-way street. You often hear about how great captains and generals inspire their men. But the truth is that the loyalty of the men in the ranks is almost never "inspired." It's either earned or it's not there at all. And as far as I know, there is only one way to earn it. Men stand up for a boss who stands up for them.

"Joe Longo wasn't found guilty of anything," Ben Marcus said. "He wasn't indicted for anything and he wasn't up on departmental charges. Until you show me otherwise, the order stands."

Just about everyone Joe ever knew was at the wake. There were cops from the precincts in Brooklyn and Queens where Joe had worked, and all the guys he knew from Mounted. There were dozens of friends and neighbors, including about twenty guys he met on the set of *The French Connection*. Joe, in fact, was in the picture. The last scene is a shootout on Ward's Island between the cops and the drug dealers. Joe played one of the bad guys. He's the one in the camel topcoat standing next to Tony LoBianco and shooting left handed. He was only on the set about a week but in that time he got to know everybody, and when he died they all wanted to pay their respects. Phil D'Antoni, who produced the picture, was there, along with a lot of the actors and crew, including LoBianco and Roy Scheider.

In addition to the Task Force people and the other cops I've already mentioned, there was also a bunch of us who used to work together in Narcotics, including myself and Eddie Egan, Juan Piedra, Dave McKibbon, and Gil Lacey. At the time, of course, Lacey's being there didn't mean a thing to me. I knew that he and Joe went back a long way and had worked together in the Brooklyn days. Later, when I learned the whole story of the Danzie incident, I couldn't understand how Lacey had the balls even to show his face at the funeral parlor. He was supposed to be Joe's friend but he had actually helped set the trap and then sat back to watch the whole thing unfold. How could he face Jeannie, hug her, and offer her condolences as though he wasn't one of the men who in effect had loaded the gun Joe shot himself with?

The fact was that Gil Lacey had sold his soul to Scala, Diamond, and all the others who were still trying to turn Joe around even after he was dead. There's no doubt in my mind now that he came to the funeral as a spy for the Internal Affairs Division. They wanted the names of every cop who was close enough to Joe to mourn him.

They also had a man on the outside who parked right across the street from the funeral parlor and took pictures of everyone who went in. I don't know what time he got there or how long he was there, but I remember that Joe's brother Chris came over and told me that someone had just told him there was a man outside taking pictures.

I ran out to see for myself, and by the time I got to the car Eddie Egan, Dave McKibbon, and a couple of other guys that Joe and I used to work with were outside, too. I remember I was ready to pull that bastard out of his car and smash his camera in his face, but luckily I didn't have to. As soon as I confronted him, he made some half-assed excuse and got the hell out of there.

It left a bad taste in the mouth, though, and I'm sure there wasn't a cop at the wake who didn't know what had happened. It was a little while after that that a rumor got started to the effect that any cop who served as a pallbearer would be subject to investigation. I don't know whether this was just one of those things that starts spontaneously or whether some weasel spread the word maliciously. But that's neither here nor there, because one of the few things that happened in those days that made me proud to be a cop was the way everyone reacted to that rumor. Guys who weren't even that close to Joe came up to me and asked if their names could be added to the list of pallbearers.

Obviously, it was impossible. There were only going to be six pallbearers—Joe's brothers Chris and Sal, me, Eddie Egan, Dave McKibbon, and a cop named Billy Olivieri who had been a rookie with Joe in Brooklyn.

After I explained the situation, a bunch of guys came up and asked if there could be honorary pallbearers in addition to the regular pallbearers. They wanted every cop in the place—there were well over two hundred of us—to form an honor guard.

I knew what they were thinking and I loved them for it, but I didn't think it would be right. The reason they wanted to do it was not just to show everyone what they thought of Joe. It was also to tell the humps taking down names where they stood. Somehow it seemed to me that a thing like this would be exploiting Joe's funeral, no matter how good the intentions were. I didn't even think it would be right to bother Jeannie about it, so I thanked them for the offer and told them I didn't think it was a good idea. In retrospect, I guess I did the right thing, because when I mentioned it to Jeannie sometime later she said she didn't think she would have wanted it. But there were tears in her eyes when she said it and I think it meant a lot to her to know how so many other cops felt about Joe and about the men who destroyed him.

When we drove out to the cemetery, there were a hundred cars in the procession. Captain Marcus marched the whole Task Force contingent in military fashion and I still remember the way I felt when he barked his command of "Present Arms" and every cop there snapped to attention and saluted Joe's coffin as it was lowered into the ground. In the background someone played "Taps" softly, and I have a vision in my mind that I can't make go away of Gil Lacey standing near Jeannie and the kids while the winches squeaked and Joe's body inched its way into the earth.

Chapter 16
Point of No Return

A COP IN a jam loses all his rights. He loses his right to the due process of law accorded to any other person accused of a crime. If he dies, he even loses the right to have his death properly investigated.

The first cars to arrive on the scene when Luke phoned in his emergency call to 911 were from the local precinct, the Ninety-fourth. Within minutes, though, a team from Internal Affairs showed up and took jurisdiction over the case. In all my years on the job, I never saw a case "solved" so quickly where there was a violent death and no eyewitnesses. There were so many loose ends that weren't followed up on.

For example, John Meglio called me toward the end of April to tell me about a strange thing that happened at the Greenpoint Hospital in Brooklyn, where Joe's body was taken by ambulance. The admittance slip lists him as D.O.A. and gives the presumed cause of death as "bullet wound to the head." But Joe was shot in the chest, not in the head. And there were no cuts, marks, or even bloodstains on his head that could have been mistaken for a bullet wound.

To be perfectly frank, at first I didn't see any significance to this. It was strange, but probably a simple mistake. I didn't understand why John was raising the question at this time. But he sounded very upset so I said I'd come over to his office and we'd talk about it.

When I got there he filled me in on what he had been doing. Jeannie had come to see him a couple of weeks earlier. She wanted his help because the Police Department had given her only the money Joe himself had paid into his benefit fund but was refusing to give her her widow's pension. They wouldn't even explain their action and her attempts to find out the reason had gotten her nowhere.

John speculated that they were denying the pension because Joe's death had been ruled a suicide. "I don't know what their reason was," he told me, "and I still haven't been able to find out. But the thing is I promised Jeannie I'd help her. Everyone I've talked to says I'm beating my head against the wall, but I have to do something. Maybe if I'd have been able to do more for Joe, he'd be alive today."

I told him he was foolish to think like that. He had done everything he could and had nothing to blame himself for. But when a good friend kills himself, I guess you can't help feeling guilty. I had gone through the same thing myself. Of course, I didn't see Joe during those last weeks like John did. But I did call him one evening to invite him to a screening of *The Godfather*. Jeannie said he wasn't in. So I called back the next morning. Again she told me he wasn't home and that she hadn't seen him or spoken to him. I remember thinking that she didn't sound like herself but I had no idea what was going on. Later, she told me that Joe was there both times I called, sullen, unshaven, refusing to talk to me because he was certain his phone was tapped and he didn't want to involve me in his mess.

After she said that, I couldn't get it out of my mind that if I hadn't been so caught up in my own affairs I would have realized from the way she sounded that something was wrong. I should have gone out there to see him, and if I had, maybe he would have opened up about what was happening to him. Maybe if we had talked about it, he wouldn't have done what he did.

So I could see why John was torturing himself about it and why he wanted to make it up by doing something to help Jeannie. But I couldn't see what the mistake in the hospital records had to do with it.

"I don't know either, Sonny," John admitted. "But all I've got to go on is these few pieces of paper—this, the autopsy report, a couple of other things like that. And I keep reading them and reading them and reading them, hoping that they'll tell me something. I must have read this admittance slip a dozen times, and I can't get it out of my mind. It says he was shot in the head. Does that mean something or is it just a mistake?"

I really felt sorry for him. I said, "The trouble with you is you think like a lawyer, not a detective. Maybe you need a partner."

He looked across his desk at me and smiled. "All right, detective," he said, "let's figure out what it means."

"No," I needled, "that's what a lawyer would do. A detective would find out what it means. Whatdya say we take a ride out to Brooklyn?"

We drove to Greenpoint Hospital in John's car and when we got there we found the intern who had filled out the admission form. At first he was as puzzled by it as we were. He was a young guy, very harried, the way interns usually are, but very apologetic about the mistake. John showed him a copy of the autopsy report and I asked him if there was anything about Joe's head or face that could have misled him into thinking there was a head wound. "If there was anything," he said, "any markings or abrasions, it'd be here in the autopsy report. But you can see for yourself, there's nothing. I guess I must have been tired, that's all."

"Are you sure?" I asked.

What I was thinking was that maybe he would remember some wound or some marks that had been left out of the autopsy report.

"I wish I could help you," he said, "but I just don't remember."

We thanked him for trying, and as we were leaving he said, "Wait a minute. Was that the guy that shot himself?"

"Yeah."

"The detective?"

"Yeah."

"Well, then, you know what it must have been? The report's right, there were no markings. But when they brought him in, I remember the attendant from the ambulance said, 'We've got a D.O.A. A cop shot himself.' Then I just took a quick look at him and they wheeled him away. I guess that stuck in my mind and I wasn't even thinking, I automatically wrote 'bullet wound to the head.' "

"Why?" John asked.

He looked at both of us like we were some kind of idiots. "Because when a guy shoots himself, he shoots himself in the head," he said.

John jumped at that. "Always?" he asked.

The intern smiled sheepishly. "No," he said, "there are exceptions to everything."

When we left the hospital John and I were both pretty confused about what we had learned, but for different reasons. On the way back to the city John was already starting to speculate that perhaps Joe hadn't killed himself. "You heard what the doctor said," he said. "When a guy shoots himself, he shoots himself in the head."

"He also said there are exceptions," I reminded him. It seemed to me John was clutching at straws.

He was quiet for a while. Then he said, "Sonny, do you remember what it was Joe said that Diamond said to him?"

It wasn't anything I could ever forget. I had heard it from John and from Jeannie and Luke. "Yeah," I said. "Work with us, go to jail, or . . ."

I stopped without finishing the sentence. Obviously, John and I were thinking the same thing. *Or blow your brains out.* That was the phrase Luke said Joe had been brooding over all through the last week. He would pace the bedroom with the lights out and he would say, "They want me to blow my brains out."

But that isn't what he did.

For a minute there John almost had me going, or I almost had myself going. Half of me wanted to believe that Joe hadn't committed suicide, that for some reason no one as yet understood he had been murdered, but the other half told me we weren't being realistic. "No," I said, "forget it, John. It won't wash. What about the note?"

When Joe died, they found a three-page handwritten note in the briefcase he had put in the trunk of the car. Neither of us had seen it, but newspaper reports based on statements made by Department spokesmen described it as a suicide note. The Department, though, refused to release the note, on the grounds that it pertained to a case still under investigation.

John nodded his head sadly.

"Look, we got something out of it," I said. "I'm gonna get that ambulance attendant and find out who told him Joe shot himself. They can't take away Jeannie's pension unless they prove it was suicide. And how can they prove anything if they already had their minds made up before they even got him into the ambulance?"

He nodded approvingly.

"What about you?" I asked.

"I want a look at that note," he said. "I don't care if I have to bring everyone into court from the mayor on down, I'm going to find out what Joe wrote and why they don't want us to see it."

Jeannie had poured out her heart to me and told me about those last two weeks. Before I talked to her it was hard for me to imagine Joe killing himself, but once I had a picture in my mind of how depressed he was, I could see that must have been what happened.

Morally, though, that didn't change the fact that they had driven him to do it. They trapped him and squeezed him until the poor guy didn't see any way out, and then they told his widow that she'd have to figure out some other way to raise her kids because her husband hadn't died in the line of duty.

Horseshit.

He was out there doing his job. Not always the way the regulations say, but the way he had to do it to make the biggest case of his life. Then he broke under the pressure they put on him as a result of the things they had led him to do. The job killed him as surely as if Danzie had shot him between the eyes when Joe broke into that room at the Americana.

But of course they didn't see it that way, and so they were compounding what they had done to Joe by denying a pension to his widow and his kids. At least that's how it looked to me. And so, even though at the time I accepted the fact that Joe killed himself, I understood John's wanting to find out why they had closed the case as a suicide before they had done a full investigation. The intervention of Internal Affairs within minutes of Joe's death had the effect of forestalling any legitimate investigation because the Homicide detectives, who were expert in handling this kind of case, had to lay back and take their cues from IAD.

Besides, it was obvious that Internal Affairs had taken control of the investigation with their minds already made up. "What? Longo's dead? Yeah, we know all about him. He was in a jam, must have shot himself."

And that was all. *We know all about him.* Just close out the case and bury him, the sooner the better.

The next day I tracked down the ambulance attendant and he confirmed what we both suspected. One of the policemen on the scene had told him that the death was a suicide. He didn't know the man's name but it was one of the investigators in charge.

I also learned that the first car to respond to the scene was a patrol car with two uniformed men from the Nine-four. Then there was a team of detectives from the Fourteenth Homicide District, and finally a whole contingent from Internal Affairs, including Chief Inspector William Gerhardt, the head of the Division. Internal Affairs immediately claimed jurisdiction over the case because Joe was under investigation.

The team from Fourteenth Homicide remained on the scene. They saw to it that Joe's hands were bagged so that tests could be done on them for gunshot residues, which is standard procedure in a shooting incident. They also had the car swabbed to test for the presence of gunpowder and they detailed two teams of uniformed men to canvass the neighborhood in order to find out if anyone had seen or heard anything.

IAD, though, took possession of the car, the attaché case found in the trunk, and Joe's gun, which was found on the floor of the car by Joe's feet. Internal Affairs also notified the commanding officer of the Fourteenth Homicide that any information on the case was to be turned over to Chief Inspector Gerhardt. Although nominally the case was still assigned to the Fourteenth, the effect of this order was that the investigation became an IAD matter. The Homicide detectives saw to it that the canvass was completed and that the tests they had already ordered were carried out, but it was clear to them they weren't expected to do more.

When I got to John's office late that afternoon to tell him what I had learned during the day, he didn't even give me a chance to talk. "No time for that," he said. "Jeannie's taking the train in, she'll be at Penn Station in about twenty minutes. It took some doing, but they said she could have the note. You'd better get down there right away before they change their minds. And stay close to her, Sonny. I don't know if she's ready for what that note might say."

If they had looked for the worst place to make a widow go to pick up the last message her husband left, they couldn't have done better

than the New York City Morgue, which is on First Avenue right next
door to Bellevue Hospital. A grim, gray building carved out of the
same dull stone that built Bellevue, the morgue provides the finishing
touch to one of the oldest and most depressing neighborhoods in New
York.

Jeannie, who had hardly said a word since I picked her up at Penn
Station, put out her hand to stop me as I reached for the door handle.
I had been out to visit her and the kids a couple of times a week since
the funeral but I hadn't realized till just then how thin her face had
gotten. She looked tired and drawn, and her eyes were frightened, the
way she had described Joe as looking during those last two weeks.

"Sonny," she asked, her voice soft and unsteady, "have you ever
seen a suicide note?"

"Yes."

"What do they say?"

"They say different things."

She nodded, as though that answer helped. Then she opened the
car door and stepped into the street. I watched as she walked around
the front of the car, looking very brave, her head held straight, her hair
blending into the yellow air of the city's twilight. Then I joined her on
the sidewalk and we walked into the morgue together.

The feeling of the morgue is exactly what you would expect if you
have never been in one. It's a feeling of death, like the feeling of an old
hospital or of a cemetery. It took us only a few minutes to transact our
business with an expressionless medical examiner who produced a
copy of the note and asked Jeannie to sign the required forms with
such cold impersonality that it almost seemed he had forgotten how to
deal with living people.

We walked back to the car without talking. I held the door for
Jeannie and then hurried around to join her. In her hand she held the
manila envelope the clerk had given her, and for a long time she
couldn't bring herself to open it. Then she took a deep breath and slid
the three long sheets of white paper from the envelope. Her lips trembling with the effort to keep from sobbing, she started to read. After
a few seconds she was crying soundlessly, and then the pages flew from
her hand toward me and she was wailing with inconsolable sorrow. I
slid over in the seat to hold her but she didn't want to be comforted.

"Sonny, please read it," she pleaded, barely able to control her
voice. "Tell me what he said."

Just holding the note in my hands gave me a strange hollow feeling, like the way I felt once when we had to exhume a body in a homicide case. For a few minutes I had trouble focusing on the page to read it.

In the upper-right-hand corner of the first of the three Xeroxed pages there were some letters and numbers that indicated that the original of the note had been logged in at the Property Clerk's Office. Each of the three pages had a date and a detective's initials down at the bottom. The blue lines on the yellow ruled pad Joe had used hardly reproduced at all in the photocopy, so there were just faint horizontal markings like the light pencil lines we used to draw in grammar school to make ourselves write straight.

There was no doubt that the note was in Joe's handwriting, even though it didn't really look like the way he normally wrote. His writing was about the worst I have ever seen, and I used to kid him that with handwriting like that he should have been a doctor. But apparently he made a special effort to make the note legible, and as a result there was something almost childish about the way it looked, a jumble of large, awkward-looking letters that flopped around the almost invisible lines like clothes drying on a windy day. At times he must have gotten carried away with what he had to say, and the writing would get flatter and faster, more like his usual scrawl. And then he must have stopped himself and made himself go back to that pathetically careful style that was halfway between printing and writing.

The note said:

I've been <u>driven</u> to this point of no return. Nothing that was done, was done with criminal intent. All the events were given in detail to our attorney's. Luke said I was crazy to think it would work, but I know in my heart it would've. I'm a very disappointed in a few things that happened. Mainly that our plan to wasn't allowed to occur. I know we would've made some tremendous cases after having C.D. in the position of having another charge to answer for. Knowing that when he came to us he would've had a load following him.

Now though, I know it was all a hoax on B.N.D.D.'s part, to make it appear as if we accepted a gratuity from C.D. That my friends, is an <u>insult</u>, so severe that I will not allow this embarrassment to affect this job or anyone I've ever been associated with. The outlook, being as bleak as it does appear, can only be made worse by the newspapers. If any of you *have any heart at all, be satisfied by this event.*

I have only been allowed to enjoy my life sporadicly. I dedicated my life to my job. I've also ignored my family to a point of disgust on my part. I finally was getting recognition in my work.

Everything I possess, relative to my job, is in the black attache case. My other gun, papers, etc.. The rest of my things are in my desk at the NYJTForce office at 201 Varick St. Please don't embarass me any further by bothering my family & friends. I have two children whom I love and a wife I adore—leave them in peace with their thoughts of me. This event will make them suffer enough.

Before I close my final words I must reiterate. Any conversation that was had with C.D. was total lies on Luke's part or mine. Those conversations apparently convinced both he and B.N.D.D. that our intentions were favorable towards their case against us. I hate to disappoint anyone but it was all lies. I must've really been convincing, that would only prove how effective I was in my job.

May God look down and show, in his own way, the wrong, unjust and malpracticed deed that has been done by B.N.D.D. and their people.

> *Goodbye to my family*
> *My Wife I adore & my two*
> *children whom I was allowed to*
> *enjoy only a short time.*

Luke will speak only truth because it is the easiest thing to remember.

> *Joe Longo*

Chapter 17
A Dead Man's Name

I COULDN'T GET Joe's note out of my mind. The thing that haunted me most about it was that he died the way he lived—as a cop. Except for three brief but touching references to his family, his last recorded thoughts were all about the job. "I've also ignored my family to a point of disgust on my part," he wrote bitterly, but couldn't refrain from adding in the very next sentence, "I finally was getting recognition in my work."

Joe's last message testified all over again to that blind dedication that has robbed so many cops of their homes and families. Every married detective I ever worked with had a problem with it, because you can't expect a woman to put up with her husband's not coming home for days on end, showing up to get a few hours' sleep, and then heading right back for more. Once in a while a young detective would brag that he wasn't going to have that kind of trouble because his wife was "very understanding." But what was there to understand? That a guy would rather be sneaking down alleys to make a coke bust than home with her? How can you understand a thing like that?

It's just the way we were. A cop lives in a man's world, where somehow there just doesn't seem to be room for a wife and family. It never surprised me that even though the Police Department has a disproportionate number of Irish and Italian Catholics, it still has one of the highest divorce rates of any occupation group in the country. Let's face it, when I say that a cop lives in a man's world, what that really means is a boy's world where you never really have to grow up. It's a wild, endless adventure with a squad room instead of a clubhouse, a real-life game of cops and robbers in which filthy shooting galleries on Lenox Avenue are the hiding places instead of the cellars and rooftops where you played as boys. We can stay out as late as we like and never have to go home unless we want to.

I could see this in Joe's note. I could see the terrible guilt about his family mixed so confusingly with the pride he took in the way he did his job. I could see, too, that to the very end he never unraveled the weird twists and turns of the Danzie case. He wanted that case so badly that he refused to believe what his senses told him. "Now though, I know it was all a hoax on B.N.D.D.'s part," he wrote, and if that had been all he wrote I would have to say that he finally understood. But he also said, "I know we would've made some tremendous cases after having C.D. in the position of having another charge to answer for." He said, "When he came to us he would've had a load following him." He said, "Luke said I was crazy to think it would work, but I know in my heart it would've."

John Meglio read Joe's note as carefully as I did, but he was looking at it from a different point of view and so he was able to see things in it that I missed. On the Monday after I picked up the note with Jeannie at the morgue, he asked me to come to his office. When I got there he left word with his receptionist that he wasn't to be disturbed. Then he closed his door and sat me down in the chair opposite his desk.

"Sonny," he began, "did you ever have a case that looked like a suicide but was really a homicide?"

"Me personally?" I asked. "No, never."

"But you've heard of such cases?"

"Sure."

"Even when there might be a suicide note?"

John wasn't the kind of man who joked about such things, but it was hard to take this line of reasoning seriously. "I think there have been cases where the note was written under duress," I said. "Or where it was forged. But Joe wrote this note himself and no one had a gun at his head."

"How do you know?" he asked with that lawyerlike coolness that could drive you up a wall.

"How do I know!" I spluttered. "How do I know what? That it's his handwriting? Because I've seen it a thousand times. That no one forced him to write it and then killed him? Because he wrote it some other time."

John smiled transparently. "Precisely," he said.

"What's precisely?"

"Precisely. He obviously wrote it someplace else because it wasn't with him in the car. It was in the briefcase in the trunk. It wouldn't make sense to write the note, get out of the car, put the note in the trunk, get back in the car and shoot yourself. Besides, there wasn't time. Luke was gone less than five minutes."

"So what's the point?" I challenged. "No one ever said he wrote it in the car."

"Then where did he write it?"

"How the fuck should I know?"

John passed his tongue over his lips before answering. "Maybe he wrote it that morning," he said. "Maybe he wrote it Sunday night. Maybe he wrote it the morning after they caught him in Danzie's basement. It makes a difference, doesn't it?"

"I guess so."

"You know it does. The note doesn't tell us anything about his frame of mind Monday morning because we don't know it was written Monday morning."

I looked skeptical.

"Don't get me wrong," John said. "I don't mean to say he didn't do it. All I mean is that they had no business closing out the case on the basis of an alleged suicide note that was written at some unknown time and place. There's something else, too. The note says he put all his papers in the attaché case. But the note itself was in the attaché case. Does that make sense?"

"Maybe he just forgot he wrote that," I suggested.

John shook his head. "Sonny," he said, "a man leaves a suicide note where it's going to be found. He doesn't hide it in the trunk of somebody else's car. Think about it. When he wrote that note he didn't intend for it to be in the briefcase when he died. He was going to have it with him. But he didn't have it with him. Why not?"

"What are you saying? He didn't kill himself?" I asked.

"No," John answered. "I'm not saying that. I'm not saying any-thing. I'm just asking you, what would you do if this was your case?"

"I don't know."

"Would you close it?"

"On the basis of the note? No."

John stood up. "Okay, Sonny," he said. "Let's do it this way. The Police Department won't tell me a thing. Maybe you can find out. If they had a good reason for saying it was suicide, then I'll buy it. But if all they have is that note, I'll take them to court and see to it that Jeannie gets what's coming to her."

John and I were both convinced that the investigation of Joe's death had not been handled properly. But neither of us was prepared for what we found after months of fighting to get the evidence and examining it for ourselves. Except for the undated note found in the wrong place and the fact that he was jammed up, *there wasn't a single other thing about the case that established suicide.*

John started the process by studying the autopsy report, which describes the path of the bullet that killed Joe. He got body diagrams from a medical text and traced it out for himself. "Bullet wound of left anterior chest 50½ inches about left heel and two inches to right of midline. Bullet passed through left fifth intercostal space, pericardial sac, in and out through anterior and posterior wall of right ventricle in its lower third and apical region, through pericardial sac, in and out through the lowermost lobe of right lung, exit from chest posteriorly by the right tenth intercostal space. Recovered in skin at 49 inches above right heel and four inches to right of midline."

The autopsy report also mentions "confluent spots of blood on the right hand."

Those bloodstains were a mystery. They should have been on the hand that held the gun, because when a bullet hits the heart the last beat of the heart pumps a jet of blood through the wound. But John's diagrams showed that the bullet had traveled in a downward path from front to back and from Joe's left to his right. How could a man hold a gun in his right hand and shoot himself in such a way? Besides, Joe was left handed. If he shot himself, wouldn't it have been with his left hand? Then how come his left hand was clean?

One afternoon in the middle of May John drove out to Brooklyn and interviewed Dr. Alvin Goodman, the Kings County Deputy Chief Medical Examiner who had performed the autopsy. He was a man in his late fifties with a thick walrus mustache and bushy gray hair. When John told him what he wanted, Dr. Goodman got his records from the file and studied them for almost ten minutes. Then he tossed the folder onto his desk, looked up, and said, "All right. Now what do you want to know?"

"Did Detective Longo shoot himself?" John asked.

"Yes."

"With which hand?"

"The right."

"How do you know that?"

"Because of the bloodstains on the back of the hand."

"You're absolutely certain of that?"

"Yes."

"Couldn't his right hand simply have been in the vicinity of his chest?"

"It's possible."

"For example, if he steadied the muzzle of the gun with his right hand?"

"It's possible."

"But actually shot with his left?"

"No, that's not possible."

"Why not?"

"Because there are no bloodstains on his left hand."

"Perhaps his right hand shielded his left?"

"No, Mr. Meglio, I'm sorry," Dr. Goodman said. "If it had been a smaller wound perhaps. But there was blood everywhere, even in his socks. If his left hand had been anywhere near the wound it would have been stained."

"Is that what you told the police?" John asked pointedly.

Dr. Goodman bristled. "I would have told them exactly what

happened, if they asked me," he snapped. "He shot himself with his right hand. Now if you have no further questions, I have work to do."

"Thank you very much, doctor. That's very helpful," John said, not pushing the point. "There's something else, though. Is the angle of the wound consistent with shooting by the right hand?"

Goodman's face went red and he started to say something but stopped himself. He grabbed the autopsy report from his desk and studied the description of the wound. "It's not inconsistent," he said.

"What does that mean?"

"It means it's possible."

"Possible?" John challenged. "Is that adequate?"

"Adequate?" Dr. Goodman exploded, rising from his seat. "Of course it's adequate. The man shot himself. What more do you want?"

"Just an answer to one more question," John said coldly. "Did you know that Detective Longo was left handed?"

"No," Goodman answered. "Good day, Mr. Meglio."

If this were a work of fiction, these last chapters would tell how John and I gradually pieced together the evidence that proved that Joe Longo was murdered, then tracked down his killers. In real life, though, things don't often work out that neatly. Besides, anyone operating on his own, without official authority to question anyone and without the investigative resources of a modern police department, has the cards pretty well stacked against him.

And when I say not having the Department's resources, that's putting it mildly. John was convinced that what he had, in fact, was their active resistance. The Department put every stumbling block in his way that they could legally get away with.

When John asked the Fourteenth Homicide District if he could check their files on the case, he was told they didn't have them any more. They said they turned everything over to Internal Affairs. John then began to pressure the Police Department for the material but got absolutely nowhere. After exhausting all normal procedures for obtaining such information, he finally got a court order to examine under oath the Homicide detective who was in charge of the case. Like many of the rank-and-file cops John ran into in the investigation, he personally had no reluctance to help but he was held back by the Department. Fortunately, although his superiors may have told him not to give out any information, they couldn't or wouldn't expect him to perjure himself. As soon as John put him under oath and asked him where the files were, he said, "They're in my office."

"How long have they been there?"

"They've been there all along, counselor. Since the day he died."

He seemed relieved to be able to tell the truth. It was obvious that he was willing to help us as much as he could. Even so, there were still some areas he was reluctant to go into. When John tried to ask him if he had been ordered to tell us that the files were not in his custody, he interrupted the question with a gesture of his hand and got up from the table. He walked to the window and studied the traffic on Madison Avenue for a few minutes. When he came back to the table, John went on with another line of questioning. Since the detective was under oath, it would have been possible to pressure him further, but it was obvious that he was under a lot of pressure already and John didn't want to do anything that might jeopardize his cooperation. At one point John asked him whether the Internal Affairs Division had taken the case away from the Fourteenth Homicide.

"I don't know if I'd want to put it that way, counselor," the detective answered coyly. "I do remember that they had an interest in the case, though."

It's a sad fact that Internal Affairs scares the average cop shitless. And with good reason. In the New York City Police Department, the federal government, and the police departments of other major cities in the United States, the Internal Affairs Division, or whatever its local variants may be called, is a set-apart force of investigators whose secret police-like powers far exceed the powers of any other branch of our criminal justice system. They can bring a cop up on departmental charges, get him dismissed from the Force and stripped of his pension for all sorts of things that aren't illegal or corrupt and wouldn't even get a guy fired from a normal job. In effect, they have the power to take away a man's job and his life savings without having to prove in a court of law that he did anything wrong.

A case in point is a young ex-detective who used to work with Gil Lacey and is now waiting on tables somewhere on Long Island. In the summer of 1969 he was home on vacation doing some repairs around the house. One evening Lacey drove out to see him. Lacey claims that in the course of the visit he handed his partner an envelope with money in it. "I told him I knew he was fixing up his house and I thought it would help," Lacey testified. "That's all that was said on the subject."

The young detective was charged with accepting a bribe and suspended from the Force. He fought the case all the way. A U.S. attorney brought Lacey's accusation before a federal grand jury, but the grand jury refused to indict the detective. A local prosecutor then tried his luck with a county grand jury. Again there was no indictment. Finally, Internal Affairs brought him up on departmental charges. He was acquitted by the Police Department. But the day before his reinstatement was to take effect, two high federal officials who had supervisory control over Lacey's activities personally called on one of the top bosses of the Department at his home and pleaded with him not to reinstate the detective. They were afraid that if word got out that a cop Lacey had testified against was cleared and reinstated, it would damage Lacey's credibility as a witness in other cases they had in the works.

The Department did as it was asked, firing a promising young detective after every legally constituted body that had heard the case found him not guilty. Whether he took the money or not is really beside the point. In this country we're supposed to have something called due process of law, and it's supposed to apply to everyone, even cops.

The point I'm trying to make is that I had no trouble understanding why no one would talk about Joe. The people downtown wanted the case closed, so it was going to stay closed. They said he shot himself, so he shot himself.

Fortunately, John wasn't a cop and had no reason to back off from a showdown with anyone. As Jeannie's attorney, he took the case to court by arguing that the premature and unsubstantiated finding of suicide robbed his client of the pension benefits she would have received as the widow of a slain police officer. There was more to John's argument than this, but at that time the most important thing was that it gave him legal standing to demand access to records of the Police Department's investigation of Joe's death.

Because of the suspicions that had been raised by the note and the nature of the wound, there were a number of things John wanted to be positive about before he would admit that Joe had committed suicide. He wanted the results of the ballistics test on Joe's gun. Was it the murder weapon? He wanted the results of the tests on Joe's hands. Had he fired a gun? He wanted a chance to examine Joe's clothes to check for powder burns. Had he been shot at close range? And he wanted to examine the contents of Joe's black leather attaché case, which, according to the note, contained "everything I possess relative to my work." Would Joe's memo book tell us anything that might throw some light on his death?

By September 1972, six months after Joe died, the following facts had been established:

No ballistics test had been done on Joe's gun. The Police Department closed the case as a suicide without ever testing to see whether the gun found on the scene was the one that killed him.

The tests for gunpowder residues were negative. The Fourteenth Homicide District cops on the scene had sent the swabs taken from Joe's hands and from the interior of the car to Washington, where the FBI performed a Neutron Activation Analysis Examination on them. This is a far more sophisticated and accurate test for gunpowder residues than the so-called paraffin test. The FBI reported no indication that the deceased had fired a gun prior to his death and no indication that a gun had been fired inside the car.

Joe's clothes had mysteriously disappeared. At first the Department refused to turn over the clothes. When John went to court for an order to obtain them, the Department answered that the clothes could not be found. They said they had given them to Jeannie. Then they said they had given them to the undertaker. Then they said they had never taken them from the hospital and they were still in the custody of the medical examiner. In any case, the clothes Joe was wearing at the time of his death have never been found. As far as anyone knows, it was the only time anything like this ever happened in the history of the New York City Medical Examiner's Office.

Joe's memo book wasn't in the briefcase. It, too, had disappeared and the Property Clerk's Office log did not list it in the inventory of the contents of the attaché case. Perhaps Joe didn't put it in the brief-case, although his note seems to say that he did. He certainly didn't leave it at home, because Jeannie has been unable to find it.

In June of 1972, just a few weeks after John started his probe of Joe's death, a grand jury heard turn-around detective Juan Piedra testify about a twenty-thousand-dollar shake that was alleged to have taken place at the McAlpin Hotel in late 1969. Joe was named as one of the cops who shared in the proceeds. What happened was that nine detectives in the elite Special Investigations Unit arrested four Colombian drug dealers in the McAlpin. The raid netted forty-four pounds of cocaine and sixteen kilos of heroin. The street value of the confiscated drugs was estimated at over ten million dollars, which made it by far the largest single seizure since the French Connection case seven years earlier. But, according to Piedra, the detectives also seized twenty thousand dollars in cash, which they divided among themselves. Joe Longo was one of the cops who made the arrest and he was named in the indictment as an unindicted co-conspirator.

I have no way of knowing whether there was any substance to the charge against Joe or whether it was just their way of telling John to back off. The fact is that Piedra's word wasn't worth much. When he testified against some other cops in an unrelated matter, Trial Commissioner Sylvester Hines disallowed his testimony and dismissed the charges on the grounds of Detective Piedra's doubtful credibility. As far as the McAlpin incident is concerned, the case against the cops Piedra named was quietly dropped. They were never even brought to trial.

Under the circumstances, John had to do a lot of soul searching. Joe couldn't be helped or hurt by anything anyone did, but his family could. John's opposition could drag Joe's name through the mud any time they wanted. All they had to do was add his name to the list any time they went to the grand jury for indictments.

On the other hand, Jeannie had taken a job and was having trouble making ends meet. Not only had Joey and Marie lost their father, but now their mother had to be away from home all day, too. She really needed the pension, and because of the way Joe died she was as entitled to it as any police widow ever was. But would it be worth it if the kids had to see their father's name smeared in the papers with some trumped up charges every time John filed a motion?

In the end, Jeannie decided that this was a chance that had to be taken. There was more at stake than just the pension. There was also the question of how Joe died. If there was any possibility that he hadn't committed suicide, she owed it to herself and the kids to find the truth. It wouldn't be fair to have them go through life thinking he had killed himself if that wasn't what happened.

So the investigation went on. By October, John's constant prodding, lawsuits, and threats of lawsuits were starting to get some results. In order to counter the charge that Joe's death hadn't been properly investigated, the Department belatedly performed a ballistics test on the gun found on the floor of the car. The results were disappointing but not surprising. The bullet taken from Joe's body matched a slug test-fired from his own gun.

In those days of Watergate and cover-ups, I wasn't at all surprised that John felt so ill at ease with the ballistics test that he hired his own expert. We've all heard so much news about falsifications by government agencies that I think a person would have to be very naive to rule out the possibility that evidence could be altered. In this case, though, if there was a cover-up, it wasn't a cover-up of Joe's death. What everyone wanted to bury wasn't the story of how Joe died. It was the story of the last two months of his life.

In the spring and summer of 1972, police corruption was a headline issue, and the so-called anticorruption agencies were being hailed as the saviors of New York. Joe's story would tear that myth apart. Because it showed how a good man could be callously destroyed. Because it showed the amoral viciousness of his persecutors. Because it showed that the men who were supposedly cleaning up law enforcement were ultimately more lawless than the cops they were trying to put behind bars. Maybe it has to be that way, but that doesn't make it right.

In the summer of seventy-two Gil Lacey came out of the closet and publicly revealed for the first time that he had been working as an undercover agent for the Knapp Commission, the United States Attorney's Office, and the Internal Affairs Division of the Police Department.

Overnight he became a celebrity, the way William Phillips and Frank Serpico had been made into celebrities before him. Lacey was the first major turnaround cop to come out of narcotics enforcement. *Life* magazine did a hero's article on him in which they melodramatically hid his face, although of course the cops he would be testifying against were all guys who worked with him and who knew damned well what he looked like. But I guess all those shots of the back of his head helped create the impression of a glamorous and mysterious superspy in a dangerous line of work. To anyone who knew the story, the text was as unreal as the pictures. Whereas most cops who testify against their brother officers do so to get out of trouble, the article said that Gil Lacey had gone into this line of work out of the purest motives. He was depicted as an honest cop who volunteered for undercover work to help in the fight to eliminate corruption.

What interested John and me in the *Life* piece, though, wasn't the nonsense about Gil Lacey's high moral principles. The article also contained a few vague allusions to Joe Longo. Joe wasn't mentioned by name, but Lacey told the writer of the piece about a narcotics detective who had shot himself while under investigation. "He was a big man, a wonderful man. He was very Italian," Lacey was quoted as saying. He also said that he was "tormented by the possibility" that other cops might think that he had something to do with the case that drove this unnamed detective to kill himself.

This unsolicited denial was our first clue that Lacey might have been in some way involved in Joe's arrest of Carlo Danzie. Until then, no one had connected him to the case. A few weeks later this suspicion was further corroborated when the *Daily News* ran an article on Lacey. Included were brief synopses of a dozen of his cases. The names of the people involved were all omitted, but one of the cases was unmistakably that of Joe and Carlo Danzie. It told of a drug dealer being flown in from Europe for the purpose of working under cover against cops. It told of his being arrested at a fashionable midtown hotel with "superb samples" in his possession. It told of his insistence on dealing only with a high-level Narcotics official in Washington. And it told of a four-thousand-dollar "shakedown" and an illegal phone tap.

But there was no mention of the fact that Danzie had repeatedly failed in his attempts to bribe the officers or of the fact that both Joe and Luke knew perfectly well that Danzie was an informant for the deputy director of the BNDD. On the contrary, the article says simply that it was "clear" to the European undercover agent that the detectives were interested in shaking him down. There is no mention of the fact that Danzie had asked to go to Europe in order to complete arrangements for an overseas drug shipment that he would turn over to Joe. There is no mention of the fact that Joe actually asked for permission to let Danzie go or of the fact that this request was at first okayed and then denied. Instead, the article depicts Danzie as "pleading" to be allowed to "flee the country." It depicts Joe and Luke as allowing him to flee after accepting a four-thousand-dollar payoff. There is no mention of the fact that it was Juan Piedra who helped Joe install the wiretap on Danzie's phone and that Luke never saw the tap or had anything to do with it. On the contrary, the article claims that Joe and Luke were arrested when the two of them installed the tap.

There is no mention of the fact that the detective in the case apparently killed himself with the weapon that was returned to him after he was supposedly arrested and then allowed to return to duty.

While all this was going on into the fall of 1972, no one could possibly realize that behind the wire-mesh gates of the Police Department Property Clerk's Office a time bomb was ticking its own secret countdown toward the explosion that would shake everyone even remotely connected to Joe or to the French Connection case. When it went off, the significance of Joe's death suddenly took on new meaning, as questions no one had thought to ask before now began demanding answers.

The way I first heard about it provides an interesting insight into the way the Internal Affairs Division works. It was sometime in the middle of December and I was on vacation. Phil D'Antoni was shooting a television movie based on a story I had written called *Mr. Inside, Mr. Outside.* We were on location in an abandoned tenement on Columbus Avenue somewhere up in the west Eighties. I was inside the building trying to help some of the actors with the technical aspect of a police scene when my partner Randy Jurgensen drove down from the Two-eight with a message for me. I was supposed to call Charlie Warshaw, who used to be my sergeant when I was in the Two-five. The last I had heard he was a lieutenant in Internal Affairs. I hadn't seen him in years.

"Hi, Sonny, how you doing?" Warshaw said cheerfully when I got him on the line. "I'm glad I was able to catch up with you. Pretty busy, huh?"

I found out later that the number I had called was one of the special numbers IAD maintains for informants. They're unlisted phones and the people who answer them don't identify themselves by name or unit.

"I try to keep on my toes," I said.

"It's not like the old days," he said. "I guess you're a movie star now, right?"

"Not really. What can I do for you, Charlie?"

"Nothing much, just wanted to touch a base with you. I haven't seen you in so long, and I was just going over some paper work—end-of-the-year stuff, you know—and I came across something about one of your cases, figured I'd pick up the phone, give you a call."

There was something about his tone that bothered me. I especially didn't like the way he was being cute and evasive about the fact that he was calling on IAD business. "Yeah, well, I'm fine. We'll have to get together some time," I said, without sounding particularly like I meant it. "I wish I could talk now but I gotta get back on the set."

"Oh, well, look, Sonny," he said, forcing a laugh, "if you can't make it, you can't make it. Whatdya say I come up there? It'll gimme a chance to see how you movie stars operate."

I told him I'd check with the director to find out when we were taking a break and I'd call him back in about half an hour. As soon as I hung up the phone I called the legal division of the Detectives' Endowment Association. There are Police Department regulations that govern procedure when Internal Affairs wants to talk to a cop. They're supposed to send a request to his commander to have him report to them. A copy of this request is automatically routed to the DEA—or the Patrolman's Benevolent Association in the case of patrolmen. This way the DEA or the PBA can send one of its lawyers to be present at the interview. The two associations fought for years to get these regulations on the books because the Department never allowed cops to have the same right to counsel that other citizens enjoy. What troubled me about Warshaw's call was that he was obviously trying to circumvent these rules by making the whole thing sound like an informal request.

The DEA lawyer, whose name was Harriman, told me to set up a meeting with Warshaw and to let him know where and when it was going to be. He promised to be there. I called Warshaw back and asked him to come up to the set. I told him Harriman would be there also.

"Harriman?" he said. "Hey, Sonny, I just wanted to ask you some questions, get some stuff straightened out. Whatdya need a lawyer for?"

"So," I said, "cmon up. You'll ask your questions. What do you care if he's here?"

There was a short pause, and when Warshaw spoke again I noticed a slight but unmistakable sharpening of his tone. "Listen, Sonny," he said, "if you want to bring a lawyer that changes the whole picture. I'll have to check it with Chief Gerhardt, see what he wants me to do."

Gerhardt was the head of the entire Internal Affairs Division. The fact that Warshaw didn't want to talk to me if I had a lawyer there and the fact that Gerhardt was involved convinced me that I had done the right thing in calling the DEA.

"Sure, you do that, Charlie," I said. "But, look, you still haven't told me what it's all about."

"I told you what it's about," Warshaw protested. "It's some old cases."

"What cases?"

I was afraid we were starting to sound like Abbott and Costello.

"Just some old stuff. Do you remember the Fuca case?"

I was so shocked I almost dropped the phone. The Fuca case was the French Connection case. It was the biggest narcotics seizure in history and certainly the biggest thing I had ever worked on.

"What kind of shit is this, do I remember the Fuca case?" I spluttered. "What about it?"

"Look, I'll get back to you, Sonny," he said and hung up.

What I didn't know was that while Warshaw was calling me from the IAD office in the Broome Street Annex, right next door at Police Headquarters, Commissioner Patrick V. Murphy was preparing for a press conference at which he would announce that the ninety-seven pounds of heroin I had found in 1962 when I arrested Patsy Fuca had mysteriously disappeared from the Property Clerk's Office. What quickly became known as the French Connection Ripoff wasn't a simple burglarly at all. After removing most of the junk, the thieves had replaced it with chalk and talcum powder in the very same bags in which it had been stored. The commissioner also explained that the Property Clerk's voucher book showed that in March of 1969, for some unknown reason, the steamer trunk and the suitcase containing the French Connection heroin had been inexplicably signed out to Detective Joe Longo. A Police Department spokesman said they were looking into the possibility that the switch had been done when the trunk was in Longo's possession.

They were also looking into the possibility that the theft had been engineered by one of the agents or detectives who worked on the case.

In other words, the routine "procedural stuff" Warshaw wanted to question me about was a multimillion dollar robbery.

Of course, as I said, I didn't know any of this at the time. I went back to work on the movie but my mind was on the French Connection case and Warshaw's call. I kept one eye on the street looking for Randy to show up with a message from Warshaw. As the afternoon dragged on and no one came, I kept trying to tell myself that I had been making something out of nothing. Maybe Warshaw had been acting so mysterious because after a few months at IAD he had forgotten that there was any other way to act.

By five o'clock I knew I wasn't going to hear from him. I called Harriman and told him there was nothing up.

"Horseshit," he said. "There's plenty up. Have you been in a cave or something? Pick up a copy of the *Post* and get your ass down here."

The headline in the afternoon paper told the whole story: FRENCH CONNECTION HEROIN STOLEN.

I raced down to the DEA office on lower Fifth Avenue, my mind a mile ahead of the car. Whenever I got stuck at a light, I read a little more in the newspaper but there were so many confusing thoughts in my head that I couldn't get a clear picture of what was going on. All I knew was that the Property Clerk's Office had lost the evidence in my biggest case, that my friend Joe's name was mixed up in it somehow, and that IAD wanted to talk to me.

The turmoil at the DEA office was a perfect match for the way I felt. The outer office was filled with puzzled and apprehensive cops waiting to talk to lawyers. At one time or another, most of them had worked with Joe. From what I could gather, some of them had received regular forthwiths to report to IAD for questioning. With others Warshaw and his crew had tried the same game they tried with me.

I had been waiting only a few minutes when Harriman stepped out of his office and scanned the faces in the waiting room. When he saw me he motioned for me to come inside. Frankly, it didn't make me feel any better to know that I was being jumped to the head of the line.

At that time the information was still sketchy and didn't go much beyond what Murphy had announced at the press conference, but

Harriman filled me in as best he could. "The way it looks now," he said, "they're rounding up everyone Longo ever worked with, everyone he ever talked to. The last hour or so I've been getting calls, they're starting to go for all the guys who worked on the case back in sixty-two. That puts you near the head of the class, Sonny. You pass both tests."

"Are you telling me I'm a suspect in this thing?" I said angrily. I think I may have been shouting.

"Don't take it out on me," Harriman answered coolly. "Everyone's a suspect. I've been on the phone all day trying to remind them that a cop's got a right to an attorney the same as anybody else. And you know what I get for an answer? 'Why should they mind answering questions if they've got nothing to hide?' I swear, I can't believe it. Any suspect that gets dragged in off the street has to be given his rights. But when they want to talk to a cop, it's still the middle of the nineteenth century."

I agreed with everything Harriman was saying, but he wasn't telling me a thing that clarified my situation. "Well, what do they want with me?" I asked.

"Beats me," he said. "You're the one who put the stuff in there in the first place. You know how it was packaged, wrapped, sealed, what kind of precautions there were. They probably need your help. On the other hand, you're undoubtedly a suspect. Everyone is. So they're probably not too sure themselves what they want to do with you. If you want my advice, we tell them to shit or get off the pot. Either they assign you to the case or they order you down for questioning. And if that happens I go with you."

The strange thing was that when Harriman gave that choice to Lieutenant Warshaw, it turned out that no one at Internal Affairs knew what to do with it. Warshaw said he'd talk it over with his superiors and then we never heard from him again. Over the next few months there was a lot of speculation in the papers and at Police Headquarters about how the ripoff had been accomplished. There were questions about where it had been located in the Property Clerk's Office, how it was wrapped and packaged, how it was secured, who had authority to move it, and so forth. And in all that time, the guy who seized the French Connection heroin and put it in the Property Clerk's Office, the only man in the world authorized to remove it, was never once questioned by the authorities who were supposedly investigating the biggest robbery in history.

I can't say for sure that the facts I had would have been any help to them, but when I think back to the way they treated me and a lot of other guys that first day, I'm not surprised that they were never able to solve the case. I don't think they ever will.

Chapter 18
Property Clerk

IN THE DOZEN years between 1960 and 1972, Narcotics detectives in the New York City Police Department seized slightly under a ton of heroin and cocaine. Although prices fluctuated wildly during that period, at 1972 rates these seizures represented a street value of approximately five hundred million dollars.

Until 1974, when the Police Department moved to its new headquarters in a modernistic brick tower tucked behind the courthouse in Foley Square, regulations required that police officers bring all confiscated property to the Property Clerk's Office on the second floor of the old Headquarters Annex at 400 Broome Street. A square building in red brick with the forbidding appearance of a nineteenth-century factory, the Annex directly faces the old granite Headquarters on Centre Street, which had been the Department's home since 1910.

Over the years, traffic flow into the Property Clerk's Office grew steadily. By 1972 the Property Clerk's staff of civilians and police officers was logging over four thousand pieces of evidence daily. Undoubtedly the world's most bizarre warehouse, the Broome Street storage facility consisted of approximately five thousand square feet of floor space crammed with a mind-boggling assortment of guns, furs, jewels, knives, televisions, cash, clothing, and dope—in short, all the tools and objects of crime.

Whenever an arrest is made, the suspect and any relevant physical evidence are first taken to the stationhouse for processing. After the evidence is vouchered and the suspect booked, everything moves downtown. The suspect is sent to the Tombs to await trial or release on bail. In narcotics cases the evidence goes first to the Police Department labs on Twenty-first Street for testing and then to the Property Clerk's Office. Although the Department of Corrections maintains a fleet of trucks for transporting prisoners and makes regular daily pick-ups at each of the local precincts, the job of getting the evidence to the lab and then to the Property Clerk is the responsibility of the arresting officer.

It may take months or even years for a case to reach its final disposition, and all that time the cop is personally responsible for the physical evidence. If there is a grand jury proceeding, he must go to the Property Clerk's Office each morning, sign out the evidence, bring it to the grand jury and then return it at the end of the day: If there's a motion to suppress, he has to go through the same ritual, and it's repeated every time there's a continuance. When the case finally goes to trial he again is required to sign the evidence out every morning and in again at night no matter how long the trial lasts. If I live to be a hundred, I'll never understand why the Property Clerk's Office isn't responsible for getting the evidence to court the way the Department of Corrections is responsible for getting the defendants there. At least there ought to be secure storage areas in each of the courthouses where evidence can be held.

Instead, the Department says that all evidence has to be stored in one place. Cops begin arriving at 400 Broome Street as early as seven o'clock every weekday morning. They congregate in the dingy second-floor hallway, where three tellers' windows look out from the fifty-foot-long wall that faces the two automatic elevators. At eight o'clock the windows open and the rush begins. Each cop in turn gives his name, rank, precinct, and shield number, as well as the voucher number of the material he wants. The clerk enters this information in a thick green cloth-bound ledger, each page of which is divided into two columns of five ruled sections with appropriately marked lines.

Behind the narrow space where the clerks stand is the storage area itself. Approximately a hundred feet long by fifty feet deep, it is filled almost entirely with chest-high wooden storage bins arranged back to back in long rows. Packed far beyond their intended capacity with weapons and stolen property, the bins spill over onto the floor, giving the place the appearance of a cheap discount store in the middle of a sale. Using the voucher number supplied by the police officer, the clerk has to locate the desired article and bring it to the front window. In the minutes this can take, other clerks wait on other cops. When evidence is brought to the window, the cop must sign the ledger at the bottom of the space filled in with the information on his transaction. Since his shield is visible, displayed either on his shirt or outside jacket pocket, it isn't necessary for him to show any additional identification.

Because of their special value, narcotics are not kept on the open shelves with the other contraband. Rather, they are secured in wooden bins inside a special fifteen-by-thirty-foot cage set at the back of the general storage area. Surrounded on three sides by a Cyclone steel fence, its fourth wall the brick of the building itself, the narcotics holding area is serviced by only one heavily padlocked door which is kept locked at all times and must be opened with a key for each transaction. Also, two steel-lined closetlike walk-in safes within the fenced enclosure are used for added protection of bulk drugs—generally quarter kilos or more.

Physically, the storage facilities are at least as safe as the average bank. In order to steal narcotics when the Property Clerk's Office is closed, a thief would first have to get past the police guards who patrol the building's only entrance. If he made it to the second floor, he would then have to get through the locked door to the Property Clerk's Office itself. Cutting through the Cyclone fence would get him into the enclosure where small narcotics are stored in miscellaneous manila envelopes containing anything from a single heavily diluted nickel bag to a couple of ounces of relatively pure heroin. But in order to get at the major supplies he would have to open the safe, which is virtually impossible to do without either knowing the combination or using explosives.

Unfortunately, there is an easier way. At least there was until 1973, when the Police Department overhauled the entire system after discovering that it amounted to little more than a cumbersome way of getting drugs into the Property Clerk's Office but a greased chute for getting them out. Well protected against forcible entry, the Property Clerk's Office employed virtually no safeguards against fraudulent removal of drugs. Those few security measures that did exist were generally ignored, so that hundreds of millions of dollars' worth of easily marketable narcotics could be had literally for the asking.

Even at its best the system was remarkably slipshod, but it was never at its best. Apparently it didn't dawn on the men who run the Police Department that the task of securing millions of dollars' worth of valuables required sophisticated techniques. With all the logic of a rich man buying a pack of chihuahuas to use as watchdogs, the Department regarded—and indeed still regards—assignment to the Property Clerk's Office as a routine desk job. To make matters worse, years ago the Police Department decided to cut corners by putting lower-paid civilians in Property Office positions that formerly were manned by uniformed officers.

The whole system was, to say the least, inadequate, and for years the Department knew that something had to be done about it. In the time-honored tradition of bureaucracies everywhere, it studied the problem and then did nothing until it was time for the next study. Then, in October 1972, an attractive twenty-three-year-old woman from Long Island walked into the offices of the Internal Affairs Division—which, coincidentally, were also located at the Broome Street Annex—and swore out a rape complaint against a New York City policeman. After checking out her story, IAD detectives were sent to arrest the policeman at his home in Little Neck. There they discovered three small packets of heroin in plastic bags bearing the seal of the Police Department Property Clerk.

At first Internal Affairs wanted to charge the cop not only with rape but also with trafficking in narcotics, but he was quickly cleared on the second count. The drugs turned out to be the evidence in an active case. He had signed them out on the day the case went to trial, then took them home with him each night in order to save hours each morning and night at the Broome Street shape-up. What he had done was against regulations but it was no crime.

The Department had long known about this expedient and relatively harmless method of circumventing its own time-consuming procedures. Figuring that every hour its men spent standing on line outside the Property Clerk's windows was that much time away from the job, it winked at the practice. This time, though, the Police Department was afraid that if the story leaked out it could result in a major scandal. The commissioner ordered a complete audit of the Property Clerk's logbooks.

Even before this order could be put into effect, the commissioner learned that a mere audit of the books wouldn't even begin to uncover all that was wrong with the Property Clerk's Office. He received a call from an upstate district attorney who had news for him that was so confidential in nature that he wouldn't give it over the phone. When the commissioner arrived at the D.A.'s office, he was told that a reliable informant had told a member of the district attorney's staff that he knew of at least one large drug deal involving narcotics stolen from the New York City Property Clerk's Office. "Tell them to check the stuff from the French Connection," the informant had said.

The commissioner raced back to the city and ordered an immediate and complete investigation of the Property Clerk's Office. In addition to examining the logbooks, the examiners were to count, weigh, and chemically analyze every packet of narcotics at 400 Broome Street. By mid December the team of detectives, auditors, and chemists assigned to scrutinize the Property Clerk's Office had made a preliminary finding that sent tidal waves of shock coursing through the Department hierarchy. On Thursday, December 14, 1972, Police Commissioner Murphy called a press conference in the large meeting hall on the ground floor of the old Headquarters building. Tense and obviously shaken, the commissioner announced that a portion of the heroin seized in the so-called French Connection case and held in the Property Clerk's Office since 1962 had mysteriously disappeared. Of the ninety-seven pounds of pure heroin originally logged in, only sixteen were still in the Police Department's possession. The rest had simply vanished. With the audit still incomplete, the commissioner had to admit that the Department had lost at least eighteen million dollars' worth of narcotics. Reluctantly answering a direct question, the usually imperturbable Murphy conceded that it was "theoretically possible" that these losses might be only the tip of the iceberg.

Other Department spokesmen were more candid. The French Connection drugs, they explained, were in two batches. A suitcase which originally contained twenty-four pounds of heroin now contained only one pound of the pure drug and twenty-three pounds of an unspecified white powder. In addition, a steamer trunk, which was on record as having held seventy-three pounds of heroin, also had been looted. Desperately trying to find one bright spot in an otherwise dismal situation, the spokesman pointed out that at first the trunk had been thought missing. It wasn't in the safe and the Property Clerk's logbooks revealed that it had been signed out to Detective Joe Longo in 1969 and never returned.

Fortunately, when the entire Property Clerk's Office was searched, the missing trunk turned up in a remote and relatively inaccessible area far from where it should have been. Analysis of its contents revealed that it still contained fifteen pounds of the original heroin and forty-seven pounds of another white substance. Eleven pounds were gone entirely, with no substitution.

There were no celebrations at Police Headquarters that Christmas. As the audit went on, it quickly became apparent that Commissioner Murphy had grossly underestimated the extent of the loss. Through December and into January, Murphy was repeatedly forced to issue updated figures with the latest tallies of the Department's losses. By early February, when the results were all in, they added up to the biggest ripoff in the annals of crime. Beside the Property Clerk job, such legendary heists as the Brinks robbery, the Hotel Pierre jewel caper, and the Nice bank robbery begin to look like petty stickups. In all, the thieves had gotten away with 261 pounds of heroin and 137 pounds of cocaine, a total that represented roughly 21 percent of all the drugs seized in New York in the eleven years since the French Connection arrests. Conservative estimates valued the haul at approximately seventy-two million dollars.

That staggering sum represents the street value only of the drugs *known* to have been stolen. But each summer the Police Department burns all the narcotics it is holding from cases closed out during the preceding year. How much of that had been tampered with? Over the years, had the Police Department been annually incinerating hundreds of pounds of talcum powder, milk sugar, and chalk? If so, then the true value of the drugs stolen from the Property Clerk's Office may run into the hundreds of millions of dollars.

No one close to the situation could fail to notice the irony involved in the Property Clerk thefts. The New York City Police Department faced the greatest robbery in history in the triple role of investigator, victim, and number-one suspect.

In February 1973, Governor Nelson A. Rockefeller assigned Special State Prosecutor Claude Bowlby to head up an inquiry into the Property Clerk thefts. An ambitious one-time assistant D.A. from Manhattan, Bowlby was given a special grand jury and a promise of complete freedom to operate with absolute jurisdiction over all state or city agencies. So far he has been unable to find an answer to the Property Clerk thefts. Until he was fired in 1976 by Governor Hugh Carey, Bowlby dealt with the problem by issuing periodic statements in which he declared that the case had been solved. His annual announcements of a solution to the puzzle of what is commonly called the French Connection Ripoff began to sound like the tease for the opening of a television police show.

In August 1973, six months after he was put in charge of the investigation, Special Prosecutor Bowlby announced the indictment of gangland figure Larry Boston on a narcotics conspiracy charge. According to Bowlby, the money found in Boston's car when he was arrested in February 1972—slightly under a million dollars—was to have been a payoff for a portion of the Property Clerk heroin. Claiming that other indictments would follow shortly, Bowlby flatly stated that six policemen were involved and that the narcotics had been taken "in large transactions, not pound by pound." When asked if undercover detective Gil Lacey was a suspect, the special prosecutor declined to comment.

In the next six months nothing happened. Then, in February 1974, the *New York Times* reported that a source close to the special prosecutor was hinting that Bowlby was once again "close" to breaking the case. Two weeks later a police sergeant named Clarence Ross was indicted for perjury before a Bowlby grand jury. Although Ross has never been linked to the Property Clerk thefts, Bowlby took the occasion to announce that with this indictment he was now "one step closer" to a solution.

In July 1975 five associates of Larry Boston, including his attorney, were charged with perjury and contempt in an inquiry into the Property Clerk thefts. The special prosecutor told reporters that Boston had paid narcotics detective Ernie Blake to engineer the caper. Blake, though, was not indicted. Indeed, although five years have passed since the Police Department discovered the theft, no one has been charged with involvement in the crime.

It is often said that when a prosecutor has evidence he gives it to the jury, but when he has no evidence he gives it to the press. For years now the French Connection Ripoff has been on trial in the newspapers. In addition to Larry Boston, there are two principal "defendants." The first is Ernie Blake and the second is Joe Longo.

Property Clerk voucher slips disclose nine transactions involving the drugs known to be missing. Six of the slips, dating from March 1969 to January 1972, were signed with Joe's name. The other three slips were signed with one or more other names which have never been publicly released. At one point the Police Department explained that it was not releasing the names because they were the names of policemen still on the Force and still under investigation. Bowlby, however, has said that the names in question are entirely fictitious. There is no disagreement on the fact that the shield numbers on all nine slips do not correspond to any shield ever issued by the New York City Police Department.

Handwriting analysis has conclusively proved that in all six instances where Joe's name appears, the signatures were forged. In fact, in two of them it is misspelled Luongo, a common Old World spelling which Joe's father Americanized when he came to this country. Additionally, the Police Department's forgery experts claim that all nine signatures were written by the same person. Whoever signed the Property Clerk voucher slips, it definitely was *not* Joe Longo.

Sadly, the fact that Joe's signatures were clearly demonstrated to be forgeries did not erase the cloud of suspicion that hung over him. Because his name had been used and because he was under investigation at the time of his death, Joe continued to be regarded as a central figure in the conspiracy, despite the fact that if he had been involved in the thefts in any way, it is ridiculous to imagine that his name would have been put on those vouchers. Whoever masterminded the ripoff had to know that unless someone talked, those logbooks were the only evidence that could ever link the perpetrators to the crime. Obviously, this master thief wouldn't want to do anything that could call attention either to himself or to anyone involved with him.

One of the most interesting aspects of the Property Clerk thefts is the fact that everyone connected with the investigation has consistently misled the public with unrealistic explanations of how the job was done. In a 1973 press conference, for example, Bowlby said that although he was not prepared to disclose exactly how the thefts were perpetrated, he did feel free to say the narcotics were removed "in large batches, not pound by pound or bag by bag." He then went on to criticize the Property Office for its laxity in permitting an imposter to sign out valuable drugs.

Yet anyone who thinks about the crime has to come to the conclusion that the drugs were never actually signed out and that the carelessness that characterized the Property Clerk's Office had nothing to do with the multimillion-dollar robbery. It is true that the officers and civilians who manned the windows at 400 Broome Street were often rather listless when it came to checking the identification of cops who signed out evidence. But simple common sense indicates that although this setup could have permitted a cop to sign out an item that wasn't his evidence, it's hardly the kind of thing anyone could bank on if he was planning to rip off hundreds of pounds of heroin and cocaine.

Besides, I know from personal experience that no one—whether it was Joe Longo or someone else using Joe's name—could have signed out the French Connection evidence. With that load and all the other big loads, the security precautions were simply too heavy. I know this because it was my evidence and I was the only one authorized to remove it. I had to take the junk to court on numerous occasions—for the grand jury, various hearings, and the trial itself, which dragged out for a considerable number of months. And each time I had to be personally cleared by the Property Clerk himself. The stuff didn't leave that safe until they checked my identification, called someone to confirm the reason I was taking the evidence, and then had me sign the logbook in their presence. In fact, once, when I had to remove just a tiny sample from one of the packets in order to send it to the government's atomic laboratory in Oak Ridge, Tennessee, the Property Clerk himself and five others stood over me while I slit one of the bags and spooned out a gram or two. In other words, the idea that one of the clerks just handed this big steamer trunk full of heroin through the window like it was a nickel bag simply doesn't square with the procedures that were in effect.

What is more, the theory that the narcotics were fraudulently signed out over the counter doesn't explain one crucial aspect of the thefts. The steamer trunk, which originally contained seventy-three pounds of heroin, had been signed out and never signed back in. Yet the trunk was not missing, as was first reported. It later turned up in the Property Clerk's Office, but not where it should have been. Can anyone be expected to believe that the thieves signed the trunk out, took it home with them, switched the contents, brought the trunk back, and then forgot to sign the logbook?

Also, the contents of the steamer trunk were different from what was found with all the other loads that were ripped off. In all the others, the heroin was switched, but the steamer trunk contained only forty-seven pounds of milk sugar. Fifteen pounds of the original heroin still remained and eleven pounds were missing entirely.

The inescapable conclusion is that the contents of this particular trunk were in the process of being switched when the commissioner's audit and analysis canceled everyone's plans and put a stop to the operation. This means that the Property Clerk Ripoff was done without the goods ever going over the counter. It is almost disappointing to realize that the biggest robbery in history involved no complicated gambits, no split-second timing, no daring, and very little imagination. Yet if anything ever stood a chance of being the perfect crime, this was it.

With any luck at all, the crime never even would have been detected, let alone solved. Dead narcotics cases hardly ever come back to life. Each year the Property Office's clerical staff, in an effort to clean house, routinely sends out thousands of form letters asking cops for permission to destroy evidence in cases that have been inactive for a certain number of years. And each year most of these requests come back approved. The Department then auctions off the salable items, dumps the weapons in the ocean, and burns the narcotics. Once a bag is burned, go prove what was in it.

Ironically, the Property Clerk Ripoff never would have been discovered if the "French Connection" himself hadn't gotten away. As anyone knows who read Robin Moore's book or saw the movie, we didn't catch the man who was responsible for getting the drugs into the country. As a result the case was still technically open. But only technically. The Frenchman, who eluded capture for years, had been a hero in the Resistance during the war and was a close personal friend of Charles De Gaulle. When he finally surfaced in France in the late nineteen sixties, the French government refused to extradite him.

Some time after that, I started receiving letters from the Property Clerk's Office asking for permission to destroy the heroin. Each time I got one of those letters I wrote across the top of it, "Evidence still needed. Case pending. Consult Brooklyn District Attorney's Office."

If it's so clear that the thefts were done from the inside, not through the Property Office's tellers' windows, two questions must be answered. Why has everyone connected with the official investigation consistently maintained that the narcotics were fraudulently signed out? And why were nine forged signatures found in the logbooks?

In answer to the first question, the theory that the thefts were accomplished by signing out the evidence broadened the case and gave the authorities virtually unlimited power to question and investigate anyone they chose. If they had said from the start that the Property Clerk Ripoff was an inside job, they wouldn't have had the ammunition they needed to go after a lot of people who had no conceivable connection with the thefts. But, by playing it the way they did, they were able to say, "Detective A worked on such and such a case, so he would have known the voucher numbers on the stuff. That makes him a suspect. I want to subpoena his bank records, I want to tap his phone, I want to question his associates." The fact of the matter is that a lot of the cases made against cops after 1972 resulted from information originally developed when they were investigated with regard to the Property Clerk thefts—investigations that wouldn't have been possible if the real nature of the crime had been acknowledged.

Now, if the nine forged signatures weren't necessary to commit the crimes, what were they doing in the logbooks? They must have been entered to cover up the thefts in December of 1972, just before the auditors and chemists arrived to conduct their investigation. At that point the thieves knew the jig was up. They knew the chemists would discover that eight loads had been switched. They knew the men taking inventory would find that the steamer trunk from the French Connection case had been removed from the safe and placed in a less secure area. Unless they did something, the circle of suspects would be narrowed.

I can imagine their panic. They can't sneak the trunk back into the safe. Someone might see. But they've got to cover their tracks. The only hope is to send the investigators off in the wrong direction. Throw up a smoke screen, make it look like someone took the stuff, switched it, brought it back. Sure, that's the thing to do. But what about that trunk? If he brought it back, where is it? Fuck it—sign it out, don't sign it in. They're not going to turn the whole place upside down. When they don't find it, they'll think he's still got it.

Okay, just put down some names. What names? Who gives a shit? Just names—real names, made-up names, what does it matter? Some poor bastard's going to have to answer a lot of questions, that's all. But so what? He can't tell them anything.

Hey, wait a minute. What about that guy that shot himself last winter? What was his name? Longo. Joe Longo. He was in a jam and he shot himself. Perfect. They'd believe it about a guy like him, a guy who gets himself jammed up.

Besides, he's dead. He's not gonna mind.

Chapter 19
Tip from a Dead Stool

JOHN MEGLIO'S LEGAL struggle to uncover the circumstances surrounding Joe Longo's death and to get Joe's widow the pension she deserved dragged on and on. He pleaded for the right to a hearing before the Police Department's Pension Board. Time after time he went to court to get an order forcing the Department to supply him with information about its investigation of the shooting.

Most of the time, it looked like he didn't stand a chance. Those of us who knew him and knew the story felt that the fight for Joe's pension had become an obsession with him. Out of a sense of debt or duty, he refused to let go. But for John, there was more involved than a feeling that he owed it to Jeannie and the kids. There was also a question of justice here. Because none of us at that time knew the full story of Joe's last two months. We knew what he had done in his misguided quest to make a big arrest involving Danzie—and we knew these weren't crimes a man deserved to die for.

We didn't know how it had all happened. We didn't know about the dogged day-by-day persistence with which Anthony Diamond,

Paul Scala, Carlo Danzie, and Gil Lacey had worked on Joe's character, probing it for weakness, undermining its strength. We didn't know how they had orchestrated events until finally, desperate and exhausted, he fell into their hands. We didn't know that when the whole story was told, it would show clearly how men like Scala and Diamond, honest men doing what is undoubtedly an unpleasant but necessary job, could become so blinded by their own self-righteousness that they could push a fellow human being to the brink of self-destruction and then step back, disclaiming all responsibility.

Above all, I think these are the reasons John kept up the fight. There were people who had to be made to face up to questions about what they'd done. Even if nothing happened afterward, even if the board continued to deny Jeannie her pension, the hearings might get at the truth, and the truth in itself is a form of justice.

In the late summer of 1975, three and a half years after Joe died, the Police Department Pension Board finally agreed to hold hearings in order to determine whether Detective Joe Longo's widow had been improperly denied her husband's line-of-duty death benefits.

The minute John heard that his request had finally been granted, he went into high gear. He bombarded the Department with demands for files, information, documents. When the Department answered with evasive explanations, he fought them in court until a judge ordered them to turn over to him all information relating to Detective Longo's career as a police officer, up to and including the investigation of his death.

In the middle of October, a uniformed police officer came to John's Madison Avenue office to hand deliver the papers the Department was required to surrender pursuant to the court order. John signed for them, told his secretary to hold all calls, closed himself in his office, and spread the contents of the envelope on his desk.

He wasn't surprised to see that it was almost all meaningless junk. There was a copy of the autopsy report, a report on the tests the FBI had done for gunpowder residues, a dozen old and irrelevant pages from Joe's personnel files. There were about thirty DD-5s—the form reports on which detectives log their daily activities on each case. Almost all of them concerned the canvass of the Driggs Avenue neighborhood, in which detectives went from door to door asking residents if they had seen or heard anything suspicious.

Then, in the middle of this mess of meaningless documents, John saw a single piece of paper with the letterhead of the New York City Police Department. As soon as he read it, he knew that it wasn't supposed to have been included in the package that was sent to him. Some unknown cop, either in the Fourteenth Homicide District or in Internal Affairs, must have slipped it in with the other papers because he knew what had happened to Joe and wanted to help.

The letter was a Xerox copy of a memo sent from a Detective Henry Stone to his commanding officer and then forwarded to the Internal Affairs Division. It was dated June 11, 1973, and said, "Re: Your qy re identity of deceased w male found in vehicle, Conduit Ave Queens, 5/27/73. Decedent is one Albert Wilkins, known to have been an informant for D.A., Suffolk Co. Contact him for further information. Decedent claimed to have information re the death NYPD Detective Joe Longo (suicide, 3/72, in Brooklyn)."

Who was Wilkins? What possible connection could there be between Joe and a Suffolk County stool pigeon? What information did Wilkins have? Had he passed it along before he died?

John immediately called Detective Stone, the author of the memo. "I can't tell you anything about that, Mr. Meglio," the detective answered firmly when John began to question him. "The whole matter has been turned over to Internal Affairs, you'll have to take it up with them."

The reaction when John called IAD was strange but not surprising. After an initial moment of shock when Internal Affairs Captain Richard Innes realized that John knew about Albert Wilkins, the tone of the conversation changed abruptly. After three and a half years of obstruction, resistance, and uncooperativeness, IAD suddenly wanted to be as helpful as possible.

"We have no objection to letting you see any of the information we have, Mr. Meglio," Innes purred. "Only don't expect much. It's just a lot of bullshit."

"How about today?"

"Today? Sure, today's fine. Just give me a minute to find out where the material is. I'll get back to you."

"That's all right," John said. "I'll hold on."

The phone clicked onto hold. A minute later the captain was back. He set up a meeting for three o'clock that afternoon at an IAD field office in lower Manhattan.

"Whom do I ask for?" John asked.

"Ask for me," Innes said. "I'll be expecting you."

The field office was located on the second floor of an ancient brick building at the corner of Broadway and Chambers Street that years ago used to house the *New York Sun*. The inside was as seedy as what you might expect if you add thirty years of neglect to the built-in grubbiness of an old-time newsroom.

A room number was stenciled on the shaded glass of the office door but there was no indication that the occupants worked for the Internal Affairs Division, or even for the Police Department in general. A tall, thick-bodied man in a shapeless gray suit, Captain Innes was already standing when John knocked and stepped through the door. "Mr. Meglio?" he asked.

There were about half a dozen scarred oak desks in the large room, each of them bare except for a telephone.

"Yes. Captain Innes?"

"That's right." Innes offered his hand. "Come with me," he said.

John followed him across the deserted office, their footsteps echoing hollowly on the rutted wood floor. Over half a century of constant traffic had warped and separated the planks. A few feet from the far wall a flimsy partition with two doors in it marked off two private offices. Innes pushed open one of these doors and motioned for John to go in.

The room was barely large enough for a desk and a few chairs, but three men were in it. They stood and introduced themselves—two inspectors and a captain, all from Internal Affairs. A bulky, old-fashioned tape recorder stood on the desk, its plug trailing off and disappearing through a hole in the partition.

One of the inspectors, an overweight Irishman with a biting style of speech that was either witty or sarcastic, seemed to be in charge. "Let's get right to the point, Mr. Meglio," he said. "I understand you want to know about the late Mr. Wilkins. Unfortunately, there's not much to tell. The only thing of significance about Wilkins is the fact that he was an informer. I can tell you that without fear that I am betraying any confidences because it became common knowledge shortly before Mr. Wilkins passed on."

John nodded his appreciation of the inspector's grim joke but said nothing.

The second inspector, a much older man with thinning hair, almost colorless blue eyes, and a pronounced stammer said, "Captain, p-p-please brief Mr. M-m-meglio on the situation." These were the only words he said all afternoon, and it's not in the least clear why anyone had felt it necessary for him to be at the meeting.

The captain took a quick drag on his cigarette and ground the butt out in a glass ashtray he held in his hand. Then he leaned forward and set the ashtray on the desk before speaking.

"May I assume, Mr. Meglio," he began, "that you have seen the memo from Detective Stone?"

John didn't answer.

"To Captain Reidecker?" the captain said, simply as an addition to his original question.

"You may assume whatever you want, captain," John said. "I was under the impression I came here to find out what you know. If it's the other way around—"

The captain cut him off. "No, of course not," he said, the almost military crispness of his bearing not in the least ruffled. "But permit me to ask you another question. Do you know who Larry Boston is?"

"Yes."

"And does the name Ilario or Larry Sciarra mean anything to you?"

"No."

"Ilario Sciarra is Larry Boston's real name. It's also the name of his nephew, his brother's son. Now Larry Sciarra—and when I use that name I'm referring of course to the nephew—was the subject of certain intelligence gathered by the district attorney in Suffolk County. And the source of that intelligence was Albert Wilkins. Do you follow me so far?"

"Of course."

"Fine. Now, the thing I want you to appreciate, Mr. Meglio, is that the Internal Affairs Division—no, I'll go that one better, the New York City Police Department—had no contact with Albert Wilkins, didn't even know of his existence until after his death. Strangled, I believe. Isn't that right, Jack?"

"Strangled," the Irish inspector said. "In his car."

"Right, in his car." The captain cleared his throat. "Now, I think you know the score," he went on. "If we had known about Albert

Wilkins, we would have had a considerable interest in talking to him. I dare say, more of an interest than you."

"He had information about the death of one of my clients," John said tersely.

"Claimed to," the captain corrected. "But it is our understanding that his information was worthless. I believe Captain Innes already informed you of that."

"He said it was bullshit."

The captain cleared his throat again. "That's very apt," he said. "Not the way I would have put it, but very apt. The point is that we never had an opportunity to question Albert Wilkins, and so the information we have is minimal. In addition to the Stone memo, the other documents and materials relevant to your interests consist of a tape recording and a transcript of that recording. Both of them were supplied to us by the Suffolk County Police Department."

As if on cue, the Irish inspector produced a tiny reel of tape, which he proceeded to thread through the machine on the desk while the captain went on speaking.

"The voice you'll be hearing is that of Albert Wilkins, at a debriefing session in his home shortly before his death. A detective was questioning him and he was going through his address book, telling whatever came to mind. What came out is somewhat incoherent but that can't be helped. And I'll tell you candidly, Mr. Meglio, this tape was re-recorded from a longer tape. There was more to the session than you'll be hearing. But you have my assurance that none of it concerns your client."

"Just hypothetically," John asked, "what if I'm not satisfied with your assurance?"

The captain shrugged and reached for another cigarette. "You're an attorney," he said. "There are courts."

The machine clicked on, and after a few feet of staticky unrecorded tape the nasal voice of a street-wise punk suddenly came from the speaker. In John's mind it was a voice that conjured up a picture of a young junkie in his twenties, long-haired and skinny, nervous, fidgety, and sharp. It was the voice of a stool pigeon, which is another way of saying it was the voice of a born loser.

Transcript
Interview: Albert Wilkins

Present: Subject
Det. Lou DiGiaimo, Suffolk Co. PD
Det. Tom Sigg, Suffolk Co. PD
Place: 4208 Conduit Ave., Queens
Date: 5/12/73

WILKINS: So, see, it was a funny relationship here. Larry Boston is Larry Sciarra's uncle. Cause Larry Sciarra's uncle is his father's brother. Awright? So the father . . . ya know, I don't want my kid fuckin around with this, that, the other thing. But Boston liked him. When he [Sciarra] come outa jail he [Boston] bought him a new Caddy . . . just for comin out, ya know, just a regular guy. Uh, the Feds, when they grabbed him and they seen who it was, they seen it was Boston's kid [inaudible]. So they called Boston and told Boston the whole story. Boston grabbed holda Larry and warned him. Said I told ya, ya know, watch what you do [inaudible].

    Uh . . . one of the guys . . . I can't remember the guy's name, was Sy . . . weird name like Sylvester or somethin like that . . . and he was explainin to us about the cop. When the cop got killed, what he [Sylvester] did is he talked to them, he said, look, he says, I want out, this, that other thing, he says things are gettin too hot. This is when the dope deal went down in Manhattan. They were takin the drugs. So he says they were all being questioned. So he says, this is gettin too hot. I don't want this. So they felt the guy was gonna crack under the strain [inaudible].

    Now what I don't understand is the partner got outa the car, went in to make a phone call. Two guys got in the backseat. Somehow they got his gun. Shot him with it. Got outa the car and that was it. Made it look like a suicide. But it wasn't a suicide. And this is . . . I got this from Larry Sciarra. And Larry don't, ya know, he don't bullshit. . . . So uh, well, ya know, like I'm gonna say, like what goes on is . . .

DET. SIGG: But why was that cop shot?

The recorder went silent, leaving the detective's question unanswered. The tape hissed for a few seconds and then the Irish inspector reached forward and clicked the machine off.

Afterword

by John J. Meglio

The story of "Joe Longo" is not finished yet. Five years after his death there are more unanswered questions than there were on the day he died. Is it a coincidence that Wilkins implies that the order to kill Joe Longo originated in the gangland operation of Larry Boston, the very man accused of engineering the Property Clerk thefts? Is it a coincidence that at the time of his death Joe was actively searching for Carlo Danzie, who had admitted his involvement with Boston on the morning after Boston's arrest? Is it possible that Carlo Danzie, the elusive narcotics dealer specially imported to New York by Paul Scala, knew more about the Property Clerk thefts than anyone has heretofore guessed? Was the mysterious stop Joe made at Hope Street, less than an hour before he died, connected with his search for Danzie? Did someone fear what Joe might learn if he found Danzie? Was he followed from Hope Street and then murdered when his partner left him alone in the car? Was his name later inserted in the Property Clerk's logbooks simply because the men who ordered his death in March needed a fall guy in December?

I don't have the answers to these questions. Perhaps Larry Boston or Carlo Danzie could have supplied some of the answers. But Danzie has disappeared without a trace, and it is widely rumored that he died in Europe in 1976 or 1977. Larry Boston was stabbed to death in the summer of 1977 by fellow inmates in the federal penitentiary at Atlanta. Unless other sources of information come to light, all I can do is draw my own conclusions, which are inevitably personal and perhaps speculative. I will say that when I heard the Wilkins tape in the IAD office I was stunned. I had no way of knowing whether Wilkins was, as the police say, a "reliable informant," but the fact that he had been murdered certainly gave anything he said a touch of credibility. Further, the recording I had just heard confirmed what I had suspected for a long time. Naturally, I was very excited.

"I assume you checked this out," I said. "I want to see all the reports."

No one answered for a few seconds. Then Captain Innes said, "There are no reports, Mr. Meglio. There was no investigation. We assessed the information you just heard very carefully, I assure you, and we concluded that there is no basis here for reopening the case."

My first thought was that they had investigated and didn't want me to know what had been found. A heated exchange followed, and in the course of it I became convinced that, incredible as it may sound, they actually had failed to follow up on a tip relating to what was purportedly the murder of a New York City detective. I told them that whether they were telling me the truth or not didn't matter. If they hadn't investigated or if they had investigated and were withholding the findings, it amounted to the same thing because I intended to raise that issue before the Pension Board and show that the mode of death of Detective Longo had not been established.

At that point I got up and left.

About a week later, Captain Innes called. He sounded very contrite. He never admitted that the Department had made a mistake in not investigating the Wilkins tip, but he did say that after our meeting the week before, they reevaluated the case and decided to check out Wilkins's information. "I wouldn't be telling you this except that I know how interested you are in the case," he said, as though he was doing me some kind of favor. "We've now investigated the matter and found that there is absolutely no basis in fact for Wilkins's allegations."

I pressed him for more information, but at first he was unwilling to say anything else. After I informed him of my intention to get a court order for the reports of this so-called investigation, he admitted that the investigation had consisted of nothing more than a phone call to Larry Boston's nephew, who was allegedly the source of Wilkins's information. The nephew, he said, "gave us his assurance" that Wilkins hadn't known what he was talking about!

This is still the official Police Department position on the matter. If Wilkins was telling the truth, then Boston or someone close to Boston may have ordered Joe killed. But the Police Department discounted Wilkins's story solely because Larry Sciara, the suspect's nephew, gave his "assurance" that it was untrue.

In 1975 a hearing was conducted before the Board of Trustees of the Police Department Pension Fund. At this hearing I presented the entire case for review and reassessment. The board, which consists of six representatives of the various police line organizations—a patrolman's representative, a sergeant's representative, a detective's representative, and so forth—and six representatives of the New York City government, split evenly in its vote, with all six line organizations voting to give Jeannie her pension, all six city officials voting against us. The tie vote meant that the original decision to deny the pension was allowed to stand, but under the law it entitled me to pursue the case in the courts. The process is a slow one and it is still going on.

While I was fighting to get Joe's widow her pension, Luke Antonelli, Joe's former partner, was dismissed from the Police Force as a result of his involvement in the Danzie incident. The illegal wiretapping charge was never filed but he was prosecuted for accepting an unlawful gratuity. When Joe died, Luke appeared to have lost his determination to fight the case. He simply pleaded guilty and threw himself on the mercy of the court.

His plea was entered in the Federal Court, Southern District of New York, before the Honorable Sylvester J. Ryan, who told the prosecuting attorney, "I have serious doubts as to whether or not I can take this plea. . . . Anything [Antonelli] did here was done in the line of his official police duties. He did all he did do, not with an evil purpose, but to make out a case. [It was] not corruptly done. . . . If he did [the acts charged in the information] as part of what he believed to be the performance of his official acts in order to make a big case, he is not guilty of any crime in my book and in the law."

How sad and ironic that the "crime" which Carlo Danzie, Anthony Diamond, Paul Scala, and Gil Lacey worked for months to trap Joe into committing should turn out to have been no crime at all! In their callous and overzealous eagerness to fight corruption, they succeeded only in causing the death of one good man and destroying the career of another. Even after he heard Judge Ryan's statement to the prosecutor, Luke refused to withdraw his guilty plea. "I don't want to fight them anymore and I don't need any goddamned vindication," he told his lawyer bitterly. "I just want to get this thing over with and get as far away from all this shit as I can."

At this point Judge Ryan accepted the guilty plea and sentenced Luke to two years of probation. Luke is now divorced and living on Staten Island. He has a new job and receives no pension or benefits from the Police Department. None of his new friends know that for thirteen years he was a cop—indeed, a top-flight narcotics detective.

Although Luke bitterly declared that he didn't want to be vindicated in the courts, he—and, of course, Joe—did receive a degree of vindication from the highest quarters of our justice system. In 1975 some of the facts surrounding Joe's death were made public by Washington columnist Jack Anderson. Anderson accused Anthony Diamond, the deputy director of the BNDD, of "engineering" the suicide of a New York narcotics detective. Senator Henry M. Jackson's Permanent Subcommittee on Investigations thereupon ordered the Justice Department to conduct an investigation. Assistant Attorney General Laurence H. Silberman was put in charge.

Silberman's staff questioned numerous witnesses, including former BNDD deputy director Anthony Diamond, who admitted that during an interrogation session he had indeed given Joe three choices —prison, cooperation, or death. In an affidavit, Special Assistant United States Attorney Paul Scala gives a sanitized version of this fateful meeting in which Diamond's statement is blandly characterized as a "passing reference to suicide."

At the conclusion of this investigation, Silberman reported his findings to the Jackson subcommittee. From the evidence available to him, the assistant attorney general was convinced that if Diamond hadn't actually "engineered" Joe's suicide, he had certainly "induced" it. Silberman concluded that Joe Longo had fallen victim to "an overzealous investigator, who jeopardized the civil rights of those under investigation, . . . an extremist."

There is one further point I feel compelled to make in order to bring the story up to date. In the course of preparing my action on behalf of Jeannie Longo, I decided that the person most likely to be in a position to provide me with information concerning Joe's last case was undercover detective Gil Lacey. Since Lacey was at that time being held in protective custody by federal marshals in the Southern District of New York, I contacted an assistant prosecutor and told him what I wanted. He promised to pass my request on to Lacey.

After a few weeks went by, the assistant U.S. attorney telephoned me at my office and told me that I could interview Lacey at the federal courthouse. We set up a meeting for the next day in the prosecutor's office.

I should point out that in the time between Joe's death and this meeting, Lacey had been a very busy man. According to his own count, he developed information that led to cases against more than fifty police officers, including at least five of his former partners. One of these partners was brought in for questioning. He was given the choice of cooperating by giving information against other detectives or going to jail. He agreed to cooperate and was released. Thinking it over that night, not knowing that Lacey had informed on him, he came to the conclusion that he couldn't betray his partner. He drove into Riverside Park and shot himself to death with his own gun.

Years later Lacey told a reporter that he tried to kill himself by taking an overdose of sleeping pills when he heard of his partner's death. He also said that he had tried to kill himself on another occasion by driving his car off a highway and that he had become physically ill and had wept uncontrollably when he was told that Joe Longo was dead.

If these things are true, they give some indication of the psychological strain Lacey was under and of what it must have cost his spirit to do the things he did. On the other hand, I must say that when I met Lacey I saw no signs that he was carrying such a burden of guilt. On the contrary, I was struck by the contrast between my friend and client Joe as I had seen him when he came to my home barely two weeks before his death, gaunt and colorless, a devastated man, and Gil Lacey, the baby-faced double agent who dressed like he was on his way to a dance, who looked plump and prosperous, who breezed glibly through his account of Joe's temptation and fall as though he were telling the story of a movie he had seen the night before.

There is no need to go into great detail concerning what I learned from Lacey. I have passed the information on and most of it is incorporated in this book. "I never thought it would come to that," Lacey said by way of justifying his role in the affair. "There were a couple of times I wanted to call him up, get word to him. You know, just warn him. But I figured he could take care of himself. I never imagined Danzie would get him. It was like watching a cat-and-mouse game between a master detective and a master spy, and right up to the end I would have bet on Joe. But then it turned out Danzie was right, Joe had this streak of vanity in him. He wanted to be a star, to make the big cases, to make the headlines. And that's what did him in. It blinded him to what was going on and made him miss things he normally would have seen. You know, he was a hell of a good detective, one of the best I've ever seen, but that ambition—not ambition, vanity; that's what Carlo called it—that was what beat him. It's a tragedy, really."

I asked Lacey whether he thought Joe had killed himself. Lacey sat straight in his chair and leaned toward me with a look of eagerness on his face, as though I finally had given him a chance to say something he had wanted to say for a long time. "To tell you the truth, I don't think he meant to kill himself," Lacey said in a tone of confidentiality, almost a whisper. "That's why he shot himself in the chest. He wanted to get some sympathy, maybe make the people who were hounding him back off a little. But instead the bullet caught his heart and he died. That's the way I think it happened."

He leaned back in his chair and studied me closely, gauging whether I believed him. For years his life had been a tangled skein of lies, of double and triple dealing. And I thought that if this lie gave him comfort, if it helped him to think that the death of the friend he helped to betray was accidental, then it wasn't my place to take that away. Like Joe, like Luke, he too, along with Scala and Diamond and Danzie, along with all of us, will be judged.